The Security of Silence

DONALD F. MEGNIN

To order additional copies of this book, contact:
Xlibris Corporation
1-888-795-4274
www.Xlibris.com
Orders@Xlibris.com
27082

The Security of Silence

Contents

Foreword

The Megnin family left France in 1685 after Louis XIV had renounced the Edict of Nantes, giving Protestants the right to live and worship as they pleased. The French Protestants, or Huguenots as they were called, sought refuge in surrounding countries. Many went to the Netherlands, others to the Dutch colony in South Africa, a few went to England, but the majority sought refuge in what later was to become Germany. Since the Thirty Years War (1618-1648), a variety of German princes welcomed the Huguenots. They were excellent farmers, craftsmen, and independent thinkers. The war had decimated the German population. Over one-third of the inhabitants had been killed since most of the battles between Catholics and Protestants raged in Germany. The local German rulers needed the skills and manpower which these new arrivals provided. If freedom of worship were guaranteed, the Huguenots were willing to serve under whichever king, prince, duke, or baron ruled the country or province into which they settled. The Megnin forbearers were a group of people who were not afraid to move about seeking their fortune wherever it might be found so long as they could worship and think as they pleased. In the late nineteenth century, my Megnin grandfather came to the United States on three different occasions. He stayed with his brother-in-law on his first trip. He then stayed with his sister-in-law and her children on each of his succeeding trips. His brother-in-law died in an accident due to someone loosening the bolts of his buggy seat causing him to fall under the wheels of a trolley. Grandfather Megnin returned to Germany each time after spending several months in the United States. He refused to learn English, and hence, found it difficult to get the kind of job which he felt suited him.

The Bartholomae family, on the other hand, as far back as anyone could determine, was an old, staid, Protestant family that traced its roots back to the Middle Ages. They had always lived in Wuerttemberg. They may have moved from town to town but were always among Germans bearing German names. The Huguenots, on the other hand, found that generations of residence in Germany still did not qualify them as "native" Germans. They could always be readily identified by their French names. Even as recently as 1975, after listening to a speech by the Austrian Hapsburg pretender to the throne in Constance, Germany, the author introduced himself to his eminence. The pretender immediately said, "That's not a German name; that's a French name!" Yes, even today in Germany name recognition is just as important as it has always been to describe "outsiders." The background of a person is automatically presumed to be known from the name he or she carries.

In the context of the highly rigid and hierarchical social structure of the late nineteenth and early twentieth centuries, these two families were brought together by chance. Neither family particularly approved of the other, initially. They came from the opposite ends of the hierarchical social ladder. This novel portrays what ensued when those two opposites met in the context of the days of social, political, and economic stress during the turbulent early decades of the twentieth century in both Germany and the United States. The status of women in this era was in the midst of a radical social change. Few men or women recognized or even wanted to acknowledge the changes which were brought on by the necessity of adjusting to the consequences of death, war, and the social, economic, and political deprivations which became part of the daily experiences of these families. The Security of Silence gives a glimpse into the unfolding drama of the woman's family, initially, and then the consequences of the choices made by the main character in her attempt to create and protect her own family in the face of what she discovered about her husband. For obvious reasons the name of one of the families has been changed to another French name. The meaning in French means mischievous which is symbolically a most appropriate name for the family. The Security of Silence begins in the late nineteenth and continues through the early decades of the twentieth century. The saga of the family continues with their emigration to the United States and their early days in America in successive volumes.

Preface

Having spent almost ten years in the aggregate, living in Germany among relatives or teaching and conducting research, it was only on one of my last trips that I discovered an old picture in the attic of my cousin's house, formerly owned by my maternal grandmother, in Vaihingen an der Enz. My cousin and her husband had purchased the house from her mother, my mother, and our two aunts. The picture was that of Michael Friederich Bartholomae, my grandfather, a newly elected member of a German business fraternity in Darmstadt, Germany in the 1890s. I was intrigued by the picture because it reminded me of how difficult it must have been for him to have achieved this honor in the rigid social environment of nineteenth-century Germany. And yet, he achieved this recognition through his own efforts in spite of the encumbrance of not having had a university education, or a father of wealth and status to sponsor his efforts. I wondered how such a man could succeed in this environment. The more I investigated his story and that of my family, the more intrigued I became about my own part in the unfolding drama that is often seen in many families but hardly ever written. It is truly a family saga with its high points and its low, with its heroes and its villains, with its outstanding personalities and its devastating predatory types. While specific names of places, persons, and events may seem real, the reader should not forget this is a novel combining fact and fiction. Any relationship, therefore, to any persons, living or dead, places, or events, are purely coincidental, and ultimately, the product of the author's imagination.

Donald F. Megnin

Chapter I

Vaihingen an der Enz

It's a little town today, nestled in the hills of northwestern Wuerttemberg, Germany, situated astride the river Enz. In the late nineteenth century, it was an agricultural village with a few sawmills, flour mills, and small shops catering to the needs of the local farmers. When Michael Friederich Bartholomae heard from his friend about the potential sale of a local printer/newspaper business, he took the train from Darmstadt to Stuttgart and then a local train to Vaihingen. Michael had never been here before. He was impressed with the location of the village. From the train station in Kleinglattbach to the village was three kilometers. With the winter wind wiping past him at the station, he decided it would be best to take a horse and buggy to Vaihingen. The gravel road passed through fruit trees and open fields. The driver told him he had come at the wrong time of the year; he should have waited until spring.

"In spring, it's beautiful out here," the driver told him. "The fruit trees are all in blossom. The fields are planted with grain and corn. Winter's not the best time to come to Vaihingen."

Michael felt the cold wind blowing through the buggy. He pulled the collar of his coat up, and pulled the rim of his hat tighter. There were patches of snow which had accumulated along the edges of the trees from the drifts. He's probably right, Michael thought to himself. It's not the best time to come for a visit. His friend, Eberhard Twielling, had written him about the business being for sale. He remembered he had told his friend to be on the lookout for a printer's shop before they said goodbye to each other in Karlsruhe. They had taken the train from Strassburg after completing their army service in Alsace. Michael had told Eberhard, "I'd really like to own my own business. I'm a printing press operator by trade, Eberhard, but there's no future in it if you have to work for someone else. Let's keep in touch. If you hear of anything for sale, let me know."

"Sure, Michael. It would be great if you could live closer to where I live. I live in a little town called Vaihingen/Enz. It's almost straight across Wuerttemberg from Karlsruhe. It's not far from Ludwigsburg, and Stuttgart is only twenty five kilometers away. Come and see me if you can. My dad's a pharmacist in the village and that's where I'm headed. I still have to finish my studies, but he wants me to take over the business. My sister wants to study pharmacology, too. My dad says it's no career for a woman."

1

"I may visit you sooner than you think, Eberhard, if you write and tell me of a business for sale in y our village."

"Well, I'll hold you to your promise, Michael. If I hear of anything, I'll let you know."

And with that the two friends left on separate trains. Eberhard went from Karlsruhe to Vaihingen, and Michael went on to Heilbronn where he lived with his father, mother, and two younger brothers. He was the oldest of the three sons. His father was a postmaster of the nearby village of Eschenbach. He had gotten this job in the service of King Ludwig of Wuerttemberg because he had received an outstanding commendation and field promotion during the Franco-Prussian War. For his wartime service he was rewarded with this appointment from the King's chancellor. It did not pay much but the pension and the house granted to him made it possible for Friederich Bartholomae to live a comfortable and respected life as one of the "petite bourgeoisie" of Heilbronn. His sons were accorded special privileges as a consequence of their father's war service. Michael went on to learn to become a pressman. His younger brothers became a salesman and a postal clerk, respectively.

A lot had happened since he and Eberhard said their good byes in the fall of '96. He had gotten a job with the Darmstadter News as a pressman. It was his second job since completing his certification as a press operator. With each new job he had received an increase in pay but he was still dissatisfied. Even after he and Maria Meyer had gotten married in September '97, he told her he really wanted to become his own boss. She encouraged him. Her own father was the city manager of Gerabronn. Even though he had a farm, he much preferred to handle the affairs of the city.

"He likes to mingle with the public. Everyone knows him and he'll do whatever he can for those who need crop insurance. If he didn't have his own insurance agency where he's his own boss, he'd probably not be satisfied either working for the city," Maria told him.

And now I'm on my way to look over a potential business to buy, he said to himself. A lot has happened since Eberhard and I left Strassburg. I've gotten married. We have a cute little daughter. Maria has given up her job as a bookkeeper in Darmstadt. This trip might prove to be one of those turning points in our lives, he thought to himself. Yes, I'll be interested in seeing what Eberhard has found for me.

The driver of the buggy took him to the Twielling Pharmacy on the edge of the market place. Michael paid him and asked, "Do you take people back to Kleinglattbach to catch the train?"

"You don't have to worry about that. There's a little shuttle train which runs between Vaihingen and Kleinglattbach that you can take. I'm sure Herr Twielling will see that you catch the train on time."

Michael entered the door to the store and saw his friend behind the counter. As he walked to the rear of the store, both he and his friend looked at each other.

"Ah, Michael! How good to see you again! You got my note about Herr Dreschler wanting to sell his printing business?"

"Hello, Eberhard. Yes, that's why I've come. I got your letter two days ago, and here I am today!"

"Can you stay overnight? We've got plenty of room. I haven't told Hannelore, but I'm sure she won't mind. I just got married last year. It's been four years since we came back from Alsace, isn't it?"

"Yes it is, Eberhard. Thanks, but I better try and catch the late afternoon train back to Darmstadt, if I can. Maria and the baby are expecting me to come back tonight."

"Oh so you're married too? I didn't know you had a family already. My wife is dying to have a child. Maybe you can tell her it's not all that much fun getting up during the night."

"It's not that bad, Eberhard. The baby is a real joy to have. Has Herr Dreschler sold his place yet?"

"No. He's had a few people look at it, but he wants to make sure the new owner will keep his employees at least for the first year. The last person was willing to buy it, but he refused to sign the paper committing him to the binding employment contract for the employees. So Dreschler said, "Too bad. I'm not selling the business without my employees." I thought you better know this before we call on him. If you're not willing to hire his five employees, Michael, there's really no point in talking to him."

"What? He has five employees? He must have a bigger operation than I thought."

"He also publishes the Enz-Bote. It's the region's only newspaper. He doesn't have much of a circulation. But every time someone comes into the village from the countryside, they want to buy a newspaper. And that's almost every day. So he has a few hundred papers that he publishes three times a week. Then he also has his printing business: church bulletins; wedding announcements and invitations; lots of ads for clothes, farm crops, cattle, and horse sales; business signs; etc. He has plenty to do, Michael. He can use all of the employees he has. Oh, I forgot. He also has a bookstore where he sells stationery along with his printing business."

"Wow. It's a bigger operation than I thought. How much does he want for it? Do you know? I may not be able to afford it."

"I don't know. Why don't we go over and take a look at it before you decide whether or not you can afford it, Michael. It may not be as much as you think. But first let me introduce you to my wife."

Eberhard took Michael up the back stairs to their apartment just over the store. As they entered the living room, Eberhard called out, "Hannelore? We've got company!"

Hannelore came out of the kitchen and dried her hands on her apron as she approached her husband and his friend.

"Hannelore, this is my friend I've told you about, Michael Bartholomae. He's interested in looking over the Dreschler printing business. Michael, this is my wife, Hannelore."

Michael took her hand and brought it briefly to his lips. "How do you do, Frau Twielling. I'm honored to meet you."

"Oh, he's so gallant, Eberhard. The pleasure is mine. Can you stay for dinner, Herr Bartholomae?"

"Thank you very much for the invitation, Frau Twielling, but I've got to catch the late afternoon train back to Darmstadt. My wife and daughter are expecting me."

"What? You've got a daughter already? Eberhard, we should have a child too! I wish we had one," she said more to herself than to Michael. "Let me at least get you something to eat and drink before you go over to Dreschlers. Isn't that a good idea, Eberhard?"

"Yes. I'm sure Michael won't mind having some coffee and kuchen."

While Frau Twielling prepared the coffee and cake, Eberhard asked, "Would you prefer beer or some Gluewine (heated wine). Michael? The Gluewine would be good in this cold weather, don't you think?"

"Yes. That would be just the thing for this cold weather."

Eberhard went to the kitchen and brought the pitcher of hot wine and two mugs. He filled each and lifted his cup to Michael. "Here's to your health and new business, Michael. Let's hope you make a purchase with Herr Dreschler."

The two men clicked their cups together and drank the hot wine slowly. Michael was still a bit uneasy about the unknown purchase price. He hadn't heard about the condition of having to take on the employees. He was glad Eberhard had told him ahead of time. He thought he'd have to look over the business very carefully and meet the employees as well. He wouldn't want to hire someone with whom he couldn't get along.

Frau Twielling brought the coffee and kuchen to the dining room table. It already had a beautiful tablecloth on it. She then brought out her fine china plates and porcelain cups and silverware.

"Do you use sugar and cream in your coffee, Herr Bartholomae?"

"Yes, thank you."

Michael took a bite of the cake. "Oh this is excellent cake, Frau Twielling. Did you bake it?"

"Yes. I bake every day, Herr Bartholomae. I like to give our employees and family treats for their "Veschber" (coffee break).

"That's a very nice idea. Did your mother do this for your employees too, Eberhard?"

"No. My mother wouldn't have thought of doing anything like that. This is strictly Hannelore's idea. My father thinks it's going a bit too far giving our help cake and coffee. He has reservations about it, but thinks it has been a good idea. It gives Hannelore something worthwhile to do. It takes her mind off having children. I'm in no hurry, but she is!"

"Herr Bartholomae, when you buy the business and you, your wife and daughter come to Vaihingen, you must come over for dinner. I'd love to meet them. It won't be easy for your wife to come to this strange little village where she knows no one. I know. I've had to make the same adjustment she'll have to make."

"There she goes again," Eberhard chimed in. "She comes from Baben-Baden and she claims she's had a hard time getting used to our accent here in Vaihingen."

"Oh so you're an Alemaner? It must have been hard for you, Frau Twielling, moving into this "Schwabenland" (land of the Schwaebians). My wife is going to have the same

4

problem. She's from Gerabronn. If you think the accent here is hard to understand, wait until you talk to her!" Michael laughed. "I'm still trying to understand what she says at times, and we've been married for more than two years."

"Well, we'd better go over and see Dreschler, Michael. I told him about you and he was interested in meeting you. He's an old man who's been in the business for more than forty years. He and his wife never had any children. She wants him to retire and travel a bit to our African colonies before he's no longer able to walk anymore. He's having trouble going up and down their stairs. His arrangement is somewhat similar to ours. The store is downstairs, but where he has his printing shop in the basement, we have our wine cellar."

Michael took his leave and went with Eberhard over to the Dreschlers. As they came in through the door of the store, Herr Dreschler met them. "So this is Herr Bartholomae?" he asked Eberhard.

"Yes. Herr Dreschler, this is my good friend from our army days, Herr Michael Bartholomae. Michael, this is Herr Walter Dreschler, the owner of the Dreschler Printing firm."

They shook hands with each other. Michael took a quick glance around the store. It was ancient, he thought to himself. Dreschler hasn't spent much time updating the items in the store. Even the glass cases were made in the fifties, he thought to himself. He must not have done anything with his store since he bought it. Well, it's high time to make a change.

"How much are you asking for your business, Herr Dreschler?"

"Not so fast, Herr Bartholomae. Let me show you around first. You can't really make a decision before you've seen each part of the business. As you c an see, this is our store. We have all kinds of stationery supplies, pencils, different types of paper, office supply items, pens and ink. I haven't gotten into the book business. There's too much inventory with too little return on books, in case you're wondering why I don't have any to sell."

Michael was curious about the lack of any books visible in the store.

"Where do you keep yours books, Herr Dreschler?"

Dreschler thought Michael meant his account books. "They're in my office. You can see them after I've shown you the layout of the three floors first."

"No, no, Herr Dreschler. I meant where are the books you sell? Oh yes. You've already told me you don't sell any."

The store has potential, Michael thought to himself. He's got more room than he's using. The shelves were sparsely supplied with no more than three or four items on any shelf. What a waste of space, Michael thought. Dreschler introduced him to Albert Uhralt and Kurt Wimmer. Wimmer was the store manager and Uhralt was his assistant. They were probably almost as old as Dreschler himself. And he wants me to keep these two old men on my staff he asked himself? He wasn't sure how productive they were. He'd have to see how they would work out. They were both eager to make his acquaintance.

"Let's go down to the basement, Herr Bartholomae. I want you to see my presses and meet my pressmen down there."

The walls along the stairs were very worn. The wall paper was torn in places and there were hand-prints lining the handrail leading down to the basement. The steps were sloped in the middle from the years of people going up and down stairs. They were worn out from top to bottom. Ouch, Michael thought. It's a wonder someone hasn't fallen on these worn out steps. The staircase was also rather dark and more light was needed. When they entered the door of the basement, Michael was astonished to see the two presses. They were huge and very clean and well oiled. Obviously, Dreschler has a good and conscientious pressman. He must clean his presses each day. He was glad of that. Nothing bothered him more than dirty presses. At the Darmstadter News, he often complained about the condition in which the presses were left over night. The first thing he had to do some mornings was clean and oil them.

"Herr Bartholomae, as you can see we're very proud of our presses. They are among the cleanest you'll find anywhere in Wuerttemberg. The reason for it is this man right here. I'd like you to meet Herr Welker. Herr Welker, this is Herr Bartholomae. He's interested in buying the business."

"How do you do, Herr Bartholomae."

"It's nice to meet you, Herr Welker," Michael said as he extended his hand.

The noise level was pretty normal, Michael thought. He was surprised how big the presses were. They were almost as large as the ones he worked on at the Darmstadter News. There were windows on the sides of the room in addition to the overhead lighting. The brightness of the room impressed him.

"As the press operator you certainly keep the presses clean!" Michael exclaimed. "They'd be a joy for any pressman to want to work on."

"Thank you, Herr Bartholomae. That's what I tell my apprentices. The first thing they have to learn is 'keep the presses clean!'

"You've certainly done that. I'm really impressed."

"Let me introduce my two apprentices to you." He called them over. "This is Henri Joffe who comes from Strassburg. And this is Wilhelm Steiner from Aurich. Henri has just started with us and Wilhelm is finishing his journeyman-ship this next year. They're really a big help to me here in the press room."

Michael shook hands with both of them. Henri was embarrassed about his dirty hands.

"That's okay, Henri. I can wash my hands again," Michael laughed. "I've done what you've done too."

"I see you have some of the best presses in the world, Herr Dreschler. Anything made by Krupp is the best."

Dreschler nodded his head in agreement. "Let's go upstairs. I want you to see what the rest of my staff does."

Dreschler preceded Michael and his friend. He opened the door as they entered the stationery store. Herr Bartholomae, this is Herr Wimmer and Herr Uhralt both of whom you met briefly when you first came in. They've both been with me for over ten years. I've trained them to be both salesmen and bookkeepers. They know the stationery business inside out."

Since Michael had only talked with them briefly upon entering the store, he made a mental note to himself. The business is not only efficient, but Dreschler has put his whole life into it. It would be an ideal situation if I can buy it. Wimmer and Uhralt nodded recognition to Herr Twielling. "You come into the store quite often, don't you Herr Twielling, to buy your paper supplies?" Wimmer asked.

"Yes, that's right. I don't have to go to Stuttgart to buy the paper supplies I need," Eberhard acknowledged.

"Let me take you upstairs and show you our apartment, Herr Bartholomae." He led the way up the back stairs, His wife was already waiting for them.

"Frieda, this is Herr Bartholomae." She extended her hand and Michael shook it. "Hello Frau Dreschler. Your husband has been kind enough to show me all around the business."

"How do you do, Herr Bartholomae. Come in. Hello Herr Twielling," she added as the three men entered the apartment.

"Frieda, maybe you could show Herr Bartholomae around the apartment. Herr Twielling and I will go into the parlor and wait until you've shown him around."

"By all means."

Michael noticed the wall paper was very old and had been on the walls for ages. The carpets were worn and even some of the furniture appeared to have been patched. The leather seats on the couches were covered with throw rugs so the holes wouldn't be visible. Frau Dreschler took him first into the kitchen. The sink was caste iron. The ceramic covering had flaked off in spots around the edges. Maria certainly wouldn't be satisfied with this sink, he told himself. The cupboards were also badly worn and in need of fresh paint.

"I like to cook and bake, Herr Bartholomae. You can see the handles on the drawers are well used."

"I've noticed that, Frau Dreschler. Did you just bake the kuchen on the table?"

"Yes I did. I wanted you and Herr Twielling to sample some of it over coffee after you've had a chance to talk with my husband about the business."

"Thank you very much, Frau Dreschler. My mother is a good baker too. The baking aroma reminds me of my mother's kitchen." She smiled her appreciation.

These are our bedrooms. This one at the rear of the house looks out over the farmers' market. We've always used it as our guest bedroom. I once thought it might become the bedroom of our son, but we've not been fortunate enough to have any children. I did keep the Georgian style. I thought it would appeal to a young man. The next room is another smaller bedroom with a window that looks out over the chestnut trees. There's a small annex to it which could easily be used for a child's bedroom. Then this last room is our master bedroom."

Looking at the old massive furniture, Michael was reminded of his grandparents. They also had had a four poster bed similar to this one. He didn't say anything.

"I'm sure your wife will like the apartment, Herr Bartholomae. I came here as a young bride almost fifty years ago. Vaihingen is a nice friendly little town. There's everything you need right here. You can buy bread and pretzels at three different bakeries. The closest one is the best. I'm sure you have never had any pretzels like those from Schick's Bakery! And they only cost a penny a piece," Frau Dreschler emphasized.

"I'm sure it's a nice town, Frau Dreschler. Thank you for showing me the apartment."

"I don't suppose you're interested in really looking over the kitchen again, are you? There's one other feature I forgot to show you that's been one of my favorites ever since my husband and I came here."

"No, I don't mind. I want to tell my wife everything about the apartment. I'm glad it's over the store. It makes it very handy to come up for lunch and dinner."

Frau Dreschler led the way to the kitchen again at the end of the apartment. There was the sink he had noticed before with the water faucet. There was the side table on which to put the dishes after washing, a wood cooking stove on the right side of the sink, and upright cupboards along each of the three walls. Just off the kitchen was a small room Frau Dreschler described as the bathroom. There was a large copper tub and next to it another pipe and faucet.

"This has served us well," Frau Dreschler confided. "It's a little small but you really don't need much more room than enough to step in and out of the tub, Herr Bartholomae. Besides, it's right next to the kitchen so your wife can heat up the water on the stove and pour it right into the tub."

Just before leaving the kitchen, Michael saw a table next to the doorway around which, he estimated, five people could sit.

"My husband and I have most of our meals here. We only use the dining room when we have guests. The window over the sink looks out towards Heibronnerstrasse. I can see the carriages coming and going to the railway station without even moving from the sink. It's even a good spot to watch the parades go by for the May Day festivities too."

"Yes, you can see way up the street from here," Michael agreed. "Is that the railroad overpass up there on the hill, Frau Dreschler?"

"That's right. You probably came over the bridge on the little connecting train from the main trunk line."

"No. I actually came by carriage. I didn't want to wait for the shuttle train. There goes the shuttle now." Michael said as he pointed out the kitchen window. The little train was making its hourly run from the Mainline Train Station to the center of Vaihingen. The little shuttle train took both passengers and freight to the Kleinglattbach Main Station for transit east to Stuttgart and west to Karlsruhe. Frau Dreschler brought Michael to the parlor where Dreschler and Twielling were talking and smoking together.

"Well, what do you think of it, Herr Bartholomae?" Dreschler asked.

"You've got an excellent operation here. I can see why Eberhard told me about you. What is your asking price for everything I've seen today?"

"As I told you right from the beginning, I want someone who will keep my employees. I was glad you were interested in meeting all of my people. I had originally wanted twenty thousand Reichsmarks. If you keep my employees, I'll sell everything in the building for eighteen thousand Reichsmarks. It's worth a lot more than that, but I want someone who will continue to serve this community and its people like I've tried to do for almost fifty years. I don't think I can sell it for anything less than that, Herr Bartholomae."

"That sounds like a very fair price, Herr Dreschler. I'll certainly keep your employees. They look as though they're doing an excellent job. I want to compliment you also on how clean everything is. Now that I've seen your place, I'll get my funds together and pay you in cash by the fifteenth of March, if that's all right with you?"

"Fine. Since I know Herr Twielling, I won't ask you for a down payment. I'll look forward to seeing you again on March fifteenth."

Michael and Dreschler shook hands before he left. As he and his friend left for the train station, he said "Eberhard, I don't know how to thank you! This is just the sort of business I've wanted to buy. I'm sure we'll be very happy here in Vaihingen/Enz."

"That's why I wrote you, Michael. I thought it would be exactly what you were looking for. I'm glad you and your wife are going to be our neighbors. There's lots to do around here and we need a good businessman like you to publish our newspaper. You know, Dreschler had two offers. He turned them down. They wouldn't agree to take on his employees. I wasn't surprised when he offered you a better price than he asked previously."

As the train came into the station, Michael said goodbye to his friend. They shook hands and Eberhard promised he would meet him at the station again on the fifteenth of March at eight-forty five a. m.

On the long train ride back to Darmstadt, Michael thought over all he had seen. He was pleased with the Enz-Bote. It's the only newspaper in the region outside of Stuttgart, he thought to himself. Dreschler is willing to sell it to me for two thousand less than I thought it was going to cost. This gives me some money with which to continue the business and I'll still have enough to move us from Darmstadt to Vaihingen. His only apprehension was his promise to keep all of the employees. He didn't mind keeping the pressman and his two apprentices, but the two old salesmen . . . . Well, we'll see, he told himself. It it's going to cost too much, I'll have to let them go. In the meantime, I'll have to view them as an asset. If I keep them, he thought to himself, the townspeople might be more sympathetic to me as a newcomer. By showing good will, the townspeople may reciprocate by continuing their newspaper subscriptions and buying items in the store. It's a risk, but it's one I have to take.

When he arrived in Darmstadt, he could hardly wait to tell Maria about the new business. "It's located on one of the two main streets of the village, Maria. One street leads to Stuttgart and the other to Heilbronn. The business is located on Heilbronnerstrasse which leads to the main railroad trunk-line about three kilometers outside the village in a place called Kleinglattbach. It's also located only a block down the street from the church. Almost everyone has to go past it on their way to the little train station in the village. It's an ideal location."

"What's the apartment like, Michael? Can we buy the furniture and everything else in the business?"

"Yes we can. The furniture is old but it's solid. There are four bedrooms, a dining room, parlor, and a kitchen with a small bathroom next to it upstairs over the store. The first floor houses the stationery store and the basement houses the presses. It has everything we could want. I've had to promise to keep Dreschler's five employees. That's the only aspect of the purchase about which I feel apprehensive. He did reduce his price by two thousand Reichsmarks as an incentive for keeping his employees."

"You mean we have five employees already without even starting?" Maria asked incredulously.

"That's what I had to agree to, otherwise he wouldn't have sold me the business. Eberhard thinks we shouldn't have any problem meeting our payroll. When people see we've kept his employees, they'll keep coming. He says 'if you do favors for your neighbors, they'll do the same for you' were his exact words."

Maria had her doubts about meeting such a large payroll every two weeks. She did recognize how enthusiastic Michael was with the prospects.

"We'll have to visit Papa right away. He told me if you found anything you thought worth buying, he would help us. Shall I write and say we'll be in Gerabronn on the tenth of March?"

"That would be just right, Maria. It would give us a few days before I have to return to Vaihingen. I have to be there on the fifteenth. I told Dreschler I'd buy the business on that day."

On the tenth of March, Michael, Maria, and the baby took the train to Gerabronn. Upon their arrival Maria's mother greeted them as they knocked on the front door.

"So this is the little lady you've written us about?" she said as she greeted Maria and Michael.

"Yes and she can walk already, Mother." Maria took Emilie's hand and led her around the living room.

"That's very unusual, Maria. A baby that can walk at six months is really rare. What's this about your moving to Vaihingen/Enz? Aren't you already far enough away from us in Darmstadt? Why do you want to go way down there? It'll take more than a day by train to get there from here! Why don't you move to Gerabronn, Michael? There must be some business around here you can buy!"

Maria's father came to the door after hearing his wife greet their guests.

"Now Friederika, don't start in on that again!" Gustav Meyer cautioned. "You know there's no newspaper business for sale around here! If that's where they want to live and work, that's their business. We've been through this argument a number of times."

"Don't tell me what I can or can't say!" Friederika scolded. "I think they should move closer to us. It's more important that we see them regularly than where they work!"

Michael wasn't about to get into an argument with his mother-in-law. He sat at the dining room table and listened. I surely wouldn't want to live around this old battle ax very long, he thought to himself. He was sure he'd say something to offend her if he started to explain why they were moving to Vaihingen.

"Michael," Maria cautioned him on the train, "Don't get into an argument with my mother! It'll only make things harder for my father. He's the one we have to deal with, not Mama."

"Okay Maria. But I surely wouldn't want to be married to her! She's the most critical person I've ever met. I don't see how your father puts up with her! She'd drive me crazy!"

Gustav Meyer had had Maria's letter requesting a loan of fifteen thousand Reichsmarks. When Friederika Meyer said she had to go shopping, her husband gave Maria and Michael the fifteen thousand Reichsmarks.

"This amount, plus what you've saved, should be enough, shouldn't it? You'd better put it in your purse, Maria, and don't say anything about it to your mother. She's still upset we're giving out so much money for a business we've never even seen. But I know the two of you will do well."

"We'll pay you back each month, Father," Michael promised. "You'll have to come and visit us after we're settled in. We've got plenty of room for you and Mother when you come to visit."

"Yes, Father," Maria implored. "Do come and visit us this summer. From what Michael has described, Vaihingen is a fascinating old village with a castle in its center. There's a river that runs at the base of it, surrounded by farmland. I can hardly wait to see it!"

After lunch, Michael, Maria and the baby left Gerabronn, much to the dismay of Friederika Meyer.

"What? You're leaving already? You've only just arrived!"

"Michael has to be in Vaihingen on the fifteenth of March, Mother. We've got a lot of things to do to get ready for the big move."

"We'll go visit them this summer, Friederika. From what they've been telling me, they've plenty of room," Gustav told his wife.

"How would you know? You haven't even seen the place!" she retorted hotly.

"No I haven't, but they've told me about it and it sounds great. Anything Maria approves of, is okay with me."

"I suppose you've given them the money already too?"

"Yes I have. It's what we agreed. And yes, I'm going to loan money to Luise and Christian too."

"What?" Maria exclaimed. "You're lending them money too? What for?"

"They want to buy a bakery here in Gerabronn. Your mother insisted if I lend you money to buy a newspaper, the least I can do is to offer the same to your sister," her father answered sheepishly.

"But can you afford that much money, Father? Isn't that a lot to loan out?"

"That's exactly what I've been trying to tell him, Maria," her mother said emphatically. "But he won't listen to me! I keep telling him he should invest his money in more land for the farm and buy a few houses here in Gerabronn. That would be much safer. After all, you and Michael have never owned a business. What if it should fail? Then where would we be?"

"Friederika, I've told you before. Shut up!" Gustav said harshly. They're not going to fail! I'm just doing what your father did for us! I'm helping them get started. What are parents for if not to help their children? We've already got enough land on this farm! And a few more houses in Gerabronn won't produce as much income as these loans will. I'd much rather loan money to deserving young people than invest in real estate! Unless there's income derived from it, there's no gain in capital!" he almost shouted at her.

It wasn't very often Gustav Meyer yelled at his wife. But when he did, she became very quiet. She just looked at him as though he were mad.

"You just wait, you old goat!" She turned on her heels and went into her bedroom. She didn't even bother to say good bye to the Bartholomaes.

Gustav Meyer apologized for his outburst. "Don't listen to what she said. She thinks we should be saving our money for retirement. It also bothers her you're going so far away from here. She'll get over it. I know you'll succeed."

"But Father," Maria said apprehensively. "Maybe we shouldn't have asked you for the loan in the first place. She wiped her eyes. "I didn't know Mother was so opposed to the idea," and started to cry.

"Now that's not necessary. You go ahead as you've planned. We've still got enough to live on in retirement. She feels we never have enough of anything."

Maria and Michael said goodbye to Maria's father. "You're a pretty little lady," he said to Emilie as the Bartholomae family boarded the train for Darmstadt. "I'm sure you're a real joy to your mother and father."

Maria and Michael were silent most of the way back. Each one wondered what the future would bring in moving to Vahingen/Enz. They had a lot of work to do to get ready for their move. March fifteenth was fast approaching. If they were going to move on the first of April, they had to pack their things and be ready for shipment to the train station. Fortunately, they had little furniture of their own. They had a furnished apartment and only their bedding, sheets, towels, clothes, baby toys, dishes, kitchen utensils and a desk had to be packed and crated. Maria began packing as soon as they returned from Gerabronn. Michael arranged for a horse and wagon to take them and all of their things to the train station.

On March fifteenth, he returned to Vaihingen. His brief case was filled with Reichsmarks he had saved plus those given to him by his father-in-law. He also had a small suitcase for one change of clothing should he miss the evening train back to Darmstadt. As the little train pulled into the Vaihingen station, he saw Eberhard Twielling waiting for him on the platform.

"Hello Michael," Eberhard said as he extended his hand.

"Hello Eberhard. This is the big day."

"That's right. You're going to become the owner of the Enz-Bote today."

"Are you sure you can take time off from work to go with me to Dreschlers?"

"That's no problem. My sister can take care of the pharmacy while I'm gone. She has three other women to help her. I do the same for her when she has something she wants to do on occasion. The drug store pretty much takes care of itself. The only thing we have to do is make sure the shelves are stocked each day. I hate to admit it, but the store could probably go on without me, if the truth were known," he laughed.

Michael didn't laugh. "No Eberhard. You're being much too modest. I'm sure your sister would have a hard time keeping the business going if you weren't here. It's impossible for a woman to run a business. The salesmen wouldn't treat her very fairly at all. No. It's a good thing you and your sister are working together. I haven't seen any business yet where a woman's in charge. She couldn't survive in a man's world!"

"You're right, Michael. While I was in the army, my parents had to help my sister, especially my father. If he weren't around, the salesmen would say, 'I'll come back when I can talk to the boss'. Even though my sister has a degree in pharmacology, she didn't have the respect she deserved. Even the customers want to talk to me or my father if he's in the store. They don't want to talk to a woman about business matters and especially not about any personal health problems!"

The two friends didn't say any more until they came to the Enz-Bote.

"What would you prefer, Michael? Do you want to talk to Dreschler alone, first, or do you want me to go with you?"

"If you have the time, Eberhard, it would be helpful if you came along. You can be my witness in this transaction. I'm sure he'll have Welker there to assist him in the sale and maybe even a lawyer."

"You're right. Dreschler will most certainly have his attorney there to oversee the signing of the Bill of Sale he's drawn up. I wouldn't be surprised if it's Karl Schiller. He's part of a law firm that's the oldest in the village. His grandfather started it in 1845. I'm almost sure Dreschler will have him there too. He's another man you've got to meet sooner or later."

Michael and Eberhard entered the Dreschler store promptly at nine a. m. Walter Dreschler, Wilfried Welker, and Karl Schiller were waiting for them.

"Ah Herr Bartholomae and Herr Twielling. We've been expecting you. Let me introduce my attorney, Herr Schiller, to you." They shook hands.

"I've met you before, haven't I?" Schiller asked Twielling. "Yes. A few times at the Turnverein festivities," Twielling answered.

"You remember my pressman, Herr Welker, don't you, Herr Bartholomae?"

"Yes. I remember you. You're the man that keeps the presses in such good shape." Welker beamed. "I try to do my best, Herr Bartholomae."

As Eberhard shook hands with Schiller he said, "I thought you would be here, Karl. I told Herr Bartholomae you were probably Herr Dreschler's attorney."

"If you don't mind, Herr Dreschler, I'd like to have Herr Twielling here as my witness in this transaction. I see you have your attorney. If I need a witness, then I'd like to have him serve in this capacity."

"Not at all, Herr Bartholomae. I've brought along Herr Welker for the same purpose."

"Gentlemen," Schiller began. "If I could have your attention. Let's sit down at Herr Dreschler's conference table and look over the Bill of Sale I've drawn up. It involves the sale of the Enz-Bote newspaper, the stationery store and all of its contents, the presses, the household and office furnishings, the inventory, and all miscellaneous household goods for eighteen thousand Reichsmarks in cash. Here is the agreement listing all of the above items and the amount. You two gentlemen, Herr Twielling and Herr Welker will sign the agreement at the bottom. Herr Bartholomae take your time in reading over this document. If there is anything with which you disagree, now is the time to voice your objection. Otherwise, the sale is final with your signature and the transfer of funds to Herr Dreschler."

Michael sat down at the table and read through the document very carefully. Frau Dreschler brought in coffee and kuchen to the conference table. The others ate and drank their coffee as he continued reading. All of the items were listed as originally agreed by Dreschler. The names of all of the employees were also in the document stating what they did, how much money they received every two weeks, and the statement 'each of these individuals will continue to work for Herr Michael Friederich Bartholomae for the foreseeable future, but not less than one year from the date of this signed agreement. If they should terminate their employment sooner, it will only be at their discretion.'

"Herr Dreschler, what if your employees should want to leave my employment after one month? Where would this leave me?"

"That's a very good point, Herr Bartholomae. It certainly would leave you in very dire circumstances, especially if more than one of these persons decided to work elsewhere."

Turning to Welker, Dreschler asked, "Herr Welker, don't you think it would be fairer if all of you agreed to stay with Herr Bartholomae for at least one year from this date exactly as he has promised you? You would have guaranteed employment with Herr Bartholomae for at least one year."

"Yes. That's true. We only thought of ourselves. But it has to be fair for Herr Bartholomae too. I don't think the others would mind if that were written into the agreement."

"Then you'll add that statement to the agreement, Her Schiller?"

"Yes. I've already made a note of it. It'll be in the final document as a codicil."

"Other than that addition, I think it covers everything else. I'm willing to sign it," Michael said.

Schiller brought out his straight pen and ink and had Michael's, Dreschler's, Twielling's, and Welker's signatures written on the document. Michael then opened his briefcase and took out the eighteen thousand Reichsmarks which he had tied into neat little bundles of one thousand Reichsmarks each. He had taken the extra two thousand Reichsmarks out and left them with Maria. Dreschler counted the eighteen bundles and had Schiller count them too so there would be no mistake in the amount. When they were both satisfied all of the money was there, Dreschler stood up and shook hands with Michael.

"Herr Bartholomae, the Enz-Bote and the entire building and contents are now yours. My wife and I shall be out of the apartment by the first of April, as we had originally agreed. I want to compliment you on your willingness to take on my employees. There were others who were willing to buy the business, but none of them wanted to enter into the employment contract. I'm sure you'll be as successful in this business as I have been. Anyone who is willing to think of his employees as an essential part of his business, will surely succeed."

Michael shook hands with Dreschler, Welker, Schiller and Frau Dreschler. "You're like the son we've never had!" Frau Dreschler said tearfully as she shook his hand.

"Thank you Frau Dreschler. I hope we can be as successful as your husband has been." Michael smiled and kissed her hand.

Michael and Eberhard left with the signed documents and receipt. Schiller promised he would bring the codicil to the store after they moved in.

"Well Michael, you did it! Congratulations! Can you come over to my house before you go home? My wife and I would like to share some champagne with you and toast your new enterprise."

"Thanks Eberhard. I'd like that. But I'll have to be back at the station by twelve o'clock to catch the train."

"Oh you'll have plenty of time. I won't let you get drunk," he laughed. Hannelore Twielling was waiting for them. Eberhard had said after the purchase, he wanted to bring Michael back to the house to celebrate. She baked a special kuchen for the occasion and made fresh coffee. As she heard them climbing the stairs to their apartment, she met them at the door.

"Are you now the new owner of the Enz-Bote, Herr Bartholomae?"

"He is, Hannelore. Our friends are going to move in on the first of April," Eberhard told her.

"That's great, Herr Bartholomae!"

"Yes. I'm really looking forward to moving this next month."

Frau Twielling had set three glasses filled with the best of Schloss Kaltenstein's wine on the dining room table. Eberhard took up a glass, handed one to his wife, and the third to Michael. "Michael, here's to you and your new enterprise. May you have many years of success as the new owner of the Enz-Bote."

"And to you, your wife, and daughter," Frau twielling added. "May you have many more children! When you and your family arrive, Herr Bartholomae, I want you to come to our home for dinner. Your wife won't be in any position to cook on your first day in Vaihingen."

"Thank you very much Frau Twielling. This is a very auspicious beginning to what I hope will be many years of friendship with the two of you. My wife comes from a region much different from here. She'll feel like you did upon your arrival in Vaihingen. You've had to get used to to living among Schwaebians too!"

"Yes, but it's not hard when you have as good a husband as I have, Herr Bartholomae. My Eberhard is a gem of a person. He and his family made me feel right at home. Even though I'm an Alemaner, I've come to feel more and more at home here. I'm sure your wife will make the transition as easily as I have."

"Thank you. I hope so. The kuchen is delicious, Frau Twielling. I hope you can teach my wife to bake as good a kuchen as this. She's a good cook, but she doesn't do any baking. My mother is the baker in our family."

"I'd be glad to teach her."

"Michael, I don't want to rush you but you said you wanted to catch the noon train back to Kleinglattbach for the connecting train to Darmstadt. It's almost eleven thirty," Eberhard reminded him.

"You're right. I'd better be going. Frau Twielling, it's been a real pleasure to have seen you again. When Maria and I arrive with the baby, we'll be delighted to join you and your husband for dinner."

Frau Twielling said good bye to Michael. "Don't forget, we'll expect you for dinner when you arrive."

"That's right Michael. If Hannelore promises you a dinner, she'll do it."

Eberhard and Michael made it to the station just as the train was pulling in. Michael had already purchased his return ticket. As he got on he shook hands with his friend. "Eberhard, you've been my friend now for several years. I'm certainly grateful for all you've done. You told me about Vahingen and that the newspaper was for sale. I'm really indebted to you. I hope I can repay you for all your help."

"Don't mention it, Michael. I've just done what any friend would do. What are friends for, if you don't help them? Once you're established here in Vaihingen, I'm sure we'll see a lot more of each other. I'm just glad Dreschler didn't sell his newspaper to someone else."

Michael got on the train and sat at a window overlooking the platform where Eberhard stood. As the train pulled out, they waved good bye to each other. "See you on the first," Eberhard called out. The train went slowly down the track. Michael saw the castle one last time. Yes, he said to himself, this is going to be a great place to live and work with friends like the Twiellings. Maria will have someone to talk to who's also had to learn how to adjust to a new part of the country.

Upon his arrival back home, Michael told Maria all about his trip and purchase. He went into detail about the agreement, the attorney and the Twiellings.

"Frau Twielling had to make the adjustment of moving from one part of Germany to another. She had to adjust to a little town in Wuerttemberg from the state of Baden. I'm sure it must have been difficult for her at first. She seems to have overcome the difficulties very well. She's invited us to dinner on the day we arrive in Vaihingen. She understands how difficult it would be for you to try to cook on our first day in Vaihingen."

"What? She would do that? She must be quite some person. And I haven't even met her yet. That's going to be a very good introduction to our new community. We'll have to think of something we can bring the Twiellings."

The next two weeks went by very quickly. Not only did Maria finish the packing, she also had time to write to Frau Twielling a letter of thanks for her hospitality to her husband.

> Dear Frau Twielling!
>
> I am very much looking forward to meeting you. My husband and I are very pleased to accept your invitation to join you for dinner on the day of our arrival in Vaihingen/Enz. We will also have our little daughter, Emilie, with us if you don't mind. She's a toddler now and beginning to talk. We should be arriving around eleven a. m. After we start to unpack our bags and look over our apartment, we will come to your home at twelve noon. Thank you again for your kind invitation.
>
> Very sincerely yours,
> Maria Bartholomae

Michael gave his letter of resignation to the editor of the Darmstadter News.

> Dear Herr Reibolt!
>
> I am hereby submitting my resignation effective on the thirtieth of March, 1900. I have purchased a small newspaper in Vaihingen/Enz, Wuerttemberg and will take over ownership on the first of April.
>
> I have enjoyed my years of association with you and your colleagues very much. You have provided me with just the right type of management experience I needed to become the owner of a newspaper myself. Thank you for the opportunity of managing your presses these past seven years. The experience has been invaluable and very much appreciated.
>
> With high regards to you and your associates, I am
>
> Very respectfully yours,
> Michael Friederich Bartholomae

The editor was not at all pleased with his letter of resignation. He called him into his office and told him in no uncertain terms how disappointed he was.

"So, Herr Bartholomae, you're leaving us? We certainly never expected, when we made you our press manager, you would quit so abruptly. If I had known earlier, I would not have made you my assistant! Your resignation leaves us no choice but to sever your employment with us as of this next Monday. I expect you to have all of your belongings out by noon and that you will drop off the key in my office before you leave this building."

"Herr Reibolt," Michael said conciliatorily, "I'm more than willing to stay until the thirtieth. You won't have to pay me. I'll gladly assist you in getting a replacement and help train him. I'm sure the school in Schwaebish-Hall would have a number of pressmen to recommend to you."

"That won't be necessary! I'm sure we'll find a replacement! I'm just angered and surprised you didn't even ask my advice before buying the newspaper!"

"I really didn't want you to get upset, Herr Reibolt. First, I wasn't sure I'd be able to get the money together, And second, I didn't think you really cared about an ordinary pressman like me."

Michael extended his hand. Reibolt refused to shake hands. He shook his head and turned away.

"Good bye, Herr Reibolt. I'm sorry you feel this way," Michael said before he left.

On the way home that evening, he thought over what had transpired. I tried to be as helpful as I could, he told himself. If he doesn't want my help in training my replacement, I'll have several more days to get ready for our move. He did feel badly, however. He knew Reibolt didn't know a thing about the presses. What's he going to do in the meantime? He'll have to depend on Seibolt. He's a good journeyman. He can probably run the presses with assistance from the apprentice. I certainly hope so for Reibolt's sake. There are too many people who read the Darmstadter News. If he doesn't want my help, then that's his problem.

Over the next several days, Maria and Michael packed all of their things in boxes. Years later when Emilie had her own first child, her mother told her "You were a source of joy to us. Each afternoon I looked forward to taking you in the baby carriage for long walks along the Eschenbach Creek. The breeze was fresh and you fell asleep as soon as we reached the bank of the creek. I walked for an hour pushing you along the roadway on the creek's edge then returned home to make afternoon coffee for Papa and me."

It was a daily routine Maria continued as long as she could after moving to Vahingen. Ownership of the newspaper and store, however, changed her routine radically.

On the first of April, Michael bought the train tickets for their trip to their new home. He had arranged to have their things brought to the station the day before. When the landlord came to say good bye and collect the key, they were all ready to take the carriage to the station.

"So, Herr and Frau Bartholomae, you have everything in order for your departure I see," Herr Friedenburg, the landlord said.

"Yes, Herr Friedenburg. We're all set to leave. Thank you for renting your apartment to us. We've had a good place to live here in Darmstadt." Michael told him.

"You're most welcome. Here's a little something for your daughter to play with as she gets older." He handed Maria a small papier-mâché doll dressed in a formal brown gown and hat.

"Thank you very much, Herr Friedenburg," Maria and Michael said almost in unison. "I'm sure she'll enjoy playing with it when she gets a little older."

They shook hands with Herr Friedenburg. He also shook little Emilie's hand. "My, she's an attractive little girl, Frau Bartholomae. Take good care of her in your new home," he said as he waved good bye.

The driver drove the carriage down the street to the train station as all three Bartholomaes waved to Herr Friedenburg for the last time.

Chapter II

Moving to Vaihingen/Enz

It was a beautiful spring day on April 1, 1900, when the Bartholomaes arrived by train in Vaihingen/Enz. Michael hired a horse and wagon to take them and their things to their new home and business. The station was in Kleinglattbach. It was three kilometers from Vaihingen. It would have cost too much to move everything via the little freight train from the main trunk line into Vaihingen. As it was, the wagon ride was over a delightful roadway through the fields and orchards surrounding the village. Maria was amazed to be able to see village after village from the top of the hill just outside Kleinglattbach.

"Look over there, Maria," Michael said as he pointed toward the castle. "There's Schloss Kaltenstein! See how it dominates the surrounding countryside?"

"Oh, what a beautiful view! And look over there, Michael. There's another dip on the horizon and then the bright orange color of the roof tiles nestled in the valleys. If Vaihingen is anything like this panoramic view, it's going to be a beautiful place to live!"

Michael and Maria oohed and aahed all the way to Vaihingen. The castle in the distance was, indeed, an impressive site. Its stark silhouette stood out from the surrounding countryside. Even though they were almost at the same height on the hilltop coming into the village, its features gave evidence of its strength and formidability. As they came down the hill and approached the village, Maria asked, "What's that smell, Michael?"

Vaihingen was wreathed in the usual intermingled aroma of horse and cow manure together with the abundance of pear, plum, cherry, and apple blossoms that blessed the countryside each spring.

"Maria, what does your father's farm smell like this time of year? Have you forgotten? The farmers have spread the manure over their fields, and that's what you smell together with these beautiful fruit blossoms!"

"Ah yes. I had almost forgotten. I've lived in Darmstadt too long!" Maria said sheepishly. "I'll get used to it. But the fragrance of these fruit trees . . . It's almost overwhelming!"

As the driver came down the hill and drove under the railway bridge, Michael pointed ahead of the horses. "There it is, Maria! That's our new business!"

Maria looked to the left and to the right and saw only huge houses on each side of the road.

"Which one, Michael? I only see houses. I don't seen any businesses!"

"Look straight ahead of you. See that big yellow stucco building ahead of us on the left? That's it."

Maria looked straight down the street. There, just where the street seemed to narrow, she saw the building. Across the front of it was a large sign Der Enz Bote. "You mean that's it?"

"Exactly!"

As the driver came closer, she saw the sides of the building and the store. "Oh, that's a big building, Michael. You mean this is what you bought?"

"Exactly! Wait until you see the apartment. It's a lot bigger than the one we had in Darmstadt."

Maria did, indeed, like the apartment and business combination. She could help keep track of the finances, she thought to herself. After she looked over the apartment, she said, "Do you think we could find someone to help take care of Emilie? I'd have more time to look after the books then."

"Why don't you just settle in first, Maria?" Michael suggested. "There's plenty of time for that. I've got Wimmer and Uhralt to look after the books for the time being. Once we're moved in and you have things the way you want them, we'll take over the bookkeeping. Don't worry about it for now. Besides," Michael went on, "we're invited over to the Twiellings' for dinner today."

"Oh, that's right. I had forgotten. It's a good thing. We don't have anything to eat in the house!"

"We can go shopping this afternoon. I'm sure Frau Twielling will tell us where to shop for milk and bread and the other things that we'll need," Michael assured her.

While Michael and the wagoner moved their things into the apartment, Maria went through it to decide which items she would keep and which ones she would throw out. Let's see, she said to herself, the furniture can stay as well as the kitchen items. But we don't need these old brooms, curtains, and bathroom brushes. It's a good thing I brought them all with me. When she looked for the toilet, she found it in the basement at the far end of the press room. We'll have to keep this window open and get this stench out of it, she said almost out loud. Michael had told her it had to be located here.

"Each spring a local farmer comes to clean it out. He throws the contents directly into his manure wagon from the alley door. It's the only place that's practical to clean out each year. Everyone does the same. It's better than throwing it in the street!" Michael said. Maria had brought her chamber pots from Darmstadt. Since she was used to emptying them daily into the toilet, it now meant she had to walk a longer distance to the rear of the building. I guess I'll get used to it, she told herself.

"I think you've made a good purchase," Maria told Michael. "I think we'll get along here just fine."

"I'm glad you like it, Maria. Since you couldn't look it over with me, I had to make the decision myself. You had to nurse Emilie, and you were also pregnant again so I had to make the choice. It's not as big a city as Darmstadt, but the people I've met are real friendly."

After the wagon was unloaded, Michael washed himself while Maria changed Emilie's diapers. She put on the newest dress and shoes that she had bought for Emilie in Darmstadt. She wanted the Twiellings to see her daughter at her best. She also put a pretty little bonnet on her so that she looked every bit the spring flower Michael called her. Michael changed into his good suit. Maria put on her finest dark green dress with the big bustle and wore her new broad-brimmed hat. They then walked the two blocks to the Twielling's. The church bell rang twelve o'clock just as Michael rang the doorbell.

"Ah, Herr Bartholomae, you're exactly on time! How nice to see you again," Hannelore Twielling said. "And this is your wife and daughter?" she asked as she extended her hand to Maria. Maria had picked up Emilie and was holding her as they came in the doorway.

"Yes, Frau Twielling," Michael said. "This is my wife, Maria, and my daughter, Emilie." Maria shook hands and said, "How nice of you to have us over for dinner, Frau Twielling."

"And this is your beautiful little girl?" Frau Twielling asked as she looked at Emilie "Let me hold her. I haven't held a child in a long time. I hope I have a girl as sweet as you are, little Emilie!"

She gave her a big kiss on her cheek. "You're so fortunate in having a child, Frau Bartholomae. We don't have any yet," she said sorrowfully.

Herr Twielling came to the door. "Well, Michael, so you've finally brought your wife and daughter to Vaihingen? What does your wife think of the business?"

"It's a lot bigger than I thought," Maria said. "We'll have our work cut out for us here."

"Yes, Eberhard. This is my wife Maria," Michael answered.

"Very nice to meet you, Frau Bartholomae. And this is Emilie?"

"How do you do, Herr Twielling," Maria said. "Yes, this is our daughter."

"Look how bright her eyes are, Eberhard! And look how nicely she's dressed!" Hannelore Twielling exclaimed. "Come in, Herr and Frau Bartholomae. Dinner's ready."

Frau Twielling carried Emilie into the dining room. Emilie looked to see where her mother was. Maria indicated with her eyes it was okay for her to be carried by Frau Twielling. She placed her on a little high chair.

"This is what my parents gave us last year," she went on. "They think it's time for us to have children!"

"Hannelore, don't get started on that again," Eberhard told her. "We haven't even been married a year yet!"

"I wouldn't worry, Frau Twielling," Maria said. "You'll have a child before you know it! Michael and I were surprised when Emilie arrived and now I'm pregnant again. It won't take long."

"I certainly hope not, Frau Bartholomae. I'd like to have a little daughter like Emilie. She's so cute!"

Eberhard poured wine for each of them from the bottle which Michael had brought. It was a dark red Mossel wine which he had first tasted in Darmstadt.

"Here's to you and your wife, Michael. May your years in Vaihingen be prosperous and happy ones. We feel honored to have you with us and look forward to many more years of pleasant times together."

"And to you and your wife, I want to thank you for your hospitality and kind invitation to join you for dinner. I trust our years together will be a continuation of the friendship which began in the Wuerttemberg Rifles Division," Michael replied.

The dinner was a very good one, with boiled potatoes, roast beef, green salad, and green beans. Frau Twielling made a special onion kuchen for dessert. As they left, Maria gave Frau Twielling a book she had bought in a Darmstadt bookstore.

"Frau Twielling, I saw this book in Darmstadt and thought you might like to have it. My brother, who's a doctor, gave me this book when he heard I was pregnant. It's an excellent introduction to becoming a parent."

"Oh, thank you very much, Frau Bartholomae. *When You Become Parents*," she read the title out loud. "I certainly hope that's true one of these days. See, Eberhard? Now we'll know what to do when we have our first child." she chided her husband.

On their way home, Maria said to Michael, "Frau Twielling is very nice. But she certainly does want a child of her own pretty badly, doesn't she?"

"I agree. But I don't think Eberhard is in any hurry. He wants to wait until he's thirty. He'd like to build a house out in the country first. He told me once that's what he missed most when he was growing up. His parents didn't build a house in the country until his father retired. He wants his children to experience grass under their feet and a garden with trees and flowers. "No," Michael said slowly, "I'm afraid it's going to be some years yet before Frau Twielling has any children."

Michael made friends very easily in Vaihingen. He was a tall man, well built, with a large frame and a booming voice. As was the practice at that time, he had a small mustache and wore pince-nez glasses. The latter were used mostly for reading, and he carried them on a long tassel around his neck. He kept his bookshelves stacked with the latest editions and added new supplies to the stationery section as they were needed.

"Herr Wimmer," Michael said shortly after they had moved in, "I want you and Herr Uhralt to be sure to have whatever supplies teachers or pupils might need for school. There's no need for them to go to Stuttgart to buy their books and papers. I want you to give me a weekly list of items that we need and I'll see to it that we have them."

"Certainly, Herr Bartholomae. Herr Dreschler didn't seem to think that was necessary, but if that's what you want, we'll do it," Wimmer promised.

Uhralt chimed in, "Herr Dreschler didn't want a lot of children around his store, Herr Bartholomae. He was afraid they might knock something over!"

"Well, that may have been Herr Dreschler's wish, but I want people to feel free to come into my store anytime they need something. If we don't have it, I want you to tell them we'll try and get it for them. There's nothing worse than a dissatisfied customer to ruin a store's reputation!"

"Yes, sir, Herr Bartholomae. I just thought I'd tell you what Herr Dreschler used to say," Uhralt replied sheepishly. "I didn't mean to object to what you want, Herr Bartholomae."

Michael didn't say any more to his store employees. He wanted to see what kinds of lists they presented him each week. When there were requests for such items as notebooks, tablets, and erasers added to the list, he felt his employees had gotten the message.

Wilfried Welker and the two apprentices were doing an excellent job with the presses. They needed little, if any, guidance. Michael undertook to increase the weekly ads. Dreschler had a few firms that had stayed with him ever since he bought the business. The news items were pretty much announcements of meetings, birthdays, church notices, births, and deaths in and around the village. Rarely were there any items of importance about the country as a whole. Occasionally, articles about the Wuerttemberg king and his family were carried, but only if they were sent directly to the attention of Herr Dreschler.

"Who are our reporters, Herr Welker?" Michael asked his pressman.

"We haven't really had any, Herr Bartholomae. Herr Dreschler wanted to hire someone when he first got started, he once told me, but I've never seen anyone hired for that position."

"How does the news of the region get reported?" Michael asked.

"Generally, local people stop in each Monday and drop off items they think might be of interest to the community. Sometimes there's hardly anything to report. And other times, we had too much. Herr Dreschler told us never to print more than four sheets of news items and ads. He didn't think people could read very well anyway," Welker continued. "Put in as many pictures as you can, Herr Dreschler told me. People can at least understand the ads. We always had lots of pictures in them."

"Well, I want you to put this notice in next week's *Enz-Bote*," Michael said sternly. "Wanted: a man who is interested in becoming a reporter for the *Enz-Bote*. Five Reichsmarks per week. Interested persons should apply at the office Monday through Saturday, 8-12 a.m. or 1-6 p.m."

"I don't think there's anyone around here who's capable of being a reporter," Welker said offhand.

"I didn't ask you if you thought there was anyone who might be interested, Herr Welker. I only told you to run this ad in next week's edition!"

"I'm only trying to save you from disappointment, Herr Bartholomae. I'll put in whatever ad you want. As I said, Herr Dreschler tried it, but it didn't work."

"Herr Welker, I want this understood right from the beginning. If I want your advice, I'll ask you. Otherwise, I'll make my own decisions. Is that clear?"

"Certainly, Herr Bartholomae. I meant no harm. I'll put the ad in next week's issue."

Michael was irritated by his pressman's reluctance. Just like in the store, he thought. Wimmer and Uhralt told me what Dreschler did and didn't do. I don't care what he did.

I want to establish this newspaper and business as the most important in the region. No wonder we don't have any news of any consequence. There's no one here to do it, he muttered to himself.

After this first encounter, Welker proved to require little, if any, guidance in printing the local paper. Michael knew the presses were very well kept. He decided he would go from business to business, not only making his acquaintance known to the villagers, but also to drum up business for his printing service. Before the end of the summer, he had contacted every businessman in the village. He also had become acquainted with many of the farmers in and around Vaihingen. He attended the weekly horse and cattle markets on the street just behind the store. As much as he disliked the advice he had received from Welker about not finding anyone interested in becoming a reporter, he was greatly chagrined that not a single man stopped by to apply for the job. In his visits on businesses and farmers, he encouraged them to let him know if anyone had any news of interest for the community.

"Just drop me a note or stop in the office. I'll see that it gets into the newspaper."

Week by week, more and more information filtered through his office for publication. By the end of the first year in Vaihingen, Michael's business had become an established fixture in the community. The sales of the newspaper had quadrupled, he hired an additional pressman, and he and Maria were expecting their second child. Michael hoped it would be a boy. He very much wanted someone to follow in his footsteps and eventually take over the business. He never told anyone he was sorry his first child was a girl, but Emilie always sensed his disappointment when he introduced her to his friends.

"This is my daughter, Emilie. We had planned to call her Emil, if she were a boy, but since she's a girl, Emilie is the next best thing to Emil," he said jokingly. It was only later in life that she realized there was more truth than humor in his comment. Her mother told her her father thought she would be a boy. After all, every Bartholomae going back four generations had had a boy as their first child.

Life seemed more than good to the Bartholomaes. Michael and Maria were accepted in this little village even though they were not natives of it. Their business was thriving. Michael was making a name for himself among the local town officials as well as among the local people. When he was seen on the streets, he was greeted with "Gruess Gott, Herr Bartholomae!" (Good day, Mr. Bartholomae.)

When a farmer on the outskirts of Vaihingen let it be known he was interested in selling a hectare of land along the subsidiary train line just beyond the underpass, Michael went to look it over. The field started at the south side of Heilbronner Street and went up the hill toward the cemetery. There were a variety of apple, cherry, plum, and pear trees on it full of ripening fruits. Green grass and clover grew between the rows of fruit trees which the farmer cut for his cows. This is just the place I've been looking for, he said to himself. I can build a little summer house on it and have a place for our children to play. He walked to the Greiner farm and asked to speak with Herr Greiner.

When he knocked at the door of the farm house, Frau Greiner came to the door. "Herr Bartholomae, what a surprise to see you! What can we do for you?"

"Gruess Gott, Frau Greiner. Is your husband home?"

"I'm sorry but my husband isn't here just now. He's out in the barn milking the cows. Could he stop and see you tomorrow?"

"That's all right, Frau Greiner. I'll go out to the barn and talk with him."

"But you'll get all dirty, Herr Bartholomae!"

"That's okay. I'll be careful."

Michael made his way out to the barn, stepping carefully around the pile of manure just outside the door. The door to the barn was just twenty meters from the door to the house. He went in and found Herr Greiner milking one of his large Simmenthaler cows.

"Gruess Gott, Herr Greiner. I'm Herr Bartholomae and I've heard you want to sell a hectare on the edge of Vaihingen just beyond the railway underpass."

"Hello, Herr Bartholomae. If you don't mind, I'll keep on milking. Yes, I want to sell a hectare. Are you interested in buying it?"

"Yes, I am. What are you asking for it?"

"Two hundred Reichsmarks."

"That's quite a lot, Herr Greiner."

"I don't think so. A neighbor of mine got one hundred Reichsmarks for half a hectare that's near the train station. That's a fair price."

"Let me think about it, Herr Greiner."

"Don't wait too long, Herr Bartholomae. I've got another man that's talked to me about it too. He says he wants it for the future when he has children."

"I'll let you know by Friday, Herr Greiner."

"The other man said he'd give me one hundred seventy-five, but I told him that's not enough. So, unless he comes back and gives me what I'm asking, it may still be available on Friday, Herr Bartholomae."

Michael returned home quickly. He wanted to talk it over with Maria. They had made a profit that first year and had a savings account in the bank. It wasn't that he couldn't afford it; he wanted to have her approval since she was the bookkeeper for the business. She knew all about cash flows, debits, and credits. She also had been concerned with the ad he had run for a reporter.

"Why do you think we need a reporter, Michael? Five Reichsmarks a week is two hundred sixty a year! If we could save that much each year, we would build up a goodly sum with which to buy something else. You know we need a contingency fund just in case we have some emergency."

He had gotten angry with Maria on that occasion. He really wanted a reporter to build up the sales of the newspaper.

"How else are we going to increase our sales if we don't have access to more news? You sound just like Welker! He told me we wouldn't find a reporter around here. Dreschler tried it and couldn't find anyone!"

Dreschler hadn't had a single applicant for the job, Michael recalled to himself. It wasn't necessary to get angry either with her or with Welker, he reminded himself. As he came into the office, he saw Maria working on the books. They had decided to hire a local girl to help her take care of Emilie and to clean the apartment. This allowed Maria more time to undertake the bookkeeping chores for the business. She was getting bigger, he thought, as he saw her sitting at her desk. She was now six months pregnant with their second child. He was pleased with how well things were going with the business and the family.

"Maria, guess what? I've found just the piece of property that we can use for the summer cottage I want to build."

"You want to buy some more land? Why don't we pay off this mortgage first, Michael, before we buy something else?"

"Yes, but this is a whole hectare, and it's right past the underpass on Heilbronner Street. The farmer won't have it very long, I'm sure. He's already got someone else interested in buying it! He's asking two hundred Reichsmarks. There are about ten fruit trees of various kinds and a beautiful sloping meadow coming down from the cemetery. Why don't you go with me a minute, and we'll both take a look at it?"

"Two hundred Reichsmarks? That's almost as much as you wanted to pay a reporter!" Maria said with a laugh.

Michael didn't appreciate the humor at his expense. He ignored her rejoinder.

"Come on, Maria. Get your coat on and we'll walk up the street and look it over. You need to get out and walk more anyway. Didn't the doctor say you should walk at least two kilometers a day until your eighth month?"

Michael got her coat and held it while she slipped into it. "It's not very cold out, Michael. I don't need a coat."

"Put it on anyway. It may be colder by the time we come back."

Maria took his arm, and they walked up the hill to the field just outside Vaihingen. As they went under the railroad bridge, they saw two morning doves sitting in the giant sycamore trees on the edge of the property. The male was cooing loudly to his mate and making amorous gestures toward her.

"Look, Maria. What do you think he's interested in doing?" Michael laughed.

"You males are all alike, aren't you?" Maria replied tauntingly.

"We know a good thing when we see it, Maria." He squeezed her arm lovingly.

"It's just like this field. Take a look up the hill. The hectare goes almost to the cemetery gates. We could build a little cottage on it, and the children can come and play here during the day. We can put in a sandbox for them. And in the winters they can use their sleds for sliding. It would be a great place for you to come with them. We'd have plenty of fruit each season too!"

"It's a beautiful field, Michael. But two hundred Reichsmarks seems awfully high. Why don't you offer him one hundred ninety?" Maria countered.

"Greiner already has another man interested in it. I don't think he'll sell it for less than two hundred."

"If you can buy it for less, I wouldn't be opposed," she finally said.

"I'll talk to him again, but if he won't take less than two hundred, I'll buy it anyway."

Since they were almost to the castle, they continued their walk to its ramparts overlooking the Enz and the broad fields below.

"Isn't that a beautiful view, Maria? Look out to the west. You can see Illingen. Toward the south there's Aurich. And toward the east, there's Enzweihingen. And to the north there's the hill with the whole village of Vaihingen below it."

"It's beautiful, Michael. We're very lucky to have found this place. It's just the kind of setting in which to raise our children. I hope Papa and Mama come to visit us next summer. I'm sure they'll be as impressed with Vaihingen as we are."

They stood together arm in arm, leaning against the castle ramparts and looked out over the broad vistas before them. "Yes, this is great place to live and have a family," they said almost in unison.

They walked back in silence, each in their own thoughts. Michael thought about what to say to Greiner about buying the field; Maria, what the new baby would look like in a few more months.

On Friday afternoon at five o'clock, Michael went to see Herr Greiner again. Greiner was in the cow barn milking his cows.

"So, Herr Bartholomae. What have you decided?" he asked as he continued to milk his cow.

"Herr Greiner, I'll make you an offer. I'll give you one hundred ninety Reichsmarks for the hectare. I've looked it over and decided that would be more than a fair price for it."

"Impossible!" Greiner retorted. "I could sell half of it for almost that amount!"

"We only want it as a playground for our children, Herr Greiner. We're not going to build a house on it. Maybe a garden house, but nothing substantial. I'd like to be able to have our children experience something of the outdoors, just like you do. I want them to breathe the fresh air and have the feel of grass under their feet and enjoy the songs of the birds. They can't really do that in the village. Your field would be ideal for them. What do you say? One hundred ninety-five and I'll take it off your hands?"

"Herr Bartholomae, for the sake of your children, I'll take it. But I want you to promise me I can come cut the hay off of it each summer for the next five years. If that's agreeable with you, I'll accept your offer."

"You've got a deal, Herr Greiner. I'll have my attorney draw up the papers for the sale."

Greiner had just completed milking the cow and stood up with his pail in one hand and the milk stool in the other. He set the stool down and shook hands with Michael. It was agreed he would sell his field for one hundred ninety five Reichsmarks, and he had the right to make the hay on it for five years.

Michael felt he had achieved success. He paid a little more than Maria had wanted, but he did get his field. Maria was disappointed he had promised to let Greiner harvest the hay for five years.

"How can you build a summer cottage on it now? Herr Greiner will object that you have broken your agreement to let him harvest the hay."

"I don't think he'll mind when I tell him I want it for our children. It'll only take up a little space. It won't ruin his hay field."

"Are you sure? Don't you think you better tell him what you're planning to do? Otherwise, he'll sue you for breach of contract, Michael. That would not be very good for the newspaper."

"All right, I'll go and talk to him again. But I still think you're making a mountain out of a mole hill."

After Michael had the bill of sale drawn up by Karl Schiller, he took it over to Greiner for his signature and the transfer of the property to himself.

As Greiner was signing the deed transferring the hectare to Michael, he mentioned "Oh, by the way, you wouldn't mind if I build a little cottage on one end of the lot for the children, would you?"

"Herr Bartholomae, an agreement is an agreement. You agreed you would let me cut the hay from the field for five years. How could I do that if you build a cottage on it?" Greiner asked.

"I would just build it on the top end. It would hardly take any of the hay away from the rest of the field," Michael countered.

"What does it say in this agreement, Herr Bartholomae? It says, 'Herr Walter Greiner has the right to harvest the hay from the one hectare field for five years which he this day conveys to Herr Michael Friederich Bartholomae.' That means exactly what it says. You cannot remove any part of it from what I want to harvest!"

Michael got upset with Greiner. "What do you mean I can't do with my field whatever I want to do, Herr Greiner? I'm not going to take more than ten square meters for the cottage. Surely that won't disrupt your hay-making capability from the field?"

"Herr Bartholomae, I've said it before. I'll say it again. The agreement says I have the right to make hay on this hectare for the next five years. Period! You cannot exclude any part of it from this agreement."

"Nonsense! I can do with my land whatever I choose. If you're going to be this disagreeable about the contract, consider it torn up. I'll pay you your two hundred Reichsmarks, and my attorney will see to it that the deed is duly drawn up and recorded without any exclusions written into it!"

And with that, Michael took the agreement and tore it up. "That's what I wanted in the first place, Herr Bartholomae. But if someone doesn't pay me my price, then I'll make the conditions so disagreeable that he'll see the benefit of my original offer. But I will be willing to cut whatever amount of hay you'll allow me after you've built your cottage."

Michael paid the two hundred Reichsmarks. He felt he had been had. "I'll see what's left of the field after I build the cottage, Herr Greiner." He realized Greiner had gotten the better of him. He would wait and see about making a deal. He didn't want to rush into anything ahead of time.

Michael Friederich Bartholomae II was born on August 11, 1901. He was the long-awaited successor to Michael's business. At least that's what he hoped would be the case. Michael II was a big baby with blue eyes and light brown hair just like his father. In contrast to Emilie, who looked very much like her mother, with dark brown eyes and dark brown hair, Michael II was almost blond. With the baby's arrival, Michael wanted to invite all of their friends to come to a celebration dinner at the Alte Ente, a restaurant on the banks of the Enz River. He invited the Twiellings, the Schillers, the Conradts, the Rapps, and the Meyers. Maria didn't feel much like celebrating. It had been a hard birth for her.

"I don't think I can go, Michael. I'm still a little weak. If you want to have a party, why don't you go ahead and have the party without me. I'm sure they'll understand."

"We can't invite people to come, Maria, if you don't attend your own party. How would that look to our friends?"

"You're the one who has invited them, Michael. I wanted you to wait until Fritzle is a little older. Christmas would be early enough for me," Maria said reproachfully.

"It's too late now. I've already arranged the party."

After her two-week bed stay, Maria got dressed for the party. Michael had agreed she could leave right after dessert. Michael hired a carriage to take her to the restaurant and home again. She would never have made it on foot. He had to lift her into and out of the carriage. She was not strong enough to get in and out by herself. When Michael and Maria arrived at the Alte Ente their friends greeted them with "Hoch soll sie leben, hoch soll sie leben, drei mal hoch!" (Three cheers!)

It was a festive evening at the Alte Ente. One round of toasts after another was offered by each of the men. Maria had learned to sip her wine for each toast. Michael drank a half a glass with each toast. Eberhard Twielling, on the other hand, was almost out from the repeated toasts. By the time dinner was served, he could barely keep awake. Hannelore Twielling had the waiter bring him coffee so he could wake up enough to eat. By the time dessert was served, he had laid his head on the table and was fast asleep. Frau Twielling ordered a carriage and took him home shortly after dessert and coffee. The driver helped take him into their house, and she put him to bed. The rest of the party broke up shortly thereafter. Michael gave each man a bottle of the best Wuerttemberger wine the Alte Ente had in stock. Maria found out later the whole evening cost them 150 Reichsmarks!

"How can we save money when you spend it like that, Michael?" she asked perplexed.

"We only have our first son once, Maria. I wanted our friends to celebrate the occasion of Fritzle's birth with us."

Unfortunately, Michael Friederich Bartholomae II lived only nine months. He died of diphtheria before doctors discovered what was wrong with him. Michael and Maria were devastated. Michael's plans for a successor were all for nought. Maria cried uncontrollably for two days. Even little Emilie couldn't understand why she didn't stop crying.

"What's wrong with Mama?" she asked her father. "Why is she crying? Does something hurt her?"

"You're too young to understand, Emilie. When you're older you'll know why she's crying."

It was only after Grandfather and Grandmother Meyer came for the funeral that Maria began to get a hold of herself. Grandmother tried her best to console her.

"It's not that bad, Maria. You're still young. You can have many more children. After all, I've lost two infants myself. It's one of those features of life you'd better get used to. What God gives, he also takes away. It doesn't help to continue to cry over what you can't change."

Grief-stricken though they were, Michael and Maria did, indeed, try again. This time they had another little daughter, Luise, born in 1902. Michael was bitterly disappointed. No one noticed it, except Maria. He became busier than ever in the business. Maria suggested they should have more help. Adolf Uhralt had retired, and since there was no one else to help Herr Wimmer, Maria had assumed more of the responsibility in running the store. She not only kept the books, she now had to assist in ordering items and in shelving them when they arrived. Michael hired a young woman to assist her.

"Now that we've hired Fraeulein Weidling, you can spend more time with Emilie and Luise, Maria," Michael told her. Maria thought that was a good idea. She taught Fraeulein Weidling how to keep track of the paper supplies.

"Fraeulein Weidling, when the inventory is down to the last five items on any of the shelves, it's time to place a new order."

"*Ja*, Frau Bartholomae. I'll let you know when I place a new order for books or paper."

With Herr Wimmer and Fraeulein Weidling, the store was not only making a profit, it had increased its line of items to include typewriters, ribbons, and wrapping paper in addition to the books and school supplies. As the business grew, Michael and Maria had another one of those arguments over money. Maria wanted to expand the help in the financial end of the business. Michael, on the other hand, didn't want too many people familiar with his accounts.

"Michael, I think we need a bookkeeper to help me in the office. I can't keep up with all of the new accounts, plus doing all of the washing, cooking, ironing, cleaning, shopping, and caring for our daughters! It's getting to be too much for me!"

"What? I don't want outsiders knowing what our finances are. That's no one's business but ours. If you need help, I'll assist you. But we're not hiring someone else to do what we should do!"

"That's fine, but I still need help caring for the household. Even with your help, I still can't keep up with everything a housewife is supposed to do!"

"Why don't we have my mother come and live with us? Since Father died, she's all alone. I'm sure she wouldn't mind living here in Vaihingen."

"We'd have to pay her, Michael. I wouldn't feel comfortable simply having her work here for nothing!"

"I think we can arrange that. I'm sure she'd probably like a little extra money. I don't think she gets a very large amount from Father's pension."

Michael's mother, Frau Hetwig Bartholomae, had only been a widow for three years. Grandfather Bartholomae was the village postmaster in Eschenbach. It was a good position. He was in His Imperial Majesty's (King Ludwig of Wuerttemberg) service. It was an office he was granted as a consequence of his distinguished service during the Franco-Prussian War of 1870-71. He was a postal clerk when the war broke out. As a reservist in His Majesty's Wuerttemberg Rifles Division, he was called in when the south German states agreed to go to war against France on the side of Prussia. He was a corporal at the time of his call up. During the attack of the Third Army (of which the Wuerttemberg Rifles Division was a part) on Paris in November 29, 1870, he led an assault party against the French lines attempting to break through on the "twin hearts" of the Wuerttemberg defense system (the villages of Villeiers-sur-Marne and Coeuilly). The assault party, under his leadership, captured the French Army courier who bore the dispatches from General Auguste Alexandre Ducrot informing the high command of his proposed attack on the German positions. August Bartholomae was given, not only a medal, but a field promotion to sergeant-major. After the war, he got his appointment as a royal postmaster. He held the post for thirty-one years. He died at age fifty-seven of pneumonia. At first Grandmother Bartholomae didn't know how she was going to survive without her August. She had a small pension from his service, but she wondered if it would be sufficient. She felt obligated to help her second son, Paul Bartholomae, because of his heart condition.

Michael wrote his mother and asked if she might like to come and live with them in Vaihingen/Enz.

Dear Mother,

We are very pleased with how business is going here in Vaihingen. It's not only a very pleasant village but also an enterprising one. We have had so much business since we moved here, I've had to hire three additional persons to work in the store and on the presses. We really need someone now who has the bookkeeping skills and background necessary to keep our Company's books. Maria has the requisite training and skills to handle our finances. However, as you know, we now have two little girls who need full-time care and attention. Unfortunately, Maria cannot do all of the cooking, washing, house cleaning, and caring for our daughters, plus take care of our books. We were wondering, Mother, if you would like to come and live with us so that you could help Maria care for and look after our children. We will gladly pay you for your services.

Please give this employment/living arrangement serious consideration. We would be only too happy to have you live with us as long as you would like to stay.

Give our best regards to Paul and Friederich and their families. Maria and I shall look forward to your response with grateful appreciation.

Your loving son,
Michael, with wife Maria

Hetwig Bartholomae was overjoyed with the letter. She enjoyed being around children. Whenever Michael, Maria, and the girls visited her in Heilbronn, she read stories to Emilie and Luise, took them for walks, and baked cookies while the girls "helped." Grandmother Hetwig gave Michael's offer careful consideration. She felt she could be a real help to her son and daughter-in-law. She now knew what she could do with her house. With the death of her August three years earlier, she wondered what she was going to do with all of the room she had in her big house. She had already invited Paul, her second son, and his family to come and live with her. He took up her offer. She lived in the downstairs apartment, and Paul and his family lived on the second floor.

The same evening she received Michael's letter, she went upstairs to talk to her son Paul and his wife, Madel.

"Paul, Michael wants me to come and live with them in Vaihingen/Enz. They need help with their two girls while Maria works in the store. What would you think if I rented my apartment and moved to Vaihingen?"

"But Mother, you don't even know if you would like it in Vaihingen. What would you do if you wanted to come back and didn't have your apartment anymore?" Paul asked plaintively.

"I'll like it, Paul. You and Madel don't need me. She takes good care of your two girls. Michael and Maria must need me; otherwise, he wouldn't have written inviting me to come."

Paul went out to the kitchen and got his wife to come into the living room to discuss what his mother should do.

"What? She wants to leave Heilbronn?" Madel was shocked. "But she doesn't even know anyone there, except Michael, and she barely knows Maria! She'd get homesick in a very few days!"

"Well, come into the living room and tell her that. She doesn't listen to me."

"Mother, Paul tells me you want to go to Vaihingen/Enz. Who do you know there besides Michael? You hardly know Maria! What would you do if you wanted to come back to Heilbronn and you had rented your apartment? Where would you live?"

"I'm sure I'll like it in Vaihingen. After all, Michael and his family have been here a few times, and I get along very well with Maria. I'm sure it'll be all right if I move down there with them."

"If you won't listen to us, at least let us move downstairs and we'll rent our apartment. How would that be?" Paul asked.

"That's all right with me. You can look after the apartment for me, and I won't ask for any rent," his mother offered.

"Well, if you want to leave us and go to some place you've never been and where you don't have any friends, then that's your decision! We won't keep you. Don't you think you ought to ask Fritz about whether or not you should move?"

"I'm sure he and Emilie won't mind. Since they've gotten married, I hardly even see him anymore. Besides, he's like your father. As a postal official, he could be moved at any time anywhere in Wuerttemberg. He may not even be here in Heilbronn much longer. But I will talk with him before I go," she promised.

The very next evening, Hetwig Bartholomae visited her youngest son, Friederich, and his recent bride, Emilie. In contrast to Madel, Emilie Bartholomae was an outgoing and friendly young woman whom the whole family liked very much. Michael had a hard time accepting Madel, on the other hand. She was only solicitous of her husband's well-being. If Paul said he was tired and wanted to rest, Madel made sure their daughters were quiet. She also reminded Michael about his promise to help his brother, Paul, whenever he needed it because "of his heart condition." Even Michael's two girls preferred to visit Aunt Emilie and Uncle Fritz rather than Aunt Madel and Uncle Paul when they went to visit Grandmother Bartholomae. They were more fun to be with even though they didn't have any children while Uncle Paul and Aunt Madel had two girls about the same ages as Emilie and Luise.

Fritz and Emilie Bartholomae lived only three blocks from his mother. As Frau Hetwig Bartholomae rang the door bell, she wondered if they heard it. She had come by on occasion only to find no one came to the door after she rang the doorbell. She rang it again. There was still no answer. I'd better try knocking on their window, she told herself. Certainly, if they're home, they'll hear that. She used her house key and tapped on their bedroom window. Fritz opened the window and asked, "Who is it?"

"It's me, Fritz. It's your mother! I need to talk to you and Emilie right away. Your brother, Michael, wants me to move to Vaihingen/Enz."

"Okay, just a minute. I've got to get my pants on!"

It seemed a long time that she stood at the door waiting for her son to open it. Finally, she heard the dead bolt unlock and the key in the door which opened it.

"So, finally. You didn't have to get all dressed up for me. I just wanted to talk to you and Emilie for few minutes."

"That's all right, Mother. It's nice you stopped by. I'm sorry I was sleeping when you knocked on the window. Why didn't you ring the doorbell?"

"I did! But neither of you heard me. That's when I tapped on your window," she laughed as she kissed her son and daughter-in-law.

"I've already talked with Paul and Madel about it, and I promised him I'd talk with you too. Michael wants me to come to Vaihingen and take care of their two girls while

Maria works in their store. You don't mind, do you? I hardly ever see the two of you anymore anyway. You're always so busy with your jobs," she said teasingly.

"That sounds like an excellent idea, Mother. I'm sure Michael will pay you, too. I don't think you could get any better arrangement than that. Maria's a real business woman. I can see why she would need some help with her girls. I think she would rather work in the store than wash and sew!" Fritz laughed.

"Of course, your friends are here, Mother," Emilie said. "You'll have to get acquainted with a lot of new people in Vaihingen. But that shouldn't be a problem for you. After all, they're all Schwaebians down there too!"

"What's going to happen to your apartment, Mother?" Fritz asked.

"Paul has already asked me if they could move into it, and they'll rent their upstairs apartment."

"Paul's always thinking ahead, isn't he? I'll bet he won't pay you any rent, either," Fritz added.

"Why should he? I'm not using it if I'm living in Vaihingen. Besides, with his heart condition, it will be better for him not to have to walk upstairs all the time."

"You certainly are a good-natured woman, Mother," Emilie said emphatically. "I wouldn't let anyone use my apartment without paying me rent!"

Hetwig packed her bags and moved to Vaihingen that next Saturday. Fritz took her to the station, and since she had written Michael, when she was coming, he waited for her at the main trunk line in Kleinglattbach. They then took the local train into Vaihingen, arriving at one o'clock. Maria had prepared dinner for them. Grandmother Bartholomae was very pleased when she saw the bedroom which had been set aside for her.

"This is perfect," she told Michael and Maria. "I can look out at the horse and cattle market from my window. That's what I've missed living in Heilbronn. I don't see many farm animals where I live," she laughed.

The next several years saw an increase in the size of Michael's business as well as in his family. Lina was born in 1905. On the hectare Michael had purchased on the outskirts of the town, he had a weekend cottage built among the fruit trees. It was close to the village, yet far enough away to give them the feeling they were leaving for a weekend whenever they went there. Grandmother Bartholomae took the girls to the cottage as often as possible. She wanted to make sure they were outside several hours a day in the "clean, fresh air" as she reminded them.

"Come along, girls. Get your hats and coats on. We're going to get a breath of fresh air" was almost a daily ritual for them.

When Lina was a baby, Grandmother wheeled the baby carriage with Lina in it. Emilie and Luise went on ahead, hand in hand. Occasionally, Luise would try to run away from Emilie, and she would have to run after her to keep her from running into the street.

"Luise, you behave!" Grandmother would scold. "Take Emilie's hand and walk nicely up the path. You don't want to be run over by a carriage, do you?"

These were idyllic days for the girls. They spent hours each day among the fruit trees and in the cottage. Grandmother packed a lunch for them and brought drinks so they could stay until late afternoon. As the four of them left, Maria watched from the door until they had walked the three and one half blocks to the "garden," as Grandmother called it.

Maria thought Grandmother Bartholomae was an excellent baby-sitter. At one Reichsmark per day, she was worth far more than she and Michael were paying her. Besides, Grandmother truly enjoyed being with the girls. She knew all kinds of stories and games which she taught them such as: Can you name what I'm looking at? Which person am I thinking about? She also played checkers, *muehle ziehen,* and hide-and-seek, which was one of the girls' favorites. Yes, if it weren't for Grandmother Bartholomae, I would never have been able to keep the books for Michael, Maria thought. She would never have had the time. The children had a wonderful place to play. Other richer families had their gardens right next to their homes and could keep their children in their own yards. The Bartholomaes didn't mind walking a short way to get to "their yard." Besides, it was far better than having to play on the cobblestones in the streets all day. Most of the village children had no other choice but to play in the street. For those who lived in the village with no fields or "gardens" nearby, there was no alternative. At least the cobblestones around the houses kept the mud out of them in the springtime. Before the cobblestones were placed in the streets, the streets often became nothing more then muddy ruts following a heavy rain or after the snow melted. Many villages in the early nineteenth century, like Vaihingen, had nothing but cobblestones around their houses.

Michael became increasingly influential in village politics. He was persuaded by the regional chairman of the National Party to run for city commissioner on a platform loyal to both King Ludwig of Wuerttemberg and the Kaiser. His editorial pages always included his own support for the Kaiser's plans to build up the prominence and importance of the German Empire. One of his more memorable tracts was in support of the Naval Funding Bill of 1908. He wrote:

> Only through support of this bill to build six additional dread-noughts can Germany be assured that no one will attack us on the high seas. We must protect our empire and the only way we can do this is by insuring our government that the people of Germany are behind this effort to build the strongest Navy to keep up with the strength of our army. The Kaiser's government must be given the money it needs to build these ships. If we do not, as Admiral Tirpitz has said, "No one will respect Germany's right to defend herself and her empire against the entente navies which now surround us and seek to limit our right to defend German interests wherever they may be in the world. An empire of our size needs a large navy to protect German nationals from China to Africa, to the South Pacific." We need these ships to survive in the

> international competition with Great Britain which is becoming
> increasingly hostile to German interests. We can only overcome Great
> Britain's advantage by building a fleet as powerful as hers.

Editorials such as these pleased not only the national government but the local voters as well. Michael was elected with a three-to-one plurality over his nearest rival for city council. The following year he was elected president of the council. Much to Maria's concern, he and the other councilors often spent Sunday afternoons during the hot summer days down by the Enz drinking beer and wine while discussing the city's business. When Lina asked one day where her Papa was, Maria said, "Let's take a walk along the Enz this afternoon, and I'll show you where he is."

Grandmother wasn't interested in going with them. "If you don't mind, Maria, I'll stay home this afternoon. It's too far for me to walk."

"We won't be gone too long, Grandmother. I just want the girls to see where their father is practically every Sunday afternoon. I wish he'd spend more time with us. Why does he have to go down there every Sunday?" she asked herself as much as her mother-in-law.

Grandmother Bartholomae didn't answer. She knew Maria was angry. She had suggested to Michael a few times already that he should spend more time with his family on the weekends. Michael rarely got angry with his mother, but on this occasion he told her, "What I do on Sundays is my own business! I'm at home six days of the week, and the only time I have to discuss village business is on Sundays!"

She really wanted to remind her son he spent two or three evenings of the week attending council meetings. But she thought better of it. She could already see the tension building between Michael and Maria. She evidently thought there was no need to add more fuel to the fire between them.

Maria took the girls along the sidewalk down to the Enz. A dirt road ran along both sides of the river. The sidewalk had been one of Michael's favorite accomplishments for Vaihingen. It took him three years of intense lobbying to convince his fellow councilors that sidewalks would be an enormous improvement for the village streets. The councilors were proud of the fact that Vaihingen was one of the first of the smaller towns in Wuerttemberg to put in cobblestone roads in the early seventies. The two main streets bisecting the city had been completed in 1874. The stones had been hauled in from the surrounding fields by the local farmers who thought the idea of getting rid of their stones by building roads with them was a good one. The council had been overwhelmed by the response to their request for local citizens to bring their smaller stones to the village square. They were placed in successive patterns to become cobblestone streets. Michael had used the same argument for improving the village's streets by putting in sidewalks as the previous generations had done putting in cobblestone streets.

"If we use cement, the *troittoir* (sidewalk) will improve both the looks of the village as well as provide a comfortable place for people to walk, especially down to the Enz."

"Do you know who built this sidewalk?" Maria asked her daughters.

"No. Who, Mama?" Emilie asked.

"Papa had the idea for it and he had it built. Wasn't that a good idea?"

Maria had mixed feelings about Michael's work on city council. She was proud of what he had accomplished in a relatively short time. But she resented the hours of time the position took away from her and their family. She had remonstrated with him any number of times, but he got angry and told her he had more important things to do. "So?" Michael blurted to her one time. "You want me to become a hen just like the rest of you? I'm surrounded by nothing but women here at home. I'm outnumbered. You and Mother have a lot more in common with our daughters than I do! If we had a son, I'd spend more time at home, but we don't! Don't tell me about spending more time at home. You don't even want anymore children!"

That comment hurt Maria deeply. She knew Michael wanted a son more than ever. "If only Fritzle hadn't died," she often said out loud as she cried to herself. From what Maria told Grandmother Bartholomae, she knew he resented having only girls.

"He wanted to try again soon after Fritzle died," she told Grandmother. "We did try, but then we had Luise and Lina. We didn't have a son. I know he wants a son more than anything, Mother. He wants to try again, but I don't know if I can take it. What if we have another daughter?"

Grandmother Bartholomae understood how Maria felt. "I wanted to have a daughter after our three sons were born, but August wouldn't think of it. We've got enough to do to raise our sons. We don't need any girls, he said. They'll only cost us more money!"

"I'll admit I've become more distant from Michael, Mother," Maria said. "Whenever he becomes amorous, I make up one excuse after another. I usually say I've got to finish my bookkeeping or I haven't entered all of the accounts payable yet from last week—anything to turn him away. You've probably noticed he spends less and less time at home. He sets more and more meetings for the council in the evenings. If there is little business to transact, either Herr Twielling or Herr Schiller suggests, 'Fritz, what about having a beer before we go home?' and he listens to them."

"I understand, Maria, but there's not much you can do about it if you don't want anymore children."

Maria took the girls down to the opposite side of the river from the Alte Ente.

"Let's be very quiet so that Papa doesn't hear us, okay?" she whispered. "We'll just stroll by and see if we can see him."

"There's Papa," Emilie exclaimed. "Where?" Luise asked. "I don't see him."

"There." She pointed to the man sitting on the end of the large table just inside the doorway of the inn."

"Where?" Lina asked.

"Emilie's right," Maria said. "He's sitting in the corner by the big tile stove!"

"I see him!" Lina cried. "I do too!" Luise agreed.

"Not so loud, Lina. We don't want Papa to know we see him!" Maria cautioned. "Okay. Let's go home, girls. Now you know where Papa goes on Sunday afternoons."

The walk back up the hill was anything but quiet.

"Why does Papa spend so much time at the Alte Ente?" Luise asked. Why doesn't he stay home with us?"

"He could go to the garden with us, couldn't he, Mama?" Lina asked.

"He's President of the Council," Emilie said in defense of her father. "He's a very busy man, isn't he, Mama?" she asked.

"He's that, all right," she agreed. "But why does he have to come down here so often?" She seemed to ask herself more than her daughters.

That evening, as they were getting ready for supper, Lina blurted out "We saw you at the Alte Ente this afternoon, Papa, but you didn't see us!"

"What were you doing at the Alte Ente?" he asked, surprised.

"We weren't at the Alte Ente. We were just across the river from it," Maria answered.

"That's not a good idea, Maria! What are the other elite families doing on a Sunday afternoon? They certainly don't go for walks along the Enz!" he said in some irritation. "Why don't you take the girls to our cottage and let them play in the meadow? It's a lot better for them there!"

Maria had heard this all before many times. She wasn't concerned about the frequency of his absences until a neighbor told her, "Frau Bartholomae, take a walk along the Enz some Sunday afternoon and see what goes on at the Alte Ente. You should see the girls that work there. And they call them waitresses? If my husband went down there all of the time, I'd let him know a thing or two!"

She took a stroll down there soon afterward and was appalled at the loud voices and raucous laughter which reverberated through the valley from the beer garden just outside the restaurant. After that first visit, she asked Michael, "How can you men get anything done there with all of that noise?" Michael got very angry. "That's none of your business! We get our work done, and that's the important thing. We make plans for our meetings and talk with the local people and drink with them so we know what's going on in the village. Your father does the same thing! So what if we drink a little and have some fun now and then? It's what every man needs. He has to get away from home occasionally and see how the rest of the world lives!"

The girls were very quiet. They didn't like these arguments which kept popping up from time to time between their parents. Maria wasn't pleased with his reply, but she couldn't deny that her father did exactly the same thing in Gerabronn. She wondered if she were becoming as obnoxious as her mother. Whenever her father wanted anything, her mother would say, "Now Gustav, you know we can't afford that! Why do you always want to spend money? Why don't you save more? What are our children going to do if we don't leave something for them after we're gone?"

Maria remembered even requests for seconds during a meal that were denied to her father with the words "No Gustav, you've had enough. Everyone only needs one helping. Look at you, you're becoming fat in your old age!"

Maria thought it best not to quiz Michael anymore. No, she said to herself, if that's what he wants to do, he'll do it whether I like it or not. I suppose if we had a son, Michael might spend more time with us.

Maria let Michael talk her into trying one more time for a son. "If we have a son, will you spend more time with us, Michael?"

"Of course, Maria. I feel outnumbered by so many girls in the house. If we have a son, I'll stay home on Sunday afternoons. I'll even cut down on the number of council meetings each week."

Maria had become very fearful of becoming pregnant again. If she could be assured it would be a boy, she'd be thrilled to try again. "If I knew for sure we'd have a boy, I wouldn't mind having another child, Michael. But three girls is enough!"

Michael promised Maria he'd only schedule two council meetings a month. "We shouldn't have any interruptions in the evenings anymore. After all, it is the summer vacation season."

The summer of 1909 was a very busy one, sexually, for the two of them. To the great disappointment of Michael and to the utter dismay of Maria, the next child was not a boy but another girl! In contrast to the three older girls, baby Maria had blue eyes and blond hair, just like Michael. She was also the largest of the girls at birth. She was twenty-one and one-half inches long and weighed almost eight and one half pounds. Her birth was also the hardest for Maria. She had had to lie down each afternoon for the last two months of her pregnancy. She could hardly sit at her desk very long before she complained her back ached. She had to get up and walk around each hour. The doctor told her she should rest as much as possible every day. She shouldn't be sitting for long periods of time.

Michael had been so concerned about her during the pregnancy he hired Helmut Friedle to keep their books. "It's obvious you can't keep up with the bookkeeping, Maria. Dr. Bauer wants you to get as much rest as possible. We don't want to take a chance on losing this baby."

And now, in spite of all of their precautions and anticipations, they had another little girl. When the midwife came out of their bedroom and said "Herr Bartholomae, you have another daughter!" Michael almost couldn't believe what he had heard. He turned very pale and sighed. "Have you told my wife?"

"I did, but I don't think she heard me, Herr Bartholomae. She's really tired. She's sleeping now."

"Don't tell her. I'll tell her when she wakes up."

Michael sat still for sometime. He came into the living room very quietly. He looked as though he wanted to cry. His two brothers each had a son: Wilhelm and Otto. But Michael, as the oldest of the three boys, still didn't have any. He desperately wanted a son to follow in his footsteps. Who will take over the business? He asked himself, "What will I tell Maria? It'll be a real shock for her. She really didn't want this last child. She only did it as a favor to me, I'm sure." He felt sorry for himself and for his wife. The midwife came in and said, "Herr Bartholomae, your wife is asking for you."

Maria saw the disappointment on Michael's face even though he tried to smile.

"What's wrong, Michael? Is it another girl?"

He nodded his head and fell on the bed next to her. Maria cried. Michael held her in his arms and said nothing for what seemed a long time.

"You're disappointed, aren't you?" she asked through her sobs.

"The little girl resembles my side of the family. She's blond and blue eyed," he told her. "Maybe the next one will be a boy."

"Michael, I'm sorry, but I can't possibly go through another pregnancy!" She sobbed all over again.

"Now, now, you don't have to think about it. Let's wait until you get up again. We've got four healthy daughters. That's what counts right now," he said consolingly.

"But you wanted a boy so badly, Michael. How come others have boys and we only have girls?" she broke down in a new torrent of tears.

"That doesn't help anything, Maria. You're only wearing yourself out. We've got plenty of time to talk about the future. Let's not even think about having another child. Let's wait and see how this baby grows before we discuss the subject again."

Maria cried even harder for a few more minutes. She finally asked for the baby. The midwife brought her in. "What a pretty baby you have, Frau Bartholomae," the midwife said. "Why, just the other day I delivered one that had a misshapen face. It was hard to look at."

Maria took baby Maria in her arms and let her suckle. She gradually felt relieved Michael hadn't seemed more disappointed than he was. They both smiled as little Mariele fell asleep on her nipple.

"I guess she's had a hard time too," Michael said. "Maybe you should both sleep for a while."

He bent down and kissed her and the baby. "I'll see you later. You'd better get some sleep."

Michael went downstairs to the office. Friedle was just finishing his entries for the day.

"Well, Herr Friedle, I'm a father again. We just got our fourth daughter!" Michael said with a mixture of pride and astonishment.

"Another girl, Herr Bartholomae? Isn't it about time you had a boy?" He laughed as he said it.

"We had one, but he died at nine months."

"I'm sorry, Herr Bartholomae. I didn't mean to make fun of your child."

"That's okay. Most people can't understand why we only have girls and no boys."

"Herr Bartholomae, I don't want to raise this question now, but I think I have to. What is this amount of one thousand Reichsmarks for Paul Bartholomae? Is this a relative of yours?"

"Yes. He's my younger brother. Didn't my wife tell you anything about him?"

"No, she didn't. That's why I'm asking you. His name is carried on the books from month to month, but there's been no entry of any payment."

"That's because we only pay him once a year. He's a clerk in a department store in Heilbronn. He has a heart condition which means he can only work four hours a day.

I promised I would pay him one thousand Reichsmarks each year to help him meet his expenses."

"Oh, so that's it. I wondered if I had missed a payment along the way."

"No. We usually send it to him around Christmas of each year. There's still plenty of time for this year. Frau Bartholomae probably carried his name on the books, so she wouldn't forget by year's end."

"Then I'll just continue to carry his name from month to month also," Friedle said.

After Friedle left the office for the day, Michael thought back over what he had said about his brother. He and Maria had had a real verbal battle about his brother shortly after they had moved to Vaihingen from Darmstadt. Paul had been diagnosed with a heart condition that required him to have bed rest each afternoon. The doctor also told him he should not undertake any stressful work. Since he worked as a clerk in a large clothing store, he had arranged for part-time employment. Paul had then written Michael to ask if he would he be able to help him if ever he needed money. Michael agreed to send him one thousand Reichsmarks each year whether he asked for it or not. It was this largess which infuriated Maria.

"Why don't we see what he needs each year rather than promising him one thousand Reichsmarks? How do we know we can afford such a large amount? How many years are you going to do this? We don't know how long he's apt to live! We're not operating a social security system for your family!" she told him angrily.

"What do you mean we're not operating a social security system for my family? Paul can't work more than four hours a day. What are he and his family supposed to do? We can't simply let them become wards of the state!" he retorted.

"I'm not saying we shouldn't help your brother, Michael, but what I am saying is, suppose you were in his situation? Would he help you? I've never seen him go out of his way to help either you or Fritz. He's only wanted each of you to help him whenever he's needed money. Do you remember who helped pay for his wedding? Do you remember when he asked you for an additional hundred Reichsmarks so he and Madel could go on a honeymoon in the Black Forest? He's never paid you back one cent! He even asked Fritz to pay for their first month's rent. Michael, your brother may not really be as sick as he claims. And you've promised to pay him one thousand Reichsmarks a year?"

Michael stormed out of the apartment and went downstairs to the press room. He, Welker, and the two apprentices spent the rest of the day cleaning the presses. The two apprentices, under the direction of Welker, usually did this themselves on Saturday mornings. They were surprised when Michael told them, "As soon as the weekly paper is printed, we're going to clean the presses!"

Michael knew she was probably right. She took care of the bookkeeping and had all of the figures at her fingertips until Friedle took over. He simply didn't like the idea she should want to limit what he could spend on his family. The previous year she had forgotten to send Paul his yearly allowance. He wrote Michael a letter in which he included the statement "If I don't receive the money within the next two weeks, I'm going to kill myself! We can't get along without your help!"

Maria was ready to have him carry out his threat. She didn't really think he would ever do it. But Michael insisted she send him a money order immediately "or I'm moving out!"

That was the last time Maria ever crossed Michael over paying his brother's yearly fee. It's a sheer waste of our good money, she told herself. I suppose with Grandmother Bartholomae in the house, I have a lot more help. I think instead of paying this yearly fee to Paul, we should really be paying Mother a bonus for her services." It took something of the sting out of her venom when she sent the yearly allowance off to Paul.

Since Grandmother Bartholomae continued to receive the monthly pension from the Royal Wuerttemberg Postal Service, after her husband died, she felt she didn't need any help from Michael.

"Living with you and your family, Michael, is enough. I don't need anything more. I enjoy living here with you, Maria, and your four daughters. They keep me young and alive. It's far better than just knitting and crocheting day and night!"

A few days after the birth of Mariele, Michael told Maria, "I guess we'll only have girls."

She detected his great disappointment. "Michael, I'm ready to quit now. I don't think I can go through another pregnancy and have another girl. I can't take it anymore. When little Fritzle died, I almost couldn't bear not becoming pregnant again. But now I don't think I could stand it if we were to have yet another girl."

Michael knew what Maria was saying. There would no longer be any intimacy between them. And even if there were, it would be highly circumscribed and limited. As President of the City Council, Michael spent more and more of his time at the office in the courthouse and at the Alte Ente. Maria knew if she wished to talk to him about some aspect of the business, she would have to wait until he came home in the evening. He was doing less and less in the business. It was running smoothly with only his brief daily oversight. A few hours each day sufficed, it seemed. It became apparent to Maria that as a successful newspaper publisher and president of the council, he preferred to be out in public more than being at home. As Council President, it was expected he would preside over the important yearly events of the village. He enjoyed speaking before the large crowds that jammed the market place each spring with the opening of the week-long May Day festivities. The three older girls loved to ride in the horse-drawn carriage with him and Maria at the head of the village's annual May Day parade. The entourage began at the market place and wound down to the Enz playground on the edge of the village. As Council President, he was next in line to the Mayor as the most prominent figure. His speeches were one of the yearly highlights of May Day. While the Mayor gave a perfunctory speech about the opening of the festivities, Michael drew upon the statistics of what the empire had achieved. He believed the Germans should continue to be prosperous and leaders of the world in industry and technology. He also reiterated the need to build a navy that would parallel Germany's military might.

"Once we've achieved the standard of living of Great Britain, we will have no further need to feel inferior to Britain's claim of world supremacy. We will become the leaders of the world before the next decade is over, and Great Britain will be in the position of trying to catch up with us!"

This ringing summary of his speeches always brought the crowds to their feet, and the cheers and applause were deafening. Michael supported the position of the Kaiser vis-a-vis Great Britain, and the public loved it. Ever since the Franco-Prussian War, nationalism was stressed throughout Germany. January 18 was another one of those truly great days in Vaihingen as it was in the rest of the country. Michael's greatest speeches were saved for this date each year. It was the anniversary of the founding of the Second German Empire in 1871. Not only was it an official holiday but it was both expected and encouraged that special activities and parades would highlight this event each year. Michael dressed himself in his army uniform and asked all of the men of the village to do the same on this date. He had been especially proud of his designation as an honorary major of the King's Wuerttemberg Rifles upon becoming President of the Council.

He also led the parade of retired army veterans and of the men and women's turnverein. They marched to the military tunes of the village band and ended with speeches by representatives of the King's state government. Most residents felt Michael's speeches were much better than those of the representatives of King Ludwig's government. In fact, his introductions of these individuals were often better than their speeches. He was a storyteller of renown, and the public came to expect a "good story" as part of anything he had to say.

Chapter III

A Sudden Change

It was the day before Emilie's birthday Michael complained to Maria, "I've got a terrific stomachache. I think I'll spend the day here in my office. I don't think I'll go out today."

"It's probably something you ate at the Alte Ente," she said reproachfully. "You go there too often. You hardly ever come upstairs for dinner anymore, especially if you're in the village somewhere. Mother makes really good dinners. Maybe you should eat more of her food and less of that restaurant food. You'd feel better."

It bothered Maria that he was spending so much time down there. She didn't want to believe what she was hearing from some of their neighbors. "The reason men like to go there is because the waitresses are 'so friendly.'" Some of the older gossips even claimed the waitresses lived upstairs. "They take their favorite guests up to their rooms when they're through work."

Maria didn't want to believe it, but whenever she found some reason to complain about the Alte Ente, she did so. Michael knew how she felt and he often told her, "The food's almost as good as Mother prepares. It's just more convenient to stop there when I'm downtown than walking back up the hill for dinner."

The pain persisted. On Emilie's birthday, Maria said, "Maybe you should see the doctor?"

"No. I'll be all right. Just let me sit in the sun this afternoon. If I don't feel better by tomorrow, I'll see a doctor."

Maria didn't think anymore about it. She had more than enough to do arranging for her daughter's birthday party that afternoon. Emilie wanted some of her friends from the Latin School to come for dinner. Then they'd go to their cottage to play.

Grandmother cooked Emilie's favorite meal of roast pork with gravy, spaetzle, green salad, and potato salad, followed by tea and birthday cake. It was her thirteenth birthday. Maria and Michael had agreed she could do whatever she wished. It was a tradition in the family. Whoever's birthday it was could have the meal of her choice and invite her closest friends for the dinner party and play for the rest of the afternoon at the cottage. Emilie's friends were all from the Latein Schule. It was the premier grammar school to which all of the village's elite (as Michael called them) sent their sons and daughters. If a student hadn't attended one of these schools, he or she could not go to the university. Michael and Maria wanted Emilie to go to the university.

"A degree is recognized by everyone as an achievement of mental excellence," Michael liked to say. Fortunately for Emilie, in the grading system used by the Latein Schule—outstanding, very good, good, satisfactory, and unsatisfactory her report cards usually recorded "outstanding," with an occasional "very good" thrown in. Most of her friends had similar report cards. Maria always told her brothers and sisters, "Emilie is one of the best students in her class!"

Because she had such good grades, Michael and Maria gave her whatever she wanted. She started piano lessons when she was six. Her friend, Clara Haff, had started piano the year before. After spending a Saturday afternoon at her house, Emilie tried to follow her lead on the piano and was surprised how readily she could play a very simply tune. When she returned home, she asked her mother, "Could I learn how to play piano like Clara? She taught me how to play "Twinkle, Twinkle, Little Star" this afternoon, Mama. It was very easy to learn."

Maria told Michael that evening "Emilie's interested in learning how to play piano."

"Good. Why don't you go to Stuttgart and pick out a piano for her? I'll talk with Frau Kuehner about giving her lessons. If a girl is to become a lady, she should know how to play piano."

Maria went to Stuttgart that very next Saturday and picked out the best piano in the music store on Koenigstrasse. "Can you ship it to Vaihingen/Enz?" she asked the owner.

"Certainly, Frau Bartholomae. That's no problem."

The piano arrived the very next week. Michael had had to arrange for it to be shipped by wagon from the Kleinglattbach station since the local train didn't take such large fragile items to Vaihingen. He hired Herr Greiner and four of his neighbors to bring the piano to their house on his large hay wagon. Michael paid Greiner twenty Reichsmarks for the transport and gave each of his neighbors two Reichsmarks for their help. It was one of the first Steinwegs to be sold in Germany costing more than what Michael paid for the hectare.

Frau Kuehner was an excellent teacher, and by the end of Emilie's first month of lessons, she could play "Kinderlein Kommet" almost without mistakes. She played for "her Papa" whenever he was home in the evenings. Before she went to bed, he'd ask, "Emilie, could you play something for me this evening?"

She soon learned what his favorites were and played a few of them. After a few months of lessons, she could play the piano while her mother and her sisters sang something for him. These evenings were among the most touching and sentimental times they had as a family. Michael often had tears streaming down his cheeks when she played his favorites like Schumann's "Traeumerei." Michael usually joined in the singing at first but before long he stopped singing because he had to blow his nose repeatedly.

That evening, after Emilie's birthday party, Michael asked her to play several sonatas for him. She was very tired after a full afternoon of fun with her friends, but she didn't want to disappoint "her Papa." She had started to play when Michael said, "Maria, you'd better get Dr. Bauer to take a look at me. The pain is so sharp I can't even sit down anymore!"

"Should I stop, Papa?" Emilie asked.

"No, no, Emilie. Keep on playing. It takes my mind off the pain."

Maria hurried over to Dr. Bauer's house. It was just down the street from theirs. She rang the doorbell, and the maid came to the door.

"Is Dr. Bauer in?" Maria asked.

"Yes, but he's just having his supper," the maid told her.

Dr. Bauer heard Maria's voice in the doorway and called out, "Frau Bartholomae, come in. I've always got time for my friends."

Maria hurried into the dining room and said, "Please excuse me, Dr. Bauer and Frau Bauer, but my husband has a terrible pain in his stomach. Could you come and take a look at him after you've had your dinner?"

"Certainly, Frau Bartholomae. I've already eaten enough. Let me get my coat and bag, and I'll go with you."

"I certainly hope it's nothing serious, Frau Bartholomae," Frau Bauer called out as they left the house.

"I hope it isn't either," Maria said over her shoulder.

"How long has Herr Bartholomae felt ill, Frau Bartholomae?" Dr. Bauer asked.

"He's had this pain for two days now, but it seemed better this morning. He didn't think I should bother you until this evening. Now he says he almost can't stand the pain in his stomach."

"It's probably something he ate," Dr. Bauer said. "Has he eaten any raw vegetables or fruits lately?"

"No, I don't think so. He hasn't had much of an appetite for two days. He's just taken some tea and bread, but that's about all I've seen him eat here at home. You know he likes to go to the Alte Ente to eat his dinners. I don't know what he's had there!" she told him with some concern. "But he hasn't been there for at least the last two days."

"Well, we'll see soon enough," Dr. Bauer answered.

When Dr. Bauer and Maria arrived, Grandmother Bartholomae had helped her son go to bed. He lay very quietly as Dr. Bauer and Maria came into the bedroom. After shaking hands and exchanging greetings, Dr. Bauer asked, "Herr Bartholomae, have you eaten any raw fruits or vegetables over the last few days?"

"No," Michael replied. "I've just had this very sharp pain in my lower right side every now and then. It seems to have gone away somewhat now."

Dr. Bauer took his time examining him. He felt around the spot where he had said the pain had been most severe. After several minutes, Dr. Bauer said, "I think we'd better have you rest here at home overnight, Herr Bartholomae. I'll give you some tablets to take for the pain, but if you still have it in this same spot tomorrow, have Frau Bartholomae call me the first thing in the morning."

Dr. Bauer didn't want to alarm Maria, but he had his suspicions after Michael told him the location of his pain. He truly hoped he would feel better by morning, but the fact that the pain was on the lower right side of his abdomen concerned him.

"That was not a good sign," he told Maria later. "You should have come to get me earlier, Frau Bartholomae! If I had known it was appendicitis, I would have sent him to the hospital right away. I knew from other cases that once the appendix has burst, it's too late!"

Michael took the tablets with water as Dr. Bauer prescribed. He almost vomited them up again, but was able to keep them down by taking additional sips of wine with the water. He slept fitfully. Maria woke each time he stirred.

"The pain's still there, Maria," Michael said.

By the time he awoke in the morning, he couldn't stand up. Maria went for the doctor immediately. Dr. Bauer took one look at Michael and said, "We've got to get you to the hospital right away. It looks like you have appendicitis. I'll have to operate immediately."

Dr. Bauer told his assistant to order the carriage for Michael. He had to be taken to the Vaihingen hospital. Dr. Bauer went on ahead to prepare the staff and operating room for surgery. When the carriage brought Michael to the door, the nurses were already waiting for him and wheeled him into the operating room. The doctor, his assistant, and two male orderlies prepared him for surgery. Dr. Bauer opened Michael's lower right abdomen and saw what he had feared: the appendix had burst. There was nothing he could do for him now. Dr. Bauer sewed him up and had him taken to a room on the second floor of the hospital. Dr. Bauer came out to the hallway where Maria was waiting. She was shocked when she saw him. She never forgot the look on his face.

"Frau Bartholomae," Dr. Bauer began, "I'm terribly sorry, but your husband is dying of a burst appendix. There's nothing we can do for him anymore. If we had gotten to him sooner, we could have cut the appendix out. But now it's too late. He's beyond anything we can do for him now."

Maria was stunned. She couldn't believe what she had just heard.

"What? He's dying? He's only thirty-nine years old. That can't be! No! I don't believe it!"

She ran crying from the hospital to her office and telephoned her brother, Dr. Ernst Meyer. "My brother, Ernst, is a doctor," she told Grandmother. "He'll know what to do for Michael!"

"Hello? Ernst?"

"Yes, this is Dr. Meyer."

"Ernst, this is Maria. Can you come to Vaihingen right away? The doctor here operated on Michael and says he's dying. There's nothing he can do for him anymore!"

"What? What's wrong with Michael? Has he had an accident?" Ernst asked.

"No! Dr. Bauer says his appendix has burst and there's nothing he can do for him now. Ernst! He's such a young man! He can't die yet." Maria broke down in sobs.

"I'll come immediately, Maria. But if it's as bad as Dr. Bauer says it is, there may not be anything anyone can do for Fritz."

"But he's still a young man!" she protested.

"I know. It doesn't seem fair. I'll get there as soon as I can."

Dr. Meyer came as quickly as he could. It took him six hours to arrive from Boeblingen by train via Stuttgart. He went immediately to the hospital and to Michael's room. Maria saw him first. The four Bartholomae girls were standing at the foot of their father's bed. Their grandmother was on his left side toward the door. Maria cried out as she hugged him. "Ernst, for God's sake, talk to Dr. Bauer. He says Michael's dying."

Michael opened his eyes. "So, they've called you too?" he said to Ernst.

"Hello, Fritz. I hear you've had a time of it with your stomach."

"Yes, the pain was really bad. I don't feel anything now."

"Don't try to talk anymore, Fritz. I'm going to check with your doctor and find out what's wrong with you."

"Where's Dr. Bauer, Maria?"

"He said he'd be in his office, just down the hall," she told him tearfully.

Ernst shook hands with Frau Bartholomae and each of the girls. "The girls are growing up, Maria. I haven't seen them since last year. I'll be right back. I'm going to talk with Dr. Bauer."

Dr. Bauer heard Ernst's voice. They met in the hall just outside Michael's door.

"Hello. I'm Dr. Bauer. You're Dr. Meyer, Frau Bartholomae's brother?"

"Yes. My sister called me and wanted me to come and examine her husband."

"I operated on him first thing this morning, Dr. Meyer. His appendix had already burst. There was nothing I could do for him. I sewed him up again and brought him back to his room. I've told Frau Bartholomae, but she doesn't believe me. She thinks you can do something to save him."

"I know. I can't do any more for him than you've done, Dr. Bauer. I'll talk to my sister. There's nothing more we can do for him other than try to make him as comfortable as possible. If only he had come to see you sooner . . ."

"That's exactly right. I could have removed his appendix before it burst."

Ernst came back into Michael's room. Everyone was very quiet. Emilie had heard what Dr. Bauer said to her Uncle Ernst out in the hall. What will we do without Papa? she thought to herself. Surely there must be something they can do for him. Maria was sitting on the bed holding Michael's hand. He had dozed off. Maria was crying quietly to herself. Grandmother sat on a chair holding Mariele on her lap. Emilie, Luise, and Lina were standing at the foot of the bed.

"Frau Bartholomae," Dr. Meyer began, "maybe it would be best if you took the girls back to the house. I have to talk to Maria alone."

Grandmother got up and said, "Come along, girls. We'd better let Dr. Meyer talk to your mother in private."

Michael woke up just as they were getting ready to leave. "Where are you going, Mother?" he asked.

"I'm going to take the girls home, Michael. Dr. Meyer wants to talk to you and Maria."

"Well, let me say goodbye to the girls."

Michael shook hands with each of them as they gave him a kiss. Mariele said, "Papa, this isn't your bed. Your bed's at home."

Michael laughed. Even Maria couldn't help smiling.

"You're right, Mariele. Papa should be home in his own bed!"

"Goodbye, Papa," Luise and Lina said in unison. Emilie started to cry as she kissed him on his cheek. "Now, now, Emilie, you're too grown up for that. You've got to help your mother until I get well again." She really started to cry. She remembered what Dr. Bauer had told her uncle in the hallway. As the girls left with their grandmother, she heard her uncle say, "Maria, it's just as I thought. Dr. Bauer told me about the operation. Fritz's appendix had already burst. Once that happens, there's nothing that can be done for him anymore. It's just a matter of time until he dies."

Maria broke down and sobbed. Michael awoke. "What's wrong? Why are you crying, Maria?" He then saw his brother-in-law. "Well, how does it look? Am I going to live or die?"

"Do you want the truth, Fritz?"

"Yes. One way or the other. It's getting late, if I'm going to die. If I live, then there's still some time to tell Maria everything that's got to be done with the business."

Ernst liked Michael. He called him Fritz even though Maria didn't like this nickname. He appreciated Michael's outspokenness. He had told his sister once when they were on vacation together with the Bartholomaes, "Fritz is a rare politician. He tells people straight out the way things are. He doesn't mind telling them what they may not want to hear. You don't find many politicians who will do that these days!"

"I've always liked your honesty, Fritz," Ernst began. "I'll tell you the truth about your illness. Your appendix has burst. If Dr. Bauer had operated on you even yesterday, he might have been able to save you. But once it's burst, there's nothing anyone can do. I'm sorry, Fritz, but it's just a matter of hours or a day or two before you'll die from the poison in your system. The only thing we can do for you is give you morphine to ease your pain."

"Well, I asked for it," Michael said. "I appreciate your telling me the truth, Ernst. Maria, you'd better go home and get Mother and the girls again. I want to say goodbye to them one last time. Then I've got lots of things to tell you before I fall asleep. Don't give me anymore morphine, Ernst. I don't want to fall asleep yet. There's too much to I have to tell Maria before I die."

Maria looked imploringly at her brother. "Isn't there something you can do for him, Ernst? He's too young to die."

"I'm sorry, Maria. There's nothing we can do for him now. You'd better go home and get the girls. He doesn't have much time left."

Maria cried all the way home. What she feared most was now going to happen. How can it be? she asked herself over and over again. If only I had gone to Dr. Bauer the next morning.

Maria came in the door just as Grandmother and the girls had finished their prayers in their Papa's behalf. Grandmother had just finished praying, "Father, please protect and preserve my son. He's all these young girls have to help them grow up into faithful servants of Thine. Nevertheless, may Thy will be done. In Jesus' name we ask it. Amen."

Through her sobs, Maria said, "Mother, get the girls ready to go back up to the hospital. Michael's dying. He wants to say good bye to the girls for the last time."

"What?" Lena asked. "How can he die when he's in the hospital?"

"Be quiet," Emilie cried. "You're too young to understand."

Luise cried and cried. "I don't want Papa to die, Mama. Can't the doctor do anything for him?"

Maria couldn't stop crying.

"The doctors are doing all they can for him, Luise. It's God's will. There's nothing anyone can do for him!" Grandmother answered on Maria's behalf.

Maria, Grandmother, and the four girls walked very quickly back to the hospital. It was only a block away. Still so shocked, they kept very quiet. Even little Mariele didn't say anything. She sensed how sad everyone was. Even Grandmother kept wiping her eyes with her handkerchief.

As they came into Michael's room, Dr. Meyer, Dr. Bauer, and the nurse had just changed his dressing and were making him as comfortable as possible.

"It's good that you came right away, Frau Bartholomae," Dr. Bauer said to Maria. "I don't think Herr Bartholomae will live much longer."

"Dr. Bauer's right, Maria," Ernst agreed. "He's slipping fast."

Maria kissed Michael's cheek, and he woke up. "So, you've come. Hello, girls. I want you girls to listen to your mother and grandmother and do what they say. The doctors told me I'm not going to live very long," Michael said slowly. Tears were welling up in his eyes. Everyone burst into tears.

"That won't help. You have to be brave and help your mother all you can. Give me a kiss, each of you."

Grandmother led little Mariele to Papa's bed. "This bed is higher than yours at home, Papa," she told him.

Michael smiled. "You're right, Mariele. And it isn't my bed either, is it?"

Everyone smiled remembering her previous visit. Each of the girls kissed their papa on his cheek. Emilie was surprised how cold it seemed. "Are you warm enough, Papa?" she asked.

He smiled. "Yes, Emilie. That's the way it is when a person dies."

"Don't die, Papa" Lina cried. "Who'll take us to Stuttgart if you're not with us?"

"Mama and Grandmother will be with you, Lina. Luise, you're almost as old as Emilie. Help her and Grandmother take care of your younger sisters, okay?"

"Yes, Papa," Luise said through her sobs.

"Grandmother, you'd better take the girls home. I've got a lot to tell Maria yet."

Dr. Meyer, Dr. Bauer, and the nurse also left with them.

"You girls have to be real brave now. Your father will soon be gone. It's not going to be easy for you," the nurse told the girls.

Grandmother didn't say anything. They were all very quiet as they went home. Each one of the girls was trying to imagine what it was going to be like without their papa there.

Maria sat and listened through her tears as Michael told her all she should do in the business for the next few weeks.

"Herr Welker has to be given his instructions each morning about which stories to print and on which page and where to put the ads. The paper supplies come from Diebold Supply in Stuttgart, and you'll have to place another order on the first of October. Herr Friedle handles all of the accounts receivable and payable."

"Michael," Maria interrupted. "I'll have to get some paper and a pencil. I can't remember everything you're telling me!" she said as she wiped her eyes repeatedly.

"Hurry up!" he said. "There's not much time."

Maria hurried out to the front desk and borrowed some paper and a pencil from the nurse. She couldn't believe Herr Bartholomae wanted to dictate all of his business instructions to her before he died.

"Frau Bartholomae, why don't you just go and listen to him. There's not much time left. He just needs to talk. You won't feel much like doing what he says when he's gone anyway," she told her.

Maria hurried back to Michael's room and sat down again. He continued to tell her what she had to do for the business.

"You'll have to call Herr Weber tomorrow and postpone our appointment." He laughed at that. "I guess you'd better cancel the appointment. We were going to discuss a new series of articles on what the council wants to do to improve the Enz River banks next year. You already know about the monthly payments on the mortgage. You might ask your father if he'll be willing to delay our payment for this month. You may want to see how business goes for the remainder of the year. Don't forget to have Emilie continue with her piano lessons and see to it that Luise and Lina continue their studies. Mother will have to spend all of her time with you now. She won't be able to spend the summers visiting my two brothers anymore. You know I've promised we'll give her thirty Reichsmarks a month to look after the girls."

Maria almost couldn't take it any longer. "Michael, don't talk anymore. I just want to sit here and hold your hand. There's not much time left."

Michael continued to tell her all that she had yet to do, but she noticed his hand was gradually getting colder. She listened and cried repeatedly. "Why, Michael? Why do you have to die?" she asked herself as much as him. Michael talked and talked. He kept thinking of things she still had to do.

"Michael," Maria said. "Don't talk anymore. It's no use. You're just making yourself weaker and weaker from the effort. I'd rather just sit here and look at you for the few moments we have left . . . ," she said tearfully.

Michael drifted off into an uneasy sleep, waking every few minutes as he recalled something else he had forgotten to tell her. Maria kissed him as his eyes closed, and he pressed her hand in his for the last time. He took one last deep sigh and was gone.

Chapter IV

A Lasting Trauma

While Maria spent the last moments with Michael on his deathbed, Grandmother Bartholomae still couldn't grasp that her son was mortally ill. Upon their return to the house, she said, "Girls, let's fold our hands, close our eyes, and pray that your father gets well again. 'Dear God, please take care of my son and father of these young girls. Please see to it that he returns sound of body to us. He is too young to die. These girls need their father. Protect him from harm and heal his sickness so that he can come home again. This we ask in Thy holy name. Amen!'"

Maria returned wearily from the hospital. As soon as she came into the living room, they knew something terrible must have happened. Her face was ashen, and she was still crying. Grandmother asked, "What's wrong, Maria? What happened?"

Through her sobs, she said, "Papa's dead! We're all alone now!" She sat down on Michael's easy chair and took all of the girls on her lap, even Emilie. They all cried together.

"What will we do, Mama?" Emilie asked. "How can we get along without Papa?"

"What's going to happen to us now?" Luise asked. "Will we be sent to an orphanage?"

"I don't want to be sent away, Mama," Lina cried. "I want to stay with you!"

"Let's not talk about it now," Maria said. "We've got to bury Papa first." With this comment, she burst out in a new stream of tears. All of the girls and Grandmother cried. Grandmother couldn't stop wiping her eyes. When she saw Dr. Meyer, she asked, "Was there nothing you could do to save my son?"

"No, Frau Bartholomae. I'm afraid Michael's appendix must have burst a couple of days ago. Once the poison had spread throughout his body, there was nothing anyone could do for him. It's too bad he didn't go to the doctor right away when he first felt the pain. If Dr. Bauer had operated on him at that time and taken out the appendix, Michael would still be here. But as it was, it was simply too late."

Maria pulled herself away from the girls and told Grandmother, "I've got to go to the cemetery and pick out a plot for Michael's grave. Can you look after the girls for me until I come back?"

"Why, certainly. The girls and I will be all right. I know what you're going through, Maria." Grandmother hugged Maria and said, "When my August died, I didn't know what I was going to do. I went through each day one step at a time. There's nothing anyone can do about it. When God calls, we have to answer, whether we're prepared or not."

Maria liked Grandmother Bartholomae. She often told Emilie, "Papa was fortunate in having such a mother. She does whatever she can to help out. Even when she doesn't feel well herself, she always wants to be sure she has done all she can before lying down. She's totally different from your Grandmother Meyer. If Grandmother Meyer didn't like something, she told the person right away. Even your grandfather has to listen to what she says, or she gets very angry with him."

Maria asked Ernst to go with her to help pick out a grave site for Michael. They walked up Heilbronner Strasse until they came to the path leading to the cemetery. They passed right by the hectare Michael had bought for them.

"Here's the meadow Michael bought with our garden house."

"It's a beautiful place, Maria. I didn't know you had property out in the country. When did he buy this?"

"Just a few years ago. He wanted the girls to have some place outside of the village where they could go and play. And now he's no longer here to watch them," Maria said and broke down again.

"The apple trees are loaded, Maria. You've got plum trees and cherry trees too. And look at all of the wild flowers. Is that your little garden house there under the plum trees?"

"Yes. Michael had it built the very same year he bought it. The girls love to go in it and play house together. During the summer, they come here every day. I guess I'll have to keep it, if I can. He wouldn't want me to sell it. He told me it's the next best thing to peace and quiet he's seen besides the cemetery. He liked to kid around like that and say all kinds of ridiculous things."

They came to the cemetery, and Ernst held the gate open for her. The hinge was quite stiff, making the gate hard to open. They walked quietly down several rows until they came to the very edge of the grave sites.

"Here's the place, Ernst. This is where my beloved is going to be buried."

Ernst looked around and saw the tall new trees that had been planted several years before. "Yes, Maria. This is a beautiful spot. I'd like it myself. I'm sure Fritz would be pleased with it."

When Maria and her brother came back from the cemetery, she called Herr Pflaunder, the undertaker.

"Good day, Herr Pflaunder. My brother and I have picked out a grave site for my husband. You can prepare for the funeral now," Maria said and started crying again. "I'm sorry, Herr Pflaunder. I'm still not used to his death."

"That's all right, Frau Bartholomae. I understand. I feel like crying too when I think how young your husband was. I'll have his body ready to bring to the house this afternoon."

It was the custom for funerals to take place at the homes of the deceased. The body was prepared in a mortuary and then delivered to the home for the wake.

Maria then called Pastor Eueler of the Evangelical Church in Vaihingen.

"Herr Pastor, this is Frau Bartholomae. I've just spoken to Herr Pflaunder and he said my husband's body will come to our home this afternoon. Will you conduct the funeral service for my husband tomorrow?"

"Frau Bartholomae, how sorry I am to hear of your husband's untimely death. What a tragedy for you and your daughters. I'm amazed you've even taken the time to call me. Of course, I'll conduct the funeral service for Herr Bartholomae. I wouldn't want anyone else to do him this honor. He was truly a good man."

"Thank you, Pastor." Maria started crying again. "Would eleven o'clock be all right for you?"

"Certainly, Frau Bartholomae. I'll alert the director of the cemetery chapel to tell him to have it all ready for eleven o'clock. You don't have to do anything else, Frau Bartholomae. I'll talk with Herr Pflaunder too about the procession from the house to the cemetery. Would you like to have one of your daughters ride on the carriage with the driver?"

"Yes. Lina has already asked me if she could, and I said yes."

"Then it's done, Frau Bartholomae. I'll arrange with Herr Pflaunder about the order of the processional to the chapel. You won't have to concern yourself with anything else. Again, my heartfelt sympathies to you and your daughters. I've said prayers for all of you this morning when I heard the tragic news."

Pastor Ludwig Eueler had been told of Michael's death by Dr. Bauer. They had gone to the university together and had known each other for more than twenty years. After Dr. Bauer had talked with Dr. Ernst Meyer, he stopped at the rectory and told his friend about the death of Michael Friederich Bartholomae.

"Ludwig, sorry to bother you, but I've just come from the hospital. Herr Bartholomae died this morning. He had a burst appendix. There was nothing I could do for him. He waited too long to come to see me. If he had only come even a day sooner, I'm sure I could have saved him. But as it was, he thought he had a stomach ache. What a tragedy for Frau Bartholomae and her daughters!"

"Oh, oh, what a pity. He was such an energetic man. Think of all that he did for this village, Paul. I wonder how she's going to get along without him?" Ludwig asked himself as much as his friend.

"Thank you for telling me. I'll go over to see her as soon as I can." In the meantime, Maria had already called Pastor Eueler. He was just going out of the rectory when she called to ask him to conduct the service.

Pastor Eueler sat down heavily in his chair. What a tragedy, he kept saying over and over again. How in the world will Frau Bartholomae be able to manage both the business and her family? he asked himself. Surely she'll have to sell the business. A woman can't manage a newspaper. Why, she wouldn't even know where to begin, he said to himself. Well, first things first. I'm going to arrange for some of his colleagues to take part in the eulogy. He arranged with each of the councilors to take part as they wished. He also asked the Mayor and County Executive to come and say a few words at the service.

After Maria called Pastor Eueler, she told her brother, "I'm exhausted, Ernst. I don't know if I can go through with it tomorrow. There are so many things I still have to do."

"You go and lie down, Maria. Give me your list, and I'll call all of the relatives. You don't have to do that."

Ernst had already called his wife, Lilly. She arrived early in the afternoon. Ernst called his parents and gave them the bad news about Michael.

"Father, Maria's husband has just died."

"What? How can that be? We were going to visit them again this next month! We didn't even know he was sick!"

"He had appendicitis, Father. The appendix had already burst by the time the doctor here operated on him. There was nothing anyone could do for him. I'm calling on Maria's behalf to tell you that the funeral is tomorrow here in Vaihingen. Do you think you can make it? It would be a big help to Maria if the two of you could come. You can stay here. Could you let the others know in Gerabronn? I've got to call Michael's brothers and tell them."

"Sure, Ernst. We'll be there, and I'll spread the word around here."

Ernst next called Michael's two brothers. Paul wasn't at home so he talked with Madel, his wife.

"Frau Bartholomae, this is Dr. Meyer. I'm Frau Maria Bartholomae's brother. I'm sorry to have to inform you that your brother-in-law, Herr Michael Friederich Bartholomae, has just died."

"What? That can't be! Paul just talked with him last month! He wasn't even sick!"

"That's just the tragedy of it. He wasn't sick. He had a ruptured appendix, and that's what killed him. The funeral is tomorrow."

"Oh, I'm very sorry, Dr. Meyer. I'll tell my husband. I don't know if we can come, but I'll give him the message."

Dr. Meyer then called Michael's youngest brother. "Herr Bartholomae? Is that you?"

"Yes, this is Friederich Bartholomae. Who is this?"

"Herr Bartholomae, this is Dr. Ernst Meyer, your brother Michael's brother-in-law."

"Oh yes, Dr. Meyer. I remember you from Michael's wedding. What's the occasion for this call?"

"I've got very bad news for you. Your brother died this morning of a ruptured appendix."

"Oh my God. Poor Maria! What's she going to do with four daughters to raise? How's Maria doing, Dr. Meyer?"

"She's doing as well as can be expected. She's still somewhat in a state of shock, I think. It'll really hit her after the funeral. The funeral is tomorrow."

"We'll be there. Thank you for calling. Goodbye, Dr. Meyer."

"Goodbye, Herr Bartholomae. Could you let the rest of your family know about the funeral?"

"I will, but I don't think they'll be able to come. They're getting pretty old."

There were so many people in attendance that the night before the funeral the Bahnhof Hotel was filled to capacity. The overflow had to be housed in the Bierstube Am Markt. It was not the most elegant of accommodations, but at least most of those who stayed overnight had a bed upon which to sleep. Dr. Meyer and his wife as well as Grandfather and Grandmother Meyer stayed at Maria's.

It was a very sad night for the family to have Michael in his casket in the house. Maria spent the night with him even though Ernst suggested, "Maria, there's nothing you can do for him anymore. You'll just wear yourself out sitting beside him all night."

Maria wouldn't listen; she just repeated what she had said before: "I'm going to sit by him tonight."

As each of the girls said goodbye to their papa again, they almost couldn't say the words. Between sobs, they did manage to touch him for the last time. Little Mariele asked, "Mama, why is Papa so cold?"

Maria tried to explain but only began crying again. Grandmother Meyer took Mariele by the hand and said, "Your Papa is dead, Mariele. When people die, they all feel that way."

She took the girls and put them to bed. Ordinarily, Grandmother Bartholomae would have done this, but Grandmother Meyer told her, "Frau Bartholomae, let me do it. You've got enough to think about tonight!"

The girls had a hard time falling asleep. Emilie blew her nose repeatedly from all of the crying. Luise kept saying, "I can't believe Papa's dead." After a long pause, she asked, "Emilie, why did Papa die?"

"Uncle Ernst said he had a ruptured appendix."

"What's an appendix? How can anyone die from that?"

"It's an organ in the body. Uncle Ernst said a person doesn't really need it, but if it breaks open inside a person, it can kill him from the poison that comes out of it. Uncle Ernst showed me in his doctor's book what it looks like," Emilie said sadly. While she knew what her uncle had showed her and told her, she too had a hard time believing her father was dead.

"It doesn't seem real, does it, Luise? He had such a good time at my birthday party."

"What's Mama going to do?" Luise asked. "Will we be able to stay here, Emilie?"

"I hope so. I don't want to leave Mama. I want to stay here with her."

"I do too! I don't want to be sent away," Luise started crying again.

"I asked Mama if I can ride on the hearse with the driver, and she said I could," Lina said proudly.

"When did she say that?" Luise asked.

"I asked her after she came home from the hospital. And she said I could."

"You seem to think it's going to be a lot of fun! A funeral isn't a time for fun, Lina," Emilie said sharply. "Especially not when it's going to be Papa's."

The girls started crying again.

"He's never coming back, Lina! Don't you understand that?" Luise asked.

"I'm sorry, but I can't help it. I just love horses," Lina said one more time.

The girls finally fell asleep when Grandmother Meyer came in one more time before she went to bed.

"You, girls, be quiet now. You've got to get a good night's sleep before the funeral tomorrow."

On September 25, 1912, at 10 a.m., the horse-drawn hearse came to take Michael to the cemetery chapel. Herr Pflaunder asked, "Frau Bartholomae, do you wish to walk with your family behind the carriage to the cemetery?"

"Yes, and I'd like to have all of my relatives come with me too."

"Then I'll have my apprentices go to the hotel and Bierstube to alert all of your relatives. We'll wait for half an hour so that everyone who wishes can march along behind the hearse."

Maria started crying again. Her mother came over to her. "Maria, you have to be strong. There's no sense in crying. He won't come back. Life is like that. When you think that everything is going well, there's always something that happens to spoil it."

"Fredericka, stop that," her husband told her. "Telling her to be strong isn't much of a help for Maria at all."

He took Maria in his arms and held her. Maria cried even harder. Her mother tried to soothe her but to no avail. Because their mother was crying so hard, the girls started in too. Ernst and Lilly tried to talk to her, but she was completely disconsolate. Lilly made her some tea, and Grandmother Bartholomae brought out the cookies she had baked. But Maria wasn't interested in eating or drinking anything.

"Let's go for a walk, girls," Grandmother Meyer suggested to her granddaughters. She took them outside, and they walked around the house to the market. The farmers were selling horses that morning.

"Look at all of those big horses. Aren't they nice animals?" Grandmother Meyer asked the girls. She took them over to pet some of them. One of the farmers asked, "Why are you all crying? It's a beautiful day!"

"Their father died and they're going to his funeral today," Frau Meyer told him.

"I'm terribly sorry, girls. Let me buy you all some candy," the farmer said solicitously.

"No, thanks," Frau Meyer told him. "It'll only spoil their appetites for dinner."

They returned to the house just in time to see the undertaker and his helpers put Michael in the hearse. Lina ran up to the driver and said, "Mama said I could ride on the seat with you."

The driver jumped down and lifted her up to the seat behind the horses and then climbed back up himself. Maria came out of the house with her father and mother, brother and sister-in-law, and her mother-in-law. Maria took Emilie and Luise by the hand and followed the hearse to the cemetery chapel. Grandfather and Grandmother Meyer followed next, with Grandmother Bartholomae and Mariele. Ernst and Lilly Meyer, Otto and Eva Meyer, Ernst and Emmie Neuwirth, and Sabatian and Luise Werner followed. Also in attendance were Michael's two brothers and their wives: Paul and Madel, Friederich and Emilie. Coming up the rear was a collection of nieces and nephews from both sides of the family. It was the first time any of the cousins on Michael's side had come to Vaihingen. They were almost complete strangers to the girls. They had seen some photographs of them but had never met them personally. Maria introduced her daughters to Paul and Madel, Friederich and Emilie Bartholomae, and their children.

"Emilie is my oldest, then Luise, Lina, and little Mariele," Maria said.

The girls, their aunts, uncles, and cousins from their father's side shook hands. Emilie couldn't help but be impressed with how different her father's relatives looked from those of her mother. "They look a lot like Papa, don't they Luise? Especially Uncle Fritz. He's so tall and a bit on the heavy side, just like Papa."

Luise agreed.

"He has the same blond hair and blue eyes like Papa," Emilie pointed out.

The girls started crying again although they were embarrassed crying around their cousins.

It was a slow walk up the hill to the cemetery. The horses moved slowly, and while it was a pleasant, sunny day, no one felt too hot from the walk. The hearse took Michael to the chapel where his casket was placed on a platform constructed at the front of the chapel. Pastor Eueler waited until everyone was seated.

"Dear family, relatives, and friends of Michael Friederich Bartholomae, we have assembled here this morning to pay homage to a truly great man who had become an indispensable part of our community. He leaves behind him a wonderfully strong wife and four young daughters who will no doubt miss their father tremendously in the years ahead. We pray God's blessing upon them. May his presence ever envelope their lives and be a source of strength and comfort as they face the days ahead. I've asked the Councilors, the Mayor, and the County Executive to be brief in their remarks this morning because all of you are invited to Die Rose for dinner. Herr Schiller will speak first."

"Herr Bartholomae was a special friend of mine," Herr Schiller started. "Not only did he suggest the new sidewalks throughout the village, but he wanted to encourage other businesses to locate in Vaihingen. He had contacted several firms and invited them to come to look over our village. But it was not only work that brought us together. It was the informal times that I especially remember. We often adjourned to the Alte Ente after our Council meetings, and he regaled us with his stories. Frau Bartholomae, my heartfelt condolences to you. You and your daughters lost not only a beloved husband and father, but the rest of us have lost a wonderful friend whom we shall ever remember. If you don't mind I'd like to relate to you one of many stories he told us at the Alte Ente. He was on maneuvers one night in Alsace while he was in the army and had to go to the toilet something fierce. Since his unit was just on the edge of a little village, he decided to duck into a nearby outhouse. It was completely dark and as he pulled down his trousers to sit, he sat right on the lap of the farmer who was there ahead of him. Needless to say, the farmer was surprised. He said, "Why don't you use the one next to me rather than the one I'm on?"

The congregation laughed. Even Maria had to smile at that one. She had never heard that one before.

"Yes, Fritz. We'll miss you," Herr Schiller continued. "May you ever rest in peace."

The next Councilor who spoke was Herr Hermann Weigele. He too related the pleasant times they had spent not only in the Council but at the Alte Ente.

"Most of you don't know this, but Fritz Bartholomae wanted us to buy the field along the south bank of the Enz toward Illingen. He said this would make an ideal swimming and picnic area along the river. If we had some place to put up a bath house, he thought boys and girls would be able to swim in the summers. There would be ropes separating the deeper and shallower parts of the river so that swimmers and non-swimmers could all enjoy the water.

"He was filled with good ideas. It's not only a tragedy for you and your family, Frau Bartholomae, but for us, the Vaihingen community. I'm confident he would have become a member of Parliament if he had been interested and had lived. He was a great man. He could have become even greater had he not been so cruelly plucked from our midst."

Emilie was surprised that her father had thought of providing the youth a place to swim. She had heard some of the boys along the river were already swimming in it even though the authorities didn't allow it.

The congregation blew their noses and a few sobs were heard in the chapel.

The third Councilor was Rudolph Aepfle. He was a big man who stood almost two meters tall. When he stood up no one could miss him. Maria remembered the time Michael told her of Herr Aepfle's first Council meeting.

"Now we've got to see to it that we don't spend too much money," Michael had quoted him as saying. "We don't want to create anything we can't pay for in cash. If we need new water pipelines or new streets, let's have the local people put them in and we'll reduce their taxes by the amount of their labor and the materials they use."

I couldn't believe what I was hearing. A corvee system for modern times! He must think we're still under feudalism. Michael had laughed. He hadn't thought too highly of Herr Aepfle at first but gradually grew to respect him even if he disagreed with some of his ideas. Maria wondered what he would have to say about her husband.

"Herr Bartholomae was a very strong nationalist. He wanted us to have the latest news from Berlin and from around the world. He often told us, 'What we need is some way to have direct contact with the national newspapers. We don't know what's going on around the world fast enough. I'd eventually like to hire a correspondent to work for us part time in Berlin,' he said. 'Then maybe we could create more interest in what our government is doing to promote trade and expand our empire overseas.'

"But Herr Bartholomae wasn't only interested in what was going on in the world. He was also very concerned about what was happening right here in Vaihingen. I can well recall how he once helped a poor family that had been burned out of their home. He took money out his own pocket to rent an apartment for them until they could rebuild their home. He even went with them to a bank to underwrite a loan so they could rebuild. Not many people would do something like that," Herr Aepfle said.

"But Herr Bartholomae was that kind of a person. If he saw someone in need, and he could do something for them, he did it. He didn't ask anyone else to do what he himself wouldn't be willing to do. It was a pleasure to have known him," he continued. "He was a Christian in every sense of the word."

Maria was surprised that this person whom her husband thought was living too much in the past should speak so highly of him. She didn't know he had done that for a family in Vaihingen.

The last of the Councilors to speak was Eberhard Twielling. Herr Twielling was the first person from Vaihingen Michael had gotten to know.

"Even before Fritz arrived in Vaihingen," he said, "I got to know him when we served in the army together. The story that Herr Schiller told was a true one even though when Fritz told it, he made it even funnier. We were both sharp shooters in the Wuerttemberg Rifles Division. It was my privilege to tell him about Vaihingen since this was my birthplace. When the *Enz-Bote* came up for sale, I wrote him years later and told him about it. I like to think it was my influence which convinced him and Frau Bartholomae to buy it. I'm very pleased that they did. He has been my very best friend from the time we served together in the army. On the Council he was an inspiration to all of us to improve the village in whatever way we could. Vaihingen has become an even better place to live and work since he and his family moved here. When I first told him about my village, he wanted to hear all about it. He wanted to learn about the castle. When was it built? Who built it? Is it still being used? How far can you see from its tower? The more I told him about Schloss Kaltenstein, the more interested he became in Vaihingen. He told me that 'if I ever get a chance, I'd like to live in such a village as this.' I feel it was an honor and a privilege to have known Fritz Bartholomae. I'm very glad I recruited him to run for City Council. We've had an excellent administration under his direction these past five years. We're going to miss you, Fritz," he said as he choked back the tears.

Maria started to cry again and then all of the girls. Even Mariele cried. She didn't stop. Grandmother Bartholomae took her out of the chapel. She finally stopped crying when Grandmother took her to the grave site and showed her where her Papa was going to be buried. She then came back into the chapel and sat quietly on her grandmother's lap.

Pastor Eueler read the scriptures from the Gospel of John and a few of the Psalms. He then spoke about Michael's work, where he had come from, about his parents and brothers, and finally, about Maria and their four daughters.

"Frau Bartholomae is a brave woman. Who of us would want to raise four young girls all by himself? Fortunately, she has a strong family to help her, including her mother-in-law. I'm sure her parents, her brothers, and sisters will do all they can to render her assistance in this hour of need. We do not know what lies ahead of us, indeed, nor what hour we too may be called home to the Father. We can only trust in the goodness of God to reward the faithful for their work and faith in him. Herr Bartholomae was an ideal member of our community. He was one who did what he could in his official office to alleviate some of the problems which we face here on earth. He was a very faithful husband and devoted father to his four daughters. They shall miss him greatly, and we shall miss a truly great man. He came to church regularly and often attended our Church Council to inform us of what the city was going to do each year. We appreciated his honesty and integrity. We have lost a very great friend who has been called home before his time. Frau Bartholomae, you, your daughters, your mother-in-law, and family have our deepest and heartfelt sympathy in the loss of your husband, father, son, brother, brother-in-law and uncle. As Frau Bartholomae told me before the service, she is going to put a picture of her beloved husband on his gravestone with the immortal words of St. Paul, 'Die Liebe hoeret nimmer auf' (Love never ends)"

Herr Pflaunder arranged each of the pall-bearers, with four on a side, to carry Michael's coffin to the grave site. The pall-bearers were his two brothers and Maria's brothers and brothers-in-law. It was just a short way to go. As soon as everyone was assembled, Pastor Eueler spoke the words of committal and Michael's casket was lowered into the ground. The Vaihingen Singers Society sang two songs at the grave side: "Ich hat einen Kameraden" (I Had a Comrade) and Schubert's "Liebestraum" (Dream of Love), two of Michael's favorite songs. Maria and the girls could hardly stand it anymore; they felt so weak. Everyone was crying and even Pastor Eueler had tears in his eyes as he said goodbye to them. Maria walked the girls back to the house and asked Ernst and Lilly, "Would you mind hosting the dinner at Die Rose? I don't think I can take much more of this today. I want to sleep awhile."

"Of course, Maria. We'll take your place at the dinner. The girls can go with us. I'm sure among all of us, they'll be okay," Lilly assured Maria.

Everything was ready at the restaurant. The guests were seated according to the names which Herr Pflaunder had given to the manager. The four girls were the immediate family with their Uncle Ernst and Aunt Lilly, Grandmother Bartholomae, and Grandfather and Grandmother Meyer. At separate tables all of the other uncles, aunts, and cousins were seated. There were over thirty people, which included family, the Mayor and his wife, the Councilors, friends, and the Pastor and his wife. No one stayed very long after the dinner and dessert. There was no laughter at all, and even Mariele didn't make any fuss during the meal. Everyone sat around as if in shock. Once the coffee and dessert were served, people left quietly to pack their bags at the hotel or Bierstube for the trip home. They all wanted to catch the three-thirty train if they could. Otherwise, they would have to spend another night in Vaihingen. No one seemed to want to do that.

Ernst and Lilly took the girls back to the house. Maria was still sleeping when they arrived. As soon as she heard the door open, she awoke and asked, "What time is it? Have I slept very long?"

"No, Maria," her brother answered. "It's around four o'clock, and I think we'd better get you something to eat. You haven't eaten much at all for the last two days."

"Emilie, why don't you take your sisters for a walk? Maybe you could go up to the meadow for a while," Aunt Lilly suggested.

"That's a very good idea," Grandmother Bartholomae said. "I'll go along with them and see that they come back before dark."

The next morning, Ernst and Lilly left to catch the ten-thirty train for Stuttgart. Maria was very sorry to see them go, but she knew they had three boys at home with Lilly's mother. It was another tearful parting. None of the girls wanted them to leave.

"They have to go home to their family," Maria told the girls. "We'll see them again some other time."

Maria and the girls walked Ernst and Lilly to the station. Grandmother and Grandfather Meyer had gone back to Gerabronn with the Schwaderer family. They had said their goodbyes after dinner. Maria was glad Ernst and Lilly had stayed over one more day. It helped to take her mind off Michael's absence. As they came to the train station, Lilly said, "Emilie, why don't you come to visit us over a weekend this next month? I'm sure the boys would like to see you. You can read them stories and we'll go to the zoo together. Would you like to do that?"

"Oh yes, Aunt Lilly. I'd love to do that."

"Can we go too?" Luise and Lina asked.

"When you're both a little older, and Aunt Lilly invites you, you can go there too. Emilie is the oldest and when she goes there, she can help Aunt Lilly with the children," Maria said.

The girls didn't say anymore. But Aunt Lilly said, "Yes, when you're older, you'll get a chance to come and visit us too."

The train arrived and they said goodbye to Uncle Ernst and Aunt Lilly. Uncle Ernst said, "Now remember, girls, your mother will need a lot of help to run the business. You'll all have to help her and your grandmother around the house. She won't be able to spend as much time with all of you as she has. So be good, girls, and help her all you can, okay?"

The girls all said they'd help their mother as much as they could. They didn't want their aunt and uncle to think they were ungrateful. They thanked them for coming.

As they walked back to the house, Emilie asked, "Mama, is it all right if I go visit them next month?"

"Yes Emilie. I think we can arrange that. But you'll have to help grandmother, like Uncle Ernst said. All of us are going to have to work a lot harder than we did before Papa died." She blew her nose and then all of them started crying again. Emilie thought, how in the world can we go on without Papa? What will Mama do? Lina interrupted her reverie by asking her mother, "When can I go to visit Uncle Ernst and Aunt Lilly? I'd like to go with Emilie when she goes. Why can't I go along?"

"Because you're still very young, Lina. You're only seven. When you're as old as Emilie, you'll be able to visit them too."

Luise didn't say anything. She just looked at Emilie. "I wish I were as old as Emilie. Then I could do what she does. She gets to go everywhere and we have to stay home."

Maria got upset with the girls. "You just wait until you're as big as Emilie. She's the oldest and I have to depend on her a lot. She helps with the shopping. She goes with Grandmother to the market. She runs errands for me from the store. She looks after you three girls when Grandmother or I are not at home. If either of you were the oldest, I'd have to depend on you much more too! Now I want this whining to stop right now!"

Luise and Lina started to cry, but they didn't say anything more. Emilie felt much better because Mama told them how much she did at home and how she depended on her to help. Emilie did feel sorry for her sisters, though. She just happened to be the oldest. They'll never be able to change that. I'm always going to be the oldest, she told herself.

When they got home, Mariele and Grandmother were glad to see them. Maria said to Grandmother, "I'll have to go down to the office this morning and see how the business is going. Herr Welker is very efficient, but he needs to know what has to be done from day to day. Michael said I should give him daily instructions; otherwise, he's apt to get sidetracked by constantly cleaning the presses."

"You go along, Maria," Grandmother said. "The girls and I will take care of the house. Emilie will look after her sisters while I do the cooking. We'll get along all right."

Chapter V

Vaihingen's First Businesswoman

Maria went downstairs to the office each day at 7:45 and only came up for dinner at noon. She returned to her work at one thirty and returned in the evening at six after she had closed the office and said goodbye to the staff. The girls liked the evenings best of all. Maria played games with them and read them stories while Grandmother prepared supper. When Maria was too tired to read, she asked Emilie to read out loud to her sisters while she sat and listened too. Sometimes she fell asleep on the couch and they had to wake her for supper. After supper the girls did their homework. Emilie helped Luise with her math since she was very good in math.

"Emilie, I think you can do math much better than I," her mother told her. "My father used to tell me I could do figuring quicker than he."

Emilie was very pleased with her mother's praise.

"I hope I can become as successful as you and Papa, Mama."

For the next few years, Emilie worked very hard at her school work. Maria and Michael had enrolled her in the local Latein Schule (Latin School) which was the best in the region. Anyone who went there was expected to go on to the university once they had finished. She liked math and German, especially, but also did very well in science and history. Even though her weakest subject was French, she still got a "very good" on her report card. She also excelled in religion, which everyone had to take. She liked to learn about the stories in the Bible and how people in ancient times treated each other. It was a very cruel world from what she understood of it, she thought.

On weekends during spring, summer, and fall, Emilie took her sisters up to the meadow, where they played in the garden house. In the winters, they took their sleds and rode down the hill from the garden house to the road. It was a lot of fun. Mariele was too small to ride by herself. Either Emilie or Luise would go down with her. Lina insisted on going down by herself even though she couldn't really steer the sled very well. Once she even ran into an apple tree, and fortunately, only fell off the sled as it turned over next to the tree.

"Don't tell Grandmother you hit a tree, Lina. She won't let us come up here anymore if you do," Emilie cautioned.

"I won't tell her" Lina promised.

When they returned to the house, Grandmother asked, "How was it? Did any of you get hurt? Why are you so wet, Lina?"

"I fell off the sled a few times, that's why I'm so wet."

During part of the summers, Emilie, as the oldest daughter, was allowed to visit her Grandfather and Grandmother Meyer in Gerabronn. She enjoyed going there. Grandfather was the city council president, just like her father had been. He was also the town's custodian. In addition, Grandfather Meyer was an insurance agent and spent his time writing insurance against hail and storm damage for the local farmers when he wasn't working on the town's business. She liked going with him from farm to farm because of the way her grandfather always introduced her.

"This is Emilie Bartholomae, my daughter, Maria's oldest girl. She's very smart and takes after her mother. She looks just like Maria did when she was a little girl, don't you think?" Everyone remembered Maria.

"Oh yes, Herr Meyer. She looks exactly like Maria did."

The townspeople shook hands with her, and the farmers sometimes even kissed her hand, which caused her grandfather to chuckle.

"Yes, she's a lady too. She can play piano beautifully and gets only high marks in school. I'm very proud of Emilie."

Grandmother Meyer was very different from her husband.

"I've had a very hard life," she always told everyone. "I was the second of ten children, and as the second oldest, was expected to look after my younger siblings. The oldest was a boy so that I, as the oldest girl, naturally, was expected to look after the younger ones. My mother favored her oldest son. My mother pretty much took me for granted!"

Grandmother Meyer also took it for granted the oldest child would be treated similarly. Since Emilie was the oldest girl in her family, she treated her differently from her sisters.

At each visit she told her, "Emilie, you're a lady. You don't have to work around the farm like the other grandchildren. You're going to study and become something which the rest of us are not. You're like my oldest son, Ernst. He studied too and now he's a doctor. You're going to get a good education and marry some wealthy, educated man. Mark my words, you're going to marry someone who will see to it that you continue to be treated like a lady!"

Emilie felt rather embarrassed when her grandmother told this to other people, but she felt flattered too. Her Grandmother Meyer never asked her to go out to the barn and gather the eggs or feed the pigs. She treated her like a guest in her house. Whenever she was there at the same time as some of her cousins—the Meyers, the Schwaderers, or the Neuwirths—Grandmother said, "Now, Emilie, you look after your younger cousins. Read to them or tell them stories or teach them some new games to play. I'm putting you in charge. Just see to it that they don't get hurt."

"I'll try my best, Grandmother."

Grandmother Meyer was a very forceful woman. She told Grandfather when he had to be home and how much he could eat.

"I'd like another helping of soup," Grandfather Meyer asked on one occasion.

"Gustav, you've had enough. This has to last for this evening too. You can't have another bowl. Go easy on the meat too. We don't have very much left with all these children to feed."

Grandfather Meyer took this admonishment in good humor. He didn't argue with his wife. He stopped in at one of the restaurants in town during his business rounds and had another bowl of soup. He felt this was far better than making an issue of it with her. When Emilie went with him, he asked her not to say anything to her grandmother.

"It'll only get her upset. Would you like something, Emilie?"

Since they had just eaten, she rarely wanted anything else. Occasionally she did have a piece of pie.

"It's our little secret, right, Emilie?"

Emilie laughed. "If you say so, Grandfather."

Maria did very well as a businesswoman. The *Enz-Bote* expanded its sales. Maria hired two more workers to help in the store and the press room.

"Mama, could I help you in the store after school?" Emilie asked.

"Emilie, you're going to become a lady. You're not going do anything that's in anyway connected with business or work. You're going to become a refined, educated woman. I'd like to see you marry a minister or a professor someday. That's why your father and I have given you whatever you've wanted. You're an excellent student. You play piano beautifully. You know how to take care of children. You've learned how to cook from watching Grandmother Bartholomae. I don't see any reason for you to have to work in the business. It's just not ladylike enough for you to want to do that," Maria told her daughter firmly. Neither of them ever raised the question again.

Emilie was almost fifteen when World War I started. The two pressmen had to join their army units, leaving Maria with only Herr Welker to do all of the work with the presses. She advertised for help, and two young women came to work for her in the store. She worked on the layouts for the weekly *Enz-Bote*, and Herr Welker did all of the work keeping the presses in order. Herr Welker took on a fourteen-year-old apprentice so he could help while learning the trade. Supplies became so scarce Maria had to make frequent trips to Stuttgart to try to find newsprint and ink for the newspaper. She felt uncomfortable going from office to office almost having to beg for supplies. But she had no alternative. The local townspeople depended on her to supply them with the news of the region and the country. She told Emilie, years later, "You wouldn't believe how fresh the men were in the warehouses! Frau Bartholomae, they'd say, if you need a man, just tell me. I'll get you all of the newsprint you need. Can you imagine? They wanted to trade sex for materials! If your father had been alive, they wouldn't have dared to even hint at such a proposition." Maria had to endure these taunts and innuendoes from the various suppliers. She would never have been able to keep the presses going had she not gone to the city at least once a week.

By the time Emilie finished her high school studies, there was a critical shortage of teachers in Germany. The men had all gone off to war, and young women were encouraged to take up the slack. She talked it over with her mother.

"Mama, what do you think, should I become a teacher? There's a real need for teachers now that practically all of the men have had to go in the army."

"You're right, Emilie. There's a critical shortage of men. I know from my own business. If you want to become a teacher, that's okay with me. We could use good teachers."

Emilie enrolled in the Froebel Frauen Seminar in Stuttgart to become an elementary school teacher. It proved to be an interesting and worthwhile experience for her. The other girls who enrolled were from mostly rich and well-established families. Gertrude Henne and Augusta Heer became her two best friends. They were both the daughters of successful Lutheran ministers in Wuerttemberg. Gertrude was the oldest of two girls from Heidenheim. Her father was the dean of the cathedral. Augusta was the oldest of three siblings, having a younger brother and sister. Her father was the dean of the Ulm Cathedral, the largest church in the entire state and the one with the highest spire in the world. All three of them lived together in a small house which Maria and Emilie had initially rented not far from the college. Maria had taken a day off from work to help Emilie pick it out during the summer before the semester started. It cost two hundred Reichsmarks a semester.

"This is the best one we've looked at, Emilie. Why don't you run an ad in the local paper for two other girls to share it with you?" her mother suggested. "It's expensive, but you should have the best. If you find two other girls to live with you, it'll make it even better for you. You can save on the monthly food bill, and you certainly need a telephone. I want you to call me regularly and tell me how you are doing. The others could pay part of these costs and make it less expensive for each of you."

"Do you think I can do that, Mama?"

"I don't see why not. I think you should rent this house whether you have any roommates or not. I think I can afford it. But if you can find a couple of girls to share it with you, it'll not only be cheaper for you, it'll also give you some company in this large city. Don't forget, Stuttgart isn't like Vaihingen. There are all kinds of people living here, some of whom you really don't want to associate with, Emilie."

"Okay, Mama. I'll put an ad in the newspaper. If you think you can afford the rent, I'll take it."

Emilie placed an ad in the *Stuttgarter Nachrichten*. Much to her surprise, the two girls who stopped by the same day the ad appeared were Gertrude and Augusta. They liked the house. Emilie thought they would be ideal housemates. The two girls seemed to like her as well.

"If we could share the cost of renting this house," Emilie said, "we'll have good accommodations at much lower cost for each of us."

"I'll have to ask my father first," Gertrude said. "But I really like your house. I hope he says yes."

"My father said I should make my own decisions," Augusta stated. "He said if I found a place I liked, I should go ahead and rent it. I'm sure he won't mind when I tell him who my roommates are going to be. It's a lot more fun living together than alone in this big city."

Gertrude called her father from the Post Amt and told him about the house.

"Father, I've met two very nice girls here in Stuttgart who are also going to attend the Froebel Frauen Seminar. They're renting a house and they'd like to have me join them. Would it be all right if I shared the monthly rent with them? We would share the two hundred Reichsmarks rent each month and probably share the cost of a telephone as well."

"Who are the two girls, Gertrude?" her father asked. "Where are they from? Who are their fathers? What is their profession?"

"Augusta is the daughter of the dean of the Ulm Cathedral. Emilie is the daughter of a woman who owns a newspaper in Vaihingen/Enz. Her father died a few years ago."

"What? How can she afford to send her daughter to the Froebel Frauen Seminar?"

"I don't know, Father, but Emilie was the first one to rent the house. She placed the ad in the newspaper. Augusta said yes right away because her father let her make her own decision."

"Her father's been something of a radical for a long time. I want you to be safe in Stuttgart. That's why I'm asking you these questions. You said this girl's father is dead?" Dean Henne asked.

"Yes, I think so. Emilie told me her mother helped her pick out this house. She just mentioned her father died and her mother has taken over management of the store and newspaper that she owns," Gertrude related.

"What? She's a business woman? I don't think I want you living with the daughter of a business woman!"

"Why not, Father? I think Emilie's mother is a lot wealthier than we are!"

"Where is this girl from?"

"She's from Vaihingen an der Enz."

"Well, let me check this out with my friend, Pastor Scheuer. He's the minister of the cathedral there. I don't want you to do anything, Gertrude, until I call you back. Is that understood? You wait right there at the Post Office, and I'll call you right back."

"Yes, Father. I'll wait right here."

Dean Henne called his friend, Pastor Scheuer, and got all of the information he wanted about the Bartholomaes. He almost couldn't believe what his friend told him.

"You mean she owns and manages a newspaper, Walter?"

"Yes. And not only that, she's doing a very good job of it. She's also deeply religious and attends church with her daughters and mother-in-law every Sunday morning, Albert. I don't think your daughter could find a better companion than Frau Bartholomae's daughter."

"But a business woman, Walter? Isn't she one of these cigarette-smoking, loud-talking, aggressive females that turn our stomachs?"

"Not Frau Bartholomae! She's one of the bravest, most remarkable women whom I've ever met. Just stop to think of it, Albert. Her husband dies at age thirty-nine of a burst appendix. She has four daughters ranging in age from thirteen to two and a half. She's never managed a business before. She has to be responsible for not only the region's only newspaper, but a stationery store and presses. She's doing all of this work and still is a very faithful and loyal church attendee. She's a very brave woman, in my opinion."

"Did her husband attend the university?"

"I don't think so, Albert. But he was a very fine man. He was president of the village council, head of the Nationalist Party, and from what Pastor Ludwig Eueler told me before he left Vaihingen, Herr Bartholomae could easily have been elected to the Reichstag, if he had chosen to run."

"So you wouldn't have any hesitation in recommending Fraeulein Bartholomae as a roommate for my daughter Gertrude to live together in Stuttgart?"

"Absolutely not, Albert. She's just like her mother—very generous, kind, and gracious. Both she and her mother are about the farthest removed women from the cigarette smoking-type that you will ever find."

"Thank you very much, Walter. I wanted to check out Frau Bartholomae before I gave permission to my daughter to move in with Fraeulein Bartholomae and Augusta Heer."

"Is Augusta the daughter of Dean Heer, of the Ulm Cathedral?"

"Yes. That's the one."

"Well, aren't you concerned about his theological radicalism? I wouldn't be surprised if his daughter is a chip off the old block, Albert. I'd be much more concerned about her than I would be about Emilie Bartholomae."

"No, that's okay. At least he's a university graduate and has studied theology at one of our best theological schools. I think I have more in common with him than with a man who was a newspaper owner-publisher."

Dean Albert Henne called his daughter after talking with his friend from Vaihingen. She was beginning to wonder whether or not her father was going to call.

"Hello? Father?"

"It's me. I talked with Pastor Scheuer in Vaihingen, and he tells me the Bartholomae family is a very good one, even if her father didn't attend the university. I want to meet Frau Bartholomae someday, Gertrude. From what Pastor Scheuer told me, he thinks she's the most remarkable woman he's ever met. So I guess it'll be all right if you move in with Augusta and Emilie. But be careful. Stuttgart is a very big city. Don't go out alone. Make sure the three of you are always together, okay?"

"Yes, Father. Thank you very much for letting me move in with them."

Gertrude hurried to tell her friends the good news. She ran most of the way from the post office to the house, a distance of eight blocks.

"I had to wait," Gertrude said, as she came in the door. "Papa called Pastor Scheuer in Vaihingen, Emilie, to find out about your mother. He thinks running a newspaper is a man's job. He wasn't sure I should be associating with the daughter of a business woman!" All three of the girls laughed.

"Wasn't he concerned about my family?" Augusta asked.

"No. He knows your father. They went to the same university and seminary together. He wasn't concerned about your family." They all laughed again.

"Evidently, Emilie, my father's so impressed with your mother, he wants to meet her someday. Your pastor must have given her a very strong recommendation. He said she was not only very religious, but she was also a devoted supporter of the church. He still is impressed with what a good job your mother is doing as the owner-publisher of your newspaper.

"Papa has a hard time, Emilie, accepting the fact that your mother is a businesswoman. He still can't believe a woman can carry on a business, especially running a newspaper!"

"Your father's a typical male, Gertrude," Augusta said. "Just because a woman is in charge, he thinks that's impossible. I wonder what he would say if I were to become a minister. Not that I would, but he would probably be opposed to that too, wouldn't he?"

"You're right about that, Augusta. He thinks we should all become good housewives. Just like the Kaiser always says, 'Kinder, Kirche, Kueche!' (Children, Church, and Kitchen)."

The three girls felt a real bond developing among them.

"How fortunate I am to have found you two as housemates," Emilie said. "If my mother hadn't suggested it, I wouldn't have met you two!"

Emilie felt really proud of her mother. If a dean of one of the largest churches in Wuerttemberg still couldn't believe what Mama was able to do to provide for us, she thought to herself, she must really be an outstanding woman. As if Augusta were reading Emilie's thoughts, the former said, "It is highly unusual for a woman to carry on a business which her husband had founded. Your mother is probably the only one in the whole state, if not the country, who's doing that. I've never even heard of any other woman ever trying to do what your mother is doing. She must really be a very special person, Emilie."

It was the start of a friendship which lasted all of their lives. Each one grew in appreciation of the others. Even when they were apart, they wrote copious letters to each other wherever they happened to be. Emilie received them even when she moved to America years later.

Chapter VI

Emilie's Education

The professors at the Froebel Institute were old, Emilie thought, but very nice. All of the younger professors had been called into the army. Professor Doktor Fritsch was her favorite. He taught psychology and the philosophy of education. She was very interested in learning that a child needed to find his own way in life and that a parent or teacher could assist a child in achieving his greatest potential by matching talent with opportunity in learning to become whatever he wanted to become. Emilie felt that was what her mother and father had always tried to do for her. When she wanted to learn to play piano, for instance, both of them said, "That's a good idea, Emilie." Not only did they provide her with a piano but also a teacher. If she said, "Papa, I want to travel," they took her with them on trips to the Black Forest and Lake Constance. She really felt she was learning a new method of teaching by helping a child do what he wanted to do, and she had a talent for doing so, just like her parents had done for her. It wasn't necessary to hit a child to make him mind the teacher. She had seen this done in the Latein Schule and in the religious education classes very often, when a pupil didn't give the right answer. She liked this new approach much better. She liked the idea of learning something new right along with the child. She learned how to structure situations for learning to take place by having various tools available and a positive attitude toward the child, so that he could grow to learn what he had to know and at the same time expand his knowledge. This approach enabled him to go beyond what he had learned, to what he still wanted to learn. Cultivating the child's interest was a key to understanding what innate talents he had to build upon for his whole lifetime. Gertrude and Augusta also agreed that Dr. Fritsch's lectures were by far the best they had ever heard.

After two years of study, Dr. Fritsch asked the class, "Who among you would take time out from your studies to teach school?"

The girls were surprised he asked this question. They all wanted to teach.

"There's a critical shortage of teachers in our country schools these days due to the war. The men have all been called to serve in the army. Even some of your professors have had to go. There are literally no teachers available in some of the smallest villages in Wuerttemberg. Even those of us who are in our sixties and seventies have been called back into the classroom. But our children need new and fresh young teachers. We don't need those who use the stick on our children to force them to learn their subjects! That's not education!" he continued. "All of you are already far ahead of where most of the teachers are in the use of modern teaching methods. Which ones of you would volunteer to take time off to teach in the elementary schools until the war is over? It would be an excellent opportunity for you to try out some of the ideas you've been learning here. When the war's over, you can always come back and get your degree."

Every one of the students volunteered to take on a teaching position for the war's duration. Dr. Fritsch told them, "Start looking in your own hometowns first. You'll not only be close to home, but it will save you money. You can live at home and teach either in your hometown or nearby."

Since the summer term was over, Gertrude, Augusta, and Emilie took his advice and located jobs in their own neighborhoods. Before they went home, they cleaned up the house for the last time and told their landlord what they were going to do.

"I'm both pleased and disappointed, ladies," he said. "I can understand your decision, however. I know this has to be done during the war. But I hope I'll see each of you again after the war is over," he said sadly. "I've already lost a son in France and another one was wounded in Russia." He couldn't go on. The three girls cried together with Herr Waful. The war was already killing far more men than had been predicted at its beginning.

"Goodbye, Herr Waful. We hope we can come back after the war. Your house was a delightful place to live! And it was only two blocks from the Seminar," each of them told him. "We hope we can come back, but none of us really knows what's going to happen over the next few years," Emilie told him. "I just hope the war doesn't last much longer. So many friends and neighbors have been called up and several of them have already been killed on various fronts, just like your son, Herr Waful. My Mother told me it's getting harder and harder to get supplies for the newspaper. Everything is being diverted to the war effort. She might even have to shut down the paper for the duration, if she can't get newsprint anymore."

Frau Bartholomae was glad Emilie came home. She thought getting a teaching position for her wouldn't be much of a problem in the Vaihingen area. She had already heard there was a position open in Enzweihingen, just down the Enz River from Vaihingen. The principal had advertised a position for a kindergarten/first grade teacher starting in August. As soon as Emilie arrived home, her mother told her about the position in Enzweihingen. Emilie took the little train there the very next day to talk to the principal.

"How do you do, Herr Binger. I'm Fraeulein Bartholomae. My mother told me about an ad you had placed in her newspaper saying you had a position open for next August."

"Yes. I'm looking for a kindergarten and first grade teacher."

"Dr. Wilhelm Fritsch, a professor at the Froebel Frauen Seminar, asked us students if we would be willing to take time off from our studies to help the war effort by being teachers for the duration."

"Oh yes, I know Dr. Fritsch. How long have you studied at the Froebel Institute, Fraeulein Bartholomae?"

"I've just completed my second year. I would like to finish my studies after the war."

"That's very commendable, Fraeulein. We desperately need teachers. Could you start in August? I am authorized to offer you one hundred gold Reichsmarks per month. Usually we wouldn't be required to pay you that much without your degree, but since you're a Froebel student, I'm offering you the same salary as any beginning teacher in our school. We're pleased to have a student from the Froebel Institute as a teacher. Would you know if any of your classmates are looking for a position?"

"I'm sorry, Herr Binger, but all of my friends have gone home to their villages and gotten jobs there."

"Well, just in case you hear of someone who is still looking for a position, we have another one open," Herr Binger said. "We start on the first of August. Enjoy the rest of your summer, Fraeulein Bartholomae."

Emilie returned home as fast as she could. She didn't even wait for the next train. She walked along the banks of the Enz and got home an hour before the train came through. She had walked so fast she was almost out of breath.

"Guess what, Mama?" she said breathlessly.

"What is it, Emilie? You're all out of breath!"

"Herr Binger wants me to teach first grade next August!"

"That's wonderful, Emilie. Finally, one of my girls has gotten a good position. I was beginning to wonder how many more years it was going to be before one of you would achieve some honored profession," she said teasingly. "You can always complete your studies after the war. In the meantime, you'll be a big help to have around home again. Your grandmother is getting older and she can use your help with your younger sisters."

"I can pay for my room and board, Mama. You won't have to pay for me anymore," Emilie offered.

"What? Do you think I'm so poor that you have to support me? You just help your grandmother after school and on weekends. That'll be pay enough for living here again."

Emilie gave her mother a hug and kissed her.

"I'm very proud of you, Mama. Dean Henne says you're a really remarkable woman. He wants to shake your hand. He doesn't think a woman can run her own business, let alone a newspaper!"

"Is that Gertrude's father?"

"Yes. He called Pastor Scheuer and asked all kinds of questions about you. Paster Scheuer gave you a wonderful recommendation. He said you were one his best parishioners!"

"Why did he call Pastor Scheuer?"

"Gertrude couldn't move in with Augusta and me until her father gave his approval, Mama. He said he wanted to be sure that the people she lived with were good Christian girls from good Christian families."

"And I suppose he didn't like the fact I was a widow?"

"Yes, Mama. He wondered how you could afford to send me to the Froebel Institute without Papa's support."

"Well, Emilie, that's just one more example of what I face almost every day. The men I have to deal with just can't see a woman being a boss! They want to know who's sending me. Why doesn't the boss come himself they usually ask? Yes, even the dean of a cathedral wants to know who we are and what's the basis of our support. I don't think I want to meet him, Emilie. He probably thinks we are nobodies because Papa didn't attend the university."

Emilie didn't carry on the conversation any longer with her mother. She could see she was getting upset with Gertrude's father. I'm sure if she could meet him, he'd be able to see what a remarkable woman she is, just like Pastor Scheuer said, she told herself. I think Dean Henne would change his mind about women if he knew a businesswoman like Mama.

Emilie was pleased her sisters welcomed her back home too. Each one of them expressed pleasure in the fact she was now a teacher. Even little Mariele took her to school on her last day of classes to introduce her to her teacher.

"This is my big sister," she said to Fraeulein Ruebber. "She's a teacher too!"

"I was recruited, just like you," Fraeulein Ruebber told Emilie. "I haven't finished my studies yet, either. I have one more year to study and then I want to get my master's degree. Look around you," Fraeulein Ruebber continued. "As you start teaching, ask yourself, 'How many men do I find in the classrooms?' You'll soon answer your own question. None at all under sixty. What kind of a future is that for these children?"

"It's only until the war is over," Emilie suggested. "Then the men will be coming back."

Fraeulein Ruebber laughed rather cynically. "The men will be coming back home, you say? Haven't you been reading between the lines of our newspaper, Fraeulein Bartholomae? How much longer can we go on like this? We've already lost thirty of our men from Vaihingen! The food is getting scarcer. America is now at war with us! How much longer can we absorb these losses of men and materials?" She wiped her eyes as she got more and more heated in her recitation. Emilie only learned later from her mother Ingrid Ruebber's fiancee had been killed at Verdun.

Chapter VII

Entering the Teaching Profession

Grandmother Meyer always said, "Emilie is a lady. She doesn't have to learn how to do all of the household chores. She'll hire someone to do them for her when she gets married."

That quote stuck in Emilie's mind for the rest of her life, even though her experience later would be far from anything remotely related to becoming a regal lady. Why did she call me a lady? Emilie would ask herself. I work in the kitchen right along with Grandmother Bartholomae. I help her cook, clean and wash, and take care of my younger sisters. I really can't understand why Grandmother Meyer thought I was a lady!

When she started teaching first grade in Enzweihingen, she felt anything but ladylike. She had to arrive at eight o'clock every morning, six days a week. She had to get her room ready and her materials she was going to use that day sorted out. She had to clean the room after school each afternoon before she went home. She even had to wash the windows since the janitor, who had always done them, was now in the army. If Grandmother Meyer could see me now, she told herself, she'd think twice before calling me a lady.

On her first day as a teacher, she waited at the door to her classroom for the first children to appear. They came with their mothers clutching little snack sacks in their hands. The mothers were very friendly, and many of them knew Emilie's mother. Whenever they went shopping for school supplies, they came to her store since it was the nearest to Enzweihingen. Each mother said, "Good morning, Fraeulein Bartholomae. I know your mother very well since we've shopped in her store for many years." And the mother would say "This is Haensle" or Gertrude or Christina or Wilhelmina or Fritzle or whatever name the little first grader had. Emilie had twenty little first graders that first year. Most of them had to walk several blocks from their farms to get to school. The main houses and barns were located in the village. The farmers went to their fields around the village by ox cart or by horse-drawn wagons, exactly as they did in Vaihingen. Emilie got to know each of the children very well by the middle of the school year. Their mothers invited her to visit them in their homes, and she became acquainted with the whole family that way. Those children that lived on farms were especially lucky because they always had enough food. Practically all of the mothers gave her eggs or bread to take home. When she'd protest, they'd say, "Take it! Your mother and your sisters need some good food. We've got plenty here on the farm!"

Emilie lived about three kilometers from Enzweihingen in Vaihingen. On days when the sun was shining, she loved to walk along the banks of the Enz to and from Vaihingen. There were fields along the way, and whenever she came, the local farmers would take off their hats and wave them as she walked by. Most of them were old men who were helping their daughters-in-law on the farm while their sons were off to war. She felt sorry for them because they looked so old and many were quite stooped when they walked. But she knew there was nothing they could do. They had to work; otherwise, the work wouldn't get done. The children in her class were just too small to do such hard work. She often talked with her mother about how hard the farmers had to work. Her mother agreed. "There's nothing harder that I can think of other than working as a miner in a coal mine. I've heard there are now women working in factories in Stuttgart because of the shortage of men. This would never have occurred if the war hadn't happened. After a long pause, she said, "You know, Emilie, the war is going to make a lot of women work for a living. There are so many young men who have been killed in battle. Their wives and sweethearts will have to work just like I've had to these past years. When your father died, I thought I'd never be able to go on without him . . . But I have. And I can see there are going to be many more women like me, unfortunately. After this war is over, there are going to be millions of women who will have to learn to do the same. It's not easy. I certainly don't wish this singleness upon them, but I can see it coming."

Emilie was amazed at her mother. It was the first time she had ever heard her talk about her father in these terms. Emilie still missed him terribly, and she started to cry.

"Emilie, you're going to have to get over the loss of Papa. I still miss him, probably even more than you do, but there's nothing we can do to bring him back. Your sisters seem to have accepted the fact that he's gone. They don't talk about him anymore. Even Grandmother Bartholomae has accepted the fact. You're a young woman now, Emilie. You have to put the past behind you."

Emilie still missed her Papa. She would never overcome the loss of him entirely. She knew what her mother told her was true, but it was still hard for her to accept even several years after his death. He was never very far from her thoughts. What would Papa do in this situation was often a question she almost subconsciously asked herself?

The first year went by quickly. She learned all of the children's names, where they lived, what their parents did, which ones were the better pupils, and which ones were slower. She did arrange with the principal to have a piano brought into her classroom after the first month.

"If you can arrange with Herr Binger to have a piano brought into your classroom, Emilie, I'll buy it," her mother offered shortly after she told her how much she missed not having a piano in the classroom. With such a generous offer, Emilie approached the principal and told him what her mother had said.

"What? Your mother is willing to buy a piano to use in your classroom? We certainly can't turn down an offer like that."

Shortly after this conversation with Herr Binger, Emilie and her mother went to Stuttgart and looked over a variety of pianos. They selected one that Emilie thought was suitable for her classroom. Her mother paid for it, and Herr Binger arranged to have it shipped from Stuttgart the following week. The only real problem he had was finding someone to haul it from the Enzweihingen train station to the school. There were no trucks available anymore. They had all been confiscated for the war effort. He finally found a local farmer who had a large wagon and three strong horses to bring it to the school. When the farmer asked who was going to lift it on and off the wagon, Herr Binger answered, "Why don't you ask some of your neighbors if they could help us? There are only two of us men left here at school. We're certainly not strong enough to do it by ourselves."

The farmer asked all of his nearby neighbors if they could help. He finally found seven old men. Herr Binger couldn't believe his eyes.

"What?" he asked the farmer. "You really think we can lift the piano?"

The farmer was from the estate of the von Neuwirth family, one of the oldest and largest estates in Wuerttemberg. He wasn't about to be insulted by this principal.

"If you don't want to help us, we'll do it ourselves!" And he started up his team of horses. The principal apologized.

"I didn't mean to insult any of you. I just wonder if we can manage it. Of course, Herr Schumacher and I will go along. We'll do the best we can for Fraeulein Bartholomae to get her piano here."

It took all seven elderly men, the principal, and his assistant, to lift her piano from the station platform onto the wagon and then off again at the school. The hardest part was getting it into the school room from the wagon. All of the men seemed to be struggling to maintain their footing under the heavy load and in not tripping over each other's feet. All of the men seemed to know Fraeulein Bartholomae. When they saw her standing at her classroom door, they brightened up and were smiling in spite of their heavy load. They put the piano down inside the door and pushed it into the corner of the room by the window where she said she wanted it. Herr Binger gave each man a gold Reichsmark and brought out two bottles of Vaihinger Schloss wine, which he proceeded to pour into nine glasses. He also poured one for Emilie, but she declined.

"No thanks, I don't drink. But thank you all very much for your hard work. I wouldn't have this piano if it weren't for all of you."

They seemed to appreciate her thanks, and each one shook her hand as they left and wished her a good time using the piano with the children. Herr Binger was glad the ordeal was over.

"Fraeulein Bartholomae, if I had known how hard it was getting your piano into your classroom, I would never have allowed it. I hadn't thought about moving it around, I guess, and didn't think about having a manpower shortage. These old farmers are stronger than I thought."

Emilie was thankful she had the piano. She played as the children sang the songs she taught them. Several of the parents told her their children taught them the same songs they had learned in class and were pleased how well they were learning them.

Emilie's favorite subject was arithmetic. One little boy, Erich Reinholder, learned not only how to count from one to one hundred but how to add several numbers together in a column as well. He was ready for the third grade in arithmetic even before he left her class. Herr Binger wondered how that had happened.

"Erich is just one of those budding geniuses who learn things very quickly, Herr Binger. He should be in the next grade in all of his subjects. He reads well, he can spell, and he writes very clearly, and his arithmetic is way above any of the other children. I think you should move him to Fraeulein Rudder's class at mid-year."

Fortunately for Erich, Herr Binger did just that. Fraeulein Rudder was so impressed with him she recommended Erich for an even higher promotion at year's end. Erich moved from Emilie's first grade to the fourth grade by the end of his first year of school. Needless to say, Frau Reinholder was shocked. She had no idea Erich was so bright. She thought he was a daydreamer at home. She had to remind him to clean up his room each day.

"How can you say he's so smart when I have to tell him what to do every day? If I didn't say, 'Erich, have you put your books back on the shelf?' Have you put your toys back into the cupboard?' He'd never be putting them away!"

Both Fraeulein Rudder and Emilie told Frau Reinholder Erich needed understanding. "If you talk with him and ask him what he's done each day, Frau Reinholder, you'll be surprised to learn what he can tell you. He listens very well and has no problem understanding instructions. In fact, if we ask the boys and girls who can tell us how many blocks are left if we take away fifteen from twenty, he's always the first to reply. Or if we ask, 'What is the fifth letter of the alphabet?' Erich knows it without even thinking. It seems he's really a very remarkable boy."

Frau Reinholder thanked the two teachers for the counsel they gave her. She said she would write the news to her husband who was serving on the Russian front.

"Even as a toddler, Erich seemed to like to put things together in rows. We thought he was just interested in putting things together for the fun of it. But now that you mention it, I have realized he has always put his toys or blocks into sets of threes or fours and then started new sets. Occasionally, he puts them all together and says, 'See how many there are now?'" Frau Reinholder related.

Fraeulein Rudder and Emilie just looked at each other. They were amazed and pleased to have had this little boy in their classrooms.

"It doesn't happen often," Fraeulein Rudder said, "but when it does, I'm overwhelmed each time. I thank God for the opportunity to be his teacher." Emilie felt exactly the same way.

By the end of her second year of teaching, she was asked by the principal to take over the kindergarten class. The previous teacher, Frau Scheible, had quit to work on her farm. Her husband's reserve unit had been called up, and she had no one else to help her mother-in-law on the farm. She wanted to stay on, but both her husband and mother-in-law said it was impossible. She was needed on the farm. Herr Binger told her she could come back anytime after the war, if she still wanted the job. Reluctantly, she quit.

"I'd very much like to come back, Herr Binger," she told him. "I love to teach kindergartners!"

Frau Scheible was only a few years older than Emilie but was still childless. "My husband and I have wanted children, but none has arrived even after five years of marriage," she told Emilie.

"We'll just have to wait until after the war," she said hopefully. "But I enjoy the little children at that age. They're so lovable. I'd like to have several of my own!" she said wistfully. Emilie couldn't help but feel sorry for her. Now she had to give up teaching and become a farmer. How sad for her, she thought.

The kindergartners were a real change after the first graders. First of all, there were more of them: twenty-five. Secondly, there were more boys than girls: fifteen boys and ten girls. Emilie was able to take her piano with her, which was very fortunate. She spent more time with them learning songs than anything else. The children liked singing and quieted down as soon as she started playing. If they tried to draw or color, before long one of the boys would start to paint on a neighbor's picture, and the argument was on. The only other time during the day they were quiet, besides nap time, was during storytelling time. Emilie had learned a lot of stories by heart. She could tell them relatively easily. The children sat on their little chairs and listened as she told them stories from the Bible or from the Brothers Grimm Tales, or from antiquity. She also took them for walks out in the countryside as often as possible. Before she could do that, she had to ask a few of the mothers if they could go along. She knew she couldn't look after all twenty five of them alone.

After their second outing, one of the mothers asked her, "Fraeulein Bartholomae, could I come and help you in the classroom? I've always wanted to become a kindergarten teacher, but I've never had the opportunity to study. I got married very early, and we started having children right away. Now that my youngest is in kindergarten, I think I have the time to do it. We've have seven children already, but I don't think we'll have anymore. My husband is in the army and our three oldest children are helping my mother on our farm, so I'm not needed much there anymore."

"That's great," Emilie said. "I can use all of the help I can get. You've probably noticed how difficult it is for one person to try to direct the energies of so many children. If you could come at least an hour each day, even that would be a real help."

"Oh, I'd like to come for the whole morning. I could bring Edward with me and be here each morning at eight o'clock. If you would like, I could help you to clean up afterward so that the classroom is ready for the next day."

Emilie couldn't have been more pleased with Frau Schilling. She was punctual, dependable, and a great help on classroom projects such as painting and drawing. While Emilie explained how the children were to draw or paint a certain kind of picture, Frau Schilling went ahead and demonstrated it for them. She was a much better drawer than Emilie and helped the individual child sketch their scenes and then to paint them. If there was a problem between two children, Frau Schilling was there to redirect their efforts toward their own drawings. When Emilie told her, "We should always try to talk quietly with the children who are having problems." Frau Schilling did exactly that. She never raised her voice and always said, "Fraeulein Bartholomae wants you to paint your picture for your favorite person. Who would that be?" The usual response was "Mama or Papa," and they would return to their project to finish as much as possible before the morning was over. Frau Schilling helped clean up after the morning class. Emilie put the paints away while Frau Schilling washed the paint brushes. Emilie swept the floor; Frau Schilling mopped it. Emilie put the books back on the shelves while Frau Schilling put the blocks away in their boxes. After a few weeks, she was no longer Edward's mother but Frau Schilling, the assistant teacher. Herr Binger was glad Emilie had help. He noticed that after Frau Schilling started helping, Emilie was spending far less time on the piano and the children were not singing as much as they did before. He was very nice about it. After the first month Frau Schilling was with her, he said, "Fraeulein Bartholomae, I hear less singing these days coming from your room. And I've noticed you don't play the piano as long anymore either. It must be the children are learning more about the Bible, history, and painting than they did earlier. You're still teaching them songs, aren't you?"

"Oh yes, Herr Binger. But I don't have to spend so much time anymore trying to separate the children who are quarreling than I did earlier. Since Frau Schilling is with me, the class has gone much better."

At the end of her second year, Herr Binger asked her to stay on with the kindergarten class. Emilie agreed, but only if Frau Schilling would stay. He talked with Frau Schilling and she told him, "Edward is going into first grade. If I can leave at the end of the morning to take him home, I'll be glad to help Fraeulein Bartholomae."

When Herr Binger told her Frau Schilling could only stay until school let out each day, Emilie was relieved.

"That's okay," she said. "So long as she's with me while the children are here, I don't mind cleaning up by myself." Frau Schilling stayed for the entire year. It was a hard year. The war was gradually drawing to a close, but the German population didn't know it. They just knew there were no more men available in their villages. Even Emilie's classmates had been called up, and those of the year after her class as well. These men were barely eighteen years old and were drafted for the western front. The war had ended in the East with the defeat of the Russians in early 1918. The men who were coming home for leave before being sent to fight in France were increasingly bitter. Frau Bartholomae couldn't believe what she was hearing from her friends whose sons were among those lucky enough to come home on a brief leave.

"There's mass starvation in Russia and Poland," they said. "Beggars are everywhere."

Even those Russian troops that had been discharged by the revolutionary government during the armistice with Germany were being called back into the Russian Army. They had to fight the communists, if they were recruited by the White Forces, or fight the capitalists if they were drafted by the new Soviet government. The German soldiers who had won in the East were told initially by their government they wouldn't have to fight anymore. But now they were being transferred to the western front. The Allies were about to break, the leaders of the government said. "We've got to finish this war before too many Americans land in France. We need your help. It'll only take one more big offensive in the West, and France will fall!"

"The German soldiers are also amazed," Frau Bartholomae told Emilie, "by how little food there is here at home. They are eating quite well at the front. What's happening? they asked. Why aren't you getting more fresh meat, milk, and vegetables?"

There were also several men who had been released from the army due to medical disabilities. They had been badly wounded and were now staying in the local hospital. Only their immediate families were allowed to visit them. The mothers and wives of these soldiers were also neighbors of the Bartholomaes, and the women couldn't help but relate what their sons and husbands told them. Emilie's mother talked daily with three of the women who had men in the Vaihingen hospital ward.

"They tell us in hushed tones the war is going badly in France. There are now more than one million American troops fighting with the French and English armies against us. The artillery barrages are unbelievable! They can't take more than a few yards at a time before the Allied artillery begins and then they're lucky if they can hold on to their positions. The survival rate among our divisions is as low as thirty percent! More and more of their comrades are giving up, if they haven't been killed first. There's very little enthusiasm for any more fighting among the troops. Why get killed when we've already lost the war?"

Frau Bartholomae couldn't believe what she heard. "How can these soldiers not believe in our victory?" she asked Emilie. "Everything we've ever had, we've given up for the war effort. We've sacrificed on food. We've sacrificed on heat in the winter. We've gone without any new clothes during the entire war. We've bought billions of Reichsmarks worth of government bonds. What do they mean, we can't win this war? We've got to win! We must win! We don't want to have to go through what the Russians have gone through. We've got to keep fighting!"

Frau Bartholomae had to sit down after this outburst. Emilie had never seen her so upset in her entire life. Even when Papa died, she seemed to cry inside of herself. She didn't want the girls to see how hurt she was. "Mama, please don't get so upset. There's nothing we can do about it. If that's the way it is at the front, it would be better for us to give up. At least then no more lives would be lost. The soldiers could come home again. There wouldn't be anymore gravely wounded like those in the hospital," Emilie tried to reassure her. Her mother got even more upset with her.

"Emilie you still don't understand, do you? I suppose it's my fault for not telling you, but I've invested over two hundred thousand gold Reichsmarks in empire bonds! If we lose the war, all of that money will be lost! Do you understand now?" she almost screamed.

Emilie sat down speechless. She couldn't say anything for a long time. Her mother kept crying. What she had said fell on Emilie like a rock. She couldn't believe what her mother told her.

"You mean all of that money you and Papa had saved could all be lost?"

"That's exactly what I'm saying! If we lose the war, we'll all have to start over again. I only have my business, and I don't know how much longer I'll be able to go on with that. Herr Welker would like to buy it, but I'm not sure he'll want to if there's no value in our Reichsmarks anymore. Do you know what our government demanded from the French after their defeat in the Franco-Prussian War?"

Emilie shook her head.

"Seven billion francs! Do you think the Allies won't expect us to pay them for all of the damage we've done to them or to the Belgians if we lose? Do you know who pays for lost wars?"

"No," Emilie answered weakly.

"The defeated!"

Frau Bartholomae didn't say anymore to Emilie that day. Emilie couldn't believe what her mother had told her. I guess I didn't want to believe it, she thought to herself.

She couldn't sleep that night. She thought of Eugen Schmidt with whom she had kept in correspondence ever since he was drafted in 1917. He was an apprentice in their printing business. He wrote to Emilie faithfully all during the war. She did the same. Their letters contained all kinds of plans of what they would do once the war was over. He wanted to marry her and become part of the business. He hoped to complete his apprenticeship and become a journeyman and finally a master printer.

"I'd like to help your mother, Emilie. I think I could learn the bookkeeping aspects of the business once I've got my master's certification. We could continue on with the business your father started. I'm sure the business could use a man's touch again. I don't mean to denigrate your mother, but business can really be very ruthless and brutal. People who are kind hearted and well-intentioned, like your mother, are often the ones who get hurt the most by unscrupulous scoundrels. Once we're married, we'll have a very wonderful life together."

Yes, she thought to herself. If I marry Eugen, I'd have a very good husband, and Mama would have a very reliable son-in-law upon whom she could depend in the business. But that Mama invested so much money in bonds, I still can't believe it!

Emilie finally fell asleep. She awoke the next morning feeling sleepy and still upset from the evening's discussion with her mother. She had tried to pray for the victory of the German troops, but somehow, she couldn't quite believe what she was saying. I do want them to win, of course, but I don't feel right about the continued killing that's going on in France, she told herself. If there are so many German soldiers who have been badly wounded on our side, don't the French soldiers feel the same way our troops feel she asked herself?. If you're wounded, it doesn't matter which side you're on. You're still hurt and you may not get over it. It's only the healthy who want to keep on fighting. The only prayer she finally uttered was "God, please bring the war to a speedy conclusion. And if it is thy will, let our side be victorious in this war."

The last few months of teaching for Emilie during the school year were difficult. Not only had the Germans lost the war, but the troops who were returning were moody, embittered, and defeated. There was only an armistice, which meant the war could resume if their government did not accept the terms of peace. The food shortage became worse than at any time during the war. If the mothers of her pupils hadn't given her fruits, vegetables, and an occasional slice of beef or pork, the Bartholomaes would have had a very difficult time having enough to eat. As it was, her mother and Luise went from farm to farm around Vaihingen asking to buy eggs, meat, or anything else a farmer might like to sell.

The newspapers were filled with all kinds of stories about food riots in some of the cities in the north and of political unrest. The Kaiser had abdicated, and the new government that was formed after the first national election since the war stopped proved to be a very radical one, from Frau Bartholomae's perspective. It was a Socialist government, and one that wanted to redistribute the wealth of the country. Frau Bartholomae was fearful even her small newspaper and store might become the target of radical elements who remembered her husband's strong support for the Kaiser's government. Fortunately for the family, she wasn't targeted by the local socialists/communists. They liked the idea that a woman was the head of a business and even asked her if she would like to become a candidate for the Wuerttemberg State Legislature under their party label. She refused.

"I've got more than enough to do looking after my business and trying to raise my three younger daughters!" She didn't need to include Emilie anymore. She saw her as a teacher who was already on the way to becoming a successful professional for whom she would not longer have to be financially responsible.

After school, Emilie walked home very quickly. It seemed each day some new event was taking place for which they were totally unprepared. The shortage of food was critical in the early spring of 1919. They couldn't understand why flour, milk, and eggs weren't available in the stores anymore. Even at the height of the war, they always had some flour. It was rationed, as were clothes and leather goods. But why don't we have more now? The war's over she thought to herself! We could always buy some foodstuffs during the war. Why aren't potatoes available anymore? It wasn't the army that needed these foodstuffs; the soldiers were back home again, Emilie mulled over in her mind. As she went up the hill to her house, an older man gave her a pamphlet with a hammer and sickle on the front page.

"I don't want it," she told him.

"Read it at least before you throw it away! You'll find out why there's such a food shortage in Germany these days . . . ," he said, bitterly.

She took it reluctantly and glanced through it as she proceeded home. On the opening page of the pamphlet was the heading "Why Are We Hungry Today?" Emilie decided to read it as she continued to walk home. The author was someone from Berlin who claimed the Allies had placed a sea blockade on Germany. Nothing could enter its seaports. All foodstuffs were seized and taken to Allied ports. Even raw materials were seized. Nothing could enter Germany so long as the armistice continued. The author went on to say only a revolution could change the conduct of the Allies. The Soviet Union would gladly assist anyone who wished to take part in planning for a world revolution. He further called for a uniting of all Germans to join in this crusade to rid the world of the capitalist swindlers who were starving women and children to death for their own gain.

Emilie had never read such a diatribe before. She couldn't believe the Allies could do such a thing!

"Mama, I just read a pamphlet a man gave me as I was walking up the street. It said the Allies have put a blockade on our ports. That's why we don't have anything to eat anymore!"

Frau Bartholomae didn't even want to see it.

"Emilie, throw that nonsense away! That's rubbish! No one would do such a thing to innocent people! I can't believe the Americans or the British would do such a thing. Perhaps the French, but certainly not the rest of the Allies!"

Emilie threw it away, but she couldn't help thinking about what the author had alleged. Suppose he were right she said to herself? There is a shortage of everything imaginable. She thought no more about it because the next day Frau Schilling brought her a huge cut of bacon which they had smoked on their farm. It lasted several days. Grandmother Bartholomae served it with eggs one meal; roasted part of it with noodles for another; and finally, made the remainder into a soup with potatoes Emilie's mother and sister had bought on one of their trips to the local farmers.

During the latter days of April, after Emilie returned home, her mother showed her the headline in a Stuttgart newspaper: "Allies Hold Germany Responsible for the War." The article went on to describe what the Allies had decided Germany must do in order for the war to come to an end. All of their colonies had to be turned over to the British, French, and Japanese. Alsace-Lorraine had to be returned to France. The new nation-state of Poland was to have access to the sea by granting much of East Pomerania to Poland, including the use of the international city of Danzig as a seaport. Plebiscites were to be held in Silesia to determine which parts would become Polish and Czech territory. The northern part of Schleswig-Holstein was to be returned to Denmark. The border with Belgium was to be straightened by giving the Belgians Eupid-Malmedy and the surrounding countryside. All railway stock was to be turned over to the French in behalf of the Allies. Likewise, all heavy guns, aircraft, Zeppelins, ammunition stocks for howitzers, and heavier guns were to be turned over to the Allied armies that were to be stationed in the Mannheim to Cologne region. All of the battleships, battle-cruisers, submarines, and merchant ships of more than ten thousand tons were to be sailed into British ports for confiscation on behalf of the Allies. The Saar was to be occupied by the French and absorbed into its economy. Emilie couldn't believe what she was reading.

"Mama, how can the Allies do this to us?" she cried. "The last line is even more ominous. It says, 'The total amount of monetary damages for starting the war still has to be assessed and will be added to the list of items for payment by Germany!' How can we ever do that?" she cried.

Frau Bartholomae didn't know. "It's going to be a very hard time for us all, Emilie. If we thought the war was hard enough for us to take, I can't imagine how we're ever going to be able to survive. The whole world is against us now!"

The newspapers were full of stories about resuming the war effort. After all, the German armies were still intact. The millions of men had simply come home but were told to be ready to return to their units should they be called to do so. None of Emilie's colleagues nor any of their neighbors thought Germany should accept these conditions of peace. The soldiers who had returned were even more bitter; so many of their friends had been killed. For what? They couldn't understand why the government had not sought to end the war earlier. There would have been a chance to distribute the war loses more evenly had they sued for peace a year earlier. This seemed to be the consensus of most of the returning soldiers.

Eugen Schmidt had also returned with his unit to Vaihingen. He visited Emilie as soon as he arrived. She was glad to see him and to see that he had survived the war intact. So many others had been wounded or were unable to even communicate with their families. He couldn't resist asking her if she would marry him.

"Let me think it over, Eugen. There's no hurry. I have to finish this school year. There'll be plenty of time this summer to make that decision."

The reason she put him off was because she wanted to talk with her Uncle Ernst first. She had discovered, quite by accident, that his younger sister had Parkinson's disease. The very next weekend, she took the train to Boeblingen and talked with her uncle, the doctor. She asked him, "Can Parkinson's disease be inherited?"

"Yes," he said. "From what we know about it, it's probably an inherited disease. It may or may not occur in successive generations, but the gene causing it is carried from generation to generation."

"Should I marry a man whose sister has it?" she asked.

"If you want to take the chance of having your children come down with it, go ahead, Emilie. But if I were you, I'd look around for a more suitable husband than one who carries this liability with him."

On her way home, Emilie couldn't help but think what her uncle had told her. If I marry Eugen, she thought to herself, Mama would have a very good man to help her in the business. He knows printing and the operation of the presses from start to finish. He's certainly very congenial and easy to talk with. He's been very faithful throughout the war in writing almost every day he could. But what if our children came down with this disease? There's nothing that can be done about it. There's no medicine that can stop it, according to Uncle Ernst. The children might live for a few years or many, but they'll always carry the gene with them.

By the time she arrived in Vaihingen, she had made up her mind. It was going to be hard to do, but she had to tell him she couldn't marry him. He could still work for her mother, she thought, if he wanted to. She was very happy, she would tell him, to see that he had come back from the war alive. He could start working as soon as he was ready.

She didn't know how he would take her rejection. But she told herself that was his problem. She had to do what she had to do, and that was to protect her future children from ever having this disease.

The next day, after Emilie came back from Enzweihingen, Eugen was waiting for her. Frau Bartholomae had told him what time she usually returned. He was sitting in the store talking with her and Herr Welker, the press operator. They both wanted him to come back to work: Frau Bartholomae, because she knew how much he was in love with her daughter, and that he would make a very helpful son-in-law in running the business; Herr Welker, because he had hopes of buying the business from Frau Bartholomae, and he needed someone who was trained as a skilled pressman.

As Emilie came in the door, Eugen stood up, took her hand, and kissed it. He kept holding it as he looked longingly at her.

"Emilie, would you like to go for a walk?"

"Eugen, I would, but I've just come from walking home from Enzweihingen. Why don't we do it another time?"

"Sure, Emilie. I don't want to wear you out. I just wanted to talk with you about our future."

"That's a good idea, Eugen. Why don't we get together this next Sunday. There's something I also want to talk with you about."

They agreed to meet the next Sunday after church and take a walk along the Enz.

"After your walk, Eugen, you can come to our house for dinner," Frau Bartholomae told him. It gave Emilie another week to think about how she was going to tell him of her decision.

It seemed like the longest week of her life. She thought over and over again how she was going to tell him. She didn't want to hurt him. But she knew what she had to say to him would wound him deeply. He was such a faithful and trusting man. He was very kind to her, to her mother, and to her sisters. He had two younger sisters himself. Emilie knew how well he got along with girls. He was quite handsome. He was learning a good trade. He wouldn't have a problem getting a job, even if her mother sold the business. He had grown up in Vaihingen and knew her father. He had often spoken of her father with great respect. It was another one of those early ties that helped to knit him closer to her family. Emilie liked Eugen. She thought she could even fall in love with him at some point in the future. She didn't feel she was really in love with him now. He was a few years older than she, which wasn't unusual for German couples. His mother was also widowed and worked in one of the local bakeries as a saleswoman. Yes, she thought, it would be so easy just to say yes to Eugen. But his youngest sister . . .

Emilie had seen her for the first time when she stopped at Frau Schmidt's to find out if she had heard anything from Eugen. He hadn't written for over a month, and Emilie was concerned something might have happened to him. He was with a Wuerttemberg artillery unit, and she had read in the newspaper that a huge offensive was launched by the German armies against the Allies in the Chateau-Thierry region before Paris.

Frau Schmidt was very gracious and asked her to come in. She knew from Eugen who Emilie was, but they had never met. She had just baked some cookies and asked Emilie to take a seat at the dining room table. As they were talking, Eugen's youngest sister came into the room. Emilie almost fell off her chair. His sister was trembling so much Emilie had a hard time reaching her hand to shake it as Frau Schmidt introduced them.

"This is Victoria," Frau Schmidt said. "She has what doctors call Parkinson's disease. She shakes almost all of the time. She can't drink anything without me holding the cup for her. When she's asleep she still shakes a little. There's nothing the doctors can do for her."

Victoria was a very pleasant girl with a very nice smile. But she couldn't talk without quivering even in her speech. She was about Emilie's age. Emilie felt truly sorry for her. What a tragedy it must be for someone that young to have to go through life like that, she thought afterward. On the way out, Frau Schmidt told said, "Victoria isn't expected to live much longer. Maybe another year or so and then she'll be dead. It would be nice if she lived long enough to see her brother one more time," Frau Schmidt sighed.

Emilie finally decided to write down her reservations in a letter to Eugen about why she couldn't marry him. She would give him the letter after dinner on Sunday afternoon. It was a very hard letter to write, but she felt she had to put her feelings down on paper. Emilie wrote:

> Dear Eugen,
>
> This is the most difficult letter I've ever had to write, but I want you to know why I can't marry you. I talked with my uncle, Dr. Ernst Meyer, who is a doctor in Boeblingen, about your sister, Victoria. He told me that Parkinson's disease is an inheritable disease for which there is no cure. If we were to get married, he said, and we had children, the gene would be passed on to them. Eugen, as much as I like you and as much as we've corresponded with each other all through these last years of the war, I believe it would be better for both of us if we did not see each other again. I'm truly sorry to have to write this letter to you, but I wanted you to understand why I can't let this illusion of yours that we might get married go on any further. Marriage is out of the question. I cannot allow myself, for the sake of how much I might like you and respect you, and for all this time that we've written to each other about our plans for the future, to let this romance continue. Goodbye, Eugen. I've very much appreciated getting to know you and might even have grown to love you, but I very much want to have children. I know it's best for us both if we don't see each other any longer.
>
> Your very affectionate friend,
Emilie

After dinner that Sunday afternoon, she gave Eugen her letter. He was thunderstruck. He was visibly shaken and blanched. Emilie thought he was going to pass out. When he regained his composure, he asked, "So that's it, Emilie? You wouldn't reconsider if I said we wouldn't have any children?"

"But I want to have children, Eugen. I couldn't imagine what it would have been like for Mama if she hadn't had us. I want to have boys and girls of my own. I can't even think about a life that doesn't have any children! People who don't have any are the loneliest people I know. They have no one in their old age. I don't want to be like them, Eugen. I know it's hard for you to understand. I like you a lot, but I can't marry you. I haven't told anyone else of my decision, but I plan to now. I'm going to tell Mama first. She likes you a lot too. I hope you'll work for her again. She could really use your help."

"You think I'd want to stay here and work in the business for your mother when I'd see you every day? No! That's out of the question. I'll go somewhere else and get a job."

He went to the kitchen and thanked Frau Bartholomae and Grandmother for the dinner. He then said goodbye to each of Emilie's sisters. And finally, to her. He shook her hand and said, "Emilie, if you ever change your mind, just let me know. I'd be forever grateful. I hope I see you again in the future."

"Thank you, Eugen. You're going to be a real good man for some woman someday. I hope you'll always be happy. I've very much appreciated knowing you."

With these final words, he left and didn't bother to turn around and wave as he left her door. Her mother couldn't understand what happened.

"We were all so friendly before dinner. Your sisters laughed at some of the stories he told about his travels during the war. What happened between you two, Emilie?"

"Uncle Ernst said that Parkinson's disease is an inherited disease, Mama. Eugen's youngest sister is dying from it. Ever since my talk with Uncle, I've been thinking and thinking about the implications of this disease. I like Eugen a lot, but I'm thinking about my children and grandchildren and their children after them. I didn't want them to inherit this disease. I wrote down my thoughts very clearly in a letter that I gave Eugen after dinner. That's why he left in such a state. I couldn't help it. There was no other way for me but to tell him I couldn't marry him. I told him he could still work for you, but he wasn't interested anymore. He said he'd see me every day and that would be too hard for him to endure."

"You couldn't really expect him to want to do that, Emilie. It would break his heart every day. Well, it's too bad, but I can understand your hesitation. I wouldn't want to marry someone under those circumstances either. You'll have to tell your sisters. They really liked him and so did Grandmother. I'll tell Grandfather and Grandmother Meyer not to expect a wedding anymore."

Chapter VIII

The Sale of the Family Business

The Versailles Treaty was signed on June 25, 1919. As far as the Germans were concerned, this was a day of infamy. Not only had they been stripped of their overseas empire, but sizable chunks of their territory were given to the Allies as well. All of their major naval vessels including all submarines, heavy guns, aircraft, zeppelins, railway stock, all ammunition supplies, army horses and wagons, and army and navy trucks had to be given to the Allies. A complete ban was placed on the production of any heavy naval vessels over ten thousand tons, submarines or aircraft. The German Army could not be larger than one hundred thousand men. Even these soldiers had an enlistment period of twelve years so that no new recruits could be brought into the army for over a decade. What was even more appalling to the Germans, however, was the enormity of the cost of the war leveled against them: thirty three billion dollars to be paid over thirty years. When Frau Bartholomae read the newspaper accounts of the treaty, she almost fainted.

"How will we ever be able to pay that vast amount of money?" she cried!

"Look what they've done to us, Emilie! I told you if we lost the war, we'd have to pay for it! But I never expected such a large amount of money! Why, we're going to be in debt for the rest of my life and yours too!"

"So this is the way the Allies have gotten back at us!" Emilie started to cry. Luise, Lina, and Mariele came into the room.

"Why are you both crying?" they asked almost in unison.

"Because we're going to have very hard times ahead of us," their mother answered.

"And I thought losing all of my money in buying the empire bonds was bad enough!" she groaned. "We haven't seen anything yet. How in the world are we ever going to pay such a large amount of money?" she kept asking herself.

"But, Mama," Luise said, "You still have the business. You still have your work!"

"That's just it. I'm not sure I'll be able to continue. Prices of all kinds of goods will go up. Our government will have to levy a heavy surcharge on all of the things we buy to help raise the money to pay such an enormous amount each year. And I thought it was bad enough during the war to get the things I needed for the business. Oh my! It's going to ruin a lot of people! Everyone of your uncles and your grandfather had invested heavily during the war, not only in bonds but in stocks. They won't be worth much once we start paying on this foreign debt!"

Emilie and her sisters sat bewildered. They couldn't understand much of what their mother was saying. When she said people might lose everything of value they had, Lina wanted to know, "What things, Mama? What will they lose?"

"They could lose their businesses. If they're not able to pay their debts because of the higher prices for the things they need, they'll go bankrupt. They'll have to sell their businesses at a fraction of what they're really worth."

"But what if they just raise their prices for the things they sell?" Emilie asked. "Wouldn't that be one way to avoid having to go bankrupt because you can't pay your bills?"

"Yes, it would be," her mother replied. "But where does it stop? What if everyone kept raising their prices week by week? The government would have to set limits on the prices that could be charged for various products. But what if you have high debts and can't make enough on the sale of your goods to offset your costs? Then what are people going to do? It costs me twelve hundred Reichsmarks a month to pay all my bills for the newspaper and the store. I'm only making a little below two thousand Reichsmarks a month now. If the rate of price increases goes up twenty-five percent, which the government has already stated prices will rise, that would only leave me with a margin of three to four hundred Reichsmarks a month to take care of our needs as a family! If the prices should go higher, I can't continue without raising my prices beyond what a lot of people would be willing to pay for a newspaper, a pencil, or a block of paper. If I can't sell the products I have, girls, we have nothing!"

Around the middle of July, Herr Welker asked Frau Bartholomae if she would consider selling the business.

"You seem to be doing well," he told her. She didn't respond right away. So he asked her again. "Frau Bartholomae, would you be interested in selling the business?"

"Possibly, but I'll have to think it over for a while first."

"Okay," Welker replied. "But I'd like an answer by the first of September. I'm also looking at another business in Horrheim."

"Yes, that'll be plenty of time."

Frau Bartholomae was a very good businesswoman. She did a very thorough review of her receipts, expenditures, and accounts receivable. She also talked with her father about what he thought the business might be worth. Since he was a city manager, he worked with such figures daily and knew how much property of all kinds was worth. He encouraged her to sell quickly while she had a buyer.

"We don't know how things are going to work out over the next couple of years, Maria. I'm afraid being in business is going to be very difficult. There will be all kinds of new taxes to pay and surcharges levied on goods coming from abroad. It's not going to be much fun anymore. Expenses are likely to go through the roof before they ever fall into the range they've been in even during the war. It's going to be the worst time for anyone in business."

"What do you think it might be worth?"

"As I recall, Fritz paid eighteen thousand for it in '99, didn't he?"

"Yes. You helped us by loaning us fifteen thousand Reichsmarks he needed to complete the purchase."

"That's right. I thought the business was worth more than you paid for it and was glad to invest in it by giving you the loan. Let me think, that was more than twenty years ago, wasn't it?"

"Yes, that's how long we've had the business. I never thought I would ever want to sell it because it meant so much to Michael. But I'm finding, since the war, I've lost my interest in continuing the business. I thought Emilie might marry someone who would be interested in coming into the business, but that's off. The younger girls are going to have to learn a trade of some kind. I don't think they're likely to marry anyone capable of entering the business. As you know, Papa, the cost of everything seems to be going up. It's not like it used to be before the war. I just hope the government will continue to honor the bonds we bought."

"I hope so too, Maria. Do you realize, in this family alone, we've invested more than one million Reichsmarks in bonds?"

"I know, Papa. I made the same mistake. If the government doesn't honor those bonds, everything we've ever worked for will be lost. We'll only have our real estate. Nothing more!"

"I'm glad we still have that, Maria. If not, we'd all be out in the street. You know, Maria, the more we talk about selling the business, the more I think you should be very careful who buys it. The property itself is worth a lot of money. It's right in the center of Vaihingen and property values at least have held up pretty well."

"Herr Wilfried Welker is the person who wants to buy it. He's been with us right from the beginning. He's a master pressman and knows the business inside out. He's had less to do with the store, but I'm sure he could manage that together with his wife and daughter."

"Why not ask for one hundred fifty thousand Reichsmarks as a starter? You can always come down in your negotiations with him."

"Do you think I could get that much for it?"

"You won't know unless you try. In fact, why not start at three hundred thousand; then you'll have more latitude in your negotiations."

"I can't believe it's worth all that money, Papa, but I'll try it and see what happens."

On July 28, Maria Bartholomae talked with Wilfried Welker about buying the business.

"So, you've decided to sell, haven't you, Frau Bartholomae?"

"Yes, even though I'm sure my husband wouldn't have decided to do so, Herr Welker."

"What price have you set for it?"

"Two hundred thousand Reichsmarks."

"What? You can't be serious, Frau Bartholomae. That's way too much. I'll give you one hundred twenty-five thousand and even that's too much."

"Herr Welker, you asked me if I would sell the business and now I've decided I would. Then you asked me how much I wanted for it, and I told you. Now you say that's way too much! You know what I've just said. If you don't want to buy it, you don't have to. But you know what I'm asking for it. If you decide you want to buy it, let me know. I'll be glad to discuss it with you again in the future."

"Frau Bartholomae, I knew your husband very well and I knew him to be an honest man. I can't believe he would have asked that much for the business. Nevertheless, let me think it over."

"Herr Welker, you've got to remember that things have changed enormously since the war. The prices before the war don't exist anymore. Everything has gone up, including property. You won't find another newspaper that you can buy this cheaply. Don't forget, we're the only newspaper in the entire region. You have to go all the way to Stuttgart before you can find another paper."

Wilfried Welker ended the conversation with "I know, you're the only one in the area, but that's an awful lot of money. Let me think it over, Frau Bartholomae."

Emilie decided to go back to Enzweihingen for another year as the kindergarten teacher. Herr Binger asked her to stay on even though she told him she would like to go back to the Froebel Frauen Institute and complete her degree.

"If you would stay one more year, Fraeulein Bartholomae, I have another young teacher who will be finished with her studies next year. She could take over your class. She only has this year to complete. I'd really appreciate it if you would stay. We can give you another two hundred Reichsmarks for the year."

"Well, all right, Herr Binger, I'll stay one more year, but I really do want to complete my degree."

When she came back from school on September 1, 1919, her mother told her the news.

"Guess what, Emilie?" her mother asked with a lilt in her voice that she rarely remembered. "I think I've sold the business! Herr Welker offered me one hundred seventy-five thousand Reichsmarks. He wants to give me fifty thousand in cash and have me hold the mortgage for the rest at five percent interest per year over a twenty-year period. I told him I would. Don't you think that was a good price for the business?"

"That's less than you originally asked, Mama."

"I know it is, but it's still higher than the two hundred fifty thousand your grandfather thought I should ask in the beginning. He had proposed two hundred thousand only as a price from which to negotiate downward. I think it'll be better this way instead of having all of the money at once. It'll give me a monthly payment of over seven hundred Reichsmarks to invest and take care of my household," she said almost exuberantly.

"That's great, Mama! What are you going to do with the fifty thousand Reichsmarks?"

"I'm going to put it in the bank for now and maybe later invest it in something else. I can get two percent a month from the bank in a savings account. I'm going to take my time. I may even get a job myself in a year or two so that I have something to do. I'm so used to working. It'll be hard to make the adjustment to stay home full-time."

Emilie hoped her mother would be happy staying at home, but she had her doubts. After all, Grandmother Bartholomae was still taking care of the household and looking after the girls. She was getting older—sixty-five, in fact—but was still working hard every day. She couldn't quite imagine her mother and grandmother getting along together if her mother started cooking. She hadn't done anything like that to speak of in over twenty years. Only at the very beginning of her marriage did Maria cook. That was way back in the nineties. She had left her mother-in-law in charge pretty much ever since she moved in with them when Emilie was a little girl. The more she thought about it, the more convinced she became it would only be a matter of time until her mother was back at work somewhere. Her mother never really felt very comfortable doing housework that she could remember.

Two months later, her mother began to work in the same bank in which she had put her money. It was also very near where she lived. She didn't have to walk more than two blocks to work. She was hired as a bank teller. The president of the bank thought it was the best place for her.

"Frau Bartholomae, you know virtually everyone in Vaihingen, and people respect you because of what you've done. It wasn't easy taking over the business after your husband died. You meet people well, and I'm sure you'll be a great asset to us in the bank. We'll give you four hundred Reichsmarks per month, and after one year, we'll give you another raise depending upon how well you like our bank."

Her mother knew what Herr Loepsinger meant.

"He just wants to see if I can do the job and if enough new people are attracted to the bank to make it worth their while to continue my employment. But in the meantime, I'll have a bit more money to invest."

Emilie was pleased her mother had made such a good adjustment to her new-found wealth. Selling the business had not been easy for her. She had had to move out of the apartment by the end of October. Herr Welker and his wife wanted to move in by November 1. Frau Bartholomae starting looking for another house shortly after Welker had talked with her the first time about buying the business. She had looked outside of Vaihingen and found a place near where she and Michael had bought the meadow. There was only one problem with it, she thought: it was too far for her mother-in-law to walk into town every day.

"I'd rather be nearer to the center of the city," she told Emilie, when the latter asked why she didn't buy the house next to the meadow.

"But Mama, it's only five blocks from where you used to live. That's not that far!"

"Maybe not for you, Emilie, but it is for your grandmother. I don't want her to have to walk into town every day in the rain and snow to buy our bread and pretzels."

Maria looked at several houses near the center of town, but each time found something she didn't like. The hill behind Ringstrasse leading up to a very nice house was too steep. The garden that came with the Herter house was too big. She already had the meadow to look after on the edge of town. She finally found the Rose, a three-story house near the very center of the town. It was on Stuttgarterstrasse. It was a huge house.

If she had company from Gerabronn, Boeblingen, or Heilbronn, she would have plenty of room for her guests. When she showed the house to her mother-in-law, she suggested, "Maria, you can take in guests with a house that large. You could set aside the basement and first floor for paying guests, and the second and third floors could be used by us and any of your out-of-town relatives. There would be plenty of room, and you could earn some extra money that way."

"That's not a bad idea, Grandmother. I think we may just do that."

Maria made a down payment with the money she received from Herr Welker and carried a mortgage for the balance of hundred thousand Reichsmarks. She started packing that same day. When Emilie came home from school, she helped her mother wrap the china, pictures, and other breakables in volumes of papers. Maria hired a mover to move all of her things from the apartment to the new house. As the last things were loaded on the trucks, Emilie and her mother went through the apartment and the business for the last time.

"I wonder what Papa would say," Maria asked, wistfully. "Would he approve of what I've done?"

"I'm sure he'd approve, Mama. He'd be very proud of what you've done ever since he died. And the price you've gotten for the business, why he'd have a hard time believing you got that much!" Emilie told her reassuringly.

"Yes, but I still feel saddened. Papa and I had such a good life here together. I guess all things have to change, don't they?" she sighed. "He's not here anymore, and the business needs some new direction. It needs someone who can cope with these turbulent times. I hope Herr Welker can handle all of the work this business involves."

"He's been here long enough, Mama. If he doesn't understand the business by now, he'll never understand it. His daughter should be of help to him too. She's studied business and bookkeeping, hasn't she?"

"Yes. But learning from books is different from learning by doing. They'll have to hire someone just to lay out the newspaper each day and get all of the stories and articles together. It's not like it used to be. People want a daily paper these days; once a week isn't enough. They've got to have the news every day. It was really getting to be too much for me. You probably didn't know this, but I had to hire two young women to help me with the news and layout of the newspaper these past few months. They didn't work full-time, but they spent twenty hours a week helping me. Herr Welker took on two more apprentices too because there was so much more work to do. I hope he can manage, but that's his problem now. I'm sorry to have to leave this place. I guess I should be thankful too for the years we've spent here."

Emilie was surprised her mother told her so much about the business. She had never even mentioned anything about it previously.

"Why didn't you tell me these things earlier, Mama?"

"I didn't want you to have to be concerned, Emilie. You had enough to do with your teaching schedule. I didn't want you to have to work in the business too. Papa told me almost in his last breath, 'Don't bring the girls into the business. The newspaper business is nothing for a young woman to enter, Maria. Make sure they go on to study and make something more of themselves,'" her mother related.

"But didn't Papa know you were also a woman and would be the only one to go on with the business? How could he say such a thing, Mama? I'm proud of what you've done. Even Dean Henne was very impressed that you were going on with the business."

"I guess Papa just took it for granted. I don't think he even gave it any thought that I was a contradiction to what he had always thought and truly believed. If Grandmother Bartholomae hadn't moved in with us and taken over the household chores, he might have had to give it some thought. I'm sure I would have had to stay home and care for you girls. It never occurred to him I was working in the business almost as much as he was right from the beginning. He treated me like a colleague in the business. When he was elected to the city council, I had to do even more of the work. As much as I loved your father, Emilie, I must admit he took it for granted that I would work in the business. I even wondered on occasion, when he was giving one of his speeches in support of the ideals of the Kaiser and the Empire or when he talked about the place of a woman was in the home with the children, whether anyone caught his inconsistency. But, you know, no one ever did. They all cheered and agreed; that's where women should be. I wonder what Papa would say today with women having the right to vote and working in all kinds of jobs during the war. Even now, there are so many millions of widows who have to work as a consequence of the war!"

Emilie was dumbfounded by what her mother told her. She would never have said this about Papa if she hadn't sold the business. It's only when people go through some significant changes in their lives that they become more reflective and thoughtful about the meaning of their lives. Yes, it's too bad Papa never made the connection between what he believed and what he practiced . . .

Chapter IX

Courtship and Marriage

Emilie first met Friederich Malin at the annual Turnverein festival in early October 1919. He was a very good gymnast excelling on the parallel bars. He had just completed his routine for the Vaihingen Club when her mother, grandmother, and all of her sisters sat at a table near his mother, aunt, sister, and brother. They were eating their lunch together. She had only seen Friederich from afar, but she knew his younger brother Karl very well. He had been in her class in the Volksschule (grade school). He was a very pleasant boy and had lots of friends in the class. Karl was grown up, one of those young men who were called up during the last year of the war because they were eighteen years old. Emilie had heard he had been badly wounded in one of the last offensives of the army before Paris in July 1918. He was still bothered by headaches from a head wound. He still, however, had his old smile and infectious laugh that she remembered from grade school. She was glad to see him again. As they talked with each other, Friederich came by and asked his brother to introduce him.

"Certainly, Fritz. Emilie, this is my brother, Friederich. Friederich, this is Emilie Bartholomae. We used to be in the same class together in the Volksschule before the war. She's now a teacher in Enzweihingen."

Friederich shook her hand. "I'm very pleased to meet you, Fraeulein Bartholomae. I knew your father from the first years when I joined the Turnverein. He was a very great man both in the Verein and in the town."

Emilie was touched by Friederich's gallantry and in calling her by her title.

"Herr Malin, you don't have to address me as Fraeulein Bartholomae. Emilie is certainly good enough."

Friederich persisted.

"I well remember the editorials your father wrote before the war, Fraeulein Bartholomae. We need more men like him to tell us the truth about what happened in the war. I'm sure if he were alive today, he'd have a lot to tell us about what happened and why we've been stuck with the Versailles Treaty! It's an outrage, that's what it is. We shouldn't have quit the war. We should have kept on fighting," he said adamantly.

"I agree with you, Herr Malin. My father would probably have taken a very different tact about the postwar era in Germany."

She couldn't help but notice Friederich talked in a very hoarse whisper. She really had to listen very carefully to understand everything he was saying.

"My brother has talked like this ever since he came back from the war," Karl added.

"That doesn't concern her, Karl," Friederich said sharply. "What would she know about the war?"

"Oh, I'm very much interested in the war. My uncles were in the war and several of our friends were killed. Just because I'm younger than you are is no reason to think I haven't experienced the war. It was a tragedy for all of us!" Emilie was getting rather heated in what she thought was a put-down by Friederich.

"I would very much like to know what happened to you, Herr Malin. You seem to have difficulty speaking very loudly," she said almost belligerently. Friederich didn't say anymore. He just gave her a sharp look as if to say, what would you know about life at your age?

Emilie returned to the table where her family was sitting. She couldn't help wondering what had happened to Karl's brother. He seemed so sour and bitter about life. The next time I see Karl, I'm going to find out what happened to his brother. He looks so angry and dour most of the time, she said herself.

The more she thought about her conversation with Herr Malin, the more upset she became. How could he think I didn't regret the loss of the war? How could he think I was too young to understand what had happened to those men who were soldiers? Whatever happened to his voice? she kept asking herself. He is a very good athlete, she thought, and he has a very muscular body. She was impressed with his mastery of the parallel bars. That's not an easy gymnastic art to learn to do so well, she thought.

Emilie didn't see Karl again for several weeks. It was on a cold November morning when she ran into him at the bakery. They shook hands and before they left she said, "Karl, I'd like to have you tell me what happened to your brother during the war."

As they went outside, Karl said, "I don't know if you want to take that much time, Emilie. You've got to go to Enzweihingen to teach and I have to go to work. I'm working for Friederich now, in fact. I'm learning to become a toolmaker in his shop."

"That's fine, Karl. Why don't we get together after church next Sunday? There's that restaurant on the Enz my father liked to visit Sunday afternoons. We can talk there over dinner."

"All right, I'll see you after church next Sunday."

Emilie had a hard time waiting for Sunday to come. She thought of all kinds of things which might have happened to Friederich. Maybe he was wounded in the throat. Or maybe he had a head wound which had made him so bitter? She didn't recall any scars being visible during the Turnverein last October. I wonder what Karl's going to tell me, she kept asking herself.

She did find out from her mother that Herr Malin had opened a machine shop in Vaihingen sometime in early 1916.

"I can't remember exactly. I do know some of my neighbors have had spare parts made by him in his machine shop."

"Do you know what happened to his voice, Mama?"

"I don't know. I only know that he came back from the army sometime in 1915 or early '16. I don't remember when."

"I'm meeting his brother, Karl, at the Alte Ente Sunday after church, Mama. I'd like to know what happened to Friederich's voice."

"He's Herr Malin, Emilie. He's a lot older than you are. I don't know where you got the idea you can call a strange man by his first name," her mother reprimanded her. "You say you want to know what happened to his voice? Now why would you want to know that? Besides, the Alte Ente is no place for a teacher to be seen! It was bad enough that your father went there."

"I chose that place because I wanted to talk with Karl without being seen or interrupted by anyone who might know me," Emilie retorted. "I'm interested in knowing what makes a man like him so seemingly bitter toward life."

"People are all different, Emilie. I only know he doesn't come from a very good family. They live down by the Enz in a ramshackle old house with a big garden. His mother has been a widow for almost as long as we've lived in Vaihingen. I really don't think you ought to even be interested in what happened to his voice or to his family, for that matter. They're not our kind of people. I don't think there's ever been anyone in that family that has gone beyond grammar school. I don't know anything about his father. I assume he must have had one, but your father and I didn't know him. Maybe you ought to let sleeping dogs lie, Emilie. Maybe you shouldn't know what happened to him. What difference will it make if you find out?"

"It'll at least satisfy my curiosity."

Emilie didn't want to let on she was intrigued by Friederich. She couldn't help but remember what a delightful boy Karl had always been. He was jovial and good-hearted most of the time. He liked to laugh and enjoyed good stories. She didn't know much about the rest of his family except what her mother did say once, that Frau Malin had had an even harder time than she did raising her family. "As I recall," her mother said, "Frau Malin's husband was much older than she was. He died when she was just a young woman in 1905, I think. She had five children to raise by herself."

The more Emilie heard about the Malin family, the more impressed she was.

"Herr Malin has started a very good business from what I've heard," her mother continued. "I think he still lives with his mother down by the Enz. They've always lived on the fringe of Vaihingen. But I really don't know too much about them," she confessed. "When you talked with Karl at the Tunverein fest, I had forgotten he had also been in your class in the Volksschule. Our paths have never crossed, Emilie. The Malin family was not one of the elite families of Vaihingen. In fact, as I recall, Frau Malin's husband had been the manager of the city's poorhouse."

When Sunday finally arrived, Emilie expected Karl to meet her in church. She looked around to see if she could find him. He was nowhere to be seen. She was dismayed. She couldn't believe he wouldn't meet her. She kept looking at the door as each person came in, expecting to see him, but Karl didn't come. She was very disappointed and angry at Karl. She had a hard time concentrating on what the Dean of the Cathedral was saying that morning. He talked about the fact it was more than one year ago that the war ended. The world was in a real turmoil. Germany was impoverished, but at least everyone now had enough to eat. The war was still raging in Russia between two contending forces: the monarchists and the communists. Business seemed to be picking up again. The veterans who returned were mostly employed. He wasn't sure about the Government in Berlin, however. They were Socialists and wanted to pay off the war debt as quickly as possible. The only problem with that was the "Entente" (Western Allies) still hadn't given the German government the full amount of what they were said to owe.

"How can a person pay his debts, if he doesn't know how much of a debt he has?" he asked rhetorically. "It's no different for a government. We've got to know what we owe before we can make plans to pay our alleged debts!"

While Emilie didn't recall much more from the sermon, she was impressed enough to feel the Germans were being taken advantage of by the Allies and by their own Government.

She was very depressed as she came out of church. Not only was Karl missing, but the sermon added to the misery which most of the parishioners were already experiencing as a people and as a congregation. She didn't stay to talk to anyone. She wanted to go home as quickly as possible. As she came around the corner of the church past Friederich's workshop, there was Karl. She was very surprised to see him. He noticed right away how disappointed she was.

"You probably thought I wasn't coming, didn't you Emilie?" he laughed. "You thought I'd broken my promise to talk with you. Well, I haven't. I just don't like to go to church anymore. Ever since I was drafted into the army, I don't care much for what the church stands for. I used to have to go to church as a boy. My mother insisted that I go even when I didn't want to. Whenever I laughed at what someone said in religious instruction, I'd get a crack over my hands with a stick. No, I don't mind not going to church anymore." He laughed as he said it. "There's no reason to go if you don't have to. I'll go if and when I want to, but I don't see that coming anytime soon."

They walked slowly down the hill through the old part of Vaihingen. The walk to the Alte Ente went right past the Malin house and garden.

"It's a good thing Friederich isn't home today. He'd wonder what we were doing together. He went to Stuttgart for the day," Karl continued. "I don't know what he does there, but he goes quite often. He usually brings goodies home for our niece."

"I didn't know you had a niece."

"Actually, I have two nieces and two nephews," Karl continued. "My oldest sister, Bertha, lives in the United States and has two children. Then there's Gretel. She has a boy and a girl. They live in Stuttgart. I live at home with my mother, her sister, and Friederich. During the war, my older sister lived with us too, and her two children. Her husband was in the army and she had to live somewhere. My next oldest sister lived with us too, off and on. She was a governess and took care of people's children before she married. She's the one who's traveled a lot. She's been to the Holy Land, Egypt, Turkey, Greece, and Italy at various times. She recently got married and is living in Kassel. During the war she lived with us too."

Karl couldn't stop talking, it seemed. What interested Emilie the most was what he was telling her about his family. She knew the house where he lived was large and old. In fact, it was somewhat ramshackled, as her mother had described it. But it was mostly in need of paint. It wasn't as bright and new as her mother's house. The garden had a large stone fence around it which kept other people out. It reminded her of an old fort. On one side, facing the river, the wall was two meters high. On the top and around the other three sides, it was only one and one-half meters high. The garden was very well cared for, from what Emilie could see of it. There were all kinds of fruit trees and neatly placed walks among the flower beds and what were probably vegetable plots in the summer. She could only see the inside of the garden from the hill as they descended to the walkway along the river.

When they arrived at the tavern, Karl opened the door for her.

"I'm going to pay for my own dinner, Karl."

"I'm making a few Reichsmarks these days myself, Emilie. I can afford to pay for both of our dinners."

The dinner consisted of noodle soup, bread, roast pork, fried potatoes, a garden salad, and black forest cake with coffee. Karl explained what happened to Friederich during the war.

"It hasn't been easy for me to get all of this information together, Emilie. Friederich isn't one to talk much about himself. But from what I remember, and from what my mother told me, Friederich's unit was called up in 1915 in what was to have been the final push to capture Verdun. He left Vaihingen in late February and was sent with his unit to Alsace for a three-week refresher and conditioning course. After completion of this training, he was assigned to the newly constituted joint Bavarian and Schwaebian Ninth Army. They were to put Verdun under final siege and capture so that the road to Paris could finally be cleared of enemy forces. On the way to Verdun, Friederich noticed he was having difficulty swallowing his food. He thought no more about it until he reached the lines. He thought it must be nerves and passed it off as something that would disappear before too long. As the big push began, and as the troops were fed at their posts, Friederich began to choke on his food. He couldn't seem to swallow anything, even swallowing water was difficult. His Sergeant Major Mueller noticed he was having problems and sent him to the medic to see what he could do for him. The medic looked in his mouth and throat and told him he had something blocking the passage to the throat. He sent him to the field hospital. The doctor examined him and told him, 'You've got a couple of polyps blocking your esophagus. That's no problem. We'll cut them out right here and in a few weeks, you'll be back with your unit.'

"The doctor prepared him for the operation, and while an orderly watched over him to see that the anesthetic was taking effect, the surgeon proceeded to operate. He made a small incision on the left side of his chin bone to lay back the skin to expose the throat. He saw the two polyps he had seen from inside Friederich's mouth. But then, he saw two more growing along the side of his esophagus. He quickly cut the four polyps out, and as he did so, he must have cut the nerves to Friederich's larynx. The surgeon sewed him up again and told him not to speak, or even try to speak, for three weeks. He issued him a medical leave, so Friederich came home during the early summer of 1915. He had been issued pieces of chalk and a slate on which to write all of his requests and responses to questions people might ask. The doctor emphasized over and over again, 'You're not to try to talk until after I've seen you in three weeks. I'll expect you back here on the thirty-first of July.' And with that he dismissed him. Friederich came home. Do you still want to hear the story, Emilie? Or have you had enough?" Karl asked.

"No, no, Karl. Don't stop! I want to hear the whole story!" Emilie persisted.

"Well, it was hard for all of us that summer. Friederich couldn't say anything even when it was very hot and he sweated a lot. Fortunately, my older sister lived with us and she, as a practical nurse, had to change his bandages every two days. It often hurt him to have the dressing removed because it stuck to the wound. But it had to be done. It was almost funny in a way, to watch him write his angry response on the slate. 'You're pulling it off too quickly. Stop and put some water on the wound,' he'd write. 'Soften it up first! You idiot!'

Between my sister, our mother, and aunt, Friederich had plenty of care. He sat all day long in the garden under the apple trees and read newspapers and books. If the pain was too much for him, there wasn't much anyone could do. He couldn't tell us. After he wrote down a hundred times 'My throat hurts,' we pretty much got used to his complaints. He seemed to sulk by the hour. If any of us asked him, 'Is there anything we can do for you,' he'd shake his hand and leave the room. He literally sat for hours alone in the garden day after day, except when it rained. Then he'd stay in his bedroom. You have to remember, Emilie, he couldn't eat anything solid. The instructions Friederich brought home with him from the front stated, in very bold letters from the doctor, 'No solid food! Liquids only!'

"It must have been hard for him to sit and watch us eat while he could only have soups, juices, and a glass of wine during each meal. We didn't have any real coffee. Whenever he wrote on his slate, 'I want something more to eat,' my mother would bring out the slip of paper from the doctor and show him. It was almost as if he were deaf. We didn't say too much to him. We only talked among ourselves. He seemed to get upset when we talked because he'd have to write down his responses. After a few days, we pretty much left him in silence. Only the most necessary questions were placed to him to which he would either write a reply or refuse to answer. Remember too, Emilie, Friederich was a man who loved to sing. He had a very strong baritone voice and often sang the baritone parts he had heard after attending an opera in Stuttgart. He sang and danced with the best of them in his day.

"On the thirtieth of July, Friederich went back to France to meet the next day with the doctor who had performed the operation. After the surgeon took off his bandages, he told Friederich it was very nicely healed. 'Now say something.' Friederich tried to speak but nothing came out. The doctor told him again, 'Say something!' Friederich tried again. Again, no sound resulted. The surgeon examined him more in detail looking as best as he could down his throat. After several minutes, the doctor asked him once more to say "yes." The doctor could see that Friederich had said the word, but still only a whisper came out. The doctor shook his head in disbelief. 'There must be something else that's wrong with you, Herr Malin. I'm going to send you to a throat specialist in Stuttgart and have him check you over. There must be something that can be done about your voice.'"

"Poor Friederich," Emilie sighed. "It must have been quite a shock to him not being able to speak after such a long silence!"

"That's not all of the story yet, Emilie," Karl continued. "Friederich went to the specialist the field surgeon sent him to see. After examining him for sometime, the doctor said, 'That idiot at the front has cut the nerves to your vocal cords! There's nothing we can do for you now, Herr Malin. Tell you what I can do for you. I can write a letter to the War Department requesting that you be medically discharged from the army due to this disability of not being able to speak anymore. I wouldn't advise you to complain to the army about the field surgeon. They'll simply write you as fit and send you back to the trenches. They couldn't care less if you can talk or not. They're going to protect their surgeon at all cost. They need him far more than they need you!'

"Friederich had to accept the specialist's recommendation. There wasn't anything else he could do. He got a medical discharge 'due to war wounds resulting in the loss of speaking capability while serving in battle at the Verdun front in July 1915.'

"He came home after serving only a little more than ten months in the war. He's not been the same since," Karl said. "As time passed, I could understand him if I paid close attention to what he was saying. But not everyone took the time. He'd get into a rage if someone seemed to ignore him after he had tried to tell him something. The family and our friends took the time to listen, but that's about all. Friederich became even more isolated from people because he thought they wouldn't understand him. 'Why should I bother to talk with them?' he told me. 'It doesn't do any good anyway.'"

"I can certainly understand why Friederich seems so bitter," Emilie answered. "I'd be upset too if no one paid attention to what I was trying to say. But how did Friederich begin his business, if he couldn't talk with people?"

"He got disability payments from the government. With this money, plus what he had saved, he bought the house and small machine shop on Church Street. For the rest of the war, business was very good. He had lots of small jobs to make parts that the bigger companies didn't want to bother with. He even started to repair motorcycles and bicycles. The New Motorcycle Company asked him to be a dealer of their products. He's been really successful. I started working for him as soon as I finished the Realschule (grammar school). He was almost finished with his own toolmaking apprenticeship. Since then, he has become a master toolmaker himself. He's taught me how to make tools and designs for different types of machine parts. Actually, it was not only convenient for me, since I started working for him right out of school, but I helped him in his discussions with various customers who had a hard time understanding him. I was with him until I was drafted in May of 1917. From that point on, our mother helped him with the customers. The housework was pretty much covered by our two sisters who were living at home at the time and our aunt, Katharine Vischer. There was plenty of help when he needed it."

Karl grew very quiet and began to eat the dinner that was served. Emilie wanted to ask him more questions but thought better of it. She couldn't help but think Friederich was truly a very remarkable, self-made man. She walked by his place every Sunday to and from church.

"Every time I enter the front door of the church, I can see his workshop just across the alley with the name Friederich E. Malin, Machine Shop, Motorcycle, and Bicycle Sales on the sign across the front of the building. I thought the family didn't want to sell the whole building, Karl. How did he become the owner of it?"

"That's right. When Herr Haefner died, his family was interested in selling only the shop. They had wanted to keep the apartment above it. Friederich told Frau Haefner, if you won't sell the whole building, I'm not interested." Karl laughed. "Friederich has always been a very good wheeler-dealer. He usually gets what he wants!"

Needless to say, Emilie was very impressed with what Karl told her. She kept asking him all kinds of questions about his family. She knew from her mother Karl's father had died when Karl was a little boy. She really had no idea how many brothers and sisters he had.

"Karl, I hope you don't mind my asking you about your family. You mentioned before you had sisters. There are three of them and they all have children?"

"No, only my two older sisters. The one in America whom I told you about is Bertha. She has a little girl and a boy. My other sister is Margaret. We call her Gretel. She has a boy and a girl."

She wanted to ask him about them, but Karl didn't volunteer any further information. He started in again after eating his main course. "Friederich was the one who supported all of us after our Grandfather Vischer died in 1908. I was just a boy at the time, but I remember my mother and aunt had a long discussion about what they were going to do to make ends meet. Grandfather had been a wagon maker, just like his father and grandfather. Grandfather was already an old man when my father died in 1905. Grandfather sold his business to his nephew and moved in with us. It was a great time for me. I had lots of company. But after Grandfather died, our mother was at a loss to know what she should do to keep us all together. Our grandmother was still living, but she was too feeble to do much around the house anymore. I remember Friederich telling our mother he was going to give her his weekly wages he was earning at the

Bosch factory in Stuttgart. Evidently, between what my mother made from selling eggs, fruits, and vegetables, and what Friederich gave her, we got along fine. We never went hungry," he said proudly. "I do know Friederich paid for the midwife training program for both of my two older sisters here in Germany. As I told you before, my sister Elise became a governess and traveled to a lot of countries with the families she worked for before the war. During the war, however, she lived with us because her boyfriend was in the army. Just last year, she got married and moved to Kassel where her husband works."

"What about Gretel? Is she still living at home too?"

"No, she's not. Since her husband came home from the army, they've gotten married and moved to Stuttgart. He also works at Bosch, where Friederich used to work."

As they finished dinner with dessert and coffee, Karl said, "You've gotten a lot more information then you probably wanted, Emilie. I hope I've not bored you with our family trivia."

"No, no Karl!" she assured him. "I've found what you've told me is fascinating! I had no idea who your family was or all that your brother has done in such a short time. I really appreciate what you've told me. I hope I haven't imposed on you too much."

They left the restaurant and after walking up the hill to her mother's house, Emilie said goodbye.

"Thanks again, Karl, for all you've told me. I now understand why Friederich seems so bitter. It's really not his fault at all."

Karl laughed, and with a twinkle in his eye, said, "You're the first person I've known who was ever interested in what happened to my brother. Other people usually say 'it was due to the war, wasn't it?' They don't follow up their own question with any interest in finding out what really happened to him. They just seem to think he must have been wounded and lost his voice in the process and let it go at that."

Emilie didn't see anymore of Karl or his family until just after Christmas 1919. Her mother took all of the girls to a concert in the city cathedral. The church was almost overflowing when they got there. They had to sit wherever they could find a seat. There were three places left on the very last row inside the church.

"Mama, you sit here with Mariele and Lina. Luise and I will find a seat somewhere else," Emilie told her.

As they walked down the aisle toward the front of the church, Friederich saw them and stood up to invite them to sit with him, his mother, and his aunt.

"There are just two places left," he said. "We'll ask the people next to us to move over."

Since the two women next to Frau Malin knew her, they volunteered to move elsewhere. Frau Malin thanked them, and Emilie and Luise took their seats with Friederich and his family. It was a splendid concert, and the applause was so great at the end the orchestra played three encores.

After the music stopped and they got up to leave, Friederich introduced Emilie to his mother and aunt. She, in turn, introduced her sister to them. Emilie excused herself and said, "Our mother and our younger sisters are waiting for us at the back of the church. I certainly enjoyed meeting you, Frau Malin and Fraeulein Vischer."

As she turned to shake hands with Friederich, he suggested, "Why don't you all join us for some coffee and dessert at the hotel? We're going to stop there on our way home, and it's right near where you live. As you know, it's an excellent restaurant and the cakes are outstanding."

"Thank you very much, Herr Malin," Emilie said. "I'll have to ask my mother." Luise had already gone back to tell her mother they were invited for coffee and cake at the Schindler. When Emilie reached her mother, her mother was quite upset.

"Emilie, how can you accept an invitation from a man you hardly know? I've never even met his mother or aunt. Besides, they live down by the Enz. We don't have anything in common with them," she tried to tell Emilie as quietly as she could. She didn't want the girls to hear. Meanwhile, Luise had already gone back to where Friederich and his family were waiting and said, "Herr Malin, we'd love to go!"

"It would be an ideal way, Mama, for us to get to know another family in Vaihingen whom we don't yet know," Emilie tried to tell her mother.

Her mother was furious. She felt the two older girls had conspired against her. When Emilie introduced her and her two younger sisters, her mother was very formal and said very little to either of the ladies. Lina and Mariele, on the other hand, asked, "Could we have some ice cream, Herr Malin?"

Friederich laughed and said, "Sure, you can. In fact, we'll all have an order of ice cream," he told the waitress.

Frau Malin tried to engage Frau Bartholomae in conversation, but she wasn't very successful. Frau Bartholomae sat there and waited quietly until everyone had finished. As soon as Mariele had eaten her last spoonful of ice cream, she stood up and said, "Herr Malin, I want to thank you for the coffee and dessert. I'm sure my daughters appreciated the invitation."

She then turned to Friederich's mother and aunt and said rather coldly, "Frau Malin and Fraeulein Vischer, we enjoyed the coffee together."

She didn't bother to shake hands with them. After each of the Bartholomae sisters shook hands with the two ladies, they left.

All the way home, Frau Bartholomae kept repeating, "How could you do that, Emilie? Accepting an invitation from a person whom you hardly know! And from that family . . . Do you know where they live? They live down by the Enz! That's the poorest section of Vaihingen! We have nothing at all in common with them!"

Lina and Mariele chimed in to say, "But, Mama, the ice cream was very good!"

Emilie and Luise laughed, which made their mother even angrier. She didn't say another word until they were home. Emilie made an effort to tell her mother about her conversation with Karl and all that he had told her about his brother. But Frau Bartholomae didn't want to hear of it. Her closing remark to Emilie was, "If your father were still living, he'd tell you exactly why we shouldn't be associating with that family. They're from the lowest segment of Vaihingen society, and we're from the elite!"

At the next Turnverein meeting, Friederich was again in attendance. This time he suggested, "Fraeulein Bartholomae, let me walk you home."

"Thank you very much, Herr Malin."

It was a frosty January night and the snow glistened from the reflected house lights. Friederich was very talkative and asked about her family.

"When did your family come to Vaihingen, Fraeulein Bartholomae?"

"My father and mother came in 1900, when they bought the *Enz-Bote.*" She told him about her sisters, aunts, uncles, and cousins. He seemed genuinely interested in everything she told him. In fact, by the time they had reached her house, he asked, "Can I come by again tomorrow evening and continue our discussion? We could go to the Schindler and have some coffee and cake. It would be much warmer than being outside."

"Yes. But would you mind if I brought my sister Luise with me? Mama has this thing about my going out alone."

"Sure. But I really want to talk with you."

"Luise is very mature for her age. I'm sure she won't mind if we talk by ourselves."

Emilie was very interested in Friederich. He seemed so sincere and listened so well to what she was saying. She really wanted to meet with him alone, but she knew her mother would never stand for that. All during the day, she kept thinking about their rendevous that evening. Friederich was a very handsome man, actually. He had a full beard with a bit of a Van Dyke cast on his chin. He was much older than she was. She tried to think how many years older he might be, from what Karl told her. As she recalled her conversation with him, she remembered he had said Friederich was born in 1888. That would make him about thirty-one or thirty-two years old. Wow, she thought. He's really a lot older than I am! She went through the motions of teaching that day, looking at her watch repeatedly to see what time it was. She didn't wait for the train after school that afternoon. She walked very fast along the Enz, not seeming to mind the snow that had fallen during the day. She wanted to get home and take a bath and get ready for the evening.

At supper, her mother asked, "Emilie, what's wrong? You've hardly eaten anything. Did you have a bad day at school?"

"No, Mama. It was actually a very enjoyable day. The snow was falling and the trees were just beautiful as I walked home this afternoon. I'm just not very hungry today."

After supper, she said to her mother, "Luise and I are going for a walk this evening. It's really beautiful outside. We'll be back in a couple of hours."

Emilie had talked with Luise and told her what they were going to do.

"What if Mama finds out? What are you going to tell her?"

"'I'll think of something," Emilie answered. "But don't say anything to her, please. I think I'm falling in love with Friederich! I just want to be with him!"

"All right, Emilie. But don't forget what Mama said about his family. She'd never approve of him!"

"We'll see." She wasn't ready to make an issue of it; at least not yet.

At seven o'clock, Emilie and Luise wanted to leave for their walk. Lina and Mariele wanted to go with them, but fortunately, their mother said, "No. You girls got all wet this afternoon after school. You're not going out again this evening."

After some crying and many tears, Grandmother said, "I'll read you a story tonight before you go to bed. But only if you stop crying." They did almost instantly. Emilie and Luise went for their walk.

Just as they reached the Schindler, Friederich caught up with them.

"I thought you weren't coming. I was on my way to your house when I saw you coming down the street."

"Oh Friederich," Emilie said. "Please don't come to the house! Mama doesn't know we're meeting you. She thinks we're going for a walk in this beautiful snow!"

Luise laughed. "Boy would she be surprised if she knew where we were."

Emilie gave her a quick look and a frown and shook her head. Luise knew what she meant and didn't say anything more.

Friederich opened the door to Schindler's for them. The waiter seemed to know Friederich and greeted him by name.

"Herr Malin, would you like a table in a quiet corner of the restaurant?"

"Yes," he said. "Somewhere, where it's quiet and we won't be disturbed."

"Yes sir, I know just the place."

He took them to a little nook at the end of the dining room next to the kitchen. It was very quiet and pleasantly surrounded by potted plants. They were almost hidden from the rest of the guests in the dining room. Emilie was glad because she didn't want anyone to recognize her. Fortunately, there were only out-of-town guests there. Luise ordered some cake and hot chocolate. Emilie ordered a black forest torte. Friederich ordered only coffee.

The conversation took off exactly where it had ended the last time she and Friederich were together. Luise knew only to listen. Friederich talked about his business and how much he was earning each month.

"I have seven employees, in addition to Karl," he said. "Actually, two of the seven are still apprentices, but once they've finished their training, I'll hire them full-time. I'm going to rent the neighboring barn next to my shop and use it as a show room. I don't have enough room in my own building. I have an upstairs, but I don't want to use it for business. This is an apartment with living quarters. Now that my sisters have both left, my mother and my aunt will have more than enough to do this next spring taking care of their garden by themselves. My mother has been helping me in the business. As you can hear," he laughed, "people have a hard time understanding me. My mother acts as my mouthpiece in the sales room. Karl does the same for me in the workshop."

"What happened to your voice?" Luise asked. "How come you can't talk like the rest of us?"

Friederich gave her very sharp look. Emilie thought to herself, why didn't I tell her about his injury? She hadn't thought Luise would ask the question in such a reproachful way. But she did. Friederich dismissed her question with "It happened during the war."

And that's all he said. Emilie gave Luise a knowing look as if to say, I'll tell you about it later. Friederich knew Emilie knew. Karl had told him about their earlier conversation. He didn't think he needed to retell what she already knew. Friederich went on to tell how he got started in his business.

"After Realschule, I spent a year traveling and studying in Switzerland. I attended the Wintertur Institute of Technology and learned basic design and started my apprenticeship in toolmaking. My Vischer grandparents, my mother's parents, had given me the money to travel and study in Switzerland. I came home after it ran out. I then started working for Robert Bosch as an apprentice in Stuttgart. I was almost finished when I got drafted and spent almost a year in the army. Due to the mistake of an idiot-surgeon, I got a medical discharge and returned to Vaihingen in late 1915. I could have returned to Bosch, but no one could understand me in the factory. It was much too noisy and the foreman wasn't about to take me into his office every time he wanted to say something to me. I just got fed up with the hassle and quit. When I talked with my mother and some of our neighbors, they suggested I buy the Haefner machine shop. The old man had died and the family wasn't interested in continuing the business. I talked with the local bank director and he said he'd loan me the money to buy it if I could raise twenty thousand Reichsmarks. I had saved my monthly army pay, and with the additional amount the government gave me as a medical severance payment, it was more than enough to make the down payment. I paid forty thousand Reichsmarks for it and have now almost paid it all off. Before the year is over, I'll be free and clear of any debt," he said proudly.

Emilie was clearly impressed with his achievements and said so. "Friederich, you're a very enterprising capitalist. At the rate you're going, you'll soon be the richest man in Vaihingen!"

He smiled. "That's what I want to be, Emilie. I want to be like my friends Adolf Conradt and Hermann Weigele. They started off with their fathers' businesses in full bloom. I want to make it possible for my sons to inherit a big enterprise too!"

After almost two hours, Emilie told Friederich, "We'll have to go home now. Mama will be wondering where we are."

"I want to invite you and your family for dinner next Sunday, Emilie. We'll go to Mayers on the Market. Shall we say at twelve-thirty?"

"I don't know, Friederich. I'll have to ask my mother what she has planned for next Sunday. I'd love to go."

"I would too," Luise said.

"Then we'll plan on it. If your mother can't make it, perhaps she can come another time," he volunteered.

"All right," Emilie answered. "Luise and I will be there for sure."

They said their goodbyes and hurried home.

"What happened to Friederich's voice?" Luise asked. "Why does he always speak in a whisper?"

Emilie told her what Karl had said about his brother and how it had changed his whole attitude toward life.

"I can certainly see why he'd be bitter," Luise said. "But he seems to like us. He doesn't hesitate to tell us everything about himself."

Emilie agreed. "The more I see him, the more I really like him, Luise. What am I going to tell Mama about this invitation for next Sunday?"

"You're twenty years old, Emilie. You've got a good position as a teacher. You don't need to depend on Mama anymore. Why don't you tell her you like Friederich and that you're going whether she goes or not?"

"Yes, that's true, but what about how she feels toward the Malins in general? Can you see her sitting down with Friederich's mother and chatting about her garden or chickens?"

"Well, if you think you really like Friederich, then you're going to have to tell her sooner or later."

Emilie didn't say anymore. They got home and their mother asked how the weather was on their walk.

"It was beautiful. It's so quiet and the sky is as clear as water filled with sparkling diamonds," Emilie reported.

Her mother was surprised at her description. "You really must have been impressed by this evening," she said. "I looked outside and it looked pretty cold and wet to me!"

Luise laughed but didn't say anything. Emilie responded by saying, "Mama, you never go outside at night. It's a really beautiful evening."

All during that week, Emilie kept thinking about Sunday. Even Frau Schilling, her assistant, noticed her absentmindedness. "Fraeulein Bartholomae," she asked, "is there something I can help you with? You seem to be miles away from here. It's not like you to forget to tell the children to take off their boots, hats, and coats in the hallway as they come into school."

"Oh, you're right, Frau Schilling! I must have been thinking about something else. I'm glad you reminded them."

For the rest of the day, she made a special effort to keep her mind on her class. She did have Frau Schilling help in the storytelling time before their nap. She knows all of the stories by heart, Emilie reminded herself, and enjoys telling them. The rest of the week went by slowly, but by Friday, she had decided to tell her mother about their invitation for Sunday. After she returned from Enzweihingen, she said, "Mama, there's something I want to tell you. I've been thinking about it all week, wondering how I should tell you. Last Sunday evening, Luise and I met Friederich Malin, and he's invited us to dinner at Mayers for Sunday afternoon. He'd like to have all of us there as his guests."

"So that's why you were out of it last Sunday evening! No, I won't go. I've told you before we have nothing in common with the Malins, and I really wish you'd stop seeing him before things get too far out of hand, Emilie. There's that very nice young man, Adolf Conradt. Why don't you get acquainted with him? His sister is a very good friend of yours, and he's from one of the best families in Vaihingen. What do you see in Friederich Malin that's so intriguing? He may be an up-and-coming businessman, but he's certainly not from the same caliber of family as ours. I don't know what to say, Emilie. I'm very disappointed you've been seeing him behind my back. I wouldn't have expected that from you!"

"I'm sorry Mama, but I don't know Adolf Conradt. Fanny may be a friend of mine, but I've only seen him once since he came back from the war. I can't just go up to him and say, 'I'd like to get to know you better.' Friederich has made every effort to be friendly with us, and I'm very pleased he thinks enough of us to invite us for dinner at Mayers. Have we had any other invitations from anyone else to go to Mayers for dinner?" she asked in exasperation.

"Emilie, you needn't get fresh with me!" her mother said sternly. "I'm only trying to help you understand you shouldn't respond to each and every invitation with alacrity. There are other men around younger than Friederich Malin. You're only twenty, and you've got your whole life in front of you. All I'm trying to say is this: take your time, slow down. There will be more eligible bachelors your age if you'll be patient enough to wait. I'm not going to dinner Sunday with the Malins."

"I don't think his mother and aunt are coming along. He only wanted our family on Sunday," Emilie said.

"You and Luise go, but the rest of us are staying home!" her mother said adamantly.

Emilie saw it was futile to argue with her. She and Luise talked about what they were going to wear on Sunday. Emilie suggested they go shopping the next morning so they'd have something new to wear.

The next day, Emilie and Luise went shopping for two new dresses at Meyers, the newest dress shop in Vaihingen. It didn't take them long to pick out their dresses. Luise picked out a very pleasant dark green dress with a red sash. It looked very smart and was shorter than most of the dresses of the day. "I like it very much. How does it look on me?" she asked.

"It's really quite stunning," Emilie said. "If you want it, I'll buy it."

"But it's so expensive, Emilie!"

"That's okay, Luise. I've been saving my money for sometime now. I can afford it."

Emilie picked out a long dark blue dress with white lilly of the valley flowers throughout the dress. She also bought a white shawl which Luise said "sets off the dress beautifully!"

They also picked out two new purses to go with their new dresses: a beige one for Luise and a black one for Emilie. As they went past the perfume shop, Emilie bought each of them a bottle of Eau de Cologne.

"We'll be going out in style, Emilie!"

The total bill was more than two hundred Reichsmarks. Luise asked, "Can you afford to pay that much?"

"It's all right, Luise. I've been saving my money for just such an occasion. It's not every day we're invited out for dinner!"

On Sunday morning, Emilie and Luise got dressed for church in their new outfits. Frau Bartholomae almost fell over when she saw them.

"What? You're going to church dressed like it's an evening at the opera?" she exclaimed.

"Mama," Emilie said, "We're just going to wear these dresses under our coats. We don't want to have to change for dinner. There won't be enough time!"

"Well, make sure you both keep your coats on in church! I don't want people to think you two are party girls. That's not the kind of daughters I've been raising!" she snorted.

Frau Bartholomae took Lina and went to church with her two older daughters. Grandmother stayed home with Mariele and began cooking the afternoon dinner. All during the service, Frau Bartholomae kept looking at her daughters to see if they kept their coats on.

When the service was over, they thanked Dean Scheuer for his message and left by the church door facing the front of Friederich's workshop. Emilie was very glad he wasn't there. It was shut just like all of the other shops in Vaihingen on Sunday mornings.

"Are you sure you don't want to come with us?" Emilie asked her mother one more time.

"Where are Emilie and Luise going, Mama?" Lina asked. "Aren't they coming home with us for dinner?"

Frau Bartholomae gave Emilie a withering look and said, "No. We're not going! Lina and I are going home for dinner. Come along, Lina. Grandmother's waiting for us!"

"Why aren't they going home with us?" Lina pleaded.

"Herr Malin has invited us for dinner, Lina," Emilie said.

Her mother hadn't even waited for her explanation before she pulled Lina by the hand and stormed off toward home. They heard Lina crying, "But I want to go too!"

Emilie and Luise walked slowly down the hill. They still had almost twenty minutes before it was time to go to Mayers on the Market.

"Why don't we walk along the Enz, Luise?" Emilie suggested. "The snow has almost melted. We can stay in the tracks left by someone else."

"That's a good idea. I don't want to get my shoes too wet. I hate wearing silk stockings when I have wet feet."

They walked as far as the fountain coming out of the hill by Aurich before turning around to walk back up to the market square. They arrived at Mayers just after Friederich had entered. He was making arrangements for seven guests when they appeared.

After greeting them, he asked, "Where's your mother and the rest of the family?"

"She couldn't make it, Friederich. As I told you last week, I wasn't sure she could come, and as you can see, she couldn't," Emilie apologized.

"Well what about your other sisters and Grandmother Bartholomae? Couldn't they make it either?" he persisted.

"No. Mama said we should go alone. It's much too expensive a place for so many people."

Emilie didn't want to tell him the real reason and Luise agreed, "It would be much too expensive, Friederich, if we all came."

Friederich helped them with their coats. He was amazed at what he saw.

"My, oh my!" he exclaimed in his hoarse whisper. "You ladies look just like fashion models out of Paris! Such beautiful dresses!"

Friederich was also dressed very well. He wore a dark blue suit with a vest and a white shirt with a high buttoned, stiff collar. He wore dark horn-rimmed glasses and looked like a minister or a teacher with his watch chain hanging across the front of his vest. His shoes were really shiny from a very high polish. He also wore a dark overcoat and a dark homburg. He had trimmed his beard so that it was really pointed at his chin, with a slight cover of dark whiskers over the rest of his face. He looked very distinguished. He took their coats to the coat room and returned for the waiter to seat them at the table he had reserved earlier.

"Are more guests coming? We've set up for seven persons," the waiter said.

"No," Friederich answered. "There will only be three of us. The rest couldn't make it."

"Would you mind sitting over by the window?" the waiter asked. "There will be another larger group coming in about half an hour."

"Of course not," Emilie answered. "We'll be glad to sit over there."

Friederich didn't take too kindly to the waiter's request and said, "No! We're going to sit exactly where I requested. If you have another group coming, that's your problem! We're going to sit right here!"

"But Friederich," Emilie protested. "It's my fault the rest of the guests aren't coming! I should have told you sooner."

"Nonsense, Emilie. We're staying right here. This is where I requested. This is where we're going to eat! Period!" he said in some anger. She didn't argue with him anymore. After all, it was his party, and she was simply one of the guests.

They sat down at the end of the long table. Friederich told the waiter to bring a bottle of champagne. Neither Emilie nor Luise had ever had champagne before. As the waiter brought it, he said, "This is the best French champagne in the house. You won't find any better anywhere, not even in Berlin!"

It tasted very good and even seemed to tickle their noses. They had more than enough even during the meal. Friederich kept refilling their glasses. Their dinner was the "Special of the House" that day: roast pork and gravy, spaetzle, potato salad, beans, and a red cabbage salad. For dessert they had black forest chocolate cake and coffee. Friederich even ordered an aperitif after dessert. Emilie couldn't drink anymore. She just sipped a little of it. Luise and Friederich finished her glass between them.

After dinner, Friederich insisted on walking them home.

"We can find our way home alone, Friederich. You don't have to escort us," Emilie protested. "We can find our way very well."

"But I want to show you my workshop," he said. "It's just up the hill in front of the church. It won't take long."

"Oh, I'd like that, Friederich." Emilie said. "I'd like to see your workshop. I see it from the outside every time I go to church."

"Your sign over the doorway really stands out," Luise said. "No one can miss it as they go past."

Friederich offered his arms to both ladies as they walked up the hill. He was obviously pleased they had agreed to look over his business. When they arrived at the side door, he took out his key and said, "Let's go in the front door. Only deliveries are made through this door."

He opened the door and held it for them to enter. Emilie was amazed to see how many bicycles and motorcycles he had in his window. They were all new and shiny. He took them to the rear of the showroom and there was his workshop. It was just as clean as the front of his store. The machines had all been cleaned and the floor was swept. He showed them two projects he was working on for the lime factory. One was a roller for a conveyor belt, and the other was a link for a conveyor chain.

"These types of projects are what we specialize in. Otherwise, we're mostly making different parts for sawmills and flour mills. We have a contract for twenty-five thousand parts per month, which keeps us busy most of the time. If there's a part that's broken on any of the motorcycles or bicycles that we sell, we make the part right here in the shop."

"What's upstairs?" Luise asked.

"I have a fully furnished apartment upstairs. Would you like to see it?"

"Yes I would."

Friederich led the way up the stairs and used another key to unlock the door to the apartment.

"My mother stays here during the week," Friederich volunteered. "On weekends, she goes home to her own place down by the Enz."

Emilie was amazed to see it was completely furnished. Even the three bedrooms had throw rugs next to the beds. The kitchen had a full array of dishes and silverware. There was even a bathtub in the apartment and running water! She thought to herself, this is an ideal place for a family to move right in. Luise said as much. "Friederich, you should have a wife and she could move right in. Everything that she will ever need is here."

Friederich was pleased and laughed. "Well, maybe that will happen one of these days..."

He looked at Emilie so intently she actually blushed. As they left the apartment and workshop, Friederich asked, "Emilie, when can we get together again? Can we take a trip to Stuttgart next Saturday? I'd like to have you meet my sister Gretel and her family."

"Oh yes. I'd like that. What time shall we plan on catching the train?"

"Let's make it early," he suggested. "How about eight o'clock?"

"That's fine. I'll meet you at the train station around a quarter to eight."

After Friederich walked them home, he shook hands with Luise and said goodbye. He then took Emilie's hand in both of his and kissed it.

"It's been a real pleasure, Emilie, to have had this time together. I'll look forward to next Saturday to be with you again."

"I will too, Friederich. Thank you very much for taking my sister and me to Mayer's for dinner today."

As Emilie and Luise walked up the stairs to their apartment, Luise said, "Well, Emilie, I think he really has a crush on you. Did you notice how he looked at you when I suggested all he needed was a wife to move into his apartment?"

"I noticed that, too, Luise. Do you really think I'm old enough for him? He's more than eleven years older than I am!"

"Emilie, that shouldn't make any difference if he loves you. He's really doing very well in his business. I wouldn't mind moving right in, if he were interested in me."

As they got to the top of the stairs, their mother was already waiting for them. She still seemed angry even after they had told her what a splendid dinner she had missed. Lina started in. "What did you have?" Luise told her.

"What did you have for dessert?"

"We had black forest cake with coffee."

"See, Mama," Lina cried, "If we had gone we would have had cake too!"

Frau Bartholomae continued to look angry.

"I'm glad we didn't go. You shouldn't eat so much cake anyway, Lina! You're getting much too heavy!"

"Mama, you should have seen Friederich's apartment!" Luise exclaimed. "He has a fully furnished house over the top of his workshop. Whatever a house needs, he has. He doesn't have a flush toilet but I don't think there are too many people here in Vaihingen who have that!"

"What? He showed you his apartment?"

"Yes, Mama. It's true what Luise said. He has everything a person needs to live over his workshop. His mother stays there during the week and helps him with his customers. You know he can't speak very loudly, so she acts as his go-between when people can't understand him."

"But what business did he have showing his place to you two?" she asked angrily.

"He's proud of what he's done," Emilie answered. "Besides, he wanted us to know how well his business is going because it's what he built up all by himself. There aren't any other men who've come back from the war who have done as much as he has!"

Frau Bartholomae was taken aback by Emilie's comment. "So, you're defending him already against me, are you? I don't want to tell you what to do, but I'd be very careful about having an older man pay me so much attention! It's way too early for him to show you his nest. He hasn't even proposed to you yet, for heaven sake."

"She's going to meet his sister and her family in Stuttgart on Saturday," Luise chimed in.

"They're leaving on the 8 a.m. train," she said almost gleefully.

"Oh my God, it's gone that far already, has it?" Frau Bartholomae sighed.

"As I've told you before, Emilie, your father and I had great hopes for you and your sisters. We wanted you all to grow up and become well-educated young ladies who would marry men of distinction and education. We didn't want you to marry beneath you. The Malins are trash in this town. They're nobodies! Can't you see you're far more educated than he is? He may make a lot of money, but there's more to life than money! There's position and status! There's your future children to think of. I was proud of you when you decided on your own accord not to marry Eugen Schmidt. You didn't want to pass on the inherited disease of his sister. But now you're sliding rapidly into another trap! If you're not careful, you'll be marrying a man who has neither education nor status. I don't know about his family history, whether there are any diseases we don't know about!"

Frau Bartholomae was exhausted after this outburst. The girls all stood still as if they had seen a ghost and made nary a sound.

"Come on girls, let's take a walk," Grandmother said. "Your mother and Emilie need to talk."

As Grandmother took all of Emilie's sisters to the hallway to put on their coats and hats, Emilie said, "Mama, you're getting upset about something that may not even happen. Friederich hasn't proposed to me. I don't even know if he likes me. He's a lot older than I am, and he's well established in his business. Why would he want someone like me as his wife? He can get whomever he wants. I'm just a teacher that doesn't even have her degree yet! He's not likely to be interested in me."

"Emilie, you represent everything he doesn't have. Sure, he's got money. But he doesn't have an education. He doesn't have the status of an old-line family in Vaihingen. He doesn't have any relatives who have held high positions in government. He's got an enormous handicap with his voice. What kind of a future would you have with a man like that?"

"I don't know if it'll ever get that far, Mama, but if he should ask me to marry him, I think I would say yes!"

"You haven't listened to a thing I've said, have you?"

"Yes I have, Mama, but you seem to forget there are not many men around here my age anymore. Those who have come back from the war are pretty sad specimens. They probably won't last too many more years. I think I've got to weigh my options very carefully. At this point, I don't see any other man with the same get-up-and-go as Friederich has. He's going to be a real catch for some woman one of these days. Besides, I've already told him I'm going with him on Saturday."

Frau Bartholomae didn't say anymore to her that day nor most of the week. Emilie went back and forth to Enzweihingen each day, taught her class, and usually walked home along the Enz. It was very soothing to see the water silently flowing past, with chunks of ice floating on top occasionally. It is hard to think that in the summer time we swim in this same river, she told herself. It looks so cold now!

On Saturday morning Emilie was already awake at five o'clock. She got up very quietly, washed, and dressed. While she was in the kitchen making breakfast for herself, her grandmother came down and talked with her.

"Emilie, this is no business of mine, but I want you to know I'm sure you'll do the right thing. You have always made good choices in what you do. I'm not at all worried like your mother. I don't think you would be making a mistake marrying Herr Malin."

Emilie laughed. "Grandmother, I very much appreciate your confidence, but really, all of you are making much more out of this series of meetings I've had with Friederich than needs to be made. We're just good friends. He hasn't said a word about getting married. I'm not even sure he would want such a young, inexperienced girl like me for a wife. Why, I barely know how to cook. Whatever I do know about cooking or housekeeping, I've learned from you."

"Ah," she said, "It'll come! I had to learn the hard way too. Your great grandmother thought I was going to marry a rich man. She didn't think I needed to learn how to cook and sew and keep house. Little did she know my husband barely made enough to keep us going during the sixties and the seventies. Even though he did have a good position as a government postal official, he never made very much salary. If I didn't have a large garden, we would have gone hungry during many a winter! If Herr Malin's mother has a large garden, then I'd say they are well enough off. They'll never go hungry, and that's what really counts in life."

Emilie gave her grandmother a big hug.

"I love you, Grandmother! Thanks a lot for your advice. I feel really good about what you've said. I'll see you this evening."

Emilie went quickly up the road to the train station pulling her scarf around her face. It was a very cold January morning. The wind seemed to blow right through her overcoat. Friederich was already waiting for her and greeted her warmly with another kiss on her hand. She wasn't quite used to that although she had seen plays where women were greeted by men in that way. The train arrived exactly on time and they got on board. Friederich picked out a cabin for them that was empty. They sat there and chatted as the train chugged its way to Stuttgart.

As the train stopped in Enzweihingen, Frau Schilling got on with her son. She saw Emilie.

"Gruess Gott, Fraeulein Bartholomae. Is there room for us in your cabin?"

Friederich started to say no but stopped when Emilie said, "Frau Schilling, this is my friend, Herr Malin."

He stood up, took off his hat, and greeted her with a bow.

"Friederich, here's one of the smartest little boys I've ever had in my class. This is her son, Erich."

Frau Schilling beamed. Friederich couldn't help but be amused when Frau Schilling started to tell him of everything Erich was already able to do. She stopped talking when Friederich said, "He probably got his intelligence from his father."

Frau Schilling and her son got off at Ludswigburg. She was going to visit an aunt of hers.

"It was very nice to have met you, Herr Malin."

"Likewise," Friederich answered.

"Frau Schilling, I'll see you again next week at school," Emilie said.

"I hope so, Fraeulein Bartholomae."

Emilie wasn't quite sure what she meant by that comment. I'll have to ask her on Monday why she said that, she thought to herself.

As the train pulled into Feuerbach, Friederich pointed out the Bosch factory where he used to work.

"It was a good place to learn toolmaking, but I'm certainly glad I have my own business now. It was much too big a factory. A worker didn't get to know anyone higher than his foreman. If he didn't like you, he could make life miserable for you. Two of the young men I started with couldn't take it anymore and quit. The boss was constantly on them to improve their skills; otherwise, they were told they could go elsewhere. They went elsewhere."

After they arrived in Stuttgart, Emilie took Friederich's arm as they walked across the street to catch the streetcar for Tuebinger Strasse. The Haussmanns lived on the side of the hill overlooking downtown Stuttgart. It was only a fifteen minute ride until they were there. The apartment where the Haussmanns lived was on the second floor of a three-story building. When they came to the house, Friederich rang their doorbell. Gretel looked out the window above them and said, "So, you've arrived! Come on up the stairs to the second landing. Our apartment is straight ahead."

As they came up the stairs, Gretel was already waiting with her two children, Richard and Grete. Friederich introduced Emilie. "Emilie, I'd like to introduce you to my sister, Gretel, and her two children. This is Richard and little Grete.

"So this is Fraeulein Bartholomae, is it?" Gretel said in a somewhat mocking tone.

"You don't mind if I call you Emilie, do you? We're a very informal family. We don't stand much on ceremony. It's 'Du' [the informal and intimate word for "you"] right from the beginning, all right?"

"Why, of course," Emilie said. "That's fine with me. I've heard a lot about you from Friederich. I'm very pleased to meet you. And these are your two children?"

"Yes. Richard, we call him Riche for short, is eight, and Grete is five."

Just then her husband came in. "This is my husband, Richard. He's also from Vaihingen. We've only lived here for not quite a year."

"How do you do, Fraeulein Bartholomae. Your mother used to own the *Enz-Bote*, isn't that right?" he asked.

"Yes. But she's sold it to Herr Welker now. He used to work for her for many years after my father died."

"Ah yes, your father was President of the City Council, wasn't he?" Richard asked.

"Yes. He tried to do his best for the town."

"My father used to work for the city when your father was council president. He thought a lot of him. Come on in and sit down, for heaven's sake. We don't have to stand here in the doorway."

"I'll make some coffee, and I've just baked a cake," Gretel said. "We'll have a chance to visit then. You children can play in your rooms until we have cake. I'll call you when it's ready."

Riche and Grete went to their rooms, and the four adults sat and talked in the kitchen until the coffee was ready.

"I hear you're a teacher?" Gretel asked. "Where do you teach?"

"I'm just an elementary teacher," Emilie said apologetically. "I'm teaching kindergarten this year in Enzweihingen."

"Listen to her," Gretel said. "She's just a teacher! Why, that's one of the most important jobs anyone can have!" she exclaimed. "And you've gone to college?"

"Well, I've only gone for two years. During the war they asked us to start teaching even though we weren't through with our studies. I still have two more years to go," Emilie answered.

"What? You don't need any more schooling if you're already a teacher," Gretel said emphatically.

"Well, I'd like to get my degree, if I could."

"Ah, we've got a lady in our midst. You're a lucky man, Fritz, to be dating her!" Richard laughed as he said it.

Emilie blushed. Friederich didn't appreciate the joke at her expense.

"Richard, she's only twenty and has a very good position in Enzweihingen. We just happened to meet one of her prize pupils on the train with his mother as we were coming here. She thinks the world of Emilie. I'm sure she does an excellent job as a teacher!" Friederich corrected him.

"Oh, I didn't mean to make fun of her," Richard said. "On the contrary, I think you're a very lucky man to be going with Emilie Bartholomae! Why, she's from one of the best families in Vaihingen!"

Emilie protested, "No, no, Herr Haussmann, my mother has had to struggle to take care of us four girls since our father died. If she hadn't had the business, I don't know what she would have done. Fortunately, my father was a very farsighted man and had made preparations for my mother to take over should he die. It's not been easy for her at all since he died. We've just been very lucky, that's all," she insisted.

"What a difference from our family, Friederich," Gretel said. "Our father died when we were small too. But our father hadn't made any preparations at all for our mother to be able to provide for us. What a difference between what Frau Bartholomae has been able to do for her family and our mother." Gretel turned to Emilie. "Don't apologize for who you are, Emilie. You are what you are and you should be proud of it. We just wish we could have been as fortunate as you! But we're not. We're just part of the working class of Vaihingen. Our family is not rich and Friederich is the first one since our great grandfather to start his own business. Our Grandfather Vischer was a wheelwright who had learned his trade from his father as he had done before him. We don't know much about our father, only that he came from Haefnerhaslach shortly after the Franco-Prussian War. We know we have relatives there yet, but we hardly ever see them. Our mother was never one who wanted to go there to visit them for any reason. Our father died in 1905. You probably don't want to hear this, but I'm going to tell you anyway."

Friederich got all red in the face. "You're not going to tell her about him, are you? She doesn't need to know that!"

"Friederich," Emilie said. "I'd like to know everything I can about your family. I'm sure it's no different from ours."

Gretel laughed. "I'll bet you never had a professor in your family recently, have you, Emilie?"

"A professor?" Emilie asked, surprised. "I didn't know there was a professor in your family, Friederich."

"Go ahead and tell her," he told Gretel. "You've already put the fat on the fire."

"Emilie, it's only fair that you know as much about our family as possible. I wouldn't be surprised if Friederich proposes to you."

Emilie was very embarrassed and blushed noticeably.

"Your cheeks are really beautifully red, Emilie, when you blush," Richard teased.

Friederich turned white as a sheet. He started to get up to leave when Gretel said, "Friederich, where are you going? We haven't had our coffee and cake yet. Sit down. I'm sure Emilie has already guessed why you wanted to bring her here to meet the rest of your family. Don't be so naive. She's a grown woman!"

Friederich started toward the door to get his coat and hat.

"Fritz, for goodness sake, don't take things so seriously. I'm sure your girlfriend wouldn't have come with you if she weren't interested in meeting us. And now that she's here, let's ask her if she wants to go or stay," Richard proposed.

"I'd very much like to stay, Friederich. I want to learn all about your family. And besides, we haven't had any of Gretel's cake or coffee yet."

Friederich reluctantly sat down again. Gretel poured the coffee and served each one a big slice of her black forest cake. She took a slice to each of the children in their rooms and came back to continue her story.

"You'll probably never hear this story again, Emilie. No one in the family seems to want to talk about it. Our father was the offspring of our grandmother and a Jewish professor who was on vacation from Heidelberg University in 1848. She worked in her father's house taking care of the guests who came over the summers for vacation in Haefnerhaslach. This professor evidently took a liking to our grandmother and got her pregnant. When she told him what she thought had happened, he said he was sorry but he couldn't marry her. He already had a family back in Heidelberg. He left her a few hundred Reichsmarks to help her raise the child, but he never returned to Haefnerhaslach. Our father was the village bastard from that point onward. That's probably why he never returned to his old village and why we haven't seen anyone from there since he died. It's not a very pleasant story, but it's one that you should know. Our Grandfather and Grandmother Malin adopted the boy and he grew up thinking he was a Malin. It was only after he was twelve years old that his mother told him who she was. He thought she was an older sister. Everyone else in the family and village knew the story. That's why he never wanted to go back there. And that's probably why you won't get Friederich to take you there either. He couldn't stand his father or his family in Haefnerhaslach. You'll have to ask him sometime to tell you why he never liked his father. Actually, none of us children did, except for Karl. He was his father's favorite and he died while Karl was just a little boy."

Emilie sat stunned and said nothing. What Gretel had told her was absolutely astounding. Even Richard was quiet for a few minutes. Then he said, "Emilie, now you know what kind of a family you're getting into. You still have time to back out if you like," and laughed robustly.

Friederich didn't say anything. He simply looked very cross at Richard, as if he wanted to hit him. Gretel broke the ice.

"Come on now, it's not that bad. We've got a very good future ahead of us. Friederich is one of the *nouveau riche* of Vaihingen. His business is booming, and he's already hired more than ten men to work in his machine shop. Maybe we did start off poorly, but from now on it looks very good, indeed. Even our mother's garden has grown in value."

Emilie agreed with Gretel. "Yes, Friederich has a very good business. He showed my sister Luise and me a couple of weeks ago, and we were very impressed with what he's done. I'm sure he'll be one of the richest men in Vaihingen the way his business is going."

Gretel offered them more coffee and cake but Friederich said, "No. We've got to get back to Vaihingen today. I've got to get up early tomorrow to go out to the lime factory to see what's wrong with the conveyor belt."

"Oh, so you're making parts for the Conradts, are you?" Richard asked.

"Yes, they had a breakdown yesterday, and Adolf stopped by to talk with me about coming out first thing Monday morning to see if I can fashion a new pulley for them."

"Well, if you're making parts for the Conradts, you must be pretty highly thought of," Richard responded.

Emilie and Friederich said goodbye to the Haussmanns. They returned by streetcar to the train station for the ride home to Vaihingen. Friederich said very little even though Emilie tried her best to get him to look at the beauty of the snow on the fir trees. The ride along the hillside leading into downtown Stuttgart was beautiful. He nodded in agreement but said nothing.

"Friederich, you don't have to feel embarrassed about your father. I'm glad Gretel told me. It's a fascinating story. You should be proud of what you've all done since his death. You must really have held the family together all these years. I'm sure your mother must have depended on you greatly for your weekly paycheck," Emilie said consolingly.

Friederich's demeanor softened remarkably. He was no longer angry and took her hand and held it. He even had tears in the corners of his eyes which he tried to wipe away.

"I'm very glad you don't mind, Emilie. Any other woman would not have wanted anything more to do with me." He then told her about Roesle Fatzler. "You might just as well hear the whole story, Emilie. I was once very much in love with a girl in Vaihingen. It was shortly before the war that I first met her. Her father was the local grocer in Enzweihingen. We met for the first time at a Turnverein festival in Vaihingen. I didn't see her again until the following year at Easter. We took up where we left off. We'd go ice skating together on the Enz in the winters and swimming in the summers. She was an excellent dancer, so we always hit it off during the festivals throughout the year. In 1915, just before I was called up for the army, we talked about getting married. I had already asked her father if I could marry her. He said, well, I'd rather have you both wait until after the war; you never know what might happen. I was very disappointed. I think she was too. We kept on seeing each other on weekends. After I entered the army, she wrote to me faithfully. It was only after I came back during my convalescence we started seeing each other again. I had been gone almost a year. She spoke to me and I answered her with my notes on the slate board, just like I did with everyone else. She said she was worried about me. She hoped I'd be able to speak again after the final examination by the doctor. She said, 'You know how much I like it when you sing to me, Friederich.' I wrote the same thing to her. I couldn't wait to sing again, but I was supposed to remain completely silent for three weeks. It was after I returned the second time from seeing the specialist in Stuttgart that she came to our house to find out what the doctor had said. When I spoke to her, she almost fell over. Almost no sound came out. 'Friederich, if you can't speak or sing, I don't think we should see each other anymore!' She left and I never saw her again. I was devastated! I couldn't believe what I had heard. In retrospect, I'm glad I didn't marry her. All she wanted to do was to sing, dance, and shop."

Emilie felt sorry for Friederich but at the same time relieved it had turned out as it did. She might have married him and I would never have had this conversation with him, she thought to herself.

"I agree with you, Friederich. She would have made a horrible wife for you. Anyone who would cast off a friendship because of a war wound doesn't deserve to be called a friend and certainly not a wife!"

Friederich was pleased by her outburst. He squeezed her hand and kissed her cheek. She felt very warm and tender toward him. She thought to herself, I really am in love with him!

They rode in silence on the train all the way back to Vaihingen. He held her hand in his and held her close to him in their compartment. As they walked to her house, Friederich asked, "When will we see each other again, Emilie?"

"Anytime you want, Friederich."

"Emilie, there's something I want to ask you."

"Certainly Friederich, you can ask me anything you like. I'd be more than pleased to try to answer."

"I'd like to have you for my wife. Will you marry me?"

"Oh yes, Friederich!" she said as her heart beat so hard she thought she was shaking. He held her for sometime and then kissed her full on the mouth. He had never done that to her before. She had never been kissed like that by any other man.

"If you don't mind," he said, "I'd like to come by tomorrow evening and ask your mother's permission, if that's all right with you?"

"Oh yes!" she said emphatically.

He kissed her again and said, "Goodbye, my sweetheart, until tomorrow."

"I can hardly wait to see you again, Friederich. Good night! I love you!"

Emilie came into the house and didn't notice her mother standing there. She was literally singing to herself.

"Well, what's gotten into you? You're all rosy and bright. And singing yet too! Does a trip to Stuttgart excite you that much?"

"I had a wonderful time, Mama. Friederich is such a charming man. He's really done a lot in his life already. I met his sister and her family, and we all had a very enjoyable time together. He's coming again tomorrow evening. He wants to talk to you, Mama. I told him it would be all right for him to come then."

Luise came into the room. "You look simply radiant, Emilie. What happened in Stuttgart to make you feel this way? Was it something Friederich said to you?"

"I can't tell you. You'll have to wait until Friederich comes again."

"I certainly hope you haven't done anything foolish, Emilie." her mother said sternly.

"Just wait. You'll find out soon enough. I really can't tell you anymore."

"I think she's got a crush on Friederich!" Luise said knowingly. Lina chimed in with "Emilie's got a boy friend! Emilie's got a boy friend!"

Even little Mariele got into the spirit of it and sang along with Lina. "Emilie's got a boyfriend! Emilie's got a boyfriend!"

Emilie scolded the girls. "Herr Malin is not a boy! He's a very grown and mature man!"

"That's enough, girls," their mother said. "Emilie's had a very nice day in Stuttgart. Herr Malin is almost old enough to be your father. He's certainly not a boy!"

The day dragged by very slowly. Emilie kept looking at the clock. Frau Schilling finally said, "Fraeulein Bartholomae, I can't help but notice your eyes are constantly on the clock. Are you looking forward to something today? Would it have anything to do with the man whom I met on the train yesterday? He seemed like a very mature man."

"Frau Schilling, I am very anxious today because Herr Malin is coming to the house this evening to talk to my mother."

"Ah, Fraeulein Bartholomae! He's going to ask your mother for permission to marry you!" she blurted out.

"Sh, sh, sh, please don't say anything to anyone about it yet. You're the first person to guess what's going to happen. I'd like to keep it a secret until after he's talked to Mama. Can I count on you to keep this secret?"

"By all means, Fraeulein Bartholomae. I won't tell a soul!"

Evening finally came, and upon her return to catch the train for Vaihingen, Herr Schilling met her on the street and tipped his hat. "It's a beautiful evening isn't it, Fraeulein Bartholomae?" and smiled broadly. Emilie guessed his wife had already told him what was going to happen.

She hardly touched her dinner that evening.

"Emilie, aren't you feeling well?" her mother asked. "You should eat something. Grandmother has made a very good dinner, and you've hardly touched it."

"I'm not hungry, Mama. I had so much to eat for lunch today. I haven't room for anything else."

Emilie was waiting for Friederich to come. Her mother was dressed in her Sunday dress and sweater. She knew he was coming and that he wanted to talk to her.

"How did things go in school today?"

"Things went well today, Mama."

Emilie wasn't really in the mood to talk about school. She was very quiet and even her grandmother knew something was on her mind. "You're unusually quiet this evening, Emilie. Did you have trouble at school with some of the children?"

"No, no, Grandmother. The children are fine. And Frau Schilling is a real big help in class. She even knows the stories and songs as well as I do."

The doorbell rang, and Frau Bartholomae told all of her daughters and mother-in-law to disappear.

"I'll talk with Herr Malin alone."

Emilie went to her room and waited. Her heart was pounding. Her palms were all hot and sweaty. She got up and walked back and forth, back and forth, for what seemed an hour. She finally heard the door shut and knew Friederich and her mother had finished their conversation. Her mother came directly into her room and sat down on a chair. She looked at Emilie for sometime without saying a word. Her face was very somber and almost cross.

"Do you know what Herr Malin wanted, Emilie?"

"Yes, Mama. He told me yesterday what he wanted to talk to you about. He's asked me to marry him," she answered almost breathlessly.

"Do you know what that means?"

"Yes I do, Mama. He's a brilliant man. He may not have the formal education of a man who has gone to the university, but he knows his business, and he's got a great future ahead of him!" she blurted out.

"But do you know about the family he comes from?"

It's the old story again, Emilie said to herself. Her mother continued: "The Malins are nothing in Vaihingen. They come from the poorest section of town and haven't had a father who has achieved anything. They are from the lowest rung of the social ladder,

Emilie. How can you want to marry someone like that? He's also more than eleven years older than you are! There's less of a difference in age between him and me than there is between the two of you. I always thought you were going to marry someone from one of the good families of Vaihingen, someone who has gone to the university. Your father would be very disappointed if he knew you wanted to marry an older man like Friederich Malin. You've been raised to be a lady, Emilie. We've never let you do any of the hard work on your grandfather's farm nor around here, for that matter. We wanted you to be cultured and well educated. We've given you the best possible upbringing, and now you want to throw it all away?" she said as she wiped her eyes. "Don't you think you owe us at least the right to expect you will marry within your social class? It may not be possible for your sisters to do so. I'm not as wealthy as I once was. But both your father and I expected great things from you . . ." Frau Bartholomae was really crying now.

"Mama, be realistic. There are no men my age around here anymore. They've either been killed in the war or are hopelessly crippled! Of the few men left in Vaihingen, Friederich Malin is by far the best of them all. He's got his own business. He owns his own home! He's got a lot of money saved up. He's got a very lively family, and even his mother is a real sparkler. She's got an unconquerable spirit and Friederich takes right after her. He may not be able to speak very loudly, but he's a very fine man and I'm in love with him! What did you tell him, Mama?"

Frau Bartholomae gradually stopped crying. "I told him I wanted to think it over for a couple of weeks. I couldn't make that kind of a decision too quickly. I had to talk with my own family first. He understood and said he would come back in two weeks to find out my decision."

Emilie saw Friederich again that next Sunday. Her mother had gone to Gerabronn to talk to her father and mother. From what Emilie could determine, most of the family was for the marriage. Only Grandmother Meyer was firmly opposed. Frau Bartholomae's brothers, sisters, father, aunts, and uncles were all for it. When she relayed this information to Friederich, he was pleased. Most of her family was behind him.

"Even Uncle, Dr. Ernst Meyer, said that the loss of your voice shouldn't be anything more than a hindrance to overcome. There's nothing medically wrong with you that he could tell."

Friederich expressed surprise at that comment.

"You mean your mother asked him if I might be mentally affected by my wound?"

"No, no, Friederich!" Emilie said defensively. "She just wondered if polyps could be inherited. He assured her that as far as medical science knew, at present, they weren't!"

Friederich felt relieved and thought he'd like to meet this doctor-uncle of hers.

"You will, Friederich—when we get married."

Emilie and Friederich went to Mayer's on the Market for dinner and had a wonderful time together. She truly felt when she was with Friederich, she was with a very strong man upon whom she could depend. He would make a good father for their children.

They agreed to meet each evening at Mayer's during the time her mother was thinking over his request to marry her. The owner had a small room to the rear of the restaurant that he allowed them to use almost for themselves. They ate together and drank some wine in a very quiet and cozy atmosphere. There was hardly ever anyone else in it except for the waitress. Friederich didn't want to come to the house since he told her mother, "I'll be back in two weeks for your answer, Frau Bartholomae."

On Monday evening, January 20, 1920, Friederich came to the house all dressed up in a topcoat, suit, white shirt with a stiff, button-down collar, a solid red tie with a gold tie clasp and gold cuff-links, and brightly shined new black shoes. He was very handsome, and even Frau Bartholomae was impressed how grand he looked. He didn't even bother to take off his coat.

"Good evening, Frau Bartholomae," Friederich said as he shook her hand.

"Good evening, Herr Malin."

Since he hadn't taken off his coat, he held his hat in his hand and asked, "Frau Bartholomae, have you made a decision yet about my marrying your daughter?"

"Yes I have, Herr Malin. You may marry my daughter, Emilie."

"Thank you very much, Frau Bartholomae. I'll see to it that your daughter is treated like a lady. I'll even provide her with a maid to clean the house each week. When we have children, I'll see to it that she has someone come to help her," he promised.

"I'll have Dean Scheuer announce your formal engagement to my daughter in church next Sunday, Herr Malin. I'd like to discuss the date of the wedding with my daughter, if you don't mind."

"Certainly, Frau Bartholomae."

They shook hands again, and this time he kissed it. Frau Bartholomae was impressed with his gallantry.

That evening, Emilie and her mother set the date for the wedding. Emilie wanted it to be the same date as her mother and father's. But her mother wouldn't hear of it.

"I want you to have it on April 11."

"Why, Mama? Why can't we get married on the twenty-first of March? That's when you and Papa got married! It's a beautiful time of the year with the flowers in bloom and the leaves all out on the trees. It's the beginning of spring. That's when I'd like to be married!"

"I want you to have it on Sunday, April 11, because that's the same day Lina is confirmed in the church. I can't afford to have two separate celebrations for the two of you."

Emilie couldn't believe what she was hearing.

"You mean you want us to get married on confirmation day so you won't have to have two different celebrations to which the family is invited?" she asked incredulously.

"That's exactly what I'm saying. I can't afford to host two big family affairs in the same year anymore. You seem to forget, I'm living off the mortgage payments from Herr Welker. I lost all of that money on those worthless war bonds. Have you forgotten how much that was? I can't afford to pay for a wedding and a confirmation ceremony at two different times. They'll both have to be on the same day," her mother said emphatically.

Emilie realized it was futile to try to talk her out of what she had already decided. She knew Lina would be very upset over her mother's decision. Her wedding would take place in the afternoon after Lina's confirmation in the morning. The family would already be gathered for the one event and then they could attend the other on the same day. The guests wouldn't even have to stay overnight, if they didn't want to.

When Lina found out about it, she was very upset. She cried and cried.

"Mama, that's not fair! It's my special day! It's been planned since last Christmas. What will my friends think when I tell them Emilie's going to get married that same day? I wanted to have my friends over for dessert and then go for a long walk along the Enz. We've talked about nothing else ever since we knew when the date was. I won't be able to be with them now. It's just not fair, Mama!"

"Lina, when you get married, I'll pay for your wedding, if I can. I don't know how things are going to work out in the future. But you girls have to understand I'm not as wealthy as I once was. I can't pay for all of the special parties and events like I used to. I may not even have enough left to send any of you to the Latein Schule anymore. I just don't have enough money! There's just enough for me to live comfortably. I'll still have to go to work, I'm sure, in order to pay for all of the things you girls have come to take for granted."

"You mean, Luise and I can't go to the Latein Schule?" Lina cried.

"Probably not. I've already talked to my mother and she's willing to have all of you come to her house to learn how to cook and sew while I'm at work. So this next fall will be your last year of the Realschule, Lina. Luise will be in Gerabronn with Grandmother and Grandfather Meyer."

This set Lina off even more. She ran from the room and went to find Luise.

"We can't go to any higher school, Luise. We've got to go to work at Grandmother Meyer's next year!" she cried.

It was now Luise's turn to be upset.

"Do you mean I won't be able to go to school like Emilie, Mama?"

"I'm sorry, Luise, but I can't afford it. We've got to make do with what we have. It would cost too much to send you and Lina to the Latein Schule. It would be better if you two would learn how to cook and sew."

Luise was very quiet. Emilie had asked her to be her maid of honor. She didn't want to think about school right now.

"Maybe things will change before next year, Mama, so we'll be able to continue our schooling," she said hopefully.

"I'm afraid that won't be possible. I've already told Grandmother Meyer you're going to be there in the fall."

Luise was heartbroken. Emilie could see it in her eyes. But there was nothing she could do about it. If her mother decided she couldn't afford to send the girls to school, that was it.

That Sunday, the engagement announcement was read by the Dean of the Cathedral during the church service. Written notice appeared in the *Enz-Bote* the next day. Emilie's two best friends, Clara and Fanny, were surprised. They knew she was dating Friederich but had not yet formally met him. They came toward them immediately after church and congratulated them. Friederich was very polite and took off his hat as Emilie introduced him. He shook hands with them. Fanny couldn't believe it.

"Aren't you going back to the institute this next year, Emilie? You still have two years to complete, don't you?"

"No. I'm also giving notice to the Enzweihingen Kindergarten that I'm quitting as of the first of March. I have a lot of things to do to get ready."

"I'm very happy for you, Emilie," Clara said. "The announcement was a big surprise. I thought you would have at least told me about it before hearing it this morning from the Dean. My mother thought she had heard from a neighbor Herr Malin was courting someone, but she didn't know who. Now it turns out to be my best friend."

The next few weeks were hectic. Not only did Emilie quit teaching, she sent out all of the invitations and announcements. She and her mother had another quarrel over this issue. Her mother wanted her to include the confirmation party announcement for Lina in the same invitation.

"Mama, we can't put both of these invitations on the same card for our guests. What will people think? It's bad enough to have both events taking place on the same day, but I won't send out my wedding invitations with the confirmation announcement on the back side."

"Emilie, you don't seem to understand. I'm trying to save money by having both events take place on the same day. If you won't put Lina's announcement on the back of your wedding invitation, will you at least put a separate announcement for her in the same envelope? I'm having them all printed by Herr Welker, so it only means stuffing and addressing the envelopes. That shouldn't be too hard for you."

When Emilie told Friederich what her mother wanted her to do, he laughed. "So, she wants to save money, does she? Well, tell you what. I'll pay for the separate posting of Lina's confirmation announcement, if you don't mind addressing the extra envelopes."

"That would be very nice of you, Friederich," she said thankfully. "I'd be more than pleased to address her announcement to our relatives. It just didn't seem to make much sense to send them both out to your relatives too. After all, they don't know her."

Only Grandmother Meyer took Maria to task for not sending both events in the same envelope.

"You could have saved yourself a lot of money, Maria. Just look at all of the separate envelopes and postage it took to send out both invitations!"

Maria didn't say anything. She didn't even tell her mother Emilie sent out both of them or that Friederich paid for the second set.

Emilie and her mother went to the seamstress right next door to where they lived. Frau Bartholomae had her wedding gown altered to fit Emilie. It fit perfectly and only took the seamstress three weeks to complete. She made a new bridal veil to match the dress. Emilie was really surprised her mother let her use her gown. She had always said she wanted to keep it as another one of those rare items of fond remembrance of her husband. But her mother suggested it herself. She did ask, however, to have it back so that if any of Emilie's sisters got married, they could also use it.

The weeks passed very quickly. Emilie got responses from everyone to whom an invitation was sent. All of her relatives said they were coming. None of Friederich's relatives from Haefnerhaslach were invited. He didn't want her to send them any. Only his Vischer relatives and neighbors from Vaihingen were invited. All of them also said they were coming. Emilie and Friederich expected a total of almost one hundred fifty guests. Her mother was overwhelmed so many were coming. She had thought if seventy-five came, that would be a large number. Lina wanted another twenty of her friends to come for the confirmation party. Frau Bartholomae decided she could only pay for a cold buffet. She really couldn't see how she could afford a sit-down dinner for that many guests. "Mayers on the Market" threw in a glass of champagne for each guest since Frau Bartholomae had them serve the cold buffet. Friederich was disappointed. He had expected a full course dinner to be served. Emilie talked with him about what her mother had said.

"Tell you what, Emilie. I'll pay for the drinks that anyone may want. I'm sure most of the guests would expect to have wine served at our wedding."

When Emilie told her mother what Friederich had offered, she was a bit upset.

"How can he pay for all that wine? If he's going to do that, then I'll pay for the cake and coffee after the meal. I'm sure there will be some persons who will drink too much!"

Friederich and Emilie saw each other almost every day. They looked over his apartment above his workshop and made plans of where their bedroom would be. They also decided which rooms could be used for the children, should they have any. There was nothing on the floors in any of the rooms.

"Emilie, if you want to buy rugs for the floors and put up curtains, go ahead. If there's anything else you want to do, that's all right too. Just tell me what you're planning so I'll know what to expect by way of any workman wanting access to the apartment," Friederich offered.

"Oh, Friederich, that's great! Do you mind if I have some of the rooms re-papered? It looks like the wall paper has been up for a long time. It would make the house so much more attractive."

"Fine, but I want to approve what you pick out ahead of time."

"Certainly, Friederich. I wouldn't think of having any work done unless you approved of it."

"There's an old neighbor of ours down on the Enz who does wallpapering. You might get in touch with him. Tell him Fritz Malin sent you. I'm sure he'll give us an honest rate for his work."

Emilie went right down to Herr Klinger the next day to talk with him about re-papering their apartment. When she met him, she was surprised how much older he was than she expected. If Friederich said I should talk with him, then I know he has to do the work, she told herself. Even though she saw him through the window, she pushed the doorbell.

"Herr Klinger?"

"Yes. Who are you?" he asked as he opened the door.

"I'm Herr Friederich Malin's fiancee. He sent me to you to ask if you would do some wallpapering for us in his apartment over his workshop next to the church."

"Ah, so you're the young woman he's going to marry? I've heard about you, but I didn't know who you were. I only knew you were a daughter of Frau Bartholomae. I've known your mother for years. In fact, I once did some papering for her in her office at the *Enz-Bote* after her husband died. Are you the daughter?"

"Yes I am."

She vaguely recalled her mother saying the person who did the wallpapering in her office had not done a very good job. Emilie had never known who it was, but now she knew. She didn't feel very comfortable talking with Herr Klinger about the job after this discovery.

"Come in Fraeulein Bartholomae. I have wallpaper samples you can look through and choose the ones you want."

While his house was old, it did look as though he had recently re-papered the office and entrance way to his workshop. His wife was working in their office, and they exchanged greetings.

"I've known your mother for a long time," Frau Klinger said. "She probably doesn't remember me, but I helped her pick out the wall paper on her office wall after she and your father first came to Vaihingen. We've known the Malins even longer. Their garden abuts ours and Frau Malin has sold us eggs for many years. We've watched Fritzle grow up. He was always such a serious boy. He wanted to get ahead as quickly as possible. He didn't like Vaihingen in those days. He had always talked about leaving and going somewhere else. He wasn't sure where exactly, but he said any place would be better than Vaihingen! And here he is, one of our more prosperous businessmen these days. It's ironic, but I'm very glad he's getting married. I told him a long time ago he should find himself a wife. That's really what he needed. But you're an educated lady, Fraeulein Bartholomae. How did the two of you ever meet?"

"I met him at a Turnverein festival."

Emilie wasn't too sure she wanted to carry on this conversation with Frau Klinger. What business was it of hers how we met, she thought to herself. "I'd like to see what kinds of wallpaper you have. Show me your bedroom paper first, then for the living room, the dining room, and finally, the kitchen," Emilie said trying to end Frau Klinger's line of questioning.

Frau Klinger pulled out several rolls of paper samples for Emilie to look at while she continued her enquiry.

"You know your fiancé could never get along with his father, don't you?" She followed up her own question with her own comment. "Yes, it's one of those cases where the son wanted to be completely separate and distinct from his father. His mother told me once she couldn't have both of them in the house any longer because they were almost always fighting. She finally had to ask her parents to take in her son. She couldn't take anymore of their battles."

Emilie was taken aback by this ongoing commentary. She finally asked, "Frau Klinger, I really came by to pick out the wallpaper for our house. Could we get back to your samples, please?" she said with some exasperation.

"Of course, Fraeulein Bartholomae. I just thought you might like to know about your prospective husband. No one else has seen him grow up as much as we have," she declared with some indignation.

"Herr Malin recommended you to me; that's why I came here in the first place. Otherwise, I probably would have gone to the Fedderers. My mother knows them quite well."

"Oh, but they're so expensive! No, no. It's good that you've come to us. I didn't mean to imply that Herr Malin isn't a good match for you, Fraeulein Bartholomae. But he comes from such a 'different' family from yours. You know his father was in charge of the poorhouse in Vaihingen, don't you?"

"Yes, I've heard that. But let's get back to the wallpaper. Do you have any with a rose pattern or some similar flower pattern for the bedrooms?"

"Yes. Here's a pretty one you may like."

Frau Klinger spread out the paper in front of her. It was a beautiful white paper with little roses surrounded by two leaves and a short stem throughout the roll.

"This is the one I want," Emilie declared.

"Do you have any pattern with a larger flower and just a bit of color in it that might be good for our living room and dining room?"

"Yes, we have a lot of those."

Frau Klinger proceeded to spread four of them out on the table. There was one with a slight accent of a greenish-yellow flower amidst a whole field of leaves and tan background that appealed to Emilie. She didn't like the others.

"I'll take this pattern for the two rooms, Frau Klinger."

"If you would want a brown-and-white pattern in squares, you would have exactly the same in your kitchen as that of Herr Malin's mother."

"No. But it might be just right for the stairway leading upstairs from the workshop. Let me see what you're suggesting."

Frau Klinger showed her the roll, and it did have its appeal.

"Yes," Emilie agreed. "I'd like that for the hallway."

Frau Klinger drew up the order and said her husband could put up the wallpaper around the first of March.

"He does a real good job. He's just gotten a bit slower than he used to be. He's getting older and his apprentice only works with him three days a week. But he'll do well by you, Fraeulein Bartholomae. Have you seen Herr Malin's mother's house? She and her sister did the wallpapering themselves. It looks like an amateur's job. There are even creases in it. My husband would have taken off all of the paper and done it over again if his apprentices had done such a poor job!"

"No. I haven't seen their house yet. I imagine I'll be seeing it before too long. Thank you and I'll expect Herr Klinger to come on the first of March."

Frau Klinger told Emilie much more than what she wanted to know about Friederich. She did recall Karl had mentioned Friederich and his father didn't get along together; that's why Friederich was raised by his grandparents. She wasn't about to raise this question with Friederich since he hadn't even mentioned much about his father, especially since Gretel told her about him that time in Stuttgart. No, she thought, I'm not going to tell him anything about what Frau Klinger said. It would only get him all upset. Besides, she was just an old neighbor who had known him since he was a little boy.

Emilie hurried back to Friederich's workshop and reported what she had picked out for the apartment. His mother was there and she thought the patterns were very nice. But she said, "Friederich, isn't that going to be very expensive having Herr Klinger do the wallpapering? Why don't you do it yourself? Or, better yet, the paper that's on the walls now still looks good. You don't really have to change it, do you?"

Friederich got a bit agitated with his mother. "This is Emilie's choice, not yours, Mother. Besides, I don't have time for paperhanging! I've got more than enough to do right here."

"It's not so bad, Friederich," Emilie said. "Your mother was just trying to be helpful."

Frau Malin didn't say anything but walked away. It was clear to Emilie he had hurt her feelings. She said goodbye to her and Friederich.

"I'll see you this evening, Friederich. You're invited for dinner at six o'clock."

The next few weeks went by very quickly. The house was re-papered and looked very pretty. Herr Klinger did a very good job and even asked a lower price than Frau Klinger had originally quoted.

The wedding dress was finished with a new lace veil. Lina was going to her confirmation classes each week and had even forgotten to be angry anymore about having her party on the same day as her sister's wedding. Around the first of April, Friederich and Emilie looked over the apartment together. It was a quiet Sunday afternoon. The apartment had been cleaned from one end to the other, including down the staircase leading to Friederich's workshop. It was a beautiful April day with the sun shining brightly, and so warm sweaters were unnecessary. They had gone for a walk along the Enz when Friederich suggested, "Let's take a look at the apartment, Emilie. It's almost ready for us to move into. Let's see if there's anything missing."

Emilie quickly agreed, "Oh yes, Friederich. I'd like that. I haven't seen it this week yet."

He held the door open for her after unlocking it. She went up the stairs ahead of him. They looked at the kitchen first. There was the water faucet he said she would have right in the kitchen. She turned it on and sure enough, the water came out into the sink. "That's great, "she said. "Thank you for putting running water into the kitchen, Friederich."

She went up to him and kissed him. He held her very tightly to him. She finally broke away.

"Our tour isn't finished yet, Friederich. Let's take a look at the dining room and living room."

She pulled him by the hand and kissed him gently on the cheek. He wanted to hold her tightly again.

"Wait Friederich. We haven't seen all of the rooms yet." She gently chided him for his impatience. He liked the two rooms.

"Let's take a look at the bedrooms." She pulled him into the smaller of the three bedrooms. "This is going to be the baby's room, Friederich. Don't you think it'll make an ideal room for our little boy or girl?" she asked coyly. He nodded his head and came closer to her. He took her head in his hands and kissed her repeatedly. She thought she was going to pass out; she got so excited. He took her by the hand and led her into their bedroom. He began to unbutton her blouse and kissed her breasts repeatedly. She got so excited she asked coquettishly, "Oh Friederich, what are you going to do to me?"

He didn't say anything. He unfastened her brassiere and put his hand under her dress. As he rubbed her thighs, her excitement grew.

"Friederich, let's lie down on the bed!"

He unbuttoned his trousers. She finished undressing. She kissed him over and over again. She didn't mind at all when his excitement matched hers. He pressed against her.

"Ouch! What was that?" she asked.

"You're a virgin, Emilie. It's only your hymen breaking."

After this initial shock of pain, she felt more comfortable.

"Do it some more, Friederich! It feels so good!"

They kept it up and she felt herself having one sensation after another.

"Ah, finally," Friederich said as he relaxed. They kept kissing each other until they fell asleep on the bed. Around five o'clock, he woke up.

"Emilie, that was wonderful. You do it so well. I think we'll have a great time together after we're married!"

"Oh, I know so, Friederich!" Emilie said ecstatically.

"Just think this is where we'll be doing it again and again!"

He kissed her again and held her close to him for sometime. These were the most caring and intimate moments she hoped she would experience with him again and again. This act confirmed her love for Friederich. She hoped it also did for him.

"I think we'd better get dressed now. I told my mother to expect us for supper this evening."

It was Emilie's first visit to the Malin house. After this fabulous Sunday afternoon, she felt much relieved.

"Oh, I didn't know we were going to your mother's house. Are you sure she's expecting us?"

"Of course. You haven't been there yet. You should at least see what the family house looks like."

They walked arm in arm through the gathering dusk of Vaihingen from Friederich's workshop to his mother's house on the edge of town. Emilie had never been there. Only that one time when she went by it with Karl on the way to the Alte Ente did she know where Frau Malin's house was. The second time in the vicinity was as a consequence of her visit at the paperhanger's shop. It was just over the garden wall from the Klingers'. When they arrived, Friederich opened the door and went inside. He didn't bother knocking. Emilie called out, "Frau Malin, can we come in?"

"You're already in," she heard a voice calling out from the living room. Frau Malin came to the front door and Friederich introduced Emilie to her again. They had only seen each other on rare occasions when Emilie dropped by the workshop, or when she reported on the wall paper selections to Friederich. They had met for the first time at the Turnverein Festival the year before. The encounters since then had been brief.

"Come in, Fraeulein Bartholomae," she said as she shook her hand. "We've met a few times before, but this is your first visit to my home. The last time I saw you was at Friederich's workshop when you were ordering wallpaper."

"Yes, Frau Malin. This is only our third or fourth meeting. I'm so glad to see you again."

"It certainly is high time you've come to visit. I was beginning to think you and your family thought you were too good to pay us a visit," she said, somewhat annoyed. "You may not know this, but my father was also on the City Council years ago and was even Council President. Just like your father but back in the seventies and eighties," she said proudly. "He had too much to do in his business to continue any longer in the Council."

Friederich led the way into the house and told Emilie to take a seat. "My mother likes to talk about her father. He was a good man. It's too bad my mother married my father. Grandfather always said, 'If only Maria hadn't married that so and so, she would have been much better off!'"

"You're still bitter about your father, aren't you, Friederich? He's been dead almost fifteen years. How much longer are you going to hate him?" Frau Malin asked.

"This is my aunt, Katharine Vischer," Friederich said as she came into the room. "She and my mother live together here in the old family home."

"I'm very pleased to meet you, Fraeulein Vischer," Emilie said as she shook hands with her.

"I'm very pleased to meet you, Fraeulein Bartholomae." She spoke in a whisper almost as quietly as Friederich's. Emilie had a hard time understanding her at first. After listening to her carefully for a few minutes, she understood her very well. She seemed rather shy and retiring. She let her younger sister do all the talking. Frau Malin told Emilie all about her family, some of which she had already heard from Friederich, Karl, and Gretel. She did want Emilie to know, however, that her father had not been as poor as they were.

"He was the only wagon-maker in Vaihingen. If anyone wanted either a farm wagon or a fancy buggy, they always came to my father's shop." Her sister tried to correct her by saying, "Actually, the business was started by our Great Grandfather Vischer. Our father barely kept it going after our brother died. Our father never really got over the loss of our brother. He always hoped he would come back to Germany and take over the business," she said in her whispered tones.

"Where did he go?"

"He went to America," Frau Malin answered. "He was our younger brother and he wanted to visit America to see if he would like it there. He promised us he would come back in a few years, but he never did. He got married over there and had a family. A neighbor played a prank on him by loosening his buggy seat. As he drove down into the city, the bolt on his seat came off and he fell under the wheels of a streetcar. My father became increasingly bitter after that," she concluded.

"I'm sorry," Emilie said.

"You don't have to be," Frau Malin answered. "That happened a long time ago. Years before you were even born."

Fraeulein Vischer invited them to sit down at the dining room table for dinner.

"We don't usually have this kind of a meal in the evening, Fraeulein," Aunt Katharine said. "But this is a special occasion. It's the first time you've come to eat with us."

She had prepared a roast chicken with gravy, spaetzle, and a salad. It was very tasty and Emilie even had a second helping.

"It tastes good but it's too dry!" Friederich said. His aunt put some more gravy on his chicken and that seemed to help him swallow.

"You know, Fraeulein," Frau Malin said, "You have to make sure every meal is moist and soft enough for Friederich to swallow. Ever since his operation, he's been unable to swallow anything that's too hard or dry."

"Yes, thank you, Frau Malin, for telling me. He's told me a few times I'll have to be careful how I cook my meals. He has trouble swallowing and I've seen him drink a lot of liquids in order to get his food down," Emilie tried to assure her.

After the meal was over, Friederich said, "Well, let's go, Emilie."

She really didn't want to go yet.

"I think I should help your mother and aunt wash the dishes, Friederich. They've done such a good job preparing what was really a great dinner. It wasn't just the usual evening snack."

"You'll get a chance to do that in the future, I'm sure," he said. "It's getting late, and I've got to get up early tomorrow."

They took their leave. Frau Malin didn't seem too happy about it, Emilie thought. I'm sure she wanted to ask me more about my family. She assured Frau Malin she would stop in again before long.

"Don't wait as long as you have this time," she scolded. "I may not be from the Vaihingen elite anymore, but I do have my pride."

"Come by when you can," Fraeulein Vischer said. "You'll soon be a member of the family."

After Friederich took her home that evening, Emilie thought over all that had happened that day: they had admired the apartment and gotten about as intimate there as they would ever be. For this, she smiled happily to herself. Moreover, she had finally gone to the Malin house and gotten better acquainted with Friederich's mother and aunt. She thought how sad it was these two old women had only each other to share their big, old house. It was not very modern in any way, but it did have a large garden and many fruit trees. I'm glad I have my nicely remodeled apartment, she thought. Friederich and I wouldn't have much privacy if we had had to move in with them.

Friederich and Emilie visited their apartment as often as they could before the wedding. They enjoyed complete privacy only on the weekends. The rest of the time, Frau Malin was there to help Friederich with his customers. Emilie and Friederich were intimate two more times before their wedding day: once, after Friederich told his mother she should go home since Emilie was going to come to look over the apartment; and then just three days before the wedding. They both felt it was the best of their unions yet.

On April 11, 1920, the Bartholomae family attended church in the morning for Lina's confirmation. Then in the afternoon, Emilie's and Friederich's wedding took place. It was a grand occasion. All of her relatives from Gerabronn, Heilbronn, Stuttgart, Boeblingen, and Tuebingen were in attendance. Even one of Friederich's cousins had come from Haefnerhaslach. His mother had written to the family and invited them to attend. The Dean conducted the service and announced that anyone who had not received a formal invitation to attend the wedding was now invited to attend the reception immediately following the service at Mayers on the Market Square. The invitation from the pulpit almost threw Emilie into a tizzy. She thought, oh my poor mother! *What will that do to her finances?* She whispered to Friederich on the way out. How could he have done that?"

"I told him to," Friederich said matter-of-factly. "I told Mayers that anyone who didn't have a formal invitation and wanted to attend the reception could do so. They should keep track of who came, and I would pay the difference."

She squeezed his hand and kissed him again. "Oh, Friederich. You're so thoughtful! But I'd better tell my mother. She looked awfully pale as we came down the aisle."

As Frau Bartholomae came to stand with them after the ceremony, Emilie whispered, "Don't worry about the extra guests, Mama. Friederich has already taken care of that."

She looked as if a great burden had been taken off of her. She went to Friederich and kissed him on the cheek.

"Thank you very much for all you've done for Emilie. Even Lina is now glad we had both events on the same day," she told him.

Frau Bartholomae introduced Friederich to each of her brothers and sisters and to her parents. They had not met him before and were a bit hard-pressed to understand what he was saying. Grandfather Meyer, especially, was getting hard of hearing.

"Herr Malin, you must speak a little louder. I'm getting hard of hearing."

"Grandfather," Emilie intervened. "He can't speak any louder. He lost his voice during the war and that's as loud as he'll ever speak. What is it you want to ask him? I'll tell you what he says. I can understand him perfectly."

"Oh yes, now I remember," Grandfather Meyer recalled. "Your mother told me about him. He can't speak anymore, can he?"

"Oh yes he can!" Emilie said adamantly. "If you listen real carefully, even you can understand him, Grandfather!"

Friederich's face turned a deep red as he walked away from Grandfather Meyer.

"I'm not going to be insulted by anyone, even if it is your Grandfather," he told her afterward. Emilie's aunts and uncles could understand Friederich after a few words had passed. Uncle Ernst told his siblings, "Just look at Friederich as he's speaking. If you can't actually hear the words, you can at least figure out from his lips what he's trying to say."

Uncle Otto invited the newlyweds to come visit him on his farm in Gerabronn. Friederich had never been to a farm and promised he'd like to do that sometime. Emilie was very pleased. Some of her best experiences had been on her grandparents' farm.

Friederich shut down his machine shop for one week so they could go on their honeymoon. He had arranged to go to a resort hotel in Wildbad in the Black Forest. He hadn't said a thing about it to Emilie, and needless to say, she was overjoyed. It was to become one of her favorite places.

Chapter X

The Early Years

Following their delightful week in the Black Forest, Emilie and Friederich moved into their "new apartment." It was over his workshop on Church Street. Since they had already had it completely renovated, they needed only to gather the rest of her things from her mother's house. Friederich's were already there. A week after they had settled in, Friederich suggested, "Emilie, why don't you ask one of your sisters to come and help you with the housework? You probably don't know this, but I promised your mother two things during our conversation over whether or not she would allow you to marry me: (1) I would hire you a maid for weekly house cleaning and washing and (2) I would buy you a piano so you could continue to play. She told me you had always been treated as a lady and didn't know how to do things like cleaning and washing."

"Is that right? I didn't know that! Why didn't you tell me this earlier?"

"I didn't want you to get upset with your mother. Besides, that's one of the reasons I married you. You're a real lady who has studied and has had certain skills and opportunities which I've never had. I think it's an excellent idea and I can well afford it."

"Oh thank you very much, Friederich!" She kissed him over and over. "You know, now that you've mentioned it, I've always wondered why I was never shown how to clean house and do the washing. Even during my year of practical training in Schussenreid, Frau Winter taught me how to cook, bake, and sew, but she never mentioned anything else about taking care of a house. My mother must have told her the same thing. I guess I'm just lucky, Friederich. I have such a good husband to look after me."

Friederich smiled. He was pleased she appreciated what he was doing for her. Emilie felt an even stronger love for him after that. How kind and considerate of him, she thought.

She went over to her mother's house that evening and told her what Friederich had said.

"So, he remembered our conversation before I gave him permission to marry you?"

"Yes, Mama. Now I know why Frau Winter never taught me anything about taking care of a house. You told her I was being brought up a lady who wouldn't need to learn these things. Is that right?"

"Yes, Emilie. Your father and I had great plans for all of you girls. We didn't want any of you to marry beneath your station. We wanted you to be well-educated, responsible young women who would marry men at least on your same social level, if not higher. We never thought that you, especially, would ever marry someone beneath our social class. But now you have. I'm glad your husband recognizes who you are and how lucky he is to have you for his wife."

"But I'm still your daughter, Mama. You and Papa have given me so much already. I'm very thankful to you for making possible what I've had. I wouldn't be the person I am today if it weren't for you and Papa, Mama."

She gave her mother a big hug and kiss. Her mother hugged her also. Emilie felt closer to her mother than ever before.

"Mama, I want to ask you what you would think of this idea of Friederich's. He suggested that since he promised you I'd have a maid, I should ask you about hiring one of my sisters to help me during the week for a day or two. He'd pay the going rate for house-cleaning help, if that would be okay with you."

"That's an excellent idea. That way your sister could earn some money and it would help me with our living expenses."

"Luise would be perfect."

"Yes, but she's going to your grandmother's. It'll have to be Lina."

"Well, okay, but I don't think she'll be too pleased with the job. You know how she feels about having had her confirmation on the same day as our wedding."

"She'll do it."

By Frau Bartholomae's decision, Lina became Emilie's first maid. Just as Emilie suspected, Lina was not happy with the job. She kept telling her, "I'm not a maid. I'm going to get an education like you did. Who wants to do someone else's dirty work?"

Actually, it worked out quite well. Since Emilie couldn't get her to scrub the floors alone each week, she offered to help. In this way, Lina didn't feel quite like her sister's maid. It also gave Emilie a chance to do some of the work herself. She didn't think it was all that hard, and once they got started, Lina worked just as hard as she did. Friederich paid her the fabulous sum of twenty Reichsmarks per week. That was more than any other maid was making in Vaihingen. While it didn't completely satisfy Lina, it did give her money to buy her own clothes and have some extra, which she saved. She was determined to go to school and finish her education.

One afternoon, when Emilie left to do some shopping, she told Lina which rooms to clean and dust. When Emilie came back, Lina was furious. She and Friederich had gotten into an argument about doing housework.

"She doesn't like to do your 'dirty work'!" Friederich said scornfully. "I told her if she feels that way about it, she should stay home and we'd find someone else who would be more than glad to do the job!"

Emilie could tell immediately from the tone of his voice, Friederich was very angry. Lina was flushed and almost shaking.

"I'm not going to do this work anymore!" she shouted.

"Now, now, Lina," Emilie said. "It can't be that bad."

"Your husband tried to spank me just because I said I'm not your maid and that I'm from a much better family than he is!"

Emilie could see Friederich getting even more upset. He probably would have struck her if she hadn't come between them.

"Friederich! She's just a young girl. Don't take it so seriously."

Friederich stopped, turned around and went storming back downstairs.

"Lina," Emilie scolded. "Don't ever say that to him again. He goes wild when you insult him about his family."

"Well, he had no right to try to spank me either!" she exclaimed indignantly. "I'm not some little girl. And I'm most certainly not a maid!"

Lina didn't want to come back, but her mother told her she must. Lina finally agreed, but only if Emilie was going to be there.

"I don't want to be left alone with him again," she told her mother.

Friederich didn't forgive her very easily. Whenever he came upstairs for a snack and she was there, he mocked, "Boy, some man is going to have a real woman when he gets you. You've got a pair of bosoms even bigger than your sister's!"

Lina blushed and made a face at Friederich. Emilie found it funny and laughed because Friederich seemed to enjoy the taunts. Lina was fifteen and did, indeed, have a very hefty bosom. She was also very stocky for her age. When Emilie talked with Frederick about her one evening after a pretty strong exchange between them, she suggested he lay off his taunts.

"It's just going to get worse if you keep teasing her. She'll say whatever comes into her mind, even if it's mean and cruel. She still has a lot of growing up to do."

During one of their exchanges, Lina blurted out, "If our father were still alive, he would never have approved of you as his son-in-law. You're just too dirty with oil and grease all over your hands every day!"

Emilie finally asked her mother, "As soon as Luise comes back from Gerabronn, could she take Lina's place in helping me? She and Friederich are like oil and water. They just can't get along with each other."

In July, Luise took over from Lina. Lina went to work for Frau Gertrude Hahn, the local minister's wife and a very good friend of Emilie's from the Froebel Frauen Seminar days. They had renewed their friendship when Gertrude's husband was transferred to the City Cathedral as an Assistant to the Dean. They saw each other regularly and often had afternoon tea together. Either Emilie invited her over, or she invited Emilie to the parsonage.

Toward the middle of July, Emilie noticed she had missed her periods for the past two months. When she met Gertrude at one of their weekly teas, this time at the parsonage, Gertrude asked, "Emilie, are you planning to have any children? Gottfried and I would like to, but he's always so indifferent to my wishes. I can't get pregnant without his help, now can I?"

"You've got lots of time for that, Gertrude. You just got married last year, didn't you?"

"Yes, and I'm still not pregnant! How is it with you? Does your husband respond to you when you're in the mood?"

"He sure does. Can you keep a secret?"

"You know I can. Remember that time when Hannah Vogel left the Seminar to visit her boyfriend who was back from France on a short pass? Did I tell anyone else about it? No! Even the Director didn't know she was missing even though she and I were living together. I can keep a secret. What is it?"

"I'm pregnant!" Emilie said, overjoyed.

"What? You just got married in April!"

"I know, but Friederich is as interested in having children as I am."

"He must be some man from what your sister told me. Did you know he made a pass at her when she was working for you?"

Emilie burst out laughing. "That's a good one, Gertrude. Lina was very rude to him and he was going to spank her, that's all it was. There was nothing more than that."

"Well, let's just ask her."

Emilie felt rather uncomfortable by this questioning of what Friederich had done. She wondered what Lina might have told her. Gertrude went to the top of the stairs and called down.

"Lina? Would you come upstairs for a minute?"

Lina came up the stairs and when she saw Emilie, she paled noticeably.

"Oh, I didn't know you were here, Emilie."

They shook hands and kissed each other on the cheek.

"Lina, tell your sister what you told me a couple of weeks ago about what her husband did to you?"

"She already knows. She was there just afterwards."

"Did you tell your sister about how he tried to put you over his knee and after that he stroked your breasts?"

Lina was clearly in distress. "I thought you would keep that a secret between us, Frau Hahn?"

"And didn't you tell me he put his hands under your dress while he was grabbing you to spank you?"

"Yes, but you weren't supposed to tell anyone! You promised me you wouldn't!"

"That's all right, Lina," Emilie said reassuringly. "Do you remember what I told you about what you were never to say to Friederich? She insulted Friederich deeply by saying his family was just a poor, uneducated bunch of working-class slobs. It doesn't surprise me at all he wanted to spank you, Lina. I've already told you that. I'm just sorry you've spread this story around by telling Frau Hahn."

"Emilie, she had to tell someone. You didn't take her seriously nor did your mother, evidently. You can't blame her for being upset with your husband even if she insulted him. People of our class don't do those sorts of things, no matter how angry we get, and you know it, Emilie!"

Emilie had had enough of this grilling. She drank her tea and before she left, she told Gertrude "I'm going to be busy for the next few weeks. I'll get in touch with you later."

"Please don't be angry with me, Emilie," Lina pleaded. "I didn't know she was going to tell you! I'm really sorry, Emilie, but I had to tell someone!"

Emilie was dismayed by what she heard. She couldn't quite believe it. I think Lina made up the story, she told herself. Friederich wouldn't do such a thing! She must have been exaggerating. She's probably still angry with us that our wedding was on the same day as her confirmation. She couldn't have told something like that to a worse person, she thought to herself. Gertrude was always one who liked to spread whatever gossip she could about another person, even if it wasn't really true.

Emilie decided not to say anything to Friederich. He'd only get upset all over again, she thought. Besides, Luise is working out very well. There's no need to stir up the past.

The summer went by quickly. Luise told Emilie about her new friend, Hermann Luipold, whom she had met at the swimming pool at the Enz. She had gone there with Lina one Sunday afternoon in early August, and he had swum over to them and introduced himself. She arranged to meet him again each week until it became too cold to swim anymore. Each time she took Lina with her. That was the only way her mother let her go anywhere. If she wanted to meet some of her friends, her sister had to go along.

"Why don't you invite him to come over here on Sunday afternoon, Luise? Then Mama wouldn't insist that Lina go along," Emilie suggested.

During most of that fall, Luise and Hermann met at the Malins' apartment. The romance between them blossomed. Friederich took a liking to young Hermann. He knew his father and uncles very well. They were local carpenters in Vaihingen and Hermann was also learning the trade. He had two more years of his apprenticeship to complete and then he would be a master carpenter. Luise finished Realschule and worked for the Malins almost full time. The further along Emilie was in her pregnancy, the more unsteady she felt. Friederich insisted Luise work for her full-time. She was more than willing to do so.

Just barely into the new year, Emilie's and Friederich's little son arrived. They named him Volkmar German Ulrich Malin. Friederich picked out the names. They were the names of friends of his from his army days, none of whom survived the war.

Emilie was in full accord with his choices. She would have preferred it if he had chosen to name him junior, but Friederich didn't want anyone else to have his name.

"That's not fair to the little boy. For the rest of his life, he'd be known only as junior. I'm very glad I wasn't named after my father. I wouldn't want to wish that on anyone," he said emphatically.

Volkmar was a very happy child. He slept a lot which made it easy for Emilie to take naps along with him. Whenever he wanted to suckle, she took him in her arms and held him. She was pleasantly surprised how delightful it was to have a little baby. Fortunately for Emilie, Luise was working for her full-time. Luise prepared all of their meals and did all of the washing and cleaning. Friederich gave her an extra ten

Reichsmarks a week after the baby arrived. Emilie felt she couldn't have gotten along without her.

One Sunday afternoon in March, after they had had dinner, Hermann came by, as usual, to talk with Luise. Frau Bartholomae hadn't seen the baby for two days and wanted to take the Malins by surprise. She paid them a visit and was shocked when she saw Hermann. Emilie saw that Luise was speechless, so she introduced him to her.

"He's a good friend of ours, Mama. He just stopped by to see how little Volkmar is doing."

Her mother seemed mollified for the moment, but she couldn't take her eyes off Hermann.

"Your name is Luipold?"

"Yes it is, Frau Bartholomae. My father has the carpentry shop on Loise Street."

"Oh," she said. She didn't say anything to him for the rest of the time she was there. Hermann excused himself after a few minutes and they said their goodbyes. Luise shook hands with him since this was the first time her mother had ever met him.

"I'll stop in again sometime."

"You're welcome any time, Hermann," Friederich said. "Best regards to your father."

Frau Bartholomae stayed the rest of the afternoon, even after Volkmar fell asleep. She asked about the young man who had been visiting.

"How did you get to know him?"

"Friederich had his father do some work for him in setting up his display window for the motorcycles and bicycles. Hermann is an apprentice at the present time, and he came along to help."

"But that's strange. Why would he come by and want to see how the baby is doing? He's only an apprentice. Besides, he was all dressed up," Frau Bartholomae continued.

Emilie could see Luise's face turning crimson. Luise excused herself. "I'll be right back. I have to get something to drink."

Frau Bartholomae looked at Emilie rather sternly and asked, "Is he trying to court Luise?"

"What would give you that idea, Mama?" she asked as innocently as possible.

"You know why I'm asking, Emilie! I wasn't born yesterday. If a young man comes to visit, it isn't to see a newborn but to see a girlfriend."

Luise came into the room just as her mother was making her statement.

"Yes, you're right, Mama," she admitted. "Hermann and I have been friends ever since last summer when Lina and I went swimming with him. I was afraid to have him come to our house. I thought you wouldn't approve. It's been great working here for Emilie. We could see each other on Sundays."

"Ah, so you're interested in a carpenter's son?" Frau Bartholomae almost spit it out. "Well, I've got news for you. I want you to stop seeing him before this gets too serious. Do you understand?" she said angrily. "If I ever find him here with you again, that's the last day you're working for your sister."

She got up and left almost without saying goodbye to Emilie and Friederich. He slowed her down when he said, "Frau Bartholomae, it may not be any of my business to tell you how to raise your daughters, but you're making a big mistake. By trying to prevent Luise from seeing Hermann, no matter what you do, it'll only make their determination to see each other that much stronger."

Frau Bartholomae was never one to let someone else have the last word: "We'll see about that."

Unfortunately, two weeks later, Hermann was once again visiting the Malins when Frau Bartholomae, Lina, and Mariele came by to see little Volkmar. This time she didn't shake hands with Hermann and looked very sharply at Luise. Hermann left immediately.

"That's it!" Frau Bartholomae said adamantly. "I warned you about him. If I ever caught you two together again, that would be your last day with Emilie. Pack your clothes. You're going home with us!"

"Now wait a minute," Friederich interposed. "She can stay here as long as she likes! What's Emilie going to do without her help?"

"That's your problem, Herr Malin. I have to look after the best interests of my daughter. That means she is not going to see Hermann Luipold again!"

"But Mama," Emilie pleaded. "Luise's been a real big help to us! I couldn't have gotten along without her since Volkmar was born. Don't be like that. Luise is almost eighteen. She knows what she wants!"

"That's just the problem! A teenager doesn't know what's best for her. I know that much better than she. She's not going to marry a carpenter's apprentice. And that's final. Let's go girls!"

Frau Bartholomae stormed out with Emilie's three younger sisters in tow.

"Friederich, what am I going to do now?" Emilie wailed. "I can't possibly do everything Luise did and take care of the baby too!"

"I'll talk with my mother. Maybe she'll be able to give you a hand once a week," Friederich said reassuringly. "Let's see how it goes."

Friederich talked with his mother and she came once a week to help clean. Emilie noticed she wasn't particularly happy about doing so. Frau Malin kept telling her how to clean and what type of soap to use. She even told her how to dust. Emilie hated dusting most of all. Whenever Volke cried, she went into his room and got him. She'd change his diaper and then let him suckle. Frau Malin didn't think she needed to give him the breast every time he cried.

"Emilie"—she started calling her that only since the wedding—"the baby isn't going to go hungry if he cries a little. It's good for his lungs to cry once in a while. You're spoiling him, that's what you're doing. I've had eight children, and not one of those who is still living ever died of hunger. And I had all of my other housework to do at the same time," she scolded. "What is it with you 'ladies'? Can't you do a little work now and then?"

After a whole day of such criticism, Emilie was exhausted. She wanted to remind her mother-in-law if it hadn't been for her spinster sister's help, she wouldn't have been able to care for all of her children as well as she did. But Emilie was afraid of her. She was such a domineering old woman. Emilie unloaded herself on Friederich after one of these "weekly helping sessions" from his mother.

"Friederich, I can't take anymore of your 'mother's help'! All she does is tell me how to clean, wash, cook, and care for little Volke. I'd rather be alone than have to put up with her every week. I want to run my own household. If I make a mistake, it'll be my own fault. I don't need to be reminded what to do, when, and how by my 'help'! Either I have a maid that I can train and depend on, or I'm going to have to have someone who can do the cooking for us. I can't do everything myself."

"Why don't you let the cleaning go? Once a month would be enough. My mother may talk a lot about cleaning, but if it weren't for my aunt, she wouldn't be cleaning the house more than twice a year!" Friederich reminded her. "The main thing for you to do is take care of the baby. If the rest of the work doesn't get done, it doesn't get done."

"But I like living in a clean house, Friederich. It's much healthier for our baby too if the floors are clean. I don't want him crawling around on a dirty floor!"

"Tell you what, Emilie. Why don't you go to the Black Forest for a couple of weeks and take some time off from your chores around here. By the time you come back, maybe I'll have found someone to help you. My mother can help me in the shop like she used to do. Besides, Karl is always around too."

"Oh, thank you, Friederich!" She gave him a long and passionate kiss.

"Wildbad would be a great place for us to go!"

Emilie left with the baby the very next Monday. They arrived in Wildbad that same afternoon. She found a nice pension at the base of the mountain where a cable car took people to the top. It was a cool, quiet little apartment with her own bath and a common eating area. The apartment, with full pension, was only forty-five Reichsmarks a week. Friederich had given her several hundred to take with her so she felt she could well afford it. She also brought the baby carriage. Volke slept in it day and night. When Emilie took him for long walks on the mountain paths, he slept. It was really an idyllic time for them. Emilie wrote Friederich every day. She told him everything they did, almost like in a diary. He also wrote back to her as often as he could. He suggested she stay for the rest of the month since he still hadn't found anyone to help her. He did write that his aunt had come and cleaned the house. He paid her ten Reichsmarks for her efforts, and his aunt seemed pleased.

During Emilie's time in Wildbad with the baby, Friederich had a visitor. Gertrude Hahn hadn't heard from Emilie for some time and so decided to pay her a visit. In fact, the two women hadn't seen each other since the confrontation over Friederich's treatment of Lina. Gertrude must have felt it was time to try to make amends. In thinking over what had happened, she thought perhaps she shouldn't have been so hard on her friend. Besides, it was a good excuse to see how the baby was doing.

Friederich had had a hard morning. He had to make a special part for the compressor at the fertilizer plant and it proved more difficult than he expected. He had to go back and forth from the workshop to the plant several times until he made the part fit. He told his mother after coming back the third time, "I'm going upstairs to get something to eat and rest a while. I don't want to be disturbed until I come back down."

"Okay. I'll not bother you. If someone wants to see you, I'll tell them to come back late this afternoon."

Instead of coming to the front entrance leading into the show room, Gertrude rang the bell and proceeded up the back stairs. She knocked on the door leading into the apartment. Friederich came to the door and asked, "Who are you?"

"I'm a good friend of Emilie Malin. Are you Herr Malin?"

"Yes. But she's not here. She's in Wildbad with the baby."

Gertrude Hahn was pleased to meet Friederich. "I'm Gertrude Hahn. I'm the wife of the Assistant Minister of the Cathedral. I've wanted to talk with you for sometime. Do you mind if I come in?"

"I'm just getting myself something to eat and drink. Come in."

He went ahead and made himself a sandwich.

"Would you like something to eat?"

"No thank you, Herr Malin. I've already eaten. Since you're having a glass of wine, I'll take one too."

Friederich poured a glass of wine for Gertrude and one for himself.

"Have a seat. Now what was it you wanted to talk to me about?."

"You may not know, Herr Malin, but your wife's younger sister, Lina, works for me in the parsonage. She told me what you tried to do to her. Herr Malin, she's just a little girl. How could you want to do that to her?"

His face reddened. "What business in that of yours? I can do whatever I want in my own house! Who gave you the authority to quiz me about my behavior?"

"I didn't mean to get you angry, Herr Malin. But why don't you pick on someone who's older? Why bother with little girls?" she asked coyly.

As she did so, she moved closer to him so that her knee rubbed against his leg. She continued to taunt him.

"Is that what someone from your class usually does? Pick on little girls?"

As she spoke, she moved closer to him. Her skirt was already much shorter than most minister's wives wore. Since she had finished her glass, he filled it again.

"You really shouldn't bother with little girls, Herr Malin, when there are plenty of grown women around."

Friederich finished his glass and looked at her for sometime. She's an attractive woman, he thought. She has very nice legs and an ample bosom.

"I can do what I want in my own house."

"Yes, but not with little girls. They'll only get you into trouble. That's why I wanted to talk to you."

She crossed her legs and her dress went even higher up her thighs. Friederich drank slowly and watched what she was doing. He began to smile as she lifted her legs even higher.

"Don't you think older women are attractive too, Herr Malin?" she asked seductively.

"They have possibilities," he answered as put his hand on her thigh. She moved closer to him. Her legs were right against his. His hand moved up under her dress. She smiled at him and said, "Lina is just a little girl!"

She slowly undressed with Friederich's help. She drew him closer to her as she moved from the chair to the couch. He smiled as he thought of what he was doing. Here was a complete stranger whom he had never met before who was interested in having sex with him. Well, he thought to himself, at least I'll enjoy it since she's so willing.

He put his head between her breasts and rubbed his mustache over her nipples.

"Oh, that feels so good, Herr Malin."

As they lay on the couch in their mutual enjoyment, she whispered, "Now doesn't this feel a lot better than with a little girl?"

"So you're one of my wife's best friends and the wife of the Minister too?"

"Unfortunately. My husband's a complete dud when it comes to sex. He has no warmth or passion at all. You may not come from the upper class, Herr Malin, but you certainly know how to give a woman satisfaction."

After the sex was over, she got up, dressed, combed her hair, and said once more, "You may not come from the right class, but you certainly know how to do it, Herr Malin. Your wife's a very lucky woman. If you won't tell anyone, I won't either. This will just be a secret between you and me."

Friederich nodded his head. They shook hands and she left the same way she came. Friederich felt more rested than he had since Emilie had gone to the Black Forest.

It was just two days short of completing a month at the Wildbad Pension when Emilie and the baby returned to Vaihingen. Friederich still hadn't found anyone.

"Why don't I talk to Mama about having Mariele come and work a few days a week for us? After all, she's a big girl for her age, and she's almost twelve. She could at least look after Volkmar for me while I go shopping or do some of the cleaning around the house."

"It's too bad we couldn't have kept Luise. Where is she now?"

"She's at my grandparents' place in Gerabronn. Grandmother is probably having her do all kinds of jobs not only in the house, but in her garden. Luise really didn't want to go there. In fact, none of my sisters have wanted to go there. Grandmother is a very hard taskmaster. She wants things done perfectly and only to her satisfaction. Even grandfather doesn't have much influence over her. Once when I was there during the war, Grandfather had asked for seconds on the soup. Grandmother said, 'No Gustav. It's got to last for this evening too!' He didn't say anymore. He just left after dinner and went to the restaurant in town and got himself a sandwich. Grandmother never knew the difference!" She laughed as she related the story.

"She must be a real battle axe," Friederich commented. "I wouldn't have let her get away with that kind of treatment."

"One has to make what adjustments are necessary, Friederich, to get along in life. I've never heard Grandfather complain. He just goes ahead and does what he feels he has to do and doesn't tell her about it."

"Well, I still think Mariele is a little too young to be a baby-sitter. But go ahead and ask your mother."

The next morning after breakfast, Emilie wrapped Volkmar in a blanket and put him in his carriage and went to visit her mother and Mariele. She knew she had to go in the morning because her mother worked at the Savings Bank in the afternoon. She rang the doorbell and her mother opened an upstairs window to look out. When she saw them, she said, "I'll be right down to let you in."

Both Frau Bartholomae and Mariele came down the stairs and opened the front door. They gave each other hugs and kisses. Mariele wanted to carry Volke up the stairs.

"Can I carry him, Emilie?"

"If you're real careful and don't let him drop," her mother said, "you can carry him upstairs."

Emilie wasn't sure Mariele was strong enough to carry him the entire length of the stairs.

"You can take him out of the baby carriage, Mariele, and when we're at the stairs, I'll carry him up, and then you can hold him again, all right?" Emilie suggested.

"All right, I think I can carry him very well, but I'll wait until we get upstairs."

When they got to the top of the stairs, Emilie gave him to her and she carried him around quite easily.

"I actually think she's strong enough to carry Volke, Mama," Emilie said. "What would you think if I wanted her to help me during the day with Volkmar and to do a little housework now and then? Would that be all right with you, Mama?"

"I'm not sure she's old enough to do that, Emilie. It would be nice if she could go over to your house in the afternoons after school while I'm working. I'd feel much better about having her with you than leaving her home alone with Grandmother. She doesn't seem to like to stay with her."

"Well, why don't we try it, Mama? If she likes being with us, and if she's able to do some work, it would be a big help for me. Let me ask Mariele what she would think of the idea."

"Mariele?" Frau Bartholomae called. "Could you come here a minute? You can bring little Volke with you."

"Yes, Mama," Mariele called out from the bedroom. "I'm coming."

She carried Volkmar on her shoulder just like an adult. Emilie was pleased how she was handling him.

"Mariele, what would you think of the idea of going over to Emilie's house each afternoon after school and helping her with Volke?"

"Oh, could I, Mama? I'd love to do that! It's so lonely here with Grandmother. I just love little Volkmar. He smiles at me all the time."

"You might have to do some work," her mother cautioned. "It wouldn't just be helping to take care of your little nephew. You might have to dust or sweep the floor or the staircase occasionally too."

"I can do that, Mama. I'm about the biggest girl in my class and even some of the boys aren't as strong as I am," she said proudly.

"Well, then, on Monday, you'll be going over to Emilie's after school and stay until I get home from the bank. I'll be home at six o'clock. Emilie will tell you when it's time to come home, all right?"

"Oh, I'm so glad! Now I won't be so lonely anymore. Grandmother is a nice old lady but she doesn't do anything I like to do. All she does is read and knit all day long. Then in the late afternoon, she cooks dinner. I hardly know she's there," Mariele complained. "I'd much rather spend time watching little Volke grow. He's so cute."

Mariele came to the Malin house each afternoon for almost the year Frau Bartholomae worked. When Volkmar was just a little over a year old, Mariele was carrying him across the living room when she tripped on the rug. She and the baby went sprawling across the floor. Volke cried and cried just as Friederich came in the door. As Mariele was about to pick him up, Friederich whacked her across the bottom so hard she flew against the wall and cried even louder than Volkmar.

"So that's the last time you're going to take care of the baby!" Friederich told her.

"But it was an accident, Friederich," Emilie said. "I don't think he got hurt."

"No!" Friederich raged. "That's the last time I want to see her here as a baby-sitter. Is that understood? Babies aren't dolls to play with!"

"Yes," Emilie said sadly. "Mariele, I guess you'd better go home to Grandmother now. Mama will be home pretty soon."

Mariele continued to sob. As Emilie took her to the door, she whispered, "You can come again, Mariele, when Friederich isn't here, or when you come with Mama."

"But I like coming here," Mariele sobbed. "I don't want to have to stay home with Grandmother. There's nothing to do at home!"

x x x

Luise spent all spring and summer at her Grandparents in Gerabronn. She wrote Hermann practically every day. It had been hard at first to do so. Her mother had asked Grandmother Meyer not to let Luise receive any letters from Hermann since she was determined to break up their romance. If it hadn't been for her Uncle Otto Meyer, she would not have received any letters.

"When I first came to the farm, Grandmother told me, 'I don't want you writing any letters to that young man in Vaihingen. Is that understood?'" she related the story to Emilie.

"Why not, Grandmother?" Luise had protested.

"Because I promised your mother I wouldn't let it happen."

"I don't think that's fair," Luise told her. "What if he writes to me? What am I supposed to do?"

"Don't you worry. I'll see to it you don't get any letters," Grandmother told her in no uncertain terms. "Besides, you'll have so much to do you won't even feel like writing to him. I'll teach you how to sew. Then one of these days, you can marry a tailor and together you can set up your own business."

Luise ran from the house into the barn and cried in the haymow. It was there that Uncle Otto found her.

"What are you crying about?" he asked solicitously.

"Grandmother won't let me write any letters to my friend in Vaihingen!" she cried. "And if he writes, she told me she's not going to give me his letters."

Uncle Otto thought it over for a while, then said, "Tell you what we can do, Luise. You write your letters to him and give them to me in an envelope, and I'll mail them from the post office. I have a post box there anyway for the farm. You can have him send his letters to you, in care of me, to my box number. When the letters arrive, I'll give them to you and Grandmother won't even know you're getting any letters."

"I was overjoyed and wrote to Hermann as faithfully as he wrote me. Even Grandmother was amazed how well I seemed to take the absence of letters from Vaihingen," Luise told Emilie. "'You must be much more disciplined than I ever gave you credit for,' Grandmother told me.

"I have to give her credit, though. I learned how to sew from Grandmother. I had already learned how to cook, wash, and clean from my previous trips to Gerabronn."

Indeed, by the time Luise came home that fall, she was well prepared to take care of an entire household. She came to see Emilie shortly after she arrived.

"Could I work for you again, Emilie?"

Emilie was overjoyed. "As far as I'm concerned, Luise, you can start right now. But let me talk to Friederich first. By the way, has Mama said anything about Hermann to you?"

"Yes. She doesn't want me to see him anymore. She doesn't know we've been corresponding with each other ever since I left for Gerabronn. That's why I'd like to work for you again. We could take up where we left off last spring, if it's all right with you."

"That would be fine with me, and I'm sure it would be okay with Friederich."

"Mama said I had to look for a job if I wanted to stay in Vaihingen. That's why I came over to see you first. I'd better be going now. I'll stop by tomorrow and find out what Friederich thinks of the idea."

Emilie couldn't wait until Friederich came upstairs that evening. While Volke was taking his afternoon nap, she had gone down to the workshop to talk with him. Frau Malin was the only one in the showroom.

"Good afternoon, Frau Malin. Is Friederich here?"

"No, he isn't. Incidentally, isn't it about time you stopped calling me Frau Malin? I am your mother-in-law and I want you to call me what Friederich calls me; Mutter!"

She paused and looked at Emilie. "Why are you down here? Shouldn't you be upstairs taking care of your little baby?"

"Oh yes, I am. He's sleeping just now so I thought I could slip downstairs for a few minutes before he wakes up."

"Well, unless a lady has a maid, she should never leave her baby alone!" she scolded.

"You're right," Emilie agreed. She still couldn't bring herself to call her mutter.

"Would you tell Friederich I came down to see him when he comes back?"

"I probably won't see him again today. He told me I should lock up. He had to go to Enzweihingen again to fix the conveyor belt at the lime factory."

Emilie went back upstairs. She was certain Friederich wouldn't mind. But she had to talk with him first before making such a decision. He usually agreed with what she proposed, but he didn't like it at all if she didn't talk with him before making any decisions herself.

It was late when Friederich came back. Emilie had dinner all ready for him. She just had to heat it up again. As they ate together, she told him about Luise's visit that afternoon.

"What would you think about having her work for us? She really doesn't want to work for anyone else. If she works for us, she can stay in Vaihingen. She would be a big help in the house, and I could help you in the business downstairs. You wouldn't have to have your mother help you so much. I talked with her this afternoon and she seemed quite unhappy in the office. She took me to task for even coming down to see you."

"That sounds like a good idea. It would give her a chance to see Hermann more often."

"Thank you, Friederich. She'll be a big help to us."

The next morning Emilie went over to her mother's to see Luise. Her mother was getting ready to go to work. Emilie waited until she was gone to tell Luise the good news. Volke was toddling all over the house, with Emilie and Grandmother close behind to see he didn't break anything. Her mother gave them a hug and a kiss before she left. "You've got a real nice boy, Emilie. I often think of what your brother might have been if he had lived. Take good care of him."

As soon as her mother left, Emilie said, "Luise, guess what Friederich said about coming to work for us."

"What?"

"He said that sounds like a good idea. Isn't that wonderful? You can stay right here in Vaihingen, and you'll get a chance to see Hermann regularly too. It's too bad Mama doesn't like him. He's really a nice guy. Friederich likes him too."

"When do you want me to start?"

"You can start today, as far as I'm concerned. But it would probably be better if Friederich talks to his mother first and lets her know it won't be necessary for her to come to the store anymore. Let's say next Monday. That should be plenty of time."

"All right, I'll be there bright and early. What time does Friederich open his shop?"

"He opens at 7 a. m."

"That's fine. I'll be there at a quarter to seven each morning. I'll have to come home in the evening, I'm sure. Mama wouldn't want me to stay overnight at your place," Luise said sadly.

"I don't see why not. Surely on weekends and holidays Mama shouldn't object. I'll talk to her about it."

Each day Luise came to work, caring mostly for Volkmar while Emilie went downstairs to help Friederich in the store. On weekends, Hermann came to their house to see Luise. The four adults did a lot together. Taking walks along the Enz; going out for Sunday dinner; and doing lots of talking. Friederich felt he had struck a responding interest in Hermann about his plans to travel abroad. Ever since Emilie knew Friederich, he had talked about going abroad. She didn't take this interest too seriously because she knew so long as his family and her own were in Germany, it wasn't likely to happen. Or so she thought.

Hermann and Luise talked more and more about getting married. They knew her mother was opposed, but if they should decide to go abroad, what could she do about it? Friederich did lots of reading about different countries. He came across an article about Brazil that really intrigued him. He told Hermann, "Brazil has all kinds of riches, if you're willing to look for them. There's even a province known as Diamante, where one can find diamonds in the mountains. That might be just the place to go, Hermann, for us to strike it rich."

"If I can take Luise along, I'll go. But first, we'll have to get married."

Emilie didn't think Hermann was serious. Knowing how her mother felt, she was sure it might be some years before that would take place. After all, Luise was only eighteen! But Hermann persisted. He talked to Frau Bartholomae about it on three different occasions. Each time she said, "No, she's too young to get married."

The last time he talked with her, she finally said, "If she wants to get married after she's nineteen, I might consider it. But not before."

In the meantime, Friederich had become more and more convinced Brazil was the place to go. He wanted Emilie to go too, but she didn't want to go. Her whole family was in Germany. She talked with him about it over and over again. When she saw how determined he was, she decided it was time to have another baby. Maybe then he would listen to her. She really thought if she were pregnant, she would certainly not be asked to go, and possibly, he might reconsider and decide not to go either.

"Why do you want to leave?" she kept asking him. "Your business is here. Your family is mostly still here. We have a very comfortable life, don't we, Friederich?"

She pleaded with him. But to no avail. Friederich was afraid economic conditions in Germany were likely to worsen at some point. The French had already occupied the Ruhr, Germany's industrial heartland. The enormous debt which the Germans were asked to pay for the war made their future very uncertain. Rumors were afloat that the Germans would have to pay billions of Reichsmarks for the next fifty years in order to pay off the debt to the Allies for having lost the war. The economic anxiety, on top of what millions of soldiers such as Friederich had suffered during the war, created an interest in millions of Germans to leave Germany and find their fortunes elsewhere. Unfortunately, Friederich was one of those for whom any future success in becoming wealthy was much stronger than his ties to his country and extended family. If it meant going abroad, then that was where he wanted to go. That's really why he had read so much about Brazil and its reputed natural wealth and resources. Emilie didn't feel she ever wanted to leave Germany. This was her home. She wanted to stay right here where she knew everyone and everyone knew her and her family.

Emilie and Friederich were both very pleased with Volkmar. He was starting to talk, and it was interesting hearing him put sentences together. When Emilie suggested it might be nice to have another little baby, Friederich agreed. She hoped if she were pregnant, he wouldn't ask her to go with him. She thought, surely he would want to go by himself and see if he liked it. He would only then come back and sell the business before they would have to move. She wanted to do whatever she could to postpone such a decision.

On a hot July afternoon, as Volke was sleeping, Friederich came upstairs and had something to drink. Emilie sat down next to him and joined him with some lemonade. He put his hand under her dress and began stroking her thighs. Whenever he did that it always aroused her. As he moved his hand from one thigh to the next, he said, "Emilie, you have really beautiful legs. Your thighs are as white as snow. I love to get between them."

"You don't know what you do to me! Can we go to bed?"

"Of course. Let me help you take your clothes off."

Before she even had time to take off her shoes, he had already taken off his pants and underpants. He kissed her over and over again as they stroked each other in bed. When each one was fully aroused in their mutual enjoyment, they had an orgasm simultaneously. It was a wonderfully satisfying feeling. He was very tender as he kissed her. He told her, "That was about as good as it'll ever get, Emilie. You certainly know how to satisfy me perfectly!"

"Oh, Friederich. Let's do it again tonight. I could do it over and over again like that."

"If you're up to it, why not?"

She could hardly wait. They did it almost every night for the month of July.

On Luise's nineteenth birthday, Hermann asked Frau Bartholomae again if he could marry her.

Try as she did, she could not bring Luise to consider marrying anyone else. At the festivals, when she accompanied her, she suggested, "Why don't you consider someone like Karl Rapp to marry? He's from a very good family, and he's educated. He'd make a very good husband for you."

Each time Luise said, "I love Hermann. I don't like anyone else! The more you try to push me toward someone else, Mama, the more determined I am to marry Hermann."

Frau Bartholomae tried her best and consulted her parents, brothers, and sisters about what she should do. Her father was all in favor of Hermann.

"He's an honest young man and has a good trade. What more do you want him to have?"

"I want someone who is an educated man. I don't think my daughters should marry beneath them. It's bad enough that my oldest married one of these 'self-made men.'"

Grandmother Meyer thought Hermann wasn't the right kind of a man. "She should marry a tailor. Since Luise now knows how to sew, a tailor for a husband would be just right for her. They could go into business together."

When she asked her brothers and sisters what they thought, they asked her, "How is Emilie getting along? Isn't her husband a tradesman too? Isn't she happy she made the decision to marry him? He's providing for her probably better than a pastor could have who is just starting out. Doesn't she have a maid helping her?"

Frau Bartholomae thought about Hermann's request long and hard. She knew she couldn't prevent them from getting married. "All right, Hermann, let's ask her what she wants to do."

Frau Bartholomae called downstairs. "Luise, come upstairs. I want to ask you a question."

Luise came up three stairs at a time. "Yes, Mama?"

"Do you still want to marry Hermann?"

"Oh yes, Mama! Very much!"

"Then you better set the date. I'm not going to stand in your way. You understand, of course, it can't be a very big wedding. I can't afford one like I had for Emilie. I've lost a lot of money over these past few years and I can't spend very much anymore."

"Frau Bartholomae," Hermann said, "I want to marry your daughter because I love her, not because of her money."

Luise and Hermann arranged for the wedding to take place three weeks later in the same church where Friederich and Emilie got married. It was a very simple ceremony and only the immediate families were invited. Frau Bartholomae didn't invite her parents because they would have had to pay for the trip themselves. Grandmother had written her, "If you can't afford to pay for our travel, then we can't come. We can't even afford to take our annual vacations in the Black Forest anymore."

None of the aunts or uncles was invited. Frau Bartholomae had only to pay for her mother-in-law, Luise, Hermann, Lina, and Mariele, besides herself. Hermann paid for his parents, aunts, and uncles who lived in Vaihingen. The more distant relatives on the Luipold side were also not invited. Friederich paid for his family's meals at the reception. He wanted to invite his mother and aunt to the wedding. Frau Bartholomae said no one outside of the immediate families would be invited. When Friederich protested, she told him, "If you want to invite anyone else to the wedding, that's your business! But it'll also have to be at your expense!"

After the wedding reception, Luise and Hermann were expected to return to their respective homes, since they had no apartment for themselves. Emilie and Friederich arranged for them to spend their wedding night in the attic of their apartment. When Emilie told Friederich they had no place to go to live together, he suggested, "Why don't you have Luise clean out the attic and we'll get some furniture and a bed up there for them to use. We don't use the attic for anything anyway."

Emilie was overjoyed for Luise and Hermann. At the reception she told them, "Whenever you want to leave, here's the key to our apartment. Can you find the little room you cleaned for me last week, Luise? It's been really transformed."

"Oh, Emilie! Thank you very much! I wondered what we were going to do. Hermann thought we should go to our own homes until we could rent a room somewhere. He hadn't had any luck yet in finding a place."

x   x   x

Emilie was pregnant with her second child by the time Friederich and Hermann arranged to go to Brazil shortly after Christmas in 1922. Hermann borrowed money from one of his aunts, and Friederich co-signed the note for him, empowering him to administer the funds during their stay in Brazil. He also was to see to it that his brother-in-law paid back the loan. Since Friederich and Hermann had been discussing this trip for over a year, they were eager to go. Hermann wanted Luise to go along. Friederich didn't think this was a good idea.

"Why doesn't she stay here with Emilie? When we find our diamonds, we can either come back and get them or send for them."

"No, I want her to come with me. I didn't marry her to leave her here. Either she goes with us, or I'm not going!"

Friederich realized if he wanted company on this venture, then Luise had to go along. He had already made arrangements to rent the business to Paul Krause as of the first of the year. He couldn't very well back out of the agreement. It was to run for one year, from January 1, 1923, to December 31, 1923. The arrangement paid him a handsome rent and more than enough for the family to live quite comfortably for the year. Emilie bid Friederich, Luise, and Hermann a very tearful goodbye at the Vaihingen train station. It was a difficult goodbye for all of them.

"How long will it be before I see you again?"

"It'll be at least a year," Friederich answered. "If we find diamonds, it may be sooner. Goodbye, my sweetheart. Take good care of Volke, and I hope all goes well with the new baby. I love you, Emilie. I'm going to miss our 'special times together'!"

"Friederich, it's almost more than I can bear. You'll be gone and I'll have the baby alone. Please come home as soon as possible! I'm going to miss you terribly," she sobbed.

The three of them were going to Hamburg to catch a freighter for Rio de Janiero. No one knew for sure if and when they would ever see each other again. Hermann's parents weren't at all pleased with his decision to go with Friederich. There was more than enough work to do right here in Vaihingen. Frau Bartholomae couldn't understand how any man could even think of taking his new bride into the jungles of Brazil. She shook her head in dismay.

"See, if I had just continued to say no, you wouldn't be going off into this wilderness, Luise!" Frau Bartholomae told her daughter.

Fortunately for Emilie, she had little Volke to take care of and another on the way. She had already made arrangements with her mother for Mariele to come over each day and stay with her to help take care of him. Since Friederich wasn't there, Mariele felt very much at home in their apartment. It was also a relief to Frau Bartholomae that Mariele had a place to go after school, besides coming home. She wasn't getting along very well with her Grandmother.

Emilie wrote to Friederich every day and told him everything they were doing. She didn't mention that Mariele was working for her. No need to anger him, she thought. Friederich also wrote almost daily, for which Emilie was very thankful. The trip over had been a rough one. The waves were twenty to thirty feet high, and the freighter rolled continuously from the North Sea practically to just outside Rio's harbor. He didn't get seasick, but came close to it a few times. Luise and Hermann endured the trip very well.

Upon reaching Rio de Janiero, Friederich, Hermann, and Luise wanted to book train tickets for Diamantina only to find one daily train going from Rio to Juiz de Fora. From there, a train went from Juiz de Fora to Belo Horizonte once a week and to Diamantina once every two weeks. They had decided, even before leaving Germany, this was to be their ultimate destination. Not only did the name indicate that diamonds were in the area, they told each other, but in these highlands the temperatures were likely to be more moderate than in the lowlands. From what Friederich had read, the Serra Do Espinhaqo mountains were rich in all sorts of minerals and precious stones.

"Hermann, this is where we should find our riches," Friederich assured him.

From Friederich's letters, Emilie was very glad not to have gone along. The hotels in Rio were far too expensive to stay in for a long time, and the hotels up-country were non-existent. They had to resort to renting rooms from Europeans who had settled there, and even these rooms were sometimes very primitive. She couldn't imagine herself staying there with a toddler. Friederich and Hermann bought a couple of donkeys in Diamantina and literally struck out into the bush. Luise stayed in Diamantina and worked for a German family. Friederich and Hermann prospected in the mountains and along the streams. After four months, Hermann had had enough. They had not found much by way of diamonds. A few precious stones, but not the outcropping of diamonds they had expected to find along the creek beds.

"Friederich, I'm going back to Diamantina and find a job. I can't take any more of this futile digging!"

"What?" Friederich asked in amazement. "You can't just walk out on me! We're in this together!"

"This digging in the creeks is ludicrous! All we've found are a few semi-precious stones! We'll never get rich this way! I'm leaving."

"You're staying right here! You're not going anywhere, Hermann." Friederich unholstered his revolver.

"So long as I have this gun, you're going to stay here until I say we leave, is that clear?"

Hermann laughed. "I thought you might try something like this. If you look in your chamber, you won't find any bullets. I've already unloaded your pistol. I'm going, Friederich, and don't try to stop me."

There was nothing Friederich could do. Hermann was much bigger and stronger than he. He couldn't force him to stay without the pistol. He watched as Hermann took one of the donkeys and struck off for Diamantina. Friederich was alone now. He had enough food and supplies for at least two more months. I'll show him, Friederich said to himself. I won't leave until I've found diamonds! They had already spent four months prospecting, with little to show for their efforts. Friederich thought, Hermann just misses his wife. He'll come back after he's been with her for a while, he thought.

Hermann returned to the family where Luise was working.

"Hello, sweetheart!" he yelled as he saw her through the fence in the garden of the family where she was working.

"Hermann! How wonderful that you came back. I've missed you terribly!"

Luise wept as he caught her up in his arms and kissed her.

"You can't imagine how I've missed you, sweetheart. It's been four long months, and I haven't thought of anything else except you and what we're going to do when we see each other again."

"Oh Hermann, I'm so glad you're back! You're not going back into the jungle again, are you?"

"No way! I'm going to stay here with you and get a job."

"Where's Friederich? Didn't he come back with you?"

"No! That son of a bitch tried to kill me! If I hadn't unloaded his pistol, I'm sure he would have used it to keep me there with him."

"What? He pulled a gun on you? I'm glad you've left him! I feel sorry for Emilie. Do you think he'll ever return from the jungle?"

"I don't know, Luise. You have to be on guard all the time out there. It's not only wild animals you know are watching your every move, but there are all kinds of men out there who would just as soon kill you for your possessions as to talk with you. It's going to be rough on him, but he's well armed."

"I'm not going to write Emilie and tell her what happened between you two. She's got enough to worry about with one little boy and another baby on the way. It would only upset her no end, and there's absolutely nothing she can do about it," Luise said.

"That's a good idea. You probably shouldn't even write your mother about it either. Just tell her what you're doing and that you hear from us occasionally. Then she won't pass on any needless worry to Emilie."

Hermann got a job with a German construction firm setting up mines in and around Diamantina. He and Luise found two rooms to rent in a house next-door to where she worked. Hermann wanted to earn enough money so they could return to Germany as soon as possible.

Friederich's letters became more and more infrequent after Hermann left. He kept moving from one stream to another, trying to find the best place to set up camp.

He wrote, "I spend most of my time digging in and near the streams. I've found several rubies and some other precious stones, but no really large diamonds yet. If I don't write as often as before, it's because I'm spending my time digging. I'd really like to be able to return to Germany with as many precious stones as I can. The donkey is the only company I have. Hermann took the other one when he left. I kept most of the provisions since I told him I needed them to stay here in the jungle. If he walked fast, he could return to Diamantina in three days."

Emilie couldn't imagine what it must be like to live under these conditions. The temperatures were cool at night, Friederich wrote, but during the day, they rose to the high eighties and low nineties even in the mountains! He had a tent for protection against the rain and mosquitoes, but there were snakes and all kinds of insects and wild animals with which to contend.

Emilie continued to write Friederich every day. When no mail came from him, she wrote him twice a day. She had so much to tell him about Volkmar and what he was doing. He was already starting to talk and made complete sentences even at two years of age. "I take him to Mother's garden on the edge of town each day. He likes to look up into the apple and cherry trees. Volkmar would say, 'They are very big, Mama. They touch the sky!' It's such a joy to have a nice little boy like him, Friederich."

If there was snow on the ground, Mariele took along a sled. She sat on it and held Volke on her lap as they raced down the hill under the fruit trees. He loved the rides. He'd say, "Let's do it again," over and over until Mariele finally said, "Volkmar, we've done it enough. Your mother doesn't want us to get all wet."

"On the way home, we stopped at Mother's house so I could play piano," Emilie wrote. "The more I play, Friederich, the more certain I am we should have a piano too."

"As soon as Friederich comes back," she told Mariele, "I'm going to ask him for a piano. I love to play, and if I don't practice every day, I'm afraid I'll forget how."

By the end of February, Emilie was very large and had difficulty walking around. She felt as though she would lose her balance. She left Mariele in charge of Volkmar during the afternoons while she took a nap. Friederich's mother came to visit them every other day since Emilie was unable to walk to her house. She wasn't a very sympathetic woman. She couldn't understand why Emilie wasn't out and about more.

"I had eight children and I couldn't afford anyone to do my housework. I also had to take care of my chickens and garden," she told Emilie at practically every visit.

When Emilie told her how much she missed Friederich, her mother-in-law said, "My husband went to America on three different occasions and I never knew whether or not he was ever coming back. He hardly ever wrote. He told me I shouldn't expect to hear from him until he stood in the doorway. And we weren't rich. He didn't leave me any money for the family. He just said, "I'm going," and left. The only times he did write were to my father, asking him to send him some money."

"That must have been very hard on you, Mother."

"I couldn't do anything about it. I had to take care of the children. There were no afternoon naps for me."

Emilie didn't look forward to these visits from her mother-in-law. She always criticized her for something. Either she was not active enough, or she should stop feeling sorry for herself.

"You should walk at least two kilometers a day, right up until you give birth. If you feel a little woozy, just take a walking stick with you to steady yourself," she admonished.

Fortunately for Emilie, her friend, Gertrude Hahn, came to visit regularly. Her son was just three months younger than Volkmar. Both women had much in common: they were both from prominent families in their respective hometowns, they both had gone through the Latein Schule pre-university program, they both were students at the Froebel Frauen Seminar, and for some unique reason that Emilie never knew, their two sons looked remarkably alike, even though Gertrude's was three months younger than Volkmar. Gertrude was always interested in hearing about what Friederich was doing and what he wrote about Brazil. Emilie was pleased she was so interested in what he was doing. Gertrude asked all kinds of questions about him and seemed genuinely interested in what news Emilie had of him. They also compared notes about their two boys. They were so similar not only in looks but in their ability to talk at such an early age. They both liked to have stories told to them. In contrast to Emilie's mother-in-law's visits, it was a pleasure to have Gertrude come and visit. It gave her a chance to talk about Friederich. It helped to relieve her anxiety about him, especially when she didn't hear from him for a week at a time. It's truly remarkable, Emilie thought. I couldn't have found a more interested friend and listener than Gertrude Hahn, when it came to talking about Friederich.

One early Saturday morning, March 30, Emilie awoke and found the contractions were beginning to become steady. The water sack had burst.

"Mariele, go get my sister-in-law, Frau Elise Brendel, will you? Tell her to come right away. The baby's coming. She'll know what to do. She's Friederich's sister. She lives with Frau Malin down by the Enz. Could you do that? Hurry!"

Mariele ran as fast as she could. She knocked on the door, and Frau Malin answered.

"Ja, Mariele, what brings you here all out of breath?"

"Gruess Gott, Frau Malin. Emilie sent me to get Frau Brendel. The baby's coming!"

Elise had already come to the door as her mother opened it.

"Mariele, I'll come right away. Let me get my hat and coat, and I'll go with you."

"Do you want me to go along too?" Frau Malin asked Elise.

"No, that won't be necessary. You might come up later and see what it is."

Emilie had only met her sister-in-law once. She knew she was a mid-wife by training. She felt comfortable with her, and Emilie knew if there would be a problem, Elise would know how to handle it. Elise had only recently returned from Kassel with her young daughter. Her husband, Friederich had once told her, was a scoundrel. He not only drank too much, he also played around with other women. Elise had given him one more chance to behave. After he had fathered another child with a third woman, she left him.

When Elise came into Emilie's bedroom, she said, "Good morning, Emmy. So you're going to have your baby today Mariele tells me?"

"Yes, Elise. I'm very glad you came. I really don't know anyone else since Frau Tischler moved away. She was the one who helped me with Volkmar's birth."

"Well, let's see what you've got for a birthing table, Emmy. The bed is the last place I want to use."

Elise quickly looked over the kitchen table and the dining room table. "Emmy, I want you to get up and sit in this chair while I get the dining room table ready for you. We need to get you high enough for me to sit in a chair and watch the progress of the baby as it comes out of the uterus."

She helped Emilie get out of the bed and into the easy chair next to it. She then took all of the sheets and bedding from her bed and put them on the table. She also put two quilts on the table she had found in the wardrobe so it wouldn't be so hard to lie on. She helped Emilie get on the table and lie down. Elise sat on a chair at the end of the table with a bucket of warm water, some towels, and a basin to catch the fluids that were constantly flowing out of the birth canal.

Elise turned to Mariele, who was standing there with Volkmar.

"So, young lady, you take your little nephew to my mother's house and leave him there. Then I want you to come right back. I'll need your help keeping the fire going. We'll need plenty of hot water. You're old enough to know where babies come from. It'll be a good experience for you."

Mariele took Volke to his Grandmother Malin's house and returned quickly. She stood next to her sister and Elise waiting for the baby. As Emilie started to scream from the pain, Mariele said, "I don't think I can stay in this room. I'm only thirteen!"

"Then go out to the kitchen and make sure there's plenty of hot water. We'll have to wash off the table and the floor before we're all through," Elise told her.

Mother Malin came over as soon as she returned from shopping. She left Volkmar with her sister. As soon as she came into the kitchen and saw Mariele holding her ears and crying, she sent her to her sister's. "This is no place for a young girl!"

Mother Malin greeted both women. She then turned to her daughter-in-law, "Emmy, you don't need to cry out so loudly. You're only having a child. You're not being slaughtered! You've already scared the wits out of your little sister. She thinks you're going to die, for heaven's sake! What will the neighbors and the men down in the shop think?"

Elise got very angry with her mother. "Now see here, Mother. I'm the mid-wife and I'm in charge. Emilie can do whatever she likes to ease her pain. If she wants to scream, then she should scream."

Frau Malin noticed Emilie shivering and covered her up.

"The poor girl's freezing," she told Elise. Elise uncovered her again.

"I told you before you are not to interfere with what I'm doing. Is that clear?"

Mother Malin stood and watched. Elise placed herself in her chair under the end of the table. If the baby came out quickly, she could catch it. Emilie again let out a loud cry, and Mother Malin chastised her again. Elise was about to send her out of the room when she said, "Here it comes!"

With one final push and cry, the baby was out. Both Elise and the baby were covered with a burst of fluid. Elise held the baby upside down momentarily until it started to cry.

"You're lucky, Emmy. You've got a little baby girl!"

Mother Malin looked at the baby. "That's too bad," she said quietly. "Friederich wanted another little boy. Oh well, the next one may be a boy."

Emilie wasn't at all interested in having another child at this point. She was just glad it was a healthy baby. "Now I have one of each," she told them proudly.

Mother Malin and Elise cleaned up the room. They also remade the bed so Emilie could at last lie in her own bed again. The table had been very hard. The two women also changed the sheets. They left the rest of the the bedroom pretty much as they had found it.

"Who does your cleaning?" Elise asked Emilie.

"Since Luise left for Brazil, I've had an older woman come in once every other week to do the cleaning."

"I wondered. I didn't think your little sister could have done all of the work. The house is remarkably clean."

"What would you expect from a lady's house?" Mother Malin asked sarcastically. "You should see how clean her mother's house is! I was there just once, but I've never seen a cleaner house anywhere. She has a professional cleaning woman scrub her floors each week and polish all of the furniture, cupboards, and staircases. If she had to do that all by herself, she could never do it. But that's the way it is among the upper classes."

Emilie had never heard her mother-in-law talk like that before. She was amazed, and frankly, a bit hurt.

"My mother isn't that rich, Frau Malin. She just likes to keep things looking nice."

Emilie realized, after she said it, she had made a mistake. She shouldn't have called her Frau Malin.

"See? That's just what I mean. Your sister-in-law is also one of those upper-class women. That's why she calls me by my married name," she told Elise, indignantly.

"I'm sorry, Mother," Emilie apologized. "I forgot you want me to call you Mother. I meant no harm."

Emilie was really exhausted and wanted to sleep. Elise sensed it was time for them to leave her alone for a while.

"You get some sleep. We'll take care of you until you're able to get on your feet again. Come along, Mother. Let's go out into the kitchen. She needs to sleep."

Emilie dozed off very quickly and slept for some time. When she awoke, she could still hear them talking in the kitchen. Mother Malin was complaining about rich women who can't do their own cooking and cleaning.

"Look at your sister-in-law, Elsie. Here she is. She's had another child and hasn't yet done a day's work in her own household since she's gotten married. Your brother not only provides her with a cleaning woman but a maid as well. When she had her first child, he sent her off to Wildbad to recuperate. Now that she's had her second, he'll probably have to send her there again," Emilie heard her say.

"What's wrong with that?" Elise told her mother. "I've worked for several rich families through the years, and I was very privileged to do so. I've traveled with them. I've taken care of their children. They have wonderful things of value in their homes, Mother. And I've been well paid. If Friederich has the money, why shouldn't he do that for his wife?"

"Elise, you don't understand. Your brother was the main means of support for all of us when you were growing up. After your father died, Friederich worked for Bosch in Stuttgart. He gave me his weekly pay, and I was able to buy food, clothing, and pay other bills for the household. We always had enough. He paid for your education and your sister's, so you both could become mid-wives and governesses. When your sister, Gretel, came home pregnant, she stayed with us. Then she got pregnant a second time, and she still stayed with us. Friederich didn't like it one bit, but I told him it was my house and she had the same right to stay just like he did. He didn't say anymore about it and kept on working. Now you've come home and you're living with us again. But Friederich doesn't live with us anymore. Since he's gotten married, he's given me a few Reichsmarks each week. But since he's gone to Brazil, I've received nothing. I've had to ask Gretel's husband for a few Reichsmarks each month to make ends meet. Who's going to take care of Emilie now? I don't have the means to do it!"

"Did Friederich say anything to you about taking care of Emilie and the children?"

"No, he didn't! Her mother works four hours a day in the bank. That leaves her out. Her Grandmother is too old to take care of a newborn. Her little sister is much too young to have this responsibility. That leaves only you and me."

Emilie continued to listen in stunned silence. She was astonished by what her mother-in-law said.

"I can't afford to take care of her! I don't even have enough money to buy the groceries we need! I've taken on the job of caring for a little girl beginning tomorrow for which I'll get one Reichsmark per day from the state. It'll help us, but not for two more mouths to feed!" she continued indignantly.

"Friederich used to be such a big help to me years ago when your father died. He pitched right in and got a job. He made enough for you, your sisters, brother, aunt, and me. But ever since he's gotten married, he hardly has time for me anymore. He hires a maid to help his wife around the house. He hires a cleaning woman to do her cleaning for her. He sent her to Wildbad for a vacation after the birth of his son, and now she'll probably want to go there again after this birth. I just don't know, Elise. He didn't say anything to me and I don't think he said anything to anyone. He probably thought someone would take care of her."

"Well, tell you what, I'll stay with her for now," Elise said. "You can have Mariele take Volkmar back to her mother's this afternoon. After she wakes up, I'll talk to Emmy.

I can't imagine Friederich not having made some arrangements with her before he left. He knew she was pregnant and would have the baby before he came back."

"You're right. It's probably better if you stay, than for me. I can't stand anyone who doesn't do her own washing and cleaning. And to think Friederich married one of these 'lady' types! Think how much money it has cost him and will cost him for the rest of his life. I just don't like to think about it!" she said vehemently. "When I think back over what I've had to put up with and the work I've had to do to raise my family, I get really mad when I see rich people able to hire others to do their dirty work!" Grandmother Malin was fuming as she left.

Emilie was stunned. She was very glad Elise didn't come in right away. She fell asleep again for another two hours. It was only when the baby started crying that she awoke. As she started to nurse her, Elise came in.

"So you're awake, Emmy?"

"Yes, the baby woke up and was hungry."

"She has a good appetite, doesn't she? That's a good sign you have a healthy baby. It looks like you have plenty of milk for her."

"Oh yes. Volkmar drank for almost nine months."

"Emmy, I've never had an opportunity to talk with you before. I only met you that one time a month ago when you stopped by the house. But I really have to know what arrangements you and Friederich have made for your convalescence. Have you arranged for someone to come and stay with you?"

"No, not really. I thought between my Grandmother and Mariele, I could take care of myself pretty much."

"But how will you do the shopping? You can't go out of the house for at least another two weeks!" Elise said. "How old is your grandmother?"

"She's almost seventy-three."

"Well, you can't expect an old woman like that to take care of you. Has Friederich left you with any money?"

"Oh yes. Herr Krause brings me the monthly rent for the machine shop and business, and that's more than enough for our needs. I send Friederich about one hundred Reichsmarks a month because we have so much left over."

"Well, if you don't mind, Emmy, I'll stay with you for these two weeks and help you get back on your feet."

Emilie was overwhelmed with her generosity.

"Thank you very much, Elise. I'll pay you for your services so you won't feel put upon by me. My bankbook is in the right hand drawer of Friederich's desk. Take out twenty Reichsmarks for now with ten for you and the rest for our groceries. Would twenty Reichsmarks a week be all right with you?"

"That's at least five Reichsmarks more than I normally receive for my services. I'll be glad to stay with you for as long as you like."

"Great! I want to thank you too, Elise, for coming and helping me with the birth. I had mentioned it to you that time I saw you, but I probably should have talked with you about it again. I'm certainly glad you came when you did. I really didn't want anyone like Frau Tischler. She was so cross and rude at the birth of Volkmar. You were a real big help. I'm glad you stayed with me instead of your mother. I don't know what it is, but she seems so angry with me all of the time. I can never seem to please her."

"She's had a hard life, Emmy. She can't stand it when others have more than she has. She thinks everyone should have the same experiences she's had, so they understand how hard life is. It's never occurred to her that when she was a young woman, she pretty much had everything she wanted. Her father was well-to-do by Vaihingen standards in the nineteenth century. He was a wagon maker with a very good business. It was only after she got married that her life became so hard. My father was something of a tyrant, especially when he started to drink. Friederich couldn't stand him because he was so cruel to our mother. Mama had to ask her parents if Friederich could stay with them because, even as a boy, Friederich fought with our father. It was only after father died that Friederich came back to live with us again. He became our main breadwinner even as a teenager," she said proudly.

"So I've heard from what Karl's told me. But why doesn't she like me?"

"It's not that she doesn't like you, Emilie. I think she's jealous of you, quite frankly. You've taken her young man and breadwinner away from her. Friederich has given you what she's never had: a maid and cleaning woman. Mother forgets that if our Aunt Katharine hadn't moved in with us after our grandparents died, she would have had to do even more work than she did. I've tried to tell her a few times, but she gets very upset about it. I once asked my aunt why she never married, and she said, 'When I look at what my younger sister has had to go through in her marriage, I didn't want any part of it!'

"I don't want to change the subject, Emmy, but do you want me to send Friederich a telegram about the birth of his daughter?"

"No. He wouldn't get a telegram any faster than my letter. I'll write to him tomorrow and tell him the good news. He only comes into town about once every two weeks, if that often."

"When is Friederich coming back from Brazil?"

"I don't know, Elise. He said he'd be back when he's discovered diamonds."

"That could be a very long time, couldn't it?"

"I really don't think it'll be too much longer. He wrote in his last letter the heat was getting to him. The temperatures were in the high nineties every day. If it weren't for the cool evenings, he couldn't have held out this long."

Elise went shopping shortly after their conversation. Emilie reflected on what Elise had told her. She felt she now had a better understanding of her mother-in-law. She was glad Elise had been so open and honest with her. She appreciated her even more now that she was becoming better acquainted with her.

One of the first things that had to be done was to go to the city Registry Office and record the birth and name of her daughter. When Elise came back from shopping, Emilie asked her to go there and record the name she and Friederich had picked out before he left. When she told Elise to record the name of Ingetraude, Elise was a bit surprised.

"Is that name a part of your family history?"

"No. It's the name Friederich liked best for a girl's name. I wanted to call her Eliesse, but he didn't like that name at all. It had something to do with a girl he knew by that name when he was a young man. He didn't seem to like her."

"Ah yes, that name is vaguely familiar to me. She was the girl who lived just down the Enz from us. Her father was a clothing store owner in Vaihingen. Eliesse Springer, I think, was her name. She was a very pretty girl and probably the most sought after of all of the girls in town. Friederich had asked her to marry him just as he went into the army. She told him they should wait until the war was over. When he came back without the use of his voice, she turned him down and married one of his best friends. He's never forgiven her for that!"

She laughed as she told Emilie the story.

"I think he's a lot better off having you, Emmy. I can't imagine any woman letting her husband go off to some strange land to try to find his fortune like you have!"

Emilie thanked her for the compliment. She knew why he had gone. There was no way she could have persuaded him not to go. She noticed in the selection of names for the baby. It had to be his name or nothing. She was afraid of him when he got angry. She couldn't reach him in any way if he were crossed. It would have been so much easier for her if he had told her why he didn't like the name of Eliesse. She certainly would have understood. But as they were discussing names just before he left, he said, "If it's a boy, we'll name him Eugen. If it's a girl, it'll be Ingetraude."

Emilie recalled when she suggested names like Michael, for a boy, or Eliesse for a girl, he got very angry. He pounded the table with his fist so hard the coffee cups almost turned over. She realized then she should never oppose what he wanted. She promised herself she would discuss this with Elise sometime. Maybe she had an insight into why he was this way.

Emilie wrote and told Friederich about their new baby:

My Dearest Friederich!

She looks just like my mother when she was a baby. Now that you have a boy, you have someone to follow in your footsteps. Now I have a little girl who will grow up to be a woman like me. I'll have someone to talk to as she grows up. Mama already calls her her little "Ingele." Volke likes to walk next to the baby carriage, and whenever we see someone on the street, he asks, "Do you want to see my little sister?"

We're very fortunate, Friederich, to have two such wonderful children.

I miss you terribly, Friederich. I wish you would come home soon

Your loving and adoring wife,

Emilie

Emilie gave him a lengthy account of the birth and how glad she was Elise had assisted. Elise mailed the letter the next day at the post office.

A few days later, after Mariele took Volkmar on a walk to visit her mother, Emilie had another opportunity to talk with Elise. She thought she might have some insight into why Friederich gets angry so quickly. Of all of the Malins she had met, she thought, Elise had some of the best insights into the behavior of people. Ingele had just had her nipple and had fallen asleep.

"Elise, why does Friederich get so angry over such little things? Has he always had such a terrible temper?" Emilie asked her sister-in-law.

"Well, let me think, Emmy." She was quiet for a few minutes. "Actually, yes, he has always had a bad temper, as I recall. Even as children, if he told us to do something, we had better do it, or else we got hit. He didn't like to be crossed by anyone. Ironic, though it seems; in some ways he was like our father, easily provoked if things didn't go his way, with a terrible temper which he seemed to control much better only as he got older. It was really only since his wound and loss of his voice that he has become so short tempered. Before he went into the army, he would try to explain why something should or should not be done in a certain way. After he came back and couldn't talk normally, he took offense if someone didn't understand him right away. He really should have become more patient and understanding because of his handicap, but instead, he's become just the opposite. It's too bad, Emmy, but that's the way he is. Yes, ever since he came back from the war."

"In other words, his handicap has made him even more volatile than he was?"

"Yes, I honestly think that's what happened to him."

Elise stayed with Emilie for a month. They discussed all kinds of things: their families, their professions, children, and also Elise's personal life.

She had met Wilhelm Brendel while in Kassel working for an industrialist's family. Wilhelm was a cabinet-maker who built a special inlaid bookcase for the Rieders, the family for whom Elise worked. He was a very skilled young craftsman who got acquainted with her while spending about three weeks at the Rieders completing the job.

"I enjoyed his company very much. He was quite handsome and had really wanted to study art. But his parents had no money to send him to school, beyond the Realschule. That's when he became an apprentice to a cabinet-maker in Kassel. He liked to take me for walks along the banks of the Fulda on my days off. I probably wouldn't have married him so soon after I'd met him, except he was being called into the army. We got married just the day before he left for the front. We wrote to each other for the next three years and even spent two furloughs together. It was during the first one that I took him to Vaihingen to meet my family. Mother didn't get along with him right from the start. He started flirting with Gretel after he had had a couple of glasses of wine. She didn't want to have anything more to do with him. She said he had put his hand on her thigh as he sat next to her at dinner. I was sitting on the other side of him so I didn't notice what was going on between them. I wondered why she had gotten up so often to walk around before sitting down again."

"Did Gretel tell you about this later?"

"Yes. She also told Mother. That's why Mother was so cool toward him."

"When did you find out about what he had done to Gretel?"

"Only after I had returned to Vaihingen with our little daughter. Gretel told me because I said I was never going back to him again."

"If you don't mind my asking, Elise, why did you decide to leave your husband?"

"Shortly after his second home leave, I had continued to work for the Rieders. I lived in their home as governess to their three children. I had gotten into an argument with the Rieders' maid over getting the washing done for the children so we could go for an outing to the Frankfurt zoo. It was then that she said, 'If you only knew about Wilhelm, you'd know you were about the fifth woman on his list. He came to visit me after he said good bye to you!'

"I was stunned. I couldn't believe he would do such a thing! I wrote to him, but he was somewhere in Russia. He never received my letter. When he came back from the war, I didn't want to confront him with this information. He had found an apartment for us in a farmhouse just outside Kassel. He got odd jobs as a cabinet-maker, and since I kept my job, we were getting along well, I thought. I became concerned when he spent more and more time in Der Alte Adler (The Old Eagle) after work. He'd come home around eight o'clock, and the smell of wine was all over him. I thought the war must have had a really bad effect on him. He kept talking about his experiences in Russia all of the time. I thought a child might make a difference in his life, so we stopped taking precautions about my becoming pregnant. After Waltraude was born, he was very gentle with her and liked to hold her while she slept. When she was about six months old, he started staying out after work again. I told him I didn't think that was a good idea.

"'How are we going to save any money for Waltraude, if you spend so much of it on wine? He said he just had to get a drink before he came home. One night when it was after nine o'clock, I went to Der Alte Adler and there he was, sitting at a table with his hand under the dress of one of the barmaids! I made a real scene and screamed at him. I told him he was nothing more than a drunken Romeo. I never wanted to see him again. I went home and packed my bags. I got Waltraude all ready and left on the next train to Vaihingen. He's written to me several times, saying he's sorry for what he did and wants us to come back. That's when Gretel told me about his behavior when he was here. I wrote and told him I would never come back."

"I'm sorry, Elise. I didn't mean to pry into your private life."

"That's okay, Emmy. This is the first chance I've had to tell anyone about what had happened. I told my mother I just didn't want to go back to Brendel. He was nothing but a drunkard."

As spring turned to summer, Emilie took both children on long walks along the Enz. They were growing well, and Emilie's mother liked to have them visit her each day. On one of her visits, her mother told her, "Emilie, this is the last year Mariele will be in school. She'll be fourteen next year and through with Realschule. I want her to spend some time with my mother so she can learn how to cook, sew, and wash. She needs to learn how to take care of a household."

"I thought she wants to become a physical education teacher?"

"She may want to, but I can't afford it. It's hard enough sending money to your sister, Lina, so she can become a kindergarten teacher. If it weren't for the Hahn family helping pay her bills, I could never afford it."

"I'd like her to help me as long as she can. She's wonderful with Volke and the baby. And they like her too!"

"For the time being, it's okay. But I just don't want you to think you can keep her full-time next year after she's through school. She needs to learn how to do other things than only take care of children," her mother said firmly.

The summer was also a time of very bad economic news for the Germans. Their whole world seemed to turn upside down. For the Malins, the money Herr Krause was paying Emilie each month for the rent of the business was proving to be less and less adequate. Friederich had left her a sizable amount in their account, but even this was no longer enough to buy food. The bottom had dropped out of the Reichsmark. It no longer had any value! She paid one thousand Reichsmarks for a gram of meat. The price of bread was going up from one day to the next. A pretzel used to cost ten pfennige. It now cost ten Reichsmarks! It literally took a suitcase of money to buy a week's groceries! Emilie went to her mother and asked, "Could you lend me a few thousand Reichsmarks, Mother? I've written Friederich, but I haven't heard anything from him in sometime. He must be prospecting and hasn't picked up his mail. Otherwise, I'm sure I would have heard from him. Our rental income isn't keeping up with the daily costs we have for groceries."

"I'm no better off, Emilie. Do you know that Herr Welker came by this morning and paid me the full amount he said he owed me for the business? He gave me eighty-thousand Reichsmarks and said that was all he owed me! I tried to reason with him that this was a temporary devaluation of our currency, but he wouldn't listen. He said the bank had paid him for his deliveries this morning, and it was exactly the amount he owed me. Can you imagine? In 1919, he promised to pay off the business on a thirty-year note! I can't ask the people who are renting my other houses to pay more rent. Their incomes haven't really gone up. It's just paper money . . . I tried to cash in some of my war bonds which the government had said it would honor in 1920. Do you know what I was told? 'Frau Bartholomae, these bonds are worthless!' I'd like to help you Emilie, but I'm afraid I can't!"

"What are we supposed to do, Mama? I talked with Herr Krause about making the rental payments equivalent to the actual value of the goods and services he sells. Fortunately, he has agreed. Can't you get Herr Welker to do the same so that the value of the business in 1919 would match that of today?"

"I'm going to ask my father what I should do." Frau Bartholomae called her father and told him what Herr Welker had done.

"You'll have to sue him, Maria."

"I don't have any money to pay an attorney, Father. Could you loan me the money to retain one?"

"I don't have any money either, Maria. Your mother and I are living off what your brothers are able to give us each month. I've lost everything I've invested during the war. My bank account is worth nothing. The Reichsmark has lost its value. I'd like to help you, Maria, you know that. Welker shouldn't get away with what he's done to you. Why don't you talk with Ernst about it? Maybe he can figure out a way to make Welker pay you in real money."

Emilie's mother took the advice of her father. She went to see her brother, Dr. Ernst Meyer, in Boeblingen. He was very sympathetic to her. He went with her to visit Herr Welker and got assurance from him he would adjust the real amount he owed her in one year's time in the new currency which the government promised would be issued in the next few months.

Karl Malin stopped by after work to visit Emilie. He had continued to work for Herr Krause when Friederich left. Friederich tried to interest him in going along to Brazil. He probably would have gone, except Karl started courting Anne Laub. When he told her he was thinking of going to Brazil, she said, "What? You must be crazy! I'd never go there! It's too hot!"

"How's Friederich getting along?" Karl asked. "We've only received an occasional card from him."

"It's much different from what he expected. He's only found some precious stones but still no diamonds. I wouldn't be surprised if he comes back home before too long. Hermann and Luise are living in Diamantina. Hermann gave up the search. But Friederich's determined to find his diamonds."

"Friederich was very angry at Anne for saying she would never go to such a hot country," Karl said. "If she hadn't opposed it so much, I probably would have gone with them. I've always wanted to travel. My father once brought home a conch shell for me and told me to put it up to my ear. As I listened he said 'That's the way the ocean sounds that I'm going to cross to go to America.' I've never forgotten that," Karl said wistfully.

"Your father went to America quite often, didn't he?"

"I think about three times. He liked it there. If he had learned English, I'm sure he would have stayed. My mother's cousin owned a paper box company in a place called Syracuse, New York. He used to stay with them when he visited."

"Yes, I've heard of that city. Your sister Bertha lives there, doesn't she?"

"Yes. She's been there for more than twelve years. Just before the war, she came one summer with her young daughter and son, Madelaine and Peter, for a visit."

"Oh, so she's been there for a long time?"

"Yes. She speaks fluent English and her husband is a machinist in a washing machine factory and makes good money."

"The reason I stopped by, Emmy, is to say goodbye to you."

"What? You're leaving? Where are you going?"

"I'm going to America. I want to see what it's like. If I get a good job, I'll send for Anne, and we'll get married over there."

"But most of your family is here in Vaihingen, Karl! Do you really want to leave everything behind you've grown up with?"

She liked Karl a lot. He was so different from Friederich. He was quiet but with a sense of humor that was infectious. He had a wonderful laugh and seldom seemed to get upset with anyone. He hadn't stopped by very much lately. With Friederich gone, he didn't think he ought to visit her without him there.

"Couldn't you wait until your brother comes back? He'll surely miss you at work. And we'll all miss you very much, Karl," Emilie said almost in tears.

"No, Emmy. I don't want to wait. I've got to start out on my own sooner or later anyway. I've learned a lot from Friederich about toolmaking. I want to see if I can use what I've learned on my own. America sounds like a good place to try it out."

"Well, I'm very sorry to see you go, Karl. I've known you the longest of almost anyone in Vaihingen."

Emilie started to cry. She gave him a hug and a kiss.

"You're very special to me too, Emmy. I'm sure we'll see each other again. If my father did nothing else, he set a good precedent for me. He traveled back and forth. I hope to be able to do that too!"

"Oh, by the way, is Volke here?"

"Yes, I'll get him."

She went to Volke's bedroom and asked Mariele and Volkmar to come out to say goodbye to Uncle Karl. "He's going to America, and that's a long, long ways away," she told them.

"Ah, Volke, I've brought something for you to listen to. It's what my father gave me a long time ago."

Karl reached into his briefcase and pulled out the conch shell he had mentioned to Emilie. He put it up to Volke's ear and asked, "What do you hear?"

"It sounds like water."

"That's exactly right, Volke!" Karl said excitedly. "It sounds like the sea over which I'm going to sail to America next week."

He let Mariele and Emilie listen to it too. Sure enough, it sounded like water flowing back and forth.

x   x   x

In late November 1923, Friederich returned from Brazil. He had been there almost eleven months. He would probably have stayed for the whole year, except that Herr Krause had not kept up in his payments in the new currency as he had earlier promised. He was still using the old Reichsmarks with a bare increase to offset the revaluation of the currency. Friederich was very angry that he hadn't kept up the payment of five hundred Reichsmarks a month in the new currency. He felt cheated. It was not only a surprise, but something of a shock to Emilie when she came to the door to see who was knocking and found Friederich standing there with all of his baggage.

"Friederich!" she shrieked. "How wonderful to see you again! I've missed you terribly!"

She fell into his arms and smothered him with hugs and kisses.

"Emilie, I've missed you very much too! You don't know what it's like to be all alone in the jungle month after month. There were times when I wondered if I'd ever make it back again. I had to sell some of my precious stones to pay for my return passage. And I never did find any diamonds!"

"I don't care, Friederich. You're home and that's all that counts. Come on in. I'll get you something to eat," she said overjoyed.

Volkmar had come out to the landing and watched as his parents were kissing each other. He didn't seem to know who this man was.

"Ah, Volke, come here! You've gotten so big already!"

Friederich reached out to pick him up, but Volke looked as though he wanted to cry.

"It's all right, Volke," his mother assured him. "This is your Papa. Don't you remember him?"

Volke shook his head and reached out to her. She took him and said, "Don't be alarmed, Friederich. He doesn't remember you. It'll take a while for him to get to know you again. By this evening, I'm sure he'll be like himself."

"Where's little Ingetraude?"

"She's in the baby room. She looks just like my mother used to as a little girl," Emilie said proudly.

"What? Do you mean to tell me she's a Meyer?"

"Well, she surely looks like it!" She took him by the hand and led him into the baby's room.

"Here she is," she said smilingly. "Isn't she a beauty?"

She awoke just then and Emilie picked her up. She laughed when she looked at her mother and then at Friederich.

"She's prettier than your mother was. She has such a friendly smile. I don't think your mother ever smiled like that."

It didn't take Friederich long to get back into the routine of family and work life again. After a sumptuous meal, they all slept awhile. Emilie could hardly contain herself. They had sex twice that afternoon while the children slept. Each time, just as he was having an orgasm, he pulled out and let it discharge into his handkerchief. It was easy for Emilie to get aroused, but it was a letdown for her not to be able to have an orgasm herself.

"Why don't we let ourselves go, Friederich," she implored. "It would feel so much better," she sighed. "You've been gone an awful long time. Couldn't we just do it without your pulling out?"

"But what if you get pregnant? We can't have another child yet."

"So long as the baby is sucking, I won't get pregnant. I want to keep her on the nipple for at least the rest of the year."

"That's okay with me."

So for the rest of the year, they did it without taking any precautions. It was by far the best sex they had ever had. As they sat at the table, Friederich ran his hand up under her skirt and played with her thighs. Emilie got easily aroused and could hardly wait until the children were sleeping to go to bed with him. His return was about the best Christmas present she could have ever wished.

The second day Friederich was home, he went downstairs to the workshop. He looked for Paul Krause. On his trip through the shop, he greeted everyone. He was pleased to see the same people were still there except for one person. He asked one of the apprentices, "Where's my brother? Is he sick today?"

"No, Herr Malin. He's gone to America! He's not been here for over a month."

"Is that so?"

Just then Paul Krause came in.

"Hello, Herr Malin? How are you? Did you find a lot of diamonds in the jungle?"

"I found some precious stones, but no diamonds. You're just the man I want to talk to. Why haven't you been keeping up your rental payments in the new currency? You're about two months behind where you should be. I'm going to ask you to pay an additional hundred Reichsmarks as a penalty for not paying what you should have been paying," Friederich said sharply.

"You can't do that!" Krause protested. "I can't afford another hundred Reichsmarks a month!"

"It's either that or I'm taking over my shop again on the first of December!"

"Well let me think it over. I still think that's too much. The currency is only now really getting stabilized."

"You've got about a week to think it over. Either you pay what you owe me, or I'm taking over again."

Friederich seemed very much sobered by his long absence. He told Emilie how Hermann had simply told him one evening while they were out in the bush, "I'm leaving tomorrow morning. I can't see myself wasting any more time out here in the jungle! We'll never find any diamonds!"

Friederich continued: "The next morning, I told him 'Hermann, you're not going anywhere. You're staying right here with me.' I showed him I meant business and unholstered my pistol. He just laughed."

Friederich narrated on: "'I knew you'd probably try something like that, Friederich,' Hermann told me. 'That's why, while you were asleep last night, I unloaded your pistol. You'll find your bullets locked in your suitcase!' And with these words, he left to return to Luise in Diamantina with the second donkey. I was very upset with him, but there was nothing I could do about it except continue working by myself.

"Before I came back to Rio de Janiero, I visited them in Juiz de Fora. Hermann had gotten a job as a construction foreman and was doing well financially. So well, in fact, he had been able to pay back the loan from his aunt. He asked me if I would loan them the money to return to Germany.

"I said, 'You've got to be joking! You expect me to loan you the money? You left me out in the jungle all by myself, you son of bitch! I wouldn't loan you the money if you were the last man on earth! If Luise wants to return with me, I'll gladly take her along. But you can stay here and rot, as far as I'm concerned!'

"Luise wouldn't think of leaving Hermann. She was too much in love with him to do anything like that. She stayed with him while I came back."

Friederich took up his business again on the first of December. Paul Krause couldn't afford the additional amount of rent.

"You can continue to work here, Paul. You're a good toolmaker. With my brother gone, I could use someone who's familiar with the entire business. I'll give you an additional ten Reichsmarks a week in pay, if you'll stay."

Paul Krause thought it over and agreed. Now that Friederich was back in business again, the question came up: who would assist him when people could not understand what he was saying? Emilie couldn't spend much time in the store with two small children to look after. Mother Malin didn't want to come anymore. She was now caring for orphans sent to her by the state.

Emilie suggested to Friederich, "If we could hire Mariele to look after the children, at least after school, I'd be free to come downstairs and help. She's gotten much bigger now. You almost wouldn't recognize her because of how she's grown."

"I still can't forget how she let Volkmar drop. It could have been a disaster!"

"Why don't we invite her over and see what you think? I'm confident she can do the job."

"All right. But if I think she's not suitable, then we'll look for someone else."

Emilie was somewhat surprised but glad he at least would look her over before saying no. She went to her mother's house.

"Grandmother, when Mariele comes home from school today, would you send over to our house? Friederich and I want to talk to her."

"Ja. Certainly, Emilie."

After school, Mariele came over. She was very apprehensive as she came into the living room.

"Sit down, Mariele. I'll tell Friederich you're here. I'll be right back."

Mariele went into Volkmar's room and found him playing with his blocks. She sat down next to him. They were building houses together as Friederich and Emilie came in. Mariele had grown into a tall, blonde young woman with blue eyes and a very different build from the rest of the Bartholomae girls. She, among all of them, most resembled her father. She was pretty with very shapely legs and a fully formed bosom. She was very attractive to look at. Emilie was really pleased with her youngest sister.

Mariele got up as they came in the door. "Hello, Friederich. It's nice that you're back home again from Brazil," she said as they shook hands.

"What? You're Mariele? I wouldn't have recognized you! You've grown up to be a very pretty young woman!" Friederich said in astonishment. "Emilie told me you had changed greatly from the last time I saw you. I wouldn't have thought it possible if I hadn't seen you for myself."

"I'm glad you're not angry with me anymore, Friederich. I've never forgotten how enraged you were at me for dropping Volkmar. I really didn't mean to do it, but you didn't seem to want to believe me then," she said apologetically.

"That was a long time ago, Mariele. Volkmar doesn't seem to have been hurt by it. Let's just forget it, all right?"

"Thanks. I promise it won't happen again!"

"Mariele," Emilie began. "How would you like to work for us after school each afternoon? You can come to our house on the way home and stay until the shop closes. Probably about five hours a day. Would that be all right with you?"

"We'll pay you one Reichsmark per day," Friederich offered. "If it works out, we'll increase it to two Reichsmarks per day, after one month."

"That would be more than enough, Friederich. You can pay me whatever you like. I don't mind. I like playing with Volke and Inge."

Emilie gave her a hug and a kiss and said, "You can start tomorrow. How would that be?"

"That's fine. I'll be here after school tomorrow."

Now that Friederich had returned, Emilie had less and less of an opportunity to visit her mother and Grandmother Bartholomae. With Mariele looking after the children each afternoon, she had more time to spend downstairs. She was really only needed when someone came into the shop to buy a motorcycle or a bicycle. If a customer couldn't understand Friederich, he would turn to her and have her tell the customer what he had said. Friederich had installed a bell behind the counter of the store which rang in the kitchen. If he needed her, he could ring the bell, and she would come down. As a result of her involvement in the business, she rarely visited her mother during the day. It also meant she played less and less on her mother's piano. During lunch one afternoon, she mentioned to Friederich, "You know, if we had a piano, the children could hear me play. They might want to learn how too. Wouldn't it be nice if we had our own piano?"

"Yes, that's a good idea. Why don't we ask your mother if she would sell hers to us? She doesn't play it, and I don't think any of your sisters know how to play, do they?"

"No. That's true. I'm the only one in the family who plays. Maybe she would sell it to us. Let's stop in to see her next Sunday after our walk."

That next Sunday, they went along the Enz to the fountain at the base of the Rozwoger hill and back. They didn't make their usual trip to Enzweihingen because they wanted to stop and see Emilie's mother. As was her custom, Grandmother Bartholomae baked kuchen every Saturday morning. Maria Bartholomae had each weekend off from work. They knew she would be home. Friederich, Emilie, and the children stopped in around four o'clock and rang the doorbell. Emilie's mother looked out from the upstairs window, and when she saw who it was, she said, "Ah, what a pleasant surprise! I wasn't expecting you today. I'll be right down."

She came down the stairs very quickly. She opened the door, and Volkmar said, "How did you make it down here so fast, Grandmother?"

They all laughed because that was just what they were thinking.

"Come in. Grandmother has baked kuchen, and I'll make some coffee and tea."

They went upstairs and Grandmother Bartholomae was already in the kitchen making the coffee.

Emilie's mother gave some chocolate to Volkmar and asked, "Can Ingele drink cocoa?"

"Yes, I think she could try a little of it. She hasn't learned how to use a cup yet, but we'll see what she can do."

As they were all gathered at the dining room table, Friederich asked, "Mother Bartholomae, would you be willing to sell your piano? Emmy doesn't have one, and as busy as she is, she needs to have one close by so she can play whenever she has some free time."

Emilie was almost sorry Friederich had asked. A frown came over her mother's face. Her mother wasn't at all pleased with the question. It pained her even to have to consider such an idea.

"Oh, oh, I don't know if I can do that, Friederich. My husband bought the piano years ago so Emilie could practice on it at home while she was taking lessons. I always thought each of the girls would learn how to play, but after he died, I didn't feel I could afford to pay for their lessons anymore. I had wanted to buy a cheaper one, but my husband said, 'No. We'll buy this one. After all, Emilie is going to play it. It has to be something special.' That's how we bought the most expensive one in the store in Stuttgart. We had to have it shipped by train to Vaihingen and then hauled by a large wagon and horses from the train depot to our house. When we moved from the *Enz-Bote* house to here, several of our neighbors wanted to buy it. But I refused. Michael had bought it, and so long as it was in the house, I felt there was still a part of him there with me. I really don't want to sell it."

"But Mama, you don't play it. Grandmother doesn't play it. Nor do any of my sisters! Who's going to play it, if I don't? It's a tremendous waste of a beautiful instrument, Mama!"

Her mother said nothing. Emilie could tell from the look on her face this line of questioning didn't please her one bit. It was true, however, which she could not deny. The piano just sat there, unused. It reminded Emilie, sadly, of her mother's life. Here was a talented, still young woman, who sat in her house surrounded by memorabilia from a long by-gone age that was no more. She was caught in a time warp of her own making, as Friederich described her once. Emilie recalled a conversation she and Friederich had about her mother as she sat and looked at her. Friederich had said: "She should dress in something other than black all of the time. All she does is think about her long-dead husband. She's prematurely cold. She needs someone to heat her up again!"

"Mama, how would it be if you came to our house once in a while and listened while I play piano? You hardly ever come to visit anymore. We always have to come to your house. If we bought the piano, I would be able to play some everyday. I know if I don't do so, I'll soon get rusty and lose my ability. Playing piano is like any other skill; you've got to use it to keep it. If you don't practice, there's no reason to learn the skill. I'm sure Papa would rather have someone play the piano than having it sit around not being used."

Emilie was sorry almost immediately after she said it. Her mother took out her handkerchief and wiped her eyes. Emilie had struck her emotionally as she hadn't been struck for sometime.

"It's easy for you to say," she said slowly. "But if a person hasn't gone through it, they'll never know how hard it is to raise a family alone. If it hadn't been for Grandmother Bartholomae, all of these years, you girls would not have had much of a home life at all. I still miss Papa very, very much. There isn't a day that goes by that I'm not thinking about him and asking myself, 'What would he do in this situation?'"

"I'm very sorry, Mama," Emilie apologized. "I know you've had a very hard life, but none of us can live in the past. If you don't want to sell your piano, that's your business." Emilie started to cry.

Friederich got angry with both of them.

"How's crying going to help change the past? There's absolutely nothing you can do about it. You can only focus on the future. I'm only trying to buy a piano; I'm not trying to change the world, for heaven's sake. Let's get realistic. I'll offer you one hundred Reichsmarks for your piano, Mother Bartholomae. I don't know how much it cost, but to me that seems a fair enough price."

"What?" she asked incredulously. "You only want to pay me one hundred Reichsmarks? I could have gotten four times that amount when we moved from our old home. But I didn't want to sell it. It's a very expensive piano. You men are all alike! Just because I'm a widow, without a husband, you think you can take advantage of me. A man with your kind of money shouldn't have any problem paying what it's really worth."

Friederich got very angry. "I'll give you one hundred and twenty, but that's it. Not a penny more! We just want it for Emilie to play at home. She doesn't have the time to come over here to play every afternoon."

Emilie stopped crying. She remembered what Friederich had said about her mother. He was very critical of her. He didn't like the perpetual black she wore almost all of the time.

Friederich had once said, "Emilie, you resemble your mother very much. In fact, from what I can see, she's as well endowed as you are! She has the same large bosom and very nice legs. She's just got to get over the death of her husband! Her demeanor and what I would describe as her haughty accent, make it impossible for me to empathize with her. I respect her for all she's done. But she's doing a grave disservice to herself by becoming a virtual recluse."

To their great surprise, she said, "I'll take your offer. But you'll have to pay to have it moved to your place."

On their way home, Friederich said, "I really thought she wouldn't take my offer. I'll be amazed if she ever comes over to hear you play it."

"I hope she will. I've always felt very close to that piano because Papa bought it for me to play."

x   x   x

Shortly after they had the piano delivered, Grandmother Bartholomae fell ill. She complained of a stomachache and went to bed.

"Do you want me to stay home this afternoon and look after you?" Maria offered.

"No, that won't be necessary. I'll stay in bed this afternoon, and maybe by this evening, I'll be able to get up again."

Maria went to work and Mariele came over to Emilie's after school, as usual. She looked in on Grandmother before she left and thought she was sleeping. She didn't want to disturb her. That evening Maria came home and looked in on Grandmother Bartholomae. She too thought she was sleeping. She closed the door very quietly to her bedroom and let her sleep. After supper she looked in on her again and noticed she didn't seem to be breathing. She went over to her and felt her pulse. There was no pulse, and her hand was cold. She felt under her chin and listened to her chest. She heard no sound of any kind. She called Dr. Bauer.

"Dr. Bauer, could you come over as quickly as you can? I can't feel any pulse on my mother-in-law. She went to bed this afternoon with a stomachache and has slept all day. When I shake her, there's no response!"

"I'll be right over, Frau Bartholomae."

Maria had no sooner hung up the telephone when Dr. Bauer rang the doorbell.

"I'm so glad you came, Dr. Bauer. Grandmother doesn't seem to be breathing at all. She was only sick this afternoon. She hadn't complained about not feeling well until today."

"Let me take a look at her, Frau Bartholomae. I really can't say what might be wrong until I've examined her."

She led him into Grandmother's bedroom.

"Grandmother, the doctor's here to see you!"

There was no response. Dr. Bauer went to her bed and felt her pulse. "There's no pulse."

He listened to her chest with his stethoscope. "She's not breathing, Frau Bartholomae. She's dead. She may have suffered a heart attack, and with no one in the house with her if she called out, there was no one to hear her. She has very quietly died in her sleep."

Maria went immediately to the Malins and told them the news. Emilie arranged with the undertaker to come and get her Grandmother. Maria called each of her two brothers-in-law, Paul and Friederich Bartholomae, and told them the news of their mother's death.

"I'd like to have her buried here in Heilbronn with Papa and the rest of our family," Fritz said.

The undertaker promised to take her to the family cemetery after the church service in Vaihingen. Pastor Hahn conducted a small family service for her in the chapel. There were only about twenty persons in attendance. Grandmother Bartholomae had never really gotten acquainted with any of her neighbors. She had made very few friends in Vaihingen. Whenever it was possible for her to do so, she took the train to Heilbronn to visit with her family and neighbors. The graveside service in Heilbronn had more than twice the number of people in attendance. Emilie's mother said afterward, "You know, Emilie, I never realized how lonely your grandmother must have been in Vaihingen. All of her friends lived in Heilbronn. She never asked if she could invite any of them for a visit. She really sacrificed herself to help us after Papa died. She must have felt guilty about going back home. She stayed with us all of these years instead of going home."

It was the first time Emilie had seen either of her uncles or any of her cousins since her father died. Uncle Paul, she remembered, had always complained about being too sick to work. Her father had given him money each year to pay his mortgage. Shortly after the burial of her father, her mother told her Uncle Paul, "I won't be able to send you any more money. It's going to be hard enough for us to get along on what I make from the business without adding any more expenses."

She didn't tell anyone about what Paul had written to Emilie's father (if he didn't receive money from Michael each year, he'd commit suicide) until Grandmother Bartholomae's funeral. Her mother never believed he would. Needless to say, after she cut him off from his yearly gratuity, he continued to work as a salesman and seemed to be providing very well for his family.

Emilie was surprised her cousins were so well brought up. She had expected them to be rather slovenly and poorly dressed. But they dressed very much to the contrary. Both of her Uncle Paul's girls were well dressed and almost as old as she and Luise.

Her Uncle Fritz worked for the postal service and his two sons were teenagers. They were also tall, blond, and blue eyed, like her sister Mariele. Emilie saw her cousins were more like her father than she was, or her two younger sisters. While she, Luise, and Lina had black hair, brown eyes, and were of a shorter stature than her father's family, only Mariele seemed at all related to the Bartholomaes.

Chapter XI

Enticement to Move On

Karl wrote long and interesting letters to the Malins from America. He had arrived in New York City and proceeded to Syracuse by train together with his baggage. He lived with his oldest sister, Bertha, her husband, Gustav, and two of their three children. The oldest daughter, Madelaine, had died of influenza in 1918.

He had no trouble getting a job, he wrote. He worked with his brother-in-law at the Easy Washer Company as a toolmaker. He was very well paid, and the wages were much higher than in Germany. There were lots of jobs, but too few people to fill them. He worked during the day, his letter continued, and at night he studied English. He felt he was making real progress. In fact, he had asked Anne Laub to come to the United States to marry him. He had sent her the money and was waiting for her answer. Friederich got very angry when Emilie read the letter to him.

"What? He's asked Anne to marry him? He doesn't know, ever since he left, she's been seeing our cousin, Eugen Vischer!"

Friederich wrote Karl a long letter telling him about her and that she was two-timing him. His cousin was also Karl's best friend before he left for America. Now Eugen was carrying on with her "as if they never knew you existed!" Friederich wrote. Friederich had seen his cousin on the street one day and asked him how he could do such a thing to his best friend, Karl. Eugen said, "That's none of your business! I can date whomever I please! If she weren't interested in going out with me, she'd tell me!"

Friederich continued his letter to Karl, telling him that he had seen the two of them at the market square. "I called her a slut! I said, 'Who do you think you are, promising yourself to my brother and then two-timing him like this with his best friend as soon as he's gone?' Do you know what your cousin tried to do? He struck me, and I had to give him a real beating. I told him, 'I never want to see you again!'"

It was not a very encouraging letter in response to Karl's. Emilie learned, almost from the beginning of their marriage, Friederich called a spade a spade. He didn't care what anyone else thought.

Gertrude Hahn also told Emilie, "Anne and Eugen spend a lot of time together up at the castle after dark. As soon as darkness falls, Eugen comes for her after work and they either go up to the castle or down to the Enz before he takes her home."

They had evidently become much more discreet after Friederich's encounter with them. They didn't want to run into Friederich again.

Grandmother Malin knew the Laub family. They lived nearby along the Enz. They struggled to support themselves by raising vegetables and fruits to sell in the weekly market. Herr Laub died some years earlier, after hearing that his son had been killed in France. Anne and her younger sister, Emilie, worked as maids in some of the finer homes in Vaihingen. One of those families was the Hahn family. Anne worked for Gertrude, Emilie Malin's friend from college days, as a maid in the parsonage until she left for America. Gertrude filled Emilie in with the details of Anne's relationship with Eugen and Karl. Anne appreciated Gertrude's interest in what she planned to do. She told her she saw Karl as the instrument of change in her life for the better.

"What are you going to tell Eugen Vischer, Anne?" Gertrude asked.

"I've already told him, 'I'm leaving Vaihingen. As soon as I can book passage, I'm going to America!'"

"What did he say to that, Anne?"

"He was really surprised, Frau Hahn. He was astonished. He tried to remind me of what he thought our future together would be like. I never promised him anything. He tried to tell me he had told me when he had saved a thousand Reichsmarks, we would get married. I told him, 'I didn't promise you anything, Eugen. I only said we'd see.' I told him it would be better if we didn't see each other again."

Eugen was heartbroken. It took him sometime to accept the fact he couldn't marry Anne Laub. Once he had reconciled himself to the fact she was leaving Vaihingen, he even wrote his cousin, Karl, a letter. He congratulated him on getting a real nice girl who was a lot of fun to be with. Karl never knew what Eugen meant by this statement. The letter Friederich had written to him about Anne he didn't want to believe. He felt his brother had overstated the relationship between her and his cousin.

Karl wrote in his letter to his brother, "Thanks for your letter of this past month. I've just gotten word from Anne she is arriving on the twenty-eighth of December. We'll get married as soon as possible. I've found a very nice apartment near Bertha and Gust for us so we'll have our own place to live. I eventually want to build a house in the outskirts of Syracuse. The land is cheap, and it wouldn't be too far to drive to work. I think you've misunderstood Anne. She's a real nice girl, and even Eugen says so. I'm sure we'll be very happy together here in Syracuse. It's too bad you won't be able to attend our wedding."

Karl also wrote to Gretel and Richard Haussmann. He told them much of what he had written to his brother: jobs were plentiful, the pay was good, and the cost of living was very cheap. When Emilie and the children visited the Haussmanns, Richard said, "There's really not much of a future here at Bosch for me. Sure, I've got a job, but I'm only a mechanic. From what Karl writes, it wouldn't be hard to get a good job in America. I'd go tomorrow if I had the money."

Two months later, the Haussmanns visited the Malins in Vaihingen. Richard had gotten a loan from his parents to buy a boat ticket to the United States. Gretel had gotten a job as a cleaning lady in some homes in Stuttgart. If worse came to worst and Richard couldn't send them enough money, she would be able to help pay for the passage for herself and their two children. They had decided Richard should go first and then send for them after he had found a job and a place to live. Gretel brought Riche and Grete to stay with her mother in Vaihingen over the summer. Friederich and Emilie saw them at least once a week. On their last visit just before Richard's departure, Friederich told him, "Richard, if for some reason your wife can't get along on what she's making, I'll be glad to help her out."

Emilie didn't understand why Gretel said to Friederich, "That won't be necessary. I'll get along on my own, thank you! You're the last person I'd ask for help!"

Emilie thought it was a very kind gesture on his part. After all, he had taken care of them before she married Richard.

In late August 1925, Richard left for America.

x   x   x

Emilie's mother got a call from her brother to come to Gerabronn. Their father was very ill, and if Maria wanted to see him alive for the last time, she should come right away. Frau Bartholomae was very upset. She was her father's favorite and had helped him in his last years before retirement to write crop insurance for local farmers. She wanted to leave immediately, but Mariele was still at school. She went over to Emilie and told her what was happening.

"Emilie, your grandfather is deathly ill. Your Uncle Ernst just called me and told me I should come immediately if I wanted to see him alive for the last time."

She broke down repeatedly. Emilie tried to console her, but they both were heartbroken by the news. Poor Mama, Emilie thought. Now she has to go through the same tragic experience again like she did with Papa's death! The thought of it produced more tears, and they hugged each other as they cried.

"Emilie, I need your help. I can still catch the nine o'clock train if I can leave now. Could you go over this afternoon and get Mariele after school? I don't know how long I'll be gone, but if she could stay with you, it would be a big help for me."

"Certainly, Mama. Don't worry about her. She can stay with us until you come back."

Emilie went over to get Mariele shortly after one o'clock.

"Why hasn't Mama come back from work today, Emilie? I'm doing my homework, but Mama hasn't come back yet."

"Mariele, Mama wants you to come stay with us until she comes back from Gerabronn."

"Why did she go there?"

"Grandfather is very ill, and Uncle Ernst thought it best if all of his children could come to see him maybe for the last time."

"What? Grandfather is sick?"

"Yes, that's why Mama left in such a hurry without saying goodbye to you. You hadn't come back from school when she had to leave to catch the train. She didn't have time. The train left at nine A.M."

"Are you sure it's okay with Friederich? I don't want to get him angry again. It's enough that I'm at your place each afternoon. What will he think if I'm there all of the time?"

"Are you still worried about the time you dropped Volkmar?"

"Exactly! How can I ever forget it? He probably would have killed me if you weren't there!" she said reproachfully

"No, no, Mariele," Emilie tried to reassure her. "That was a long time ago, and you've gotten much bigger now. Why, you're practically a grown woman. Anyone would think you were at least eighteen, and you're only fourteen."

As she got her things together, Emilie couldn't help but see Mariele had grown into quite an attractive young woman. She takes after our father's family, she said to herself. There's no doubt about it. Of all of us girls, Mariele has the fairest complexion and is of an entirely different build from the rest of us Bartholomae girls!

That evening Friederich came upstairs rather late. He had had a particularly hard day trying to improvise a latch on a string spool so that when it was full, it would stop turning instead of continuing to spill string over the factory floor. He had tried to make a number of different latches, but each time they were not strong enough to shut off the spooler. When he finished, the factory manager said, "Now that was a great job, Herr Malin! I thought we were going to have to shut down the plant until we could get another part from the factory."

Friederich had taken Paul Krause with him. Without Karl there to help him, especially in talking with other people, Paul was very helpful. He had worked with Friederich long enough to understand him. As a toolmaker himself, he could intuit what Friederich was trying to do without having him tell him. Needless to say, Friederich was exhausted. As he came in the door, there was Mariele. He hadn't seen her for sometime since she was usually gone by the time he came upstairs in the late afternoon.

"Hello, Friederich."

Friederich was still thinking about the part he had struggled to make. He was still distracted and very much involved in his own thoughts about the repair of the spooler.

"And who are you?"

"I'm Mariele. Have you forgotten me already?"

"Ah, of course. I was thinking of something completely different. How old are you now, eighteen?"

"No, no. I'm only fourteen!"

As Emilie came in from the kitchen, she said, "What do you think of my little sister? Hasn't she grown?"

"She certainly has. I wouldn't have recognized her."

"She's going to stay with us for a few days. Mama had to go to Gerabronn. Uncle Ernst said Grandfather isn't very well. He has pneumonia."

"Oh, that's pretty serious for an old man."

"That's why Mama asked me if Mariele could stay with us until she returns. It may be sometime before she comes back."

"Fine. It looks like Volke and Inge are already enjoying her stay."

There were toys and blocks spread all over the living room floor. Mariele was playing with the children and helping them build towers and bridges. She sat on the floor and her dress was up over her thighs. She really seemed to take no notice of what she was doing, or how she looked. She was completely absorbed in play with the children.

"Isn't that nice the way Volkmar and Inge play with Mariele?" Emilie smiled as she talked with Friederich. "They like her so much. I'm sure they'll get along very well together while she's with us."

During the rest of that evening, Friederich kept looking at Mariele.

"I wouldn't have recognized you if you hadn't introduced yourself," he kept telling her. He couldn't seem to get over how much she had grown.

While Mariele played with the children, Emilie cooked. Friederich read the newspaper. Mariele noticed he kept looking at her. She didn't notice her dress was often up to the top of her thighs. Friederich looked at her so intently she sneaked a peek under her dress to see if she had forgotten to put on her panties. But no, they were on. As he looked at her, he smiled. She wondered why he always looked at her. She felt uneasy but didn't know why. After the children had gone to bed, Mariele spent her time doing her homework and talking with Emilie. She didn't want to be alone with Friederich.

The children got up as early as Friederich did. Emilie got them dressed and took them with her to the bakery to buy fresh rolls and pretzels. Mariele went along holding Inge's hand. Upon their return, they ate a breakfast of rolls, pretzels, and hot chocolate before Mariele went off to school.

On the first Saturday Mariele was with them, Emilie thought she would make her a real treat of one of their favorite dinners. Mariele played outside with Volke and Inge. They came in and out of the house as the mood struck them.

The dinner was spaetzle, with roast beef, potato salad, and a lettuce salad. Emilie usually cooked the meat in a dutch oven with a combination of onions, carrots, tomatoes, parsley, salt and pepper, in water. The aroma filled the whole house. With the children going in and out, Friederich couldn't help but smell it downstairs in the store. He came up periodically for a cup of coffee and a pretzel. On one of these occasions, when Mariele came in the house, Friederich asked her, "Who's your boyfriend?"

"I don't have any! I'm only fourteen!"

"Come on now," Friederich persisted. "An attractive girl like you, and as well developed as you are, you must have several."

"Well, I don't!" she stated empathetically.

"Do you ever go down to the Enz and go swimming?"

"Of course, I do. I go down there as often as I can in the summer!"

"Well, let me know the next time you go. I'd really like to see if you can swim," Friederich teased. "You probably just pretend you can. I'll bet you just lie on the bank and watch the boys!"

"No, I don't!" she blushed. "No one has ever talked to me like that!" She got up from the table and started to cry.

"Now what's wrong with that? You don't have to be embarrassed about liking boys, Mariele."

She really started to cry. Friederich went over to her and put his arms around her and kissed her fully on the lips. Mariele pushed herself away from him.

"I don't like that, Friederich! Just leave me alone!"

She went out to the kitchen to talk with her sister.

"What's the matter, Mariele?" Emilie asked.

"Friederich's making fun of me! I don't like it when he talks about how many boyfriends I have!" Mariele dried her eyes on her handkerchief.

"You've always been a very sensitive girl, haven't you Mariele?"

"How would you like it if some older man made fun of you all of the time?" She started to cry again. "I don't like to have him make fun of me! And I'm not going to tell him when I go swimming this summer!"

"Who said anything about going swimming?"

"Friederich did. He thinks I can't swim! He thinks I just lie on the bank and watch the boys."

Emilie laughed. "Don't take it so seriously, Mariele. He's only joking with you. He likes you; that's why he's teasing you so much."

"Emilie, you must be blind. He just kissed me on the lips!" She wiped them off again.

Emilie burst out laughing. "Is that right? My husband kissed my little sister? It's probably the first time you've ever been kissed by a man, isn't it?" She made light of what Mariele told her. "I'm sure you'll have a lot more experiences like that before you grow up," Emilie said reassuringly.

"But you didn't see how he did! He held me so tightly!"

Emilie dismissed Mariele's concerns. She's too young to understand, she thought to herself. She cries very easily whenever she feels offended. "Mariele, could you put some cold water into the boiling water? It's just too hot for the spaetzle."

While Mariele added the cold water, Emilie continued cutting the dough off the end of the cutting board into the boiling water. Sometimes she missed slicing the dough into a small enough size, and a big chunk fell into the water.

"Isn't that too big a piece?" Mariele asked.

"No, it's all right. If it's too big to put in your mouth, you can always cut it up with a knife."

Exactly at twelve o'clock, Friederich came upstairs for dinner. He closed the business over the dinner hour so his men could eat a leisurely lunch. He also wanted enough time to take a short nap after dinner. Emilie sent Mariele out to find Volkmar and Inge to come in to eat. She found them playing on the church steps. Volke was trying to teach her how to jump. Since he was bigger, he kept telling her, "Jump further, Inge!" Mariele told Emilie later.

"It's time to come in and eat dinner," she told them. She helped them wash their hands before sitting down at the table. As in any German household, Friederich sat at the head of the table, his wife to his immediate right, and the next oldest person to his immediate left. The children then sit with the eldest to the left, next to the guest, and the second oldest child to its mother's right. This meant Mariele had the seat directly next to Friederich on his left, between him and Volkmar. Friederich continued his banter of the morning over dinner.

"Mariele, you shouldn't be so upset when someone compliments you on how you look. You're a very attractive young woman. Men like women who have full bosoms and nice legs."

Mariele blushed. Her golden braids and blue eyes were set off even more than usual. She tried to ignore what he had said by continuing to eat. Emilie suggested to Friederich, "She's still a young girl and embarrasses easily. Maybe you shouldn't make her feel so self-conscious about how she looks."

"What? Since when don't I have the right to say what I want in my own house? She's got to learn at some point what men find attractive!" he said angrily.

"But, Papa, I didn't mean you had no right to say what you want. I only meant it makes her feel bad."

Mariele got up and left the table crying. Volke asked, "Where is Aunt Mariele going?"

"Mariele," Emilie said, "please don't feel bad. Come back and finish your dinner. It'll only get cold!"

Emilie turned to Friederich.

"You could be a bit more understanding of her. At least wait until after we're through eating before you try to joke with her!"

"Dammit, why does everyone think I've got to watch what I say? If she wants to act like a little girl, that's her problem!"

Emilie went into the bedroom and asked Mariele to come out and finish her dinner. She sat very quietly next to Volkmar and ate. Volkmar told his parents about jumping off the church steps.

"Every time Inge jumps, she falls backward instead of forward. It was so funny to watch her! I can jump a lot further than she, can't I, Aunt Mariele?"

"Yes, but you're older too. When she's as old as you are, she'll be able to do it a lot better."

"Yes, but I'll be bigger than she and able to do it even better!"

Mariele didn't say anything but kept eating. After a few minutes, Emilie noticed Mariele was turning toward Volkmar.

"You don't have to face Volke to eat, Mariele. He can eat very well by himself."

Mariele straightened up and faced towards the front again. What Emilie didn't know was Friederich's left knee was rubbing against Mariele's right thigh. Her skirt kept coming higher and higher. She kept pulling it down, but Friederich's knee kept rubbing against her. She didn't like it. She wasn't sure why. She just didn't. Each time she sat at the table with the Malin family, she tried to put her legs as close to Volkmar as possible. Whenever Emilie told her to sit up straight, she'd move her legs forward until she felt Friederich rubbing against her. Then she'd drift off toward the left again. Emilie thought it was because she liked her little nephew so much.

Mariele announced after dinner, "I'm not interested in any boys! Besides, it'll be a long time before I ever get married!"

"You'll change your mind one of these days," Friederich taunted. "It's just a matter of time, and before you know it, there'll be some guy after you."

Mariele blushed but said nothing. After washing dishes, Mariele, the two children, and Emilie went for a walk along the Enz. Friederich stayed home and read. Later that evening, Emilie's mother called.

"Grandfather died last night. We all had a chance to see him before he closed his eyes for good. The funeral is Wednesday." She couldn't continue. She was crying too much.

Emilie hung up and cried as she told Friederich.

"Grandfather Meyer died last night. Do you think I could take Volkmar with me to his funeral, Papa? Mariele and Inge could stay here with you. You probably don't want to leave the business anyway, do you?"

"But he was my grandfather too! I want to go. I don't want to stay here!" Mariele protested.

"Why don't we all go?" Friederich proposed. "I'll put Paul Krause in charge. That way the store will stay open, and we've got more than enough to do in the shop."

Emilie packed a couple of suitcases for the children, Friederich, and herself. Mariele got her things together, and they left to catch the eight-thirty train out of Stuttgart for Gerabronn. Volkmar and Inge slept most of the trip on the laps of Emilie and Mariele. Friederich alternated between reading and sleeping. Emilie slept now and then. Mariele stayed awake the whole time. She wondered what it would be like on the farm without Grandfather.

Because there were so many relatives who came to the funeral, the Malins were housed with Aunt Emilie's family, just up the street from Grandfather and Grandmother Meyer's house. Aunt Emilie was Emilie's favorite aunt and the one for whom she was named. Some of her cousins also lived nearby so that the Malins had plenty of room at the Schwaderers. Mariele preferred to stay with her cousin's family because one of the girls was her age.

After they settled in at her aunt's house, Emilie and Friederich took the children over to visit Grandmother Meyer and to see Grandfather laid out in the living room. The stove had been turned off. The body had ice beneath it to slow its decomposition.

Grandfather looked impressive, even in death. Volkmar looked at him with his eyes wide open.

"Why doesn't he wake up, Papa?"

"Because he's dead. When a person dies, he can't wake up anymore."

"Oh," Volkmar whispered. "But he looks like he's asleep!"

"That's the way it is when a person dies. It's just like being asleep."

As soon as they had come into the house, Frau Bartholomae picked up Inge and showed her the beautiful flowers. Emilie noticed her mother had been crying. Her eyes were all red, and she kept dabbing at them with her handkerchief and blowing her nose. The death of her father reminded her all too vividly of the death of her husband. Grandfather Meyer had had the same respect and influence in Gerabronn as her husband had had in Vaihingen. Emilie recalled what her mother once told her, "If anything should happen to Grandmother Meyer, I'll move back to Gerabronn and take care of Grandfather."

Emilie couldn't help but think how unjust life had been for her mother. Not only had her husband died at an early age, but now her beloved father. Her plans to return to Gerabronn had gone awry. She did not want to return to look after her mother. Her mother had always been much too forceful and demanding a woman.

"Even as children, we had to do what Mama said, not what Papa wanted," Emilie's mother told her.

What irked Emilie's mother even more about Emilie's Grandmother Meyer was what she said during the wake, "As soon as the funeral is over, I'm coming home and finish reading the novel that's running in the newspaper."

"No, Emilie. I don't think I want to move back here anymore. Without Grandfather, it just wouldn't be the same."

After the service in the house, the entire congregation walked past Grandfather's casket for the last time. As Volkmar looked up at him, he started to cry.

"Sh, sh," Emilie told him. "You don't have to cry, Volkmar."

But he wouldn't stop. As they walked toward the cemetery, his crying got louder and louder. Friederich got upset with him and said to Emilie in exasperation, "I'll take him for a walk in the other direction. Maybe he'll quiet down."

Friederich walked away from the cemetery. Volkmar stopped crying. As soon as Friederich started toward the cemetery, he started crying again. Friederich even took him to a confectionery shop for kuchen and hot chocolate. He would, ordinarily, never have done anything like that. (He told the children whenever they asked to stop at a pastry shop on their Sunday afternoon walks, "We eat dessert at home.") At this point, he was desperate to try anything that might work. Volkmar did seem to be pacified and stopped crying. When they returned to Uncle Otto's for dinner, Emilie and her mother made a determined effort not to cry. They didn't want to set Volkmar off again. The other children kept looking at him as he ate and ate. Finally, Inge asked him, "Aren't you going to cry anymore?"

"No. It's all over now."

Mariele and her mother stayed in Gerabronn for a few more days. Emilie's mother wanted to be sure Mariele could come next year after school was out to learn housekeeping from her grandmother. Mariele wasn't sure she wanted to come, but her mother said, "All of your sisters have been here. Now it's your turn." And that was the end of the discussion as far as her mother was concerned.

x x x

After Richard Haussmann had gone to America, Emilie didn't visit Gretel as often. When she did, she made the most of it. She got along very well with her sister-in-law. She was not only a very pretty woman but honest and outspoken. Friederich referred to her as "a woman who has a tongue like a two-by-four. Once you get hit by it, you don't get over it!"

Emilie liked her a lot. Whenever she went to Stuttgart shopping, she stopped by to see her. Volkmar and Inge liked to go there too, fortunately for Emilie. She could do her shopping and come back and join them for dinner in the evening. Gretel told her more about her family, some of which she had heard before. But coming from Gretel, the stories gave her an entirely new perspective.

Emilie remembered with a certain amount of embarrassment how shortly after she and Friederich were married, she was cleaning house one morning when Gretel stopped by. Emilie was busily scrubbing the kitchen floor. She had piled all of the furniture in the middle of each room. Since it was a beautiful spring day, she had left the door open to air out the house when Gretel walked in.

"Hello, Emilie. What are you doing?"

"I'm cleaning house. I thought this is a good time to do it. With the breeze blowing, the house should dry out after its scrubbing."

"When do you think you'll get through?"

"Tonight."

"Why do you have all of the furniture piled in the middle of each room?"

"So I can wash all of the floors at the same time."

"You're going to mop the floors throughout the house at one time?"

"Yes. Is there anything wrong with that?"

Gretel burst out laughing. She took down one of the living room chairs and sat on it.

"Actually, to do the whole house, it's going to take you at least two, if not three days of steady work. You can't possibly do the whole house in just one day! You have to dust the furniture too, don't forget. What you should do, Emmy—and I'm telling you this because I like you—is take one room at a time. Begin by washing the windows, dusting the furniture, and then scrubbing the floor. You can move the furniture around as you do the whole floor. You should also start in the farthest corner of the room, with your mop and pail, and work toward the door leading out of the room. Then, as you need to, you move one piece of furniture after the other as you work backward toward the door. By the time you reach the door, you should have finished the room completely."

"Ah, so that's how it's done. I've never cleaned a house before. I wondered why it was taking me so long, and I didn't seem to be making any progress."

"Of course you wouldn't know how, Emmy! A lady with your background couldn't be expected to know how to clean house."

And now Gretel and the two children were leaving . . . Emilie made the most of that last visit with her in Stuttgart. They talked and talked until it was quite dark outside. Emilie knew Friederich would have gone to his mother's for dinner, so she wasn't in any hurry to leave.

"As soon as we're in America and we can afford it, I'm going to have my mother join us. Richard thinks I shouldn't have any problem getting a job."

"You mean your mother would go to America? Why, she's an old woman!" Emilie said indignantly.

"That doesn't matter. She would like to travel too. She just could never afford it. Our father never even thought of taking her along on his trips to America. I'm sure it must have broken her heart whenever he simply told her, 'I'm going,' and without any further consideration, he made his arrangements to go. She was left to care for the family, that son of a bitch!" she said vehemently.

It was a tearful goodbye. Emilie didn't think she would ever see her again. She had grown very fond of her, and so had the children. Riche and Grete were like an older brother and sister to Volkmar and Inge.

"Can we come again next week?" Volkmar asked.

"No, Volke. We're going to America. You'll have to come a long way if you want to visit us again!" Gretel laughed.

As soon as they got home that evening, Emilie told Friederich, "You'll never believe what Gretel told me!"

"What's that?"

"Your mother's going to America."

"What? That's impossible. I don't believe it. Why she's over sixty-five. She would never leave her old friends here in Vaihingen. I think my sister's exaggerating. Her whole life has been spent here. I can't ever see her leaving."

Nevertheless, Friederich went to see his mother the very next day. She was in one of her foul moods. She wasn't at all pleased he asked her about what he had heard.

"Are you going to America?"

"And what if I did?" she replied angrily. "What's that to you? You don't care anymore what happens to me. All you do is go visit your mother-in-law with your wife and children. But as for me, you never have time anymore. So why should you care what I do?"

Friederich wasn't prepared for this response. He felt somewhat chagrined. He had neglected his mother for the past few years. He remembered he hadn't given her any money for sometime.

"How much do you need? You know all you have to do is ask me and I'll give you what you want! Are you out of money? Is that why you want to go to America?"

Frau Malin wasn't only jealous because her eldest son hadn't visited her regularly. She was also upset because she thought he took her for granted. He had long been her major means of support until he married. Since then, he couldn't seem to be bothered, she thought. It hurt her that he neglected her. She was very fond of him and appreciated all he had done for her through the years. If only he would stop by more often, she said to herself. Friederich was upset with his mother.

"You're too old to travel that far. You'll get so sea-sick, you'll wish you hadn't left!"

"I'm still going. As soon as the Haussmanns have settled into a place of their own, they'll send me the money to come."

Friederich realized her plans had gone much further than he had originally thought.

"Tell you what, Mother. I'll give you fifty Reichsmarks now, and fifty each month. Business is going well. That should help you."

"Look at me, Friederich. I walk around in this old sweater I've mended a hundred times, and you won't even go into your workshop unless you're dressed in a shirt and tie under your workshop apron. Every Sunday you get dressed up in a suit, white shirt, and tie. Your whole family has to do the same before you'll be seen in public with them. But just look at me. I can't even afford a new dress. Do you think I like to live in this poverty? Why don't you buy me a dress and coat like you buy for Emilie? Don't you think I like nice things too? At least Gretel and Richard have always bought me what I've needed, and they've given me money regularly too! But you? You don't care about me at all. All you care about is that you're well dressed and have the best of everything! And you wonder why I want to go to America? Because I just can't live here this way any longer! Sure, I'm old, I know it. But at least they'll look after me over there. That's something you haven't done in a long time!"

Friederich was shocked. This was an indictment of his neglect of her, and he resented it. He remembered his aunt and mother had often gotten into very violent arguments over the years. But she was accusing him of abandoning her. He couldn't believe it! "Who supported you and the family after Father died? Who went out and got a job and gave you all of his pay check each week so you could buy groceries for the whole family? Who didn't say anything when Bertha came back with her two children from America and stayed with us for more than a year? Who paid for Gretel's and Elise's education? Who supported Gretel when she got pregnant not once, but twice, and came home to live with us? Who supported Elise and Waltraude after she left her husband? Who supported your sister after your father and mother died? Tell me? I thought it was time for someone else to support you for a while! If Karl and Richard haven't given you any money, why didn't you say so?" Friederich said in exasperation.

He felt drained after this explosion with his mother. His mother wasn't one to heap praise on anyone, nor was she able to share the blame.

"You should have seen for yourself that I can't get along on what I make from raising a few chickens and selling eggs! If I hadn't been able to take in foster children or rent some of my garden, I would have died a long time ago!"

191

Ah yes, the garden, Friederich thought. "What's going to happen to your garden if you leave Vaihingen?"

"I don't know! I'll probably sell it."

Friederich didn't want her to sell it to just anyone. He knew the house wouldn't be for sale. His aunt and mother had inherited it from their parents after they died. His aunt and now Elise and her daughter were living there.

"What's going to happen to your share in the house?" It wasn't much of a house, but it was theirs, and it was free of any debt.

"Katharine's going to pay me for my half of the house. That'll give me more than enough money to pay for my passage to America and still have some leftover."

"How much do you want for the garden?"

"Two thousand Reichsmarks and not a penny less!"

He thought it over. "I'll take it!" he said, much to her surprise. Friederich had often looked over her garden and thought someday it's going to be a very valuable piece of property. It was located directly behind his mother's house above the Enz. It was on the very edge of Vaihingen. If any expansion should ever take place toward Stuttgart, the village would have to expand directly through her garden. It was a bit steeper in price than he had thought he would ever pay for it, but he felt with this amount, his mother wouldn't have to worry about having money in America. It also expanded his property, and if he paid that much for it now, in the future it could really become even more valuable.

Grandmother Malin made arrangements for her trip to America through a local travel agent. When he asked her, "Frau Malin, when would you like to leave?"

"As soon as possible. There's no reason for me stay here any longer."

"Would you want to leave next week? In two weeks? A month? Or what?"

"So? There are that many boats going to America?" she asked incredulously.

"Of course. Everyone wants to go to America these days!"

"In one month, I should be all ready."

He booked her passage on the *Europa* which was to leave from Bremerhaven on the twenty-fifth of November 1925.

On the last evening of Mother Malin's stay in Vaihingen, all of her old friends and neighbors came to say goodbye. They were all in their sixties or older and knew they would never see each other again. It was a painful evening even for her, especially when Emilie's mother came to say goodbye. Frau Bartholomae had never been inside her home before that evening. She brought her a little gift to take with her to America.

"Frau Malin, I wanted to bring you a little gift to take with you from Germany. Whenever you look at, it'll remind you of Vaihingen."

It was a beautiful ceramic brooch of a little girl to wear around her neck.

Emilie had never seen her mother-in-law cry before, but that must have touched her deeply.

"Thank you very much, Frau Bartholomae. It's a beautiful gift. Won't you sit down and drink a glass of wine with us?"

"No, no," Emilie's mother protested. "You're here with your old friends and neighbors. I don't want to intrude. I just wanted to wish you well and say goodbye."

The two women hugged each other for the first and last time. Frau Bartholomae had never wanted to visit the Malin household previously. She told Emilie once, "I really don't have much in common with your mother-in-law. They're not my kind of people. They're from down by the Enz. As I've told you many times before, we're from the hill. Those of us who live up here have little or nothing to do with people from down there!"

Emilie felt sorry for her mother. The two women had much more in common than she realized. There was more than a twenty-year difference in age, but both women had been widowed when young and had had to raise their families themselves. While her mother was a businesswoman and bookkeeper, Frau Malin had had to do hard physical work. They were both very proud women who didn't let others run roughshod over them, especially not men. They both had to struggle in their separate economic milieu to make ends meet. While Emilie's mother had the status of one of the town's elite, she didn't seem to feel really at home in Vaihingen. This was not her hometown. She had only moved here because her husband had bought the business. Frau Malin, on the other hand, was born in Vaihingen. This was her hometown. She still had friends she had made as a little girl. Emilie's mother never had that closeness to anyone in Vaihingen. She always felt as though she were an outsider, which she was, and her accent always identified her as such. Frau Malin had many friends, even if she was from the lower end of town.

There was also a difference in the way the two women responded to the deaths of their husbands. Emilie's mother took the death of her husband much harder than Frau Malin did that of hers. Unfortunately, Emilie's mother's love for her Michael kept her separated from others in her own remorse. The death of Gottlieb Malin, on the other hand, seemed to have had a liberating effect on Frau Malin. She had her friends among her neighbors and felt an active part of her community. Emilie's mother, in contrast, was much more dependent upon her brothers, sisters, and cousins for her circle of friends. Emilie had never noticed this before. It was only with the farewell party for Grandmother Malin that she thought about the differences between the two women. She was struck by their many similarities, and yet, the differences always kept them apart.

Grandmother Malin looked forward to seeing Bertha, Gretel, Karl, and their families again. "Yes, I'll miss all of you very much," she told her neighbors. "I'm thankful I had you as my friends. But I'm also looking ahead to the future. Not everyone can go to America and start life all over again!"

Friederich decided he would take a few days off and accompany his mother to the boat. He felt she needed help in getting her bags on board.

"I don't think an old woman should make the long trip to the boat all by herself." Emilie had suggested it would be nice if she could go too.

"Who's going to take care of the children? You can't expect my sister and aunt to do so."

Emilie stayed home, and Friederich went alone with his mother to Bremerhaven. When they got to the ship and were boarding it, Friederich knew which cabin his mother was in. He started to carry her bags there. A crewman asked,

"Where are you going?"

"I'm taking my mother's bags to her cabin."

"Where are you going?" the crewman asked a second time.

"I told you before," Friederich said as he continued down the corridor.

"Hey!" the crewman yelled. "Why don't you answer me when I speak to you?" He grabbed Friederich's arm.

"Look, I'm taking my mother's bags to her cabin!"

"What did you say? Are you making fun of me by whispering?" the crewman asked.

"I'll show you, you son of bitch!" the crewman shouted at Friederich.

He grabbed Friederich's arm and pushed him back up the corridor to kick him off the boat. Friederich dropped his mother's bags and was about to hit him when his mother came down the corridor.

"What's the matter?" Frau Malin asked.

"This man's ignoring me when I speak to him. When I ask a question, I expect an answer!" the crewman said curtly.

"He's taking my bags to my cabin."

"Why didn't he tell me that?" the crewman asked, somewhat perplexed.

"I did, you asshole! You just didn't hear me!" Friederich whispered.

"See, there he goes again! Speak up! What did you say?"

"He can't speak any louder! It's a wound from the war!" Frau Malin told the crewman.

"Oh, I thought he was making fun of me!" He let Friederich pass.

Frau Malin's cabin was in third class. She shared a cabin with four other women. Since she was the oldest, they gave her one of the lower bunks and helped Friederich store her bags under it. They introduced themselves. One woman was from Wuerzburg. Mother Malin felt right at home with a fellow Schwob on board. The other three women were from Luebeck, Hannover, and Duesseldorf.

When Friederich shook hands with them and tried to talk with them, they couldn't understand him.

"What did you say?" they asked.

"Speak up, we can't hear you," the woman from Hannover asked in an even louder voice.

"He can't speak any louder," Frau Malin answered quietly. "He can hear very well, but he can't speak above a whisper. He was wounded during the war, and ever since, he can't speak like you or me."

"Ah yes, that damn war again! Three of us are going to America because our husbands were killed. There's nothing left for us here in Germany."

They turned to Friederich and said, "Please forgive us, Herr Malin. We didn't know you can't speak any louder."

"I'm surprised you're not going to America," the woman from Wuerzburg said to Friederich.

"You certainly don't find it comfortable living here anymore, do you? You're probably not even getting any disability payments for your war injuries either."

Friederich just shook his head but said nothing. As he bid his mother goodbye, the other women said, "Herr Malin, you don't have to worry about her. We'll see to it she gets to New York safely."

On the way back to Vaihingen, Friederich thought a great deal about what had happened and what was said. The fresh ocean breezes brought back memories of his own trip to Brazil a few years earlier. Maybe we should immigrate to America too, he thought to himself. The encounter with the crewman reminded him again of how hard it was to make people understand what he was trying to say. It's no different in my own workshop, he thought. If Emilie isn't available, I have to take people into my office and shut the door before I can even try to talk to them. Even then, I'm not sure they understand what I've said. I used to be able to talk, sing, and yell with the best of them. I can't anymore. If only I could find some place where I could be alone, where I wouldn't have to meet people all of the time . . . A place where I could do what I want!

When Friederich returned that evening, he told Emilie, "Maybe we should emigrate to America too. Most of my family is over there now."

"Oh, Friederich, I don't want to leave Germany. I like it here very much. All of my family, except for Luise, is here; all of my friends; everything that has any meaning to me is right here. In America, we'd have to start all over again. You've got a very good business. People know you. Your friends are still here and even some of your relatives. Why would you want to leave your hometown for some place that's completely foreign to you?" she asked bitterly.

Friederich didn't say anymore about it. He went back to his workshop. It was a good business, he thought to himself. Emilie's right. It would be an entirely different way of life for us to emigrate. But I've never been one not to accept a challenge, he told himself.

Oh my, Emilie thought. Friederich wants to leave Vaihingen again. I don't want to leave . . . How can he even think of such a thing she asked herself? Maybe if I got pregnant again, he wouldn't want to leave. Yes, she told herself. I'll see if I can get pregnant again. It'll take his mind off this idea of leaving Germany.

The first letter they received from America from Mother Malin was from Syracuse, New York. It was a glowing account of her arrival and reception by the family. She wrote:

Dear Friederich and family,

Karl met me at the boat in New York, and we took a train to Syracuse. It was a very long train ride. We went through some very beautiful countryside of rivers, lakes, and streams. There were many, many farms with great, big barns and silos. We must have passed thousands of cows by the time we reached Syracuse. This is a huge country! The trip took almost as long as from Vaihingen to Bremerhaven. But on the map, as you can see for yourselves, it's only a very small part of the United States. I'm living with Gretel and Richard and their two children. They have a very nice but small house on a street which not only has a German name but German neighbors all around it. Richard works with Karl and Gustav at the Easy Washer Company. They earn good money and can work overtime, if they want. The Haussmanns' house, while small, is comfortable. It has hot and cold running water with a bathtub so you can take a bath anytime you want.

There's a small back yard with grass and some fruit trees, including grapes, right behind the house. I don't even have to speak English; almost everyone around us speaks German. There's a large city park nearby where people can go swimming in the summers or take long walks. The neighborhood has great, big trees along both sides of the streets. You feel as though you live in one great big park! There's even a streetcar that goes by the end of the street where we live which can take us directly downtown into the city's center. Our neighborhood seems almost as if it were like a part of Stuttgart! The only difference between here and Stuttgart is there's more room between the houses with grass called lawns between them. So, as you can imagine, I'm very comfortable living here. I'm surrounded by my family and German neighbors. I couldn't be happier with my decision to leave Germany.

I hope you are all well and that you visit my sister regularly. I'm trying to encourage her to come to America too. Except for you, Aunt Katharine, Elise, and Waltraude, all of my family is now here. With love and kisses to the children, I remain

Grandmother Malin

After reading the letter out loud to Friederich, Emilie and he were both surprised. "Do you think she's telling the truth about having hot running water in the house, Friederich? I don't think there are more than maybe one or two families in Vaihingen that have that kind of convenience."

"Why should she exaggerate? If that's the way it is, then that's the way it is! There's no reason for her to write to tell us something that doesn't exist."

"But grass and fruit trees right in their own backyard, Friederich? There are only a handful of very wealthy people that have that here! The only gardens that I can think of are ours and a few others. And they're at the edges of town. There are only the Weigeles and the Conradts that have grass around their houses."

"Maybe America is a richer country than Germany," Friederich answered thoughtfully. "I've read the United States has a higher standard of living than we do since the war. The Americans have gotten richer since 1918, and we've gotten a lot poorer. Just look at the debt we're supposed to pay off to the Allies! It'll be a long time until we can afford to have what they have!"

Emilie didn't say this to Friederich, but she couldn't help thinking about it. How can a poor family, like the Haussmanns, afford a house with these conveniences and such ample space in a city? We're much richer than they are, and we're surrounded by cement and cobblestones around our houses! We don't have a garden right next to our house. It would be just as if we had a house on my mother's big field on the edge of Vaihingen. Somehow, Emilie couldn't quite visualize how this was possible for the Haussmanns. And yet her mother-in-law surely wouldn't lie.

Chapter XII

The Last Straw

Emilie had already decided. If Friederich is interested in going to America and I'm not, she said to herself, maybe if I got pregnant again he wouldn't be so interested in going. It worked the last time. I didn't have to go to Brazil.

In late 1926, Friederich had a hard time collecting on the debts his customers had run up in their purchases of bicycles and motorcycles. He thought by granting extensions on payments over several months, he was more likely to increase his sales. What later came to be known as "installment buying" seemed like a real advantage over his competitors. His competitors extended payments to three months, but not longer. Friederich, on the other hand, was willing to give his customers up to a year to complete their payments. When he began installment buying for his customers, the sales increased three-fold. He hired his sister, Elise, to take the place of his mother in the sales room. She was a big help negotiating the purchases of the new bicycles and motorcycles by the local farmers and townspeople around Vaihingen. The installment plan called for the customers to make monthly payments on the vehicles they had purchased. Emilie had the job of keeping track of the payments on the sales which Friederich and Elise negotiated. She reviewed the sales and the receipts weekly in order to keep up with the accounts payable and receivable. She noticed, however, several of the customers had become delinquent.

"Papa, there are about six customers who haven't paid anything since they purchased their motorcycles or bicycles. What do you think we should do?"

"Write them a letter and tell them we're going to increase the cost of the motorcycle or bicycle by ten percent unless they start paying on their account."

Emilie composed the letter and took it to Welker's store to have it typed. Welker had begun the service shortly after he bought the business from her mother. The letters became pro forma similar to the following:

Dear Herr Leiher!

As of the thirtieth of September, 1926, you purchased an NSU motorcycle from the Friederich E. Malin Machine and Vehicle Shop for two hundred Reichsmarks. You promised to pay thirty Reichsmarks monthly after your down payment of ten Reichsmarks. As of this date,

December thirtieth, 1926 we have not received a single payment! Unless you meet your payment schedule on January 15, 1927, we shall have to increase your interest payment by ten percent added to the original monthly payment schedule. I shall look forward to your next payment before the January 15th deadline.

Sincerely,

Friederich E. Malin Machine, Motorcycle and Bicycle Shop,

Vaihingen/Enz

There was no response to these letters. It was as if the customers had not even received them. There was no request for an extension or for a reduced payment schedule. There was nothing.

"Elise, you and I will have to visit these people and collect what they owe me. I'm going to have Emilie cover the store for me while you and I go next Monday to Enzweihingen and begin our collections."

"No way, Friederich! I don't mind talking to customers here in the store, but I'm not going out on any collections with you! You'll have to get someone else to do that! I'm not going."

"Why not? I can't go by myself. I've already tried and people say they can't understand me! I'll give you an extra ten Reichsmarks a week."

"No thanks! I'm not going. Get someone else to go with you. If you want me to mind the store, I will. But I'm not going on any collection campaign with you!"

Friederich stormed upstairs. He slammed the office door shut. Emilie heard him and wondered, oh oh, what's gone wrong now? He came into the apartment and cursed his sister. Emilie came to the door from the kitchen.

"What's wrong, Papa? Is something the matter in the store?"

"That sister of mine refuses to go with me to call on the delinquent customers! What does she think she's getting paid for? She refuses to go with me!"

"Maybe you can get Herr Krause to go with you."

"No, He's got to stay in the shop and make sure the Bosch parts are done right. I don't want to lose the business from the shop!"

"What are you going to do, Papa? You've got to have someone go with you."

"You're going to have to go with me. You can take care of the books at night and on weekends. You've had the experience in the store when my mother wasn't available. Yes, that's what we're going to do. We'll go to Enzweihingen tomorrow and call on a couple of the people who are the most delinquent. I'll have Dote (Katharine Vischer) come and look after the children."

"All right, Papa. I'll go with you."

The next morning Emilie and Friederich took the eight o'clock shuttle train to Enzweihingen. The farmers had long finished their work in the barn and were beginning to leave for their fields in the surrounding countryside. The women of the households had opened their windows and hung their featherbeds over the open window sills. It was their daily custom when it wasn't raining. It was believed to be healthy to air out the bedding and bedroom every day.

The shops were busy with customers entering and leaving after making their purchases. The streets were filled with horses, oxen and wagons entering and exiting the numerous barns. Since it was winter but with no snow or even freezing temperatures, the farmers could still plow their fields and get them ready for the next spring's planting. Emilie and Friederich walked up Main Street to the edge of the village and rang the doorbell on one of the smaller houses. The woman of the household looked out the upstairs window and recognized who it was.

"Ja, Fraeulein Bartholomae! What a pleasant surprise to see you! Just a minute, I'll be right down!"

Emilie couldn't believe the first customer whom Friederich had selected to call upon was the Reinholder family. Erich Reinholder was one of her kindergarten pupils during the war.

"Oh, I didn't know this is the same family whose little boy I had in my class, Papa. Do you remember that time we were going to Stuttgart on the train to visit the Haussmanns and Frau Reinholder and her son sat in our compartment with us?"

Friederich nodded his head.

Frau Reinholder opened the door. "Come right in Fraeulein Bartholomae! How nice to see you again!"

"Gruess Gott, Frau Reinholder. This is my husband, Herr Malin. He's the owner of the Motorcycle and Bicycle Shop in Vaihingen."

"Please be seated. I'll put on the coffee and come right in with some of the kuchen I just bought at the bakery."

Friederich shook hands with Frau Reinholder. "It won't be necessary for you to make any coffee, Frau Reinholder. I've come to talk to you about making a payment on the motorcycle and bicycle you bought last year."

"What did he say, Fraeulein Bartholomae? I can't understand him."

"He said he wants to talk to you about what your husband purchased from his store last year, Frau Reinholder."

"Let me tell you about Erich, Fraeulein Bartholomae. He's doing very well in the Latein Schule. His grades are among the highest in his class! You remember him, don't you? He was one of the first pupils you had in Kindergarten in 1918. You gave him a very good start, Fraeulein Bartholomae! He's enjoyed school ever since."

"I've come to collect on what you owe me, Frau Reinholder!" Friederich said. "I didn't come here to discuss your son! I want you to begin paying on the motorcycle and bicycle by next month, or I'm adding ten percent to your bill each month!"

"What did he say, Fraeulein Bartholomae? I didn't understand a word he said. Excuse me a minute. I'll put on the coffee."

As she left, Friederich scowled. "Tell her I don't want any of her coffee. I want her to pay her bill!"

"But Papa, be reasonable. I haven't seen her since I left Enzweihingen. I didn't know this was the same family of Erich Reinholder."

"Well, I'm leaving! I'm not going to be insulted any more. She keeps calling you by your maiden name."

"Papa, please wait! I haven't seen her in a long time. I'll tell her again why we've come when she comes back again."

Frau Reinholder returned with the coffee and kuchen. "So, Fraeulein Bartholomae now we can continue our conversation. You'd be surprised how tall Erich has become. Why he's even taller than I am and almost as tall as my Herbert. My husband says he's going to become an accounting specialist. He's already a big help to us with his knowledge of numbers. He's going to help with the finances at the von Neurath's estate during his summer vacation."

"I don't care what your son does! I want you to start paying me for what you bought! If you don't start, I'm going to add ten percent to your monthly bill!" Friederich said more loudly than the last time.

"What did he say, Fraeulein Bartholomae? I can't understand a thing he said."

"Frau Reinholder, my husband wants you to pay on the purchases you made in his store this past fall. Didn't your husband buy a motorcycle and a bicycle from him?"

"Oh that. The motorcycle isn't running anymore and the bicycle was stolen about a month after we got it for Erich. I'll tell my husband when he comes home, Herr . . . . What's your name again?"

"That's it! I'm leaving. Are you coming with me?"

"But, Papa, we can't just go out without finishing our coffee and kuchen Frau Reinholder prepared for us!"

Friederich put on his hat and coat and without saying another word, left.

"He's a very angry man, isn't he Fraeulein Bartholomae."

"He doesn't like it when people can't understand what he says, Frau Reinholder."

"Did he have an accident so he can't speak any louder?"

"No. The nerves to his vocal cords were cut by a careless surgeon during the war."

"Oh. Did he get discharged for it and not have to serve in the army any longer?"

"Yes. But people have a hard time understanding him. That's why I'm going with him to act as his translator. Did you understand what he said, Frau Reinholder about the motorcycle and bicycle?"

"I'll tell my husband, Fraeulein Bartholomae. He comes home from work at five o'clock."

"Your kuchen and coffee are very good, Frau Reinholder. Did you bake the kuchen yourself?"

"No, Fraeulein Bartholomae. I bought it at the bakery this morning. Let me tell you about Erich. His favorite subject is math. He says you got him started by having the boys and girls put numbers together in Kindergarten. You did an excellent job, Fraeulein Bartholomae. It's too bad you're not teaching anymore!"

"Thank you for the coffee and kuchen, Frau Reinholder. I'd better go now and see if I can find my husband."

"Goodbye Fraeulein Bartholomae. Who is the man you came with?"

"Herr Malin. He's my husband."

"You poor woman, Fraeulein Bartholomae. I wouldn't want to have to live with such a short tempered man!"

"It's not so bad, Frau Reinholder. He's really a very good provider. It's just hard for him when people don't understand what he's saying."

Friederich was seated on the bench at the train station when Emilie arrived. He barely looked at her.

"So, Papa, I'm glad you waited for me. I couldn't leave any sooner."

"To hell you couldn't! She kept calling you Fraeulein Bartholomae even after you introduced me as your husband. I'm not going to stand for that kind of effrontery by anyone! I don't care about her son. I just want them to start paying on the debt they owe me! And you sat there and drank coffee with her after she insulted me!"

"I'm sorry, Papa. I couldn't leave any sooner. I didn't know this was the Reinholder family whose son was in my class years ago. I'm sure she'll tell her husband about our visit."

"I'm not interested in having her tell her husband about our visit! I want them to start paying me what they owe me, damn it! And that story about how the bicycle was stolen a month after they had it, so what! They still have to pay for it!"

"I'm sure they will, Papa. The Reinholders are a good family. I'm sure they wouldn't have bought those items if they didn't plan to pay for them."

"That's what you think! Some of the worst cheapskates I've ever seen are those who give the impression they're honest, righteous, upstanding citizens! They try and get the best of other people at no expense to themselves!"

"Since we're here, we're going to visit another of our delinquent customers."

"I don't know, Papa, but I don't feel very well. Couldn't we wait until tomorrow?"

"No! We didn't come here for nothing! Were going to try another. I want to make as many contacts as I can each day. So far I've seen five out of the six. Each time the women claimed they couldn't understand me! Even those people who bought their motorcycles or bicycles recently should have a reminder."

"We can stop at the Schindlers. They started paying each month on their motorcycle for about four months and then stopped. It's been more than three months since they've made any payment," he stated angrily. "They live on the next street around the corner from the bakery."

In spite of not feeling well, Emilie walked to the Schindlers with Friederich. She wasn't sure she was going to make it. The encounter with Frau Reinholder was unexpected. She was both pleased that Frau Reinholder recognized her. But upset too when she kept referring to her by her maiden name. Nothing angered Friederich more than being taken for granted. Why don't people call me by my married name she said to herself?

They walked in silence to the next delinquent customer. Emilie hoped it would not be someone whom she knew. She was embarrassed for Friederich when she was called Fraeulein Bartholomae. They walked up the path to the front door and Friederich rang the doorbell.

An old man opened the door. "Ja, what would you like?"

"Is Herr Schindler at home?" Friederich asked.

"What did you say?"

"Is Herr Schindler at home?"

"I can't understand you!"

"My husband asked if Herr Schindler is at home?"

"Aren't you Fraeulein Bartholomae?"

"I used to be. This is my husband, Herr Malin. He's the owner of the Friederich E, Malin Machine, Motorcycle and Bicycle shop in Vaihingen."

"Aren't you the teacher whose mother bought a piano for the children in the Kindergarten class during the war and we had to move it from the train station to the school on one of Herr von Neurath's wagons?"

"Why yes. Did you help move the piano?"

"Yes I did. We had a really hard time lifting it off the wagon and carrying it into the school as I remember."

Emilie laughed. "That's right! Herr Binger didn't think you men could carry it. But you did!"

"Forget the old stories. Tell him why we're here!" Friederich told her.

"I'm sorry, I didn't get your name," Emilie said. "We're here to talk with Herr Schindler. Is he at home?"

"I'm Herr Schindler. What do you want?"

"Herr Schindler, my husband says you bought a motorcycle from him several months ago and you've not made any payments since then."

"Ah Fraeulein Batholomae, you want to talk to my son. He's not here right now. He's at work in Stuttgart."

"Tell him he should stop and see me or I'm going to add a ten percent interest charge on his bill each month," Friederich told Emilie.

"What did he say?"

"My husband says your son should make regular payments on the motorcycle he bought. Could you tell him Herr Schindler?"

"I'll tell him Fraeulein Bartholomae. But I don't think he has it anymore. I'll have him stop in and talk to your husband on Saturday."

"Thank you very much Herr Schindler."

"It was nice to see you again, Fraeulein Bartholomae. I've often wondered what happened to that nice teacher we had in our Kindergarten class. The boys and girls really liked you very much."

Friederich was steaming by this time. He abruptly left while Emilie said good bye to Herr Schindler. She caught up with him as he climbed the platform to the train station.

"I'm glad you waited for me, Papa. I'm sorry the people call me Fraeulein Bartholomae."

"What do they think you've been doing ever since you were a teacher? Your name is now Malin, not Bartholomae!"

Friederich didn't say anything for the rest of the day. They got on the train and sat in silence until they got back to Vaihingen. Emilie was exhausted. "I don't know if I can do this again tomorrow, Papa."

"What do you mean you don't know if you can do it again tomorrow? Of course we're going to continue to visit the delinquents. We have to! They're not going to get away with not paying for what they bought! I'm short more than six thousand Reichsmarks from all of these delinquents! If I don't hear from Reinholder and Schindler I'm going to sue them. They won't get away with not paying!"

Emilie remained quiet. She felt worse since leaving Frau Reinholder. She didn't want to say anything to Friederich. It would only make him angrier. The visit with Herr Schindler was pleasant enough. She actually enjoyed reliving the story about the transport of the piano to her Kindergarten classroom. The fact that he recognized her after all of these years was more than she could have expected. She felt gratified by the warm receptions she had gotten. I wish they would call me Frau Malin, she thought. Even when I tell them my name, they still refer to me by my professional name as a teacher.

When they arrived home she asked Dote (Katharine Vischer) to make some soup and warm up the left over spaetzle and roast beef for Friederich. "I don't want anything. I don't feel very well. I think I'll go lie down a while."

"I'll make something to eat for Friederich, Emmy. Don't you want a cup of soup too? It may do you some good."

"No thanks. I feel rather woozy. If I eat anything, I may throw up."

Dote made dinner for Friederich and Emilie went to bed. She slept for the rest of the afternoon. She awoke at five o'clock. Elise and Dote were saying good bye to Friederich and the children.

"I'm sorry I slept so long. Thanks for taking care of the children, Dote."

"Can you come again tomorrow afternoon? We should have someone here when the children come back from school. I want to visit a few more customers with Emilie."

"Ja, I can do that. But do you feel up to making more visits Emmy?" Dote asked.

"I'll feel better tomorrow. I just need a good night's sleep."

Emilie made some soup for the children and provided cold cuts and bread Friederich was accustomed to eating in the evening. He had his usual glass of Burgundy with the meal. After putting the children to bed she told Friederich

"Papa, I think I'll go to bed. I still feel a little sick to my stomach."

"Okay. We'll start tomorrow after the children are in school."

By morning Emilie still felt ill. Elise came upstairs after she arrived to check on how she was feeling.

"Good morning, Emmy. How do you feel today?"

"Not much better than yesterday. I still feel as though I'm going to throw up."

The thought of it must have stimulated her to do it. She reached under the bed and pulled the chamber pot directly next to the bed. She vomited into it. Elise held her forehead as she struggled to vomit the last of the contents in her stomach.

"I think I better get Dr. Bauer to check on you, Emmy. You're in no condition to go out calling on delinquent customers today."

"I'll be all right, Elise. I'll stay in bed this morning. Maybe you can go with Friederich today."

"Emmy I told him I'm absolutely not going on any collection visits. I don't want to do that and I'm not. If you don't feel up to it, then he won't be able to go today."

"Well, I guess I'll have to get dressed. He's expecting me to be ready by the time he's through in the shop this morning."

Before she could get up, she had another attack of nausea. Very little came up but the lower part of her stomach felt awful. She also felt cramping in her uterus.

"Maybe you better have Dr. Bauer stop by this morning, Elise. I feel as though I'm going to have a baby, but it's not time yet."

"What? Are you pregnant?"

"Yes, but don't tell Friederich, Elise. He doesn't know. Maybe it's something else."

"Well, I'm going to get Dr. Bauer. I won't say anything to Friederich. If he asks I'll tell him you have the flu and need to have the doctor check on you."

"Thanks, Elise. I hope it's not what I think it is."

Elise went downstairs and told Friederich she was going to get Dr. Bauer.

"I think she has the flu. She vomited twice and feels like she going to have to do it again. I don't think you ought to make any collection visits today Friederich unless you want to go by yourself."

Friederich went upstairs and found Emilie straining over the chamber pot.

"What did you eat that doesn't sit well with you, Emmy?"

"I've not had anything, Papa. I've not been hungry. I just can't stop trying to vomit."

"Elise has gone for the doctor. We'll soon find out what's wrong with you. Do you want anything to eat or drink? Shall I make you some tea?"

"Yes. That would be good. I could try and drink some black tea. You'll find it in the first drawer to the right of the stove. It's in a tin can with a picture of an Indian tea plantation on the outside."

While Friederich was in the kitchen heating the water for tea, Elise returned with Dr. Bauer. She led him upstairs into the bedroom.

"Ah, Emilie. How are you today? Not feeling so well from what Frau Brendel tells me."

"Hello Dr. Bauer. I'm sorry you had to come over so early this morning."

"I don't mind at all Emilie. You're still one of my favorite patients ever since your father died. Now what's wrong with you? Where does it hurt and what have you taken?"

"I've not taken anything, Dr. Bauer."

"Frau Brendel tells me you're pregnant. Is that true?"

"Yes it is. I haven't told anyone except her."

"Where is the pain most severe?"

"In my uterus, Dr. Bauer. I've been cramping steadily since Elise went to get you."

"Let me take a look at you. Frau Brendel could you take the covers off of her so I can check her over?"

Elise lifted the covers and Dr. Bauer knew immediately what the problem was. The blood and tissue was all over her nightgown and bedding.

"Well, Emilie, we don't have to look any further for now. You've just had a miscarriage. Frau Brendel and I will help you get up and put you into a chair until we can clean up your bed."

"Thank you Dr. Bauer. I'm sorry I made such a mess."

"Don't apologize. A miscarriage is often the outcome of some severe strain or stress. Have you been doing anything out of the ordinary lately?"

"Yes she has. She's had to go with her husband on collection visits among delinquent customers who haven't been paying their bills on time. These customers are some of the parents of her former pupils in the Enzweihingen Kindergarten and Volksschule."

"No wonder you've had a miscarriage. You're not suited for that kind of work, Emilie. What I want you to do is stay in bed for the next five days and have complete rest. I'll look in on you on Saturday. Your appetite will gradually come back. Will you be able to look after her, Frau Brendel? She really should stay in bed for these next few days."

"I think I can arrange that. I'm helping my brother in the store downstairs, but I can come up every half hour and see how she's doing. I can get my aunt to take care of my little girl. I'll have to look after the Malin children too when they come back from Kindergarten."

"Good. Then I'll see you on Saturday morning, Emilie. If you feel any more nausea coming on, take some hot tea and an aspirin every four hours. That should help ease the discomfort."

Dr. Bauer was about to leave when Friederich came into the bedroom carrying the hot tea and crackers.

"How's the patient, Dr. Bauer?"

"She's doing well considering she's had a miscarriage."

"A Miscarriage? I didn't even know she was pregnant! How could that be?"

"You should know, Herr Malin. I understand you've been taking her with you on your attempts to collect the debts your customers owe you. That's no job for a lady, Herr Malin. She's too refined for something like that."

"Someone has to do it. If people can't understand me, what am I supposed to do?"

"I'm telling you this is what has caused her miscarriage. She's been under a lot of stress evidently and that can trigger a miscarriage. She shouldn't be expected to do this sort of work. She's not suited for it."

"If that's all you have to say, you can leave. What I do is my own business. I don't need someone to tell me what I can or can't do!"

Friederich held the door open for Dr. Bauer to leave.

"I feel sorry for your, Emilie. I'll see you again on Saturday. If something should come up between now and then, I'm sure Frau Brendel will let me know."

"Good bye Dr. Bauer. Thank you very much for coming on such short notice."

Dr. Bauer didn't bother to shake hands with Friederich. He made his way down the front stairs. Elise accompanied him.

"Don't worry, if something comes up, I'll let you know, Dr. Bauer. I'll look after her."

"Why didn't she tell her husband she was pregnant, Frau Brendel? Was she trying to keep it a secret?"

"In a way. She told me her husband wants to emigrate to America and she doesn't want to go. She thought if she were pregnant he wouldn't expect her to go. She had done the same thing in 1922 when her husband talked about going to Brazil. When he found out she was pregnant he said he would go alone and see how he liked it before sending for her. I guess it's not going to work this time."

"It might have worked if she hadn't had to become so involved in the business, Frau Brendel. Well, for now they're still here in Germany."

In the meantime, Friederich was asking Emilie all kinds of questions.

"Why didn't you tell me you were pregnant? How was I supposed to know you shouldn't be doing this kind of work under these conditions? You've made me look like a fool!"

"I'm sorry, Papa. I thought if I got pregnant again you might reconsider about going to America. I don't want to leave Germany." She began crying. "This is my home! This is where most of my family lives. I thought if I got pregnant you might forget about leaving Germany."

Emilie was convulsed in tears. She couldn't stop crying. Friederich said

"This is the last straw. As soon as I find a buyer, we're going to America! I've had nothing but grief since my operation during that damn war! Do you think I owe any allegiance or care about what happens to this country anymore? To hell with the whole damn thing! We're going to America!